Prais~~e~~ ~~of~~
Robert S~~hearman~~

"Thrillingly unpredictable, bizarrely life~~~~ ~~~~at
writer."

—*The Scotsman*

"A writer who is not afraid to approach the big subjects, but does so from interesting oblique angles and with a light, kittenish gait. Rather profound, ingeniously plotted."

—*The Independent*

"Shearman's prose is a mixture of faux-naive mundanity and breathtaking fantasy visions. Addictive. Wonderful."

—*SFX*

"Corrosively funny, wistful, sharp, strange and black as a coffin lid, Robert Shearman is an addictive delight."

—**Mark Gatiss, Co-creator of *Sherlock***

"Shearman offers us haunting, nightmare alternatives to our world that are still somehow utterly recognizable as our own, thanks to the way he always picks out the comically mundane among the impossible and the fantastical."

—**Steven Moffat, Executive Producer and
Hugo Award-winning writer for *Doctor Who***

"His stories are like the bastard offspring of Philip K. Dick and Jonathan Carroll, but with a quirky personality that is completely their own."

—**Stephen Jones, World Fantasy Award-winning
editor of *Best New Horror***

"Shearman has a uniquely engaging narrative voice and he steers clear of genre clichés, injecting elements of horror and the surreal into a recognizably real world. As impressive as his quirky imagination is his emotional range: most of the stories are darkly humorous, but humour, horror and genuine pathos all make a powerful impact in a very short space."

—*The Times Literary Supplement*

"Shearman's stories are hard to categorize, a unique fusion of literary and the fantastic, perhaps not surprising from a writer whose credits include *Doctor Who* scripts and mainstream theatre."

—*The Guardian*

Other Books by Robert Shearman

Remember Why You Fear Me:
The Best Dark Fiction of Robert Shearman

Everyone's Just So So Special

Love Songs for the Shy and Cynical

Tiny Deaths

ChiZine Publications

THEY
DO
THE
SAME
THINGS
DIFFERENT
THERE

THE BEST WEIRD FANTASY OF
ROBERT SHEARMAN

FIRST EDITION

Distributed in Canada by
HarperCollins Canada Ltd.
1995 Markham Road
Scarborough, ON M1B 5M8
Toll Free: 1-800-387-0117
e-mail: hcorder@harpercollins.com

Distributed in the U.S. by
Diamond Comic Distributors, Inc.
10150 York Road, Suite 300
Hunt Valley, MD 21030
Phone: (443) 318-8500
e-mail: books@diamondbookdistributors.com

Library and Archives Canada Cataloguing in Publication Data Forthcoming

Shearman, Robert, author

    They do the same things different there : the best weird

fantasy of Robert Shearman / Robert Shearman. -- First edition.

Short stories.

Issued in print and electronic formats.

ISBN 978-1-77148-300-1 (pbk.).--ISBN 978-1-77148-301-8 (pdf)

    I. Title.

PR6119.H435T44 2014   823'.92   C2014-904063-6

    C2014-904064-4

CHIZINE PUBLICATIONS
Toronto, Canada
www.chizinepub.com
info@chizinepub.com

Edited by Andrew Wilmot
Proofread by Stephen Michell

 Canada Council Conseil des arts
for the Arts du Canada

We acknowledge the support of the Canada Council for the Arts which last year invested $20.1 million in writing and publishing throughout Canada.

ONTARIO ARTS COUNCIL
CONSEIL DES ARTS DE L'ONTARIO
an Ontario government agency
un organisme du gouvernement de l'Ontario

Published with the generous assistance of the Ontario Arts Council.

Printed in Canada

THEY
DO
THE
SAME
THINGS
DIFFERENT
THERE

THERE
DIFFERENT
THINGS
SAME
THE
DO
THEY

Contents

LUXEMBOURG

It's not that they thought it wasn't worth reporting, it was just a matter of deciding where to schedule it. It wasn't a human interest story, after all, and it wasn't an issue of national concern, how could this possibly affect the average British voter? And global importance, well, no, clearly not. It was something quirky, something a little whimsical, a story that would amuse rather than educate, distract rather than inform. And that's why the disappearance of Luxembourg didn't headline the news, but was announced instead somewhere just between the sports round-up and the weather.

It wasn't even as if anyone could ascertain for how long it had been missing. It's not like Luxembourg was a country people were in the habit of looking at. A housewife in Belgium said that on Wednesday she'd thought to pop across the border, go to this grocery store she knew, the milk was always cheaper there. When she found out there was no longer a Luxembourg to pop across to, nothing but water stretching off as far as the eye could see, she'd turned right round and bought her goods from the supermarket in Antwerp. She said she might end up paying a bit more, but at least they were *reliable*. And no, she hadn't bothered to report the missing nation for a couple of days. When asked why, she said she was always mislaying things, there was no point in making a fuss, they usually showed up again sooner or later.

Juliet had never been to Luxembourg. Colin had. Sometimes she'd ask him what it was like there. "Oh, you know," he'd say vaguely, and shrug. And she'd smile, and nod, and change the subject, but she didn't know, that was the whole point, why else would she be asking? Sometimes he'd be a bit more forthcoming. "It's got nice architecture," he'd say. "Yeah, some of the architecture is quite nice. Quite European." Juliet didn't know Europe very well. She'd been on a day trip to Dieppe as a schoolgirl, and there'd been that summer holiday near that beach in Tenerife. Both times it had rained. She'd asked whether one day she might go to Luxembourg with him. She still had her passport, look. And showed him the photo of her inside, with that bemused expression on her face as the flash caught her by surprise. And he'd laughed, and said, no-one *chooses* to go to Luxembourg. He'd find them somewhere better than Luxembourg, just wait and see! Maybe on their anniversary. But the anniversaries had come, and then gone, several of them now, and that photo of her in the passport was looking terribly young now, she wasn't sure the customs people would let her through.

When Juliet saw the news story, she felt the urge to call out for Colin, she thought he'd find it interesting. But then she remembered. He was on one of those business trips of his, in Luxembourg, he did a lot of business in Luxembourg these days. Even at that very moment she thought he'd be enjoying himself, sampling the drizzly weather and the architecture. She settled down to watch the whole program, stupidly she half wondered whether Colin would get a mention. But they didn't talk about Luxembourg for long, soon it was time for *EastEnders*. So she watched *EastEnders* instead. She supposed there was nothing to worry about. She supposed if there was something she ought to be doing, someone would soon tell her to do it.

The next morning Juliet got up early, watched the news before going to work. She was a bit sleepy, so may not have been concentrating hard enough, but she was pretty sure Luxembourg wasn't mentioned at all. She asked the other girls at the supermarket about it, but none of them knew what she was talking about. Mrs. Wilson, who was deputy manager, but also did turns on the pâtisserie counter, so wasn't as big a deal as she thought she was, said she'd heard *something* about a country disappearing, but was certain it was Liechtenstein. And that gave Juliet some hope, she didn't think even Colin had visited Liechtenstein, she might still have a husband after all—but that night she watched the evening news, and there was an item about it, just a very short item, and it *had* been Luxembourg the whole time. "Country still missing," said the report. "Experts baffled." They had a financial boffin in, to work out how much the nation's absence would affect share prices and the FTSE—and he concluded it wouldn't make the slightest difference. And there was an editorial about it in *The Sun*, in an article entitled "Luxem-gone!" neither the title nor the contents of which made any sense whatsoever.

All that could be said with any certainty was that a nation of some half a million souls had been yanked out of existence. Fifty miles long by thirty-five miles wide, it was as if one of the jagged jigsaw pieces that made up Europe had simply been taken from the puzzle by its cosmic player. Not that many alluded to this being the handiwork of God—it was all very well some tub-thumpers claiming it was divine retribution for the evils that Luxembourg stood for, but since no one could work out what Luxembourg's stance had been on *anything*, it wasn't very convincing. A few theories did the rounds. Some said it was because of continental drift. It was unusual, admittedly, for a landlocked country to be drifting, but just because it had never happened before didn't mean it hadn't happened now. Others blamed it on global warming. They suggested that perhaps Luxembourg had been using a higher than average number of aerosol deodorants or CFC-bearing fridges per capita, and if someone could only conduct a few surveys on the ecological habits of the Luxembourg populace, they could prove it. It was hardly their fault, they said a trifle defensively, if there was no Luxembourg populace left to survey.

But the sad truth is that there weren't *that* many theories, because there wasn't that much interest. It had only been Luxembourg, after all. For a few days the nations of the world waited to see if anyone else would vanish—and when no one did, they heaved a sigh of relief. And, it must be said, looked at their neighbours sideways on, and felt a twinge of disappointment too.

The only remaining flicker of interest was not in Luxembourg itself, but what had been created in its absence. Small as a country it may have been, but the gaping puddle it left behind was considered to be rather on the large side. France called it "La Manchette." Belgium called it "La Mer Belgique." The Germans went one better, gave it the name "Fehlenderangrenzenderlandsee"—if anyone referred to it as something else, they put their fingers in their collective ears and pretended not to understand. There were quite heated discussions between the three countries, and even hints that all or any of them might be prepared to go to war to claim this fresh territory. And then the USA stepped in and said they were all being very silly—if they were going to behave like children, none of them could have it, so there. So it was named The American Channel. Everyone seemed satisfied with that. And with this last matter solved, Luxembourg dropped off the world's radar again, and every nation on the planet could get back to what it had been doing in the first place.

Juliet didn't find that so easy. Colin may have been away on his business trips rather a lot, but her life still had revolved around him—

if not his direct presence, then at least anticipation of his weekend returns. The weekend had always been about Colin, he ran through it like lettering through a stick of rock. On Saturday they would go out and do the shopping, and that night they'd curl up on the sofa and watch a DVD. If the movie wasn't too long, or if Colin wasn't interested in the special features, afterwards they might make love. That first Saturday she'd still half expected him to turn up; the night before she had, as always, vacuumed the house from top to bottom. Not that he ever commented, but she knew he'd notice if she didn't bother, she wanted the house to be just perfect for the time he was there. She adapted quite well, considering—she just pretended it was a Thursday instead, a Thursday without work, a long Thursday evening maybe, and carried on as normal, she was quite used to being on her own. But come the second weekend she found it all quite frustrating. She didn't know how much food she should buy on the shopping run, and the DVDs weren't nearly so much fun without Colin talking through the whole thing. She looked at the house, all newly cleaned, and wondered why she'd bothered. She began to fixate on his absence. It became a solid thing, somehow; she didn't know that absence could take up space, but it did—Colin wasn't there when she got up in the morning, Colin wasn't there when she went to bed, and he insisted on not being there at any time intervening—in a strange way, his very absence filled the house more completely than his presence ever had. She supposed she mentioned Luxembourg quite a lot at work, rather too much even. Mrs. Wilson took her to one side and told her to stop going on about it, she was boring everyone to bloody death, and since Mrs. Wilson was speaking to her at that moment in her capacity as deputy manager and wasn't even in spitting distance of the pâtisserie department, Juliet supposed she'd have to listen. And that seemed fair enough, she was beginning to bore herself too. And on the third Saturday in a row, as she lay there in bed, on her own, indisputably on her own, and there was no love making to be had, not even a sniff of it, Juliet told herself it was high time she did something about it all.

She supposed there must be many people out there who'd lost family when Luxembourg vanished—but since the overwhelming majority of them had been in Luxembourg too, there was no one she could compare notes with. She decided that Colin was dead. Once she put it like that, without fanfare, without qualification, everything seemed so much simpler. And seeing that he was dead, she decided too that she really ought to be grieving, that's what was called for at times like these. She stood in the bathroom, looked at herself in the mirror, practised expressions of sorrow and loss. It was hard work. In truth, she *did* feel sad, but, thinking about it, she felt sad pretty much most of the time, she wasn't sure Colin's death had very much to do with it. She had hoped that being sad already would be a help, that it wouldn't take much of a leap to get from her normal state of faded ennui to an appropriate display of grief. But just when she thought she'd got a handle on that grief, that it was finally taking shape, she'd lose her concentration and slip back into her usual sadness again. And wonder afterwards whether she'd been kidding herself, what she'd begun to feel wasn't anything like grief, not even in the same ballpark, it was just hunger or tiredness or boredom. Juliet had no experience of mourning, didn't know what it was she was reaching for. She'd never lost anyone; her siblings, her aunts and uncles, they were all still about, all still kicking. Her parents had stayed stubbornly alive— they were getting on a bit, and Juliet couldn't see what they actually *did* with all that life, but they were there anyway, if not exactly energetic, still nowhere yet near death's door. She'd have to try to mourn a bit harder, really put her back into it, she stared at herself in that mirror of hers, she practically *gurned* with the effort. She tried to visualize Colin as a corpse. But it was no good, he always just looked asleep, it made her drowsy just to think of him, it made her want to get into bed beside him and cuddle. And if she tried to imagine him with his eyes open, the facial contortions she put him through to make him look sufficiently deceased just gave her the giggles.

Colin's family felt sorry for Juliet, of course. They'd never much liked her, this shy girl that Colin had married so suddenly, pretty but not quite pretty enough, always hanging in the background at social occasions, never speaking unless she was spoken to and not speaking anything of interest even then, always too eager to pass the phone straight to Colin without saying more than the quickest of hellos. But they didn't dislike her either; there was nothing to dislike. They could quite appreciate the awkwardness that Colin's disappearance must be putting her through, and even if their sympathies had not yet been conveyed via greeting card or phone call—they wouldn't want to interfere—they were genuine enough. But when she invited them to Colin's funeral, they were somewhat irked. "He's not been in Luxembourg a month!" his mother told her. "Some people go on *holiday* longer than that!" She went on to tell her, in no uncertain terms, that there was no body, so he couldn't legally be pronounced dead, and even if there *were* a body, it would barely have cooled yet, what was her bloody rush? And Juliet told her quietly that she needed to move on. It was time. She had to move on. And although Colin's mother might have thought that Juliet was a brazen slut, that she obviously had some new man already lined up to take Colin's place, that she'd probably *wanted* Colin dead, yes, actually *wanted* it, so she could cop off with the nearest feller, that really wasn't it at all. Juliet just didn't feel she could accept Colin had left her until there was something official to tell her so. She asked the vicar if there could be a service at the church— no, there was no body, not yet, but she thought Colin'd have preferred cremation if that was any use—and was told that, sorry as he was for her loss, it wasn't quite a loss big enough for him to help her with. So the funeral became a wake, held at her house that Sunday, and all Colin's family and friends could come and pay their respects if they wanted to. Not many did. She'd been out on the shopping run the day before, had massively overcompensated on the sausage rolls and the scotch eggs, she'd be picking her way through them for months.

As she was washing up in the kitchen, Dave came in and asked if he could help. Dave said that she was the widow, she shouldn't be doing all the work. And Juliet said he could do the drying if he liked, there was a towel hanging by the saucepans. Juliet liked the sound of "widow," it gave her a buzz, and all day long she'd been waiting to feel something. Dave was three years younger than Colin, and would look a bit like him too, if only his hair were greyer and he were a bit fatter and he wore glasses. He'd come up from Leatherhead with his wife Sheila and their four-year-old son Tim, who'd been running around the house all afternoon pretending to be a dinosaur and who was clearly not making any better a stab at this grieving thing than Juliet was. "Do you miss your brother?" she asked Dave, as she handed him a cake knife.

"Oh yes," he said. "Well, sort of. I mean, I only see him at Christmas." He dried a couple of cups, and some saucers, and a fork. "I'll probably miss him at Christmas," he said.

They carried on washing up for a while. And then something got very confused, because he was supposed to be drying, but now his hands were in the sink as well, he was washing away at the cutlery with the spare sponge. It wasn't the largest of sinks, so their hands kept on bumping into each other.

"Do you miss him?" asked Dave.

"Oh yes," said Juliet.

"Do you miss kissing him?" asked Dave.

Juliet thought about this. "I suppose I do," she said. "Yes."

"I miss kisses too."

Juliet said, "But Sheila hasn't been in Luxembourg," and Dave said, "I know." And then his face was all over hers, cheek and neck, and finally he found his way to her lips, and she thought, oh yes, I was right, I *had* been missing this. They dripped soapsuds onto the floor. He pulled away. "Sorry," he said. "Sorry. I've wanted to do that for such a long time. Forgive me. I shan't do it again." And he left the kitchen.

That night he phoned her. "Oh, hello," she said. "Did you make it home okay?"

"I've got to see you again," he whispered at her. "I'm sorry, I'm sorry." She supposed that would be all right. He said he'd make it over to her on Saturday, he'd find a reason to be out for the day, just leave it with him. And even though it was now arranged, and this was only Sunday night, he managed to find a reason to call her every night that week to confirm all was still well.

She broke her shopping habit, went out on Friday evening. The supermarket wasn't as crowded, she wondered why she'd never done it on Fridays before. And she made Dave a nice lunch for when he arrived. He didn't want her potato salad, though. The first thing he did was to wrap her in his arms and kiss her all over, even before he'd taken his shoes off, even before his coat. Realistically Juliet had known they probably wouldn't draw the line at kissing, and there might be a bit of sex involved. She just wasn't prepared for how much. "Oh God, I've missed this!" he shouted out, sometime during the fifth bout. And Juliet said she'd missed it too, and she meant it, but she thought to herself she hadn't missed it quite enough to *shout* about. Dave looked just like Colin, but they felt so very different; Juliet had imagined that in the dark she could have pretended they were one and the same, fair exchange, no robbery—but his hands were all over her, she wasn't sure where he'd want to touch next, and it wasn't in the dark, was it, even with the curtains drawn the sunlight was streaming in, she could see *everything*. And that was a bit disconcerting at first, and not necessarily all that pleasant, but it lent a definite thrill to the proceedings. Around half past five he said he'd have to head home now, it was a long drive ahead, and Saturday traffic was probably rubbish. And she surprised herself by actually minding. "Don't go," she said, "not just yet," and, uselessly, "I've got potato salad in the kitchen." "Can we do this again?" he asked her. "We've got to do this again." "Oh yes," she said. "I bloody love you," he said, and kissed her, and drove away, and although she decided it'd be better to ignore that last bit, it replayed in her head a lot over the following week.

The next Saturday she didn't bother with the potato salad. She'd had a good think about what she should be feeling during the sex, about how much pleasure there ought to be—and she was able to get that right, she was very proud of herself, she'd caught the expression exactly. And then it occurred to her—my God!—she really *was* enjoying it, without having to consciously try. That made her panic a bit, she was lying there next to Dave when she realized that Colin was fading away, he'd been there in her head but now he was disappearing, how could he just disappear like that? This was grief, she thought, finally it was here, and she wasn't sure when she cried out whether it was out of relief or the sudden loss knotted in her stomach. And Dave hadn't known why she'd cried out either, but he held her tight, he held her until she felt better and he told her that he loved her. He was using the "love" word quite a lot. She told him once in a while not to be silly, and he said it wasn't silly, the last thing in the world it was was silly, it was *love*, didn't she deserve to be loved? And she asked him if he didn't love Sheila. It wasn't meant to be accusatory, but he went very quiet. He told her he had loved Sheila, of course he had, but that love had just gone. He didn't know where. It didn't make sense. How could something as important as love just fade away? What could it be worth if it could vanish so easily and without cause? So Juliet said that maybe he'd feel the same about her one day, and he denied that, he said this was a different kind of love, this one was solid. They had sex again after that. And then he got a bit tired, and asked whether she had anything to eat. He was bloody starving! And she wished she'd made the potato salad after all.

"I've told Sheila all about us," he said one Saturday. "We're getting a divorce." Juliet wasn't entirely sure that she wanted him leaving his wife for her sake—she'd only just got used to the idea of feeling grief and feeling pleasure without now having to feel guilt as well. Dave assured her it was all right. Sheila was pretty angry, and his mother was absolutely furious for some reason, Juliet might want to avoid answering the phone for a bit. But this was good, they'd no longer be living a lie, and better still, he could now spend all weekend with her. Friday evening to Sunday! He'd stay all week, of course, but his office was in Leatherhead, he could drop his marriage but not his job, that'd be silly. And it worked fine for a while. He wouldn't want sex the minute he got through the front door any longer, there was no need, they had all the time in the world now.

He'd help her with the shopping on Saturdays, in the evening they might watch a movie. Then they'd make love, and it was fairly good, but Juliet couldn't help but notice it was getting that bit more perfunctory, the hands weren't quite so keen to explore, they stayed pretty much north of the equator. Colin hadn't been a passionate man, but he'd had his moments, it had taken two years of marriage before the sex had got stale. With Dave it had taken a little under three months. Juliet supposed it was her fault, she must just suck the spirit out of people. And she didn't *want* Dave to be like Colin, she didn't want to think of Colin at all. But it was like prodding a sore tooth, she couldn't help it, she knew Dave was so close to being his brother—she watched for the grey hairs, she put extra mayonnaise in the potato salad to fatten him up. And already as she lay beside him in bed, as they shopped, watched DVDs, she thought, he may not be Colin, but Colin Mark II could be seen peeping through. "I love you," he'd tell her, so bloody often, and she'd believe him, but she'd choose half the time not to hear. "Let's have a baby," he said to her, "a baby of our very own." "But you've got Tim," she said. "Fuck Tim," he said. "I want a son with you." And he worked hard at that, Colin had never wanted a child, that made Dave different, didn't it? Didn't it? After they'd put the work in, he'd fall asleep and she'd lie in his arms. How long would he stay with her? How long could he love her? She'd started dreaming of turning on the news one weekday morning, and finding that Leatherhead was in the headlines, that Leatherhead had vanished from the face of the earth. And that's what she wanted, too; she wanted Leatherhead to fade away, and take Dave with it, just so she'd know, just so she'd finally *know* it was over and done with. She was practising already in front of the bathroom mirror,—she was practising her grief, this time she knew just how she was going to do all those reactions. And although he hadn't vanished yet, he hadn't done a Luxembourg on her, as she cuddled next to his sleeping body she began to mourn. "I love you," she said. "Oh God, I love you." And she began to cry. This is grief, she thought, I'm getting *so* good at this! It hurt so much. If only he'd disappear.

But Leatherhead didn't disappear. And Luxembourg came back.

Mrs. Wilson said she'd seen something on the news about it last night, hadn't Juliet heard? She was surprised, she'd always thought Juliet considered herself quite the Luxembourg expert. Juliet didn't believe her, but one of the girls at the checkout till confirmed it. Juliet asked if she could take her lunch break early, just to go and check, and Mrs. Wilson said she didn't think anyone could be seen to be taking lunch at half past ten, it'd set an unfortunate precedent. And Juliet thought, sod it, and it made her feel good to think that, and she went out to her car anyway, without permission, and drove home. She turned on her mobile, and Dave was there, he'd left four messages, "Phone me," he said, and, "We have to talk." So she called him from the car. "You've heard the news?" he said. "I'm coming over. I've left the office, I'm coming over right now. We need to talk about this."

Luxembourg had been misplaced in the middle of the Pacific Ocean. Juliet hadn't known much about the Pacific Ocean, but she now found out it was *vast*; you could drop a country in it easily, no sweat, say, twice the size of Luxembourg, and never expect to find it. The people of Luxembourg hadn't even noticed for a day or so they'd been transplanted; they were a bit puzzled by the warmer weather, but they weren't going to complain. And then it dawned on them—they were aboard an enormous raft, a thousand square miles floating untethered out of the reach of civilization. They peered over the edge. They found out that as wide as this raft was, it wasn't very thick—it was just a sliver of a nation, really, no more than three feet deep. And so the authorities had set up a rota, and the population had taken it in turns to lean over the side and paddle their way to the nearest country. They had thousands of miles to cross, but they really put their backs into it, it had taken them a little less than a year before they were close enough to Samoa to get a mobile phone signal and call for help.

And the best news was, as far as anyone could determine, pretty much everyone in Luxembourg had survived the incident. There'd been a few deaths, of course—old age, illness, suicide—but it looked as if they were the sort who'd have died anyway, all the dead looked fairly old or sick or fundamentally depressed. And there'd been some instances of cannibalism, where some of the populace had panicked and thought they might be about to starve, but these cases were few and far between, and no one had been quite sure why they'd resorted to such desperate means in the first place. After all, the cattle and the vegetation had been unaffected by the vanishing act, and besides, all the grocery stores had stayed open and kept normal hours.

So there was no reason to believe that Colin wasn't alive, and well, and would soon be coming home. "How do you feel about this?" asked Dave. He was sitting with her in the kitchen, looking very stern. And she didn't know how she felt, actually, did she need to *know* just yet, why did there always have to be a reaction to everything? She said she was excited. "No, how do you feel about us? What's going to happen to us?" And she hadn't even *started* to consider that. "Do you care at all?" he asked. And he said that he loved her, that he'd told her many times, but she'd never been straight with him, she'd never given him that love back. And she wanted to say that of course she loved him, she let him share her bed and her potato salad, what was love if not that? And she *did* tell him she loved him, she did it at least once a day, she counted; she just made sure he wasn't there at the time, or made sure he wasn't conscious, or made sure he was just out of earshot—and even now she didn't say this to him, it didn't seem fair to offer up love when she'd never been sure she was free. And he called her a bitch, said that he'd ruined his life for her, abandoned his wife, his kid, it was all her fault. It wasn't her fault, she began to say, it was *Luxembourg*, Luxembourg had done this to them, it disappeared for no reason, now it had popped back, how could a small European country be her responsibility? But he was having none of it. He left the house, if she wanted Colin rather than him that was up to her. He'd see whether Sheila would take him back, maybe if he said sorry, if he apologized for the rest of his bloody life. And, as it turned out, Sheila *did* take him back, but only under very stringent conditions. Apologizing for the rest of his life was just the start of it.

Metal hoops were hammered into the ground, studding the whole coastline. Ropes were threaded through. And, on a count of three, a whole flotilla of helicopters winched Luxembourg into the air, flew over to Europe, and lowered the errant country back into position. It wasn't a perfect fit, it was hard to get it into the hole exactly. Some of the extremities had to be chopped off, they lost the whole of Schengen and all the bits of Hinkel that were worth a damn. But they did the best they could, they stamped and kicked the towns that were bulging out into place, and Luxembourg was once more part of Europe. Only three feet thick, it bobbed on the water, and everyone was warned not to walk too heavily in case they sprung a leak.

And Colin came home. "Hello," he said to Juliet. "Hello," she said back. And neither were sure what to do, they both felt a bit shy. She had wondered whether seeing him on the doorstep once more would fill her with a romantic passion, that they'd sweep each other up in their arms, and never stop kissing again, never stop making love. It wasn't quite like that, but it was affectionate, they gave each other a hug. "Would you like some lunch?" she said, and he said he would. She asked him what the ordeal in Luxembourg had been like. "Oh, you know," he replied, and shrugged. He noticed she was pregnant. That's right, she said. He said he didn't blame her, she'd have thought he was dead, he'd have done the same thing had she been the one who'd disappeared. "What was he like?" he asked. "Was he better than me?" "Oh," she said, "you know." He nodded, ate his potato salad, said he'd never ask her again. To his credit he never did. She just hoped that the baby growing inside her looked nothing like her husband, it'd be hard to explain. But a few months later out it came, and it didn't, it looked like every other baby, a bald, bad-tempered old man.

For a while for the marriage improved. They had conversations when they did the shopping, he picked movies to watch on DVD she might actually like. And the lovemaking was never exciting, not exactly, but it wasn't a ritual anymore, it felt at least like making love. "I didn't know what I was missing," he said. "I've been such an idiot." And yes, in time, it all sank back into routine again, but they'd shown each other it didn't always *have* to be like that, they could make it all work so easily if they could just get round to bothering, and maybe that was enough. And Colin was an excellent father, he knew just what to do; Juliet rather envied him that, it took her a lot of thought to decide how a mother should behave. "We're happy," he said one night to her, quite unexpectedly. "We're actually happy, aren't we?" And she agreed. They were.

One day, about twenty years later, he told her he had cancer. It was eating away at him, it had been for ages apparently. The doctor had told him that morning, that's why he had to speak to her like this, that's why he had to sound so serious, oh God, don't be upset, oh God. Because it wasn't too late, the doctor had promised him, there were treatments, they mustn't give up hope. But the doctor was wrong; it was much too late. And all the treatments in the world could do nothing but make Colin's death terribly slow. Juliet was always there for him. She drove him to the hospital. She fed him soup, even when he wasn't hungry, she told him he had to keep his strength up. And she mopped it when he threw it all up, she never commented, never made him feel bad. As she watched, he got older and weaker; his hair whitened then went altogether, his paunch disappeared into thin air. And she wished he'd vanish with the paunch. She wished she could wake up one morning and know he'd just evaporated whilst she'd slept, so painless, so simple. She now knew how to react, she could do the grieving thing now, she'd been right, it *was* easier when there was a body. And this time everyone came to the funeral, all the family were there to see him off. Not Dave, of course. Dave had died from a stroke two years previously. Juliet hadn't mourned; she'd decided then and there to save it all up for Colin.

A few weeks before he died, Colin told her he had something to confess. He didn't want to hurt her, but this was something he had to do. She waited patiently as he tried to find the words. "I was never in Luxembourg," he said.

She asked him what he meant.

"I was having an affair," he told her. And he explained how he'd lied the whole time, invented business trips just to get away from her. He'd seen this woman on and off for years, he wouldn't say her name, it didn't matter anymore—and Juliet agreed, it didn't. When Luxembourg vanished it had seemed like a godsend. His life had changed overnight, he was free, and there'd be no need for a divorce, no need to make Juliet feel bad, because it had never been her fault, it had been him, all him. A break, clean and simple. He'd moved in with his lover. They had barely lasted a month. Some relationships are better at arm's length, he said. Sometimes the reality of living together just gets in the way. He knew he couldn't go back to Juliet. How could he explain where he'd been? And then one day Luxembourg had returned. It had given him a second chance. He began to cry.

"It's okay," she said. "It doesn't matter now."

And she could barely make out his voice through the tears. "That's not it," he said. "I miss her. I'm sorry. I miss her. I'm sorry. I'm sorry." And she held him in her arms, and she kissed him. And she cried too, because she knew what he meant—it was wrong, but sometimes she felt exactly the same thing.

One day she decided to take a holiday. Her husband was dead, her son was at college. What was to stop her? She renewed her passport, had a new photo taken for it. The old one looked so young now, so gauche; the picture that looked out now at the customs officials was confident, and hard, and expressive, that was a face that had *felt* things.

There wasn't much tourist interest in Luxembourg. Even after twenty years of good behaviour, it still had its reputation. And people said they felt seasick there, especially near the edge—you could see the whole country rise and fall on the water. Juliet liked Luxembourg. She liked the architecture. She knew it wasn't the *real* architecture, of course; the surface of Luxembourg was so thin all the heavy buildings had been torn down and replaced with balsa wood replicas. But that was okay, Juliet knew that Luxembourg had to have changed, that there'd have to be a

Luxembourg Mark II. She was wise enough to know that's what happened to things that come back, things you'd thought had been lost forever.

She bought herself a caffè latte, and sat beneath the light flat board spires of Luxembourg's very own Notre Dame Cathedral—not as grand looking as the one in Paris, but perfectly okay as far as cathedrals went, perfectly acceptable, they'd done a good job. She wondered whether she was tempting fate by coming here. She wondered if it would all disappear, and take her with it, and this time there'd be no going back, no reprieve discovery in the Pacific, no last minute returns, they'd all vanish forever and never be heard of again. Well, she thought to herself, we'll see. And she decided that if she vanished, she'd just accept it. And if she didn't, she'd go home, and get on with the rest of her life. Either way, she wouldn't complain. She'd give herself, and Luxembourg, and their twin destinies, until she reached the end of her coffee. She sipped at it, without rush, and admired the architecture, and smiled, and enjoyed the day.

RESTORATION

The Curator said that it was the responsibility of every man, woman, and child to find themselves a job; that there was a grace and dignity to doing something constructive with the long days. The purity of a simple life, well led—everyone could see the appeal to that. But the problem was, there really just weren't enough jobs to go around. This made a lot of people quite unhappy. Not so unhappy that they gnashed their teeth or rent their garments, it wasn't unhappiness on a biblical scale—but you could see them, these poor souls who had nothing to do, there seemed to hang about them an ennui that could actually be smelt.

Some people said that it was patently unfair that there weren't enough jobs. The Curator could create as many jobs as he wished, he could do anything, so this had to be a failing on his part, or something crueller. And other people admonished these doubters, they told them to have more faith. It was clearly a test. But they thought everything was a test, that was their explanation for everything.

Neither group of people liked to voice their opinions too loudly, though. You never knew when the Curator might be listening. The Curator had eyes and ears everywhere.

When the job at the gallery came up Andy applied for it, of course. *Everyone* applied for it, yes, man, woman and child—and though Andy hadn't been there long enough yet to realize the importance of getting work, he still knew the value of joining a good long queue when he saw one. He obviously hadn't expected to get the job. That he might was clearly absurd. And so when they told him he'd been selected he thought they were joking, that this was another part of the interview, that they were monitoring his response to success, maybe—and he decided that the response they were looking for was probably something enthusiastic, but not *too* enthusiastic—and he managed to pull off a rather cool unsmiling version of enthusiasm that he thought would fit the bill, then sat back in his chair waiting for the next question—only starting when they made him understand there really *weren't* any more questions, that that was it, the job was his.

Andy didn't know why he'd got the job. But he still had his own hair. Or, at least, most of it—and perhaps that's what made him stand out from the other applicants. Certainly there were others he'd queued alongside who were far better qualified, and more intelligent too, who had even done revision so that they'd give good answers at the interview. When Andy had been quizzed he hadn't known what to say, and he'd just nodded his head a lot, he fluttered at them his brown and quite unremarkable curls, unremarkable in all ways save for the fact he had so many of them; he showed them off for all they were worth, that's what did him well in the end.

Andy hadn't even been to an art gallery since he was a child. He'd been taken on a school trip. He'd been caught chewing gum, and had got into trouble; then he'd lagged behind the main party and got lost somewhere within the Post-Impressionists, the teacher had had to put out an announcement for him, he'd got into trouble for that too. He knew that the gallery here would be much bigger, because everything was bigger here—but he still boggled at the enormity of it as he walked through the revolving doors. There were no small exhibits here. A single work of art would take up an entire room, and the rooms were *vast*, as you walked into one you had to strain your eyes to find the exit at the far end—the picture would run right round all the walls, and extend right up to the ceiling a hundred feet in the air. Andy couldn't stand back far enough from the art to take in the sheer scale of even a single picture; he always seemed to be pressed up close to the figures caught in the paintwork, he could honestly marvel at the extraordinary detail of each and every one of them. But seeing these figures in context, that was much more difficult. He read the plaque on the wall for one picture: "1776," it said. And now he could see, yes, the Americans jubilantly declaring their independence, and the British all looking rather sinister and sulky in the background. He went into the next room, and presented there was 1916. And 1916 was a terrifying sight—the work took in the one and a half million soldiers dying in the trenches, in Flanders, at the Somme, and it seemed to Andy that every single one of these casualties was up there stuck onto the wall, shot or blown apart or drowning in mud. It was a dark picture, but yet it wasn't all mud and blood—look, there's Charlie Chaplin falling over at a skating rink, there's Al Jolson singing, Fred Astaire dancing, there's the world's first golf tournament, that'd be fun for all.

Andy shuddered at the carnage in spite of himself—because, as he said out loud, it wasn't really there, it wasn't really *real*. And he couldn't help it, he chuckled at Chaplin too, he grinned at all those golfers putting away to their hearts' delight.

There was no one to be seen at the gallery. The rooms were crowded with so many people living and dying, but on the walls only, only in the art—there was no one looking at them, marvelling at what they'd stood for, marvelling at the brushwork even. There was a little shop near the main entrance that sold postcards. There was no one behind the cash register.

"What do you make of it?" asked the woman behind him.

He didn't know where she'd sprung from, and for a moment he thought she must have popped out from one of the pictures, and the idea was so ludicrous that he nearly laughed. He stopped short, though, because she was frowning at him so seriously, he could see laughter wasn't something the woman would appreciate, or even recognize, this was a woman who hadn't heard laughter in a very long time. He presumed she *was* a woman. Surely? The voice was high, and there was a softness to the eyes, and to the lips, and there was some sagging on the torso that might once have been breasts—yes, he thought, definitely woman. Her head was completely smooth and hairless, and a little off green, it looked like a slightly mildewed egg.

Andy tried to think of something clever to say. Failed. "I don't know."

"Quite right," said the woman. "What *can* you make of it? What can anyone make of anything, when it comes down to it?" She stuck out her hand. Andy took a chance that she wanted him to shake it; he did so; he was right. "You must be my new assistant. I don't want an assistant, I can manage perfectly well on my own, I do not require assisting of any sort. But the Curator says different, and who am I to argue? The best thing we can do is to leave each other alone as much as possible, it's a big place, I'm sure we'll work it out. Do you know anything about art?"

"No."

"About history?"

"No."

"About the conservation and restoration of treasures more fragile and precious than mere words can describe?"

"No."

"Good," she said. "There'll be so much less for you to unlearn." And

25

she gave at last the semblance of a smile. Her egg face relaxed as the smile took hold: the eyes grew big and yolky, the albumen cheeks seemed to ripple and contort as if they were being poached.

"How did you know," said Andy, "that I was your new assistant?"

"Why else would you be here?"

She said she'd take him to her studio. She led him out of the First World War, back through the Reformation, through snatches and smatterings of the Dark Ages. She walked briskly, and Andy struggled to keep up—as it was, it was the best part of an hour before they reached the elevator. "I'll never find my way through all this!" Andy had joked, and his new boss had simply said, "No, you won't," and they hadn't talked again for a while.

She pulled the grille door to the elevator shut. "Going down," she said, and pushed the lowest button on the panel. Nothing happened; she kicked at the elevator irritably, at last it began to move—and fast, faster, as if to make up for lost time. Andy was alarmed and tried to find something to hold on to, but there was only the woman, and that didn't appeal, so he stuck his hands tight into his pockets instead. The woman did not seem remotely perturbed. "Now, you might think that the gallery upstairs is huge. Well, it *is* huge, I suppose, I've never been able to find an end to it. But only a small fraction of the collection is ever on display. Say, no more than two or three per cent. The rest of the art, the overwhelming majority of it, we keep below. We keep in the vaults. And it's in the vaults that we care for this unseen art. We clean it, we protect it. We restore it to what it used to be. What's up top," she said, and she jerked a finger upwards, to somewhere Andy assumed must now be miles above their heads, "is not our concern anymore."

Andy was still catching up with what she'd said fifty metres higher, his brain seemed to be falling at a slower rate than hers. "Just two or three per cent? Christ, how many paintings have you got?"

She glared at him. She thinned her once feminine lips, she showed teeth. "They're not paintings," she said. "Never call them paintings."

"I'm sorry," said Andy, and she held his gaze for a few seconds longer, then gave a single nod, and turned away, satisfied.

The elevator continued to fall.

"My name's Andy," said Andy, "you know, by the way."

"I can't remember that. I can't be expected to remember all that."

"Oh."

"You've got lots of hair. I could call you Hairy. Except that won't last long, the hair won't last, it'll just confuse me. Tell you what. I'll call you 'Assistant.' That'll be easy for both of us."

"Fair enough," said Andy. He'd been about to ask for her name. He now thought he wouldn't bother.

And then he was surprised, because he felt something in his hand, and he looked down, and it was *her* hand—just for a moment, a little squeeze, and then it was gone. And she was doing that macabre poached smile at him. "Don't worry, Assistant," she said softly. "I used to call them paintings. I once thought they were just paintings too."

↓

"All right, Assistant. I'm giving you 1574 to practise on. 1574 is a very minor work. If you damage 1574, who's going to care?" And she unrolled 1574 right in front of him, across the table of his new studio, across *all* the studio—she unrolled it ever onwards until 1574 spread about him and over him in all directions.

"Is this the original?"

"Who'd want to make a copy?"

What surprised Andy was that the archives down below were in such poor condition. The art was stacked everywhere in random order, although he was assured by his new boss there was a system—"It's *my* system," she said, "and that's all you need to know." Some of the years were in tatters, the months bulging off the frame, entire days lost beneath dirt. "You might suppose they'd be irreparable," she told him. "1346 was in a terrible state when I started here, there was a crease in the August, running right through the battle of Crécy. But with diligence, and hard labour, and love, I was able to put it right."

It was odd to hear her talk of love, that such a word could come out of a bald, ovoid face like hers. She seemed to think it was odd too, looked away. "But diligence and hard labour are probably the most important," she added.

And although Andy had no affection for these works of art, had no reason to care, when she told him that the collection wasn't complete he felt a pang of regret in his stomach for the loss. "Ideally," she agreed, "the gallery is meant to house a full archive, from prehistory right up to 2038. But there are entire decades that have vanished without trace. Stolen, maybe, who knows? More likely destroyed. Some years were in such a state of disrepair there was nothing I could do with them, some years just decomposed before my eyes. 1971, for example, that was a botched job from the start, the materials were of inferior quality. It crumbled to dust so fast, before the spring of 1972 was out."

"What does the Curator think of that?"

She sighed heavily through her nose, it came out as a scornful puff. "The Curator's instructions are that I take responsibility for the entire collection, the whole of recorded history." She shrugged. "But I can't work miracles. That's his job."

And now here was Andy with his own year to take care of. He gave 1574 a good look. And his boss gave *him* a good look as he did so; she just folded her arms, watched him, said nothing. "It's not too bad," said Andy finally. "It's not in as bad a condition as some of the others."

"It's in an *appalling* condition," she said. "Oh, Assistant. You've been looking at all the wrong things, you don't know what's good and what's shit, but never mind, never mind, I suppose you have to start somewhere. Look again. Now. The year is *filthy*, for a start. Look at it, it's so dark. Do you think that 1574 was always this dark? Only if it had been under permanent rain clouds, and in fact, the weather was rather temperate by sixteenth century standards. Now, that's not unusual, you have to expect the original colours to darken. Natural aging will do that—pigments fade and distort from the moment the events are lived, as soon as they're set down on canvas. Rich greens resinate over time, they become dark browns, even blacks. The shine gets lost.

"But in this instance," she went on, and prodded at 1574 with her finger, so disdainfully that Andy thought she'd punch a hole right through it, "it's worse than that, because we can't even begin to *see* how badly the pigments have been discoloured. They're buried behind so much dirt and grease. And soot, actually, that's my fault, I probably shouldn't have stored it next to the Industrial Revolution. Dirt has clung to the year, and that's not the fault of the year itself, but of the varnish painted over it. For centuries all the great works of art were varnished by the galleries, they thought it would better protect them. And some people even preferred the rather cheesy gloss it put on everything. But a lot of the varnishers were hacks—the varnish wasn't compatible with the original oils of the year itself, it'd react to them. And that's when you get smearing, and blurring, and dirt getting trapped within the year as if it's always been there.

"And that's just for starters! Look at the cracks. Dancing through the night sky of March 1574 there, do you see, they stand out so well in the moonlight. Now, I admit I like a bit of craquelure, I think it lends a little aged charm to an old master. But here, yes . . . these aren't just cracks, they're *fissures*, they're causing the entire panel to split out in all directions. Pretty soon March won't have thirty-one days in it, it'll end up with thirty-two. And that's all because of the oils drying, yes? The oils go on the canvas nice and wet, then they dry, the very months dry, the days within get brittle and flaky, the whole year contracts and moves within its frame."

"And what can we do to stop that?" asked Andy.

She very nearly laughed. "Stop it? We can't stop it! Oh, the arrogance of the man! Do you think *any* of the years here are in the same condition as when they were created? They're dying from the moment the paint has dried, all the sheen and brightness fading, the colours becoming ever more dull, the very tinctures starting to blister and pop. These are precious things, these little slices of time we've been given—and from the moment a year's over, from the moment they all start singing 'Auld Lang Syne' to usher in the new, the old one is already beginning to fall apart. The centuries that pass do untold damage to the centuries that have been. There's no greater enemy to history than history itself, running right over it, scraping it hard, then crushing it flat. And some days I think that's it, all I'm doing is kicking against the inevitable, I can do nothing to stop the decay of it all, all I can do is choose the method of decay it'll face. And that's on the good days, the ones where I fool myself I'm making the blindest bit of difference—on the others, and, are you listening, Assistant, there'll be so *many others*, I feel like I'm surrounded by corpses and pretending I can stop the rot, and I can't stop the rot, who are we to stop the rot, we're working in a fucking morgue."

"Oh," said Andy. "That's a shame."

She blinked at him. Just once. Then pulled herself together.

"Frankly," she said, "1574 is a dog's breakfast. And that's why I'm setting you on to it. You're hardly likely to make it much worse. Off you go, then, 1574's not getting any younger, chop-chop."

Andy pointed out he had no idea where to start conserving and cleaning a year. As far as he knew, he was supposed to run it under a tap! He chuckled at that; she didn't chuckle back. So he asked, very gently, whether he could watch her work for a while, to see how it was done.

She took him to her studio.

"This," she said, and she tried to keep a nonchalance to her voice, "is my current project." But Andy could see how she was smiling, she was just happy to be back in front of her work again—and then she gave up trying to disguise it, she turned round to him and *beamed*, she ushered him forward, invited him to look, invited him to see how well she'd done. She'd mounted a section of the year, the rest was rolled up neatly, and it seemed to Andy that she'd made an altar of that section, that it was a place of worship. "1660," she said. "Most famous for the restoration of the Stuarts to the throne of England and Scotland, and I think that's why the Curator will like this year especially, he's very keen on the triumph of authority. But there's so much more to 1660 than dynastic disputes, really—December the eighth, there's Margaret Hughes as Desdemona, the very first actress on the English stage! And that's Samuel Pepys, the diarist, September twenty-fifth, drinking his first ever cup of tea! All the little anecdotes that throw the main events into sharp relief, history can't just be kings and thrones, if you're not careful it becomes nothing but a series of assassins and wars and coups d'état, and the colour is just a single flat grey. And that's not what we're about, is it? We've got to find the other colours, Andy, we've got to find all the colours that might get forgotten, what we're doing *is* important after all!" And she suddenly looked so young, and so innocent somehow, and Andy realized she'd bothered to remember his name.

He watched her as she worked, and she soon forgot he was there, she was lost in bringing out the light in Pepys' eyes as his first taste of tea hit home, his questing curiosity, his wonder (his wrinkled nosed disgust!)—and she was happy, and she even began to sing, not words, he didn't hear any words, she seemed at times to be reaching for them but then would shake her head, she'd lost them. And she didn't notice when he sneaked away and closed the door behind him.

☟

Over the following weeks, Andy began to fall in love with 1574.

It wasn't an especially distinguished year, he'd have admitted. It was most notable for the outbreak of the Fifth War of Religion between the Catholics and the Huguenots—but this was the *fifth* war, after all, and it wasn't as if the first four had done much good, so. It was marked by the death of Charles IX, King of France, and Selim II, Sultan of the Turks, and try as he might, Andy couldn't find much sympathy for either of them. The Spanish defeated the Dutch at the battle of Mookerheyde—when Andy picked off the surface dirt he could see all the surviving Spaniards cheering. And explorer Juan Fernández discovered a series of volcanic islands off the coast of Chile, and he named them the Juan Fernández Islands, and it was a measure perhaps of how little anyone wanted these islands discovered in the first place that the name stayed unchallenged.

But none of that mattered.

For research Andy had looked at 1573 and 1575, the sister years either side, and they were really very similar at heart, with a lot of the same crises brewing, and a lot of the same people causing those crises. But Andy didn't like them. In fact, he despised them. It was almost as if they were both faux 1574s, they were trying so hard to be 1574 and just falling short, it was pathetic, really. He'd dab away with his cotton swabs, removing the muck that 1574 had accumulated, and he poured his soul into it, all his effort and care; he gave it the very best of him— 1574 *was* the very best of him. And he loved it because he knew no one else ever would, this grisly year from a pretty grisly century all told, twelve unremarkable little months that had passed unmourned so many centuries before.

He would dream of 1574 too. Of living in 1574; he could have been happy there, he knew it. It wasn't that he needed to sleep; no one needed sleep anymore, sleeping acted as a restorative to the body and it wasn't as if his body could possibly be restored. But he went to sleep anyway, as useless as sleeping was. He slept so he could dream. 1574 would have been perfect for him, so long as he'd kept away from all those Catholics and Huguenots, they were a liability.

One day his boss came to see him. He was so enjoying the work, he was rather irritated that he had to put a pause to it and give her attention.

"You've completely smudged that night sky in October," she said.

"I was a bit too free with the solvent," Andy admitted.

"And God knows what you've done to the craquelure in Spain, it's worse than when you started."

Andy shrugged.

"You're really very good," she said. "I'm impressed."

"Thank you."

"You don't need to thank me."

Her newfound respect for his work meant that she began to visit more often. Every other day or so she'd come to peer at his 1574, clucking her tongue occasionally (in approval or not, Andy couldn't tell), tilting her head this way and that as she took it in from different angles, sometimes even brushing key areas of political change and social unrest with her fingertips. Andy minded. And then Andy found he'd stopped minding, somehow—he even rather looked forward to seeing her, it offered him the excuse to put down the sponge and give his arms a rest.

"What was your name again?" she asked one day.

Andy thought for a moment. "Andy," Andy said.

"I like you, Andy. So I'm going to give you a piece of advice."

"All right," said Andy.

"There's only so much room in a head," she said. And she smiled at him sympathetically.

". . . Is that it?"

"That's it."

"Fair enough," said Andy. And she left.

She came back again a day or two later. "It occurs to me," she said, "that the advice I offered may not have been very clear."

"No."

"You remember that I came by, offered advice . . . ?"

"Yes, I remember."

"Good," she said. "Good, that's a start. I like you, sorry, what was your name again?"

Andy sighed. He lay down his cotton swab. He turned to face her. He opened his mouth to answer. He answered. "Andy," he said.

"It's an absorbing job, this," she told him. "It kind of takes over. You fill your head with all sorts of old things, facts and figures. And memories can be pushed out. Personal memories, of what you did when you were alive, even what your name was. There's only so much room in a head."

"I'm not going to forget my own name," Andy assured her.

"I did," said his boss simply, and smiled.

"I'm sorry," said Andy.

"Oh, pish," she said, and waved his sympathy aside. "Names don't matter. Names aren't us, they're just labels. Names go, and good riddance, I don't want a name. But who we *were*, Andy, that's what you need to hang on to. You need to write it down. I did. For me, I did. Look." And from her pocket she took out a piece of paper.

"1782," the message read. "Tall gentleman, wearing top hat. Deep blue eyes, the bluest I've ever seen. And the way the corners of his mouth seem to be just breaking into a smile. Special. So special, you make him stand out from the crowd, you give him definition. Make him count."

"I carry it with me everywhere," she said. "And if I ever lose myself. If I ever doubt who I am. I take it out, and I read it, and I remember. That once I was in love. That once, back in 1782, there was a man, and out of all the countless billions of men who have lived through history, against all those odds, we found each other."

And she was smiling so wide now, and her eyes were brimming with tears.

"You don't know his name?" asked Andy.

"I'm sure he had one at the time. That's enough."

She put the paper away. "Write it all down, Andy," she said. "Don't waste your efforts on all the unimportant stuff, your job, your house, whether you had a pet or not. That's all gone now. But your wife, describe your wife, remind yourself that you too were once loved and were capable of inspiring love back."

"Oh, I didn't have a wife," said Andy.

The woman's mouth opened to a perfect little "o." She stared at him.

"I never quite found the right girl," Andy went on cheerfully.

The mouth closed, she gulped. Still staring.

"You know how it is. I was quite picky."

By now she was ashen. "Oh, my poor man," she said. "My poor man. You must have already forgotten."

"No, no," Andy assured her. "I remember quite well! I had the odd girlfriend, some of them were very odd, ha! But never the right one. Actually, I think they were quite picky too, ha!, maybe more picky than me, ha ha! Look, no, look, it's all right, it doesn't matter . . ."

Because he'd never seen her egg white face quite so white before, and her eyes were welling with tears again, but this time she wasn't smiling through them. "You must have forgotten," she insisted. "You must have been loved, a man like you. Life wouldn't be so cruel. Oh, Andy." And impulsively, she kissed him on top of the head.

"You're beginning to lose your hair," she then said.

"Am I?" asked Andy.

"You should watch out for that."

↓

She didn't visit for a while afterwards, and it wasn't surprising at first, he knew how easy it was just to get lost in the work, but after a bit he began to wonder whether he might have offended her in some way—he couldn't remember what way that might have been—and he supposed it didn't matter if he had, he didn't like her very much (or did he?—he didn't *recall* liking her, that had never been a part of it, but), but, but then he realized he missed her, that her absence was a sad and slightly painful thing, that he should put a stop to that absence, he should set off to find her. So he did. He left 1574 behind and went looking for 1660, and he couldn't work out how to get there; he walked up and down corridors of the twelfth century, and then the tenth, it was all a bit confusing, there were Vikings every which way he looked. And it began to bother him that he couldn't decide where 1660 came in history—was it after 1574, was it before? And he thought, sod it, I'll turn back, and he walked in the direction he had come, but somehow that brought him to the fifth century, and there were no Vikings now, just bloody Picts. He didn't think he could find 1574 let alone 1660, and he started to panic, and he was just about to resign himself to the idea of settling down with the Anglo Saxons, maybe it wouldn't be so bad—when he turned the corner, and there, suddenly, was Charles II restored to the throne, there was Samuel Pepys, there was *she*, there she was, sitting at her desk, paintbrush in hand, and all but dwarfed by the Renaissance in full glory.

"Hello," he said.

But she didn't reply, and he thought that maybe she was concentrating, she didn't want to be disturbed, and he could respect that, he'd have wanted the same thing—so he waited, he bided his time, so much time to bide in all around him, and he bided it. Until he could bide no more— "Hello, are you all right?" he asked, and he went right up to her, and she still didn't acknowledge him, he went right up to her face. And her eyes were so wide and so scared, and her cheeks were blotched with tears, and her lips, her bottom lip was trembling as if caught in mid-stutter, "No," she said, or at least that's what he thought it was, but it might not have been a word, it might just have been a noise, "nonononono." "Do you know who I am?" he asked, and she looked directly at him, then recoiled, it was clear she didn't know *anything*, "nonono," she sobbed, and it wasn't an answer to his question, it was all she could say, each "no" popping out every time that bottom lip quivered. "Do you know who I am?" he asked again, "I'm . . ." and for the life of him at that moment he forgot his own name, how ridiculous, "I'm your assistant, yes? I'm your *friend*." And he moved to touch her, he wanted to hold her, hug her, something, but she slapped him away, and the tears started, she was so very frightened. "I'm your friend," he said, "and I'll look after you," and he knocked aside the slaps, he held on to her, and tight too, he held on as close as she'd let him, and he felt her tears on his neck, and they weren't warm like tears were supposed to be, oh, they were so *cool*. "I'm your friend, and I'm going to look after you, and I'll never stop looking after you," and he hadn't meant to make a promise, but it was a promise, wasn't it?, and "Just you remember that!", but she didn't remember anything, not a thing—and he held on to her until she *did*, until at last she did.

"Andy?" she said. "Andy, what's wrong?" Because he was crying too. And she looked so surprised to see him there, and so glad too—and he thought, *Andy*, oh yes, *that* was it.

↧

One day, as Andy was sponging down a particularly anonymous Huguenot, she came to him. She looked awkward, even a little bashful.

"I've been thinking," she said. "You can give me a name. If you like."

Andy turned away from 1574. "I thought you didn't want a name."

She blushed. "I don't mind."

"All right," he said. "What about Janet?"

She wrinkled her nose.

"You don't like Janet?"

"I don't," she agreed, "like Janet."

"Okay," he said. "Mandy."

"No."

"Becky."

"No."

"Samantha. Sammy for short."

"Tell you what," she said. "You give it a think, and when you come up with something you like, you come and find me."

"I'll do that," said Andy.

He resumed work on his Huguenot. The bloodstain on his dagger-gouged stomach shone a red it hadn't shone in hundreds of years. Andy worked hard on it, he didn't know for how long, but there was a joy to it, to uncover this man's death like it was some long lost buried treasure, and make it stand out bold and lurid and smudge-free.

Next time she came she was wearing a ribbon. He didn't know why, it looked odd wrapped around her shiny bald forehead. Why was the forehead so shiny? Had she done something to it? "I've been thinking," she said.

"Oh yes?"

"What about Miriam?"

"Who's Miriam?"

"Me. I could be Miriam."

"You could be Miriam, yes."

"Do you like Miriam?"

"Miriam's fine."

"Do you think Miriam suits me?"

"I think Miriam suits you right down to the ground," said Andy, and she beamed at him.

"All right," she said. "Miriam it is. If you like it. If that works well for you."

"Hello, Miriam," he said. "Nice to meet you." And they laughed.

"I love you," she said then.

"You do what, sorry?"

"I think it's so sad, that no one ever loved you."

"I don't know that *no one* ever loved me . . ."

"And at first I thought this was just pity for you. Inside me, here. But then it grew. And I thought, that's not pity at all, that's love." She scratched at her ribbon. It slipped down her face a bit. "I mean, I might have got it wrong, it might just be a deeper form of pity," she said. "But, you know."

"Yes."

"Probably not."

"No."

"Probably love."

"Yes."

"I want you to know," she said, "what it feels like to inspire love. You inspire love. In me."

"Well," he said. "Thank you. I mean that."

"Do I inspire love in you?"

"I hadn't really thought about it," said Andy.

"Would you think about it now?"

"All right," he said. "Yes. Go on, then. I think you do."

"Oh good," said Miriam.

She left him then. He got back to his dying Huguenot. The Huguenot seemed to be winking at him. Andy didn't like that, and swabbed at the Huguenots' eyes pointedly.

When Miriam returned the ribbon was gone, and Andy thought that was good, it really hadn't looked right. But, if anything, the forehead was shinier still. And there was a new redness to the lips, he thought she must have spilled some paint on to them.

"If it is love. Not just pity on my part, confused politeness on yours. Would you like to *make* love?"

"We could," Andy agreed.

He hadn't taken off his clothes for years now. But they were removed easily enough, it was just a matter of tugging them away with a bit of no-nonsense force. Miriam's clothes were another matter, they seemed to have been glued down, or worse—Andy wondered as they tried to peel them off whether some of the skin had grown over the clothes, or the clothes had evolved into skin, or vice versa—either way they weren't budging. It took half an hour to get most of the layers off, but there were patches of blouse and stocking that they couldn't prise away even with a chisel.

They stood there—he, naked, she, as naked as they could manage without applying some of the stronger solvents.

"You go first," she said, and he thought he could take the responsibility of that—but then, as he came toward her, he stopped short, he couldn't recall what on earth he was supposed to do. He looked at her, right at her egg face, and she was smiling bravely, but there were no clues offered in that smile, and he looked downwards, and it seemed to him that both of her breasts were like eggs too, perched side by side on top of a rounded belly that was also like an egg—her whole hairless body was like a whole stack of eggs inexpertly stitched together, God, he was looking at an entire omelette! And though she wasn't beautiful, it was nevertheless naked flesh, and it was vaguely female in shape, and his prick twitched in memory of it, in some memory that it ought to be doing *something*.

"I do love you," he said. "I love you too," she replied. And they approached the other. And they reached out their hands. And their fingers danced gently on each other's fingers. And he stroked his head against her chest. And she bit awkwardly at his nose. And they bounced their stomachs off each other—once, twice, three times!—boing!—and that third bounce was really pretty frenzied. Then they held each other. They both remembered that part.

The next time she came to visit him in his studio, they had both completely forgotten they'd once tried sex. And perhaps that was a blessing. Andy was absorbed in an entirely new Huguenot corpse, and she seemed to have grown new clothes. But she remembered her name was Miriam now, and so did he; they clung on to that, together, at least.

1574:

In February, the so-called Fifth War of Religion breaks out in France between the Catholics and the Huguenots; the Fourth War had only ended six months previously. War Number Four didn't, as you might gather, end very conclusively. The Huguenots were given the freedom to worship— but *only* within three towns in the whole country, and *only* within their own homes, and marriages could be celebrated but *only* by aristocrats before an assembly limited to ten people outside their own family. King Charles IX dies shortly afterwards. He was the man responsible for the slaughter of thousands of Huguenots in the St. Bartholomew's Day Massacre. Reports say that he actually died sweating blood; he is said to have turned to his nurse in his last moments and said, "So much blood around me! Is this all the blood I have shed?"

And then:

In November, the Spanish sailor Juan Fernández discovers a hitherto unknown archipelago. Sailing between Peru and Valparaíso, and quite by chance deviating from his planned route, Fernández stumbles across a series of islands, no more than seventy square miles in total area. Fernández looks about him. There are bits of greenery on them. They're a bit volcanic. They're not much cop. He names them after himself, and you can only wonder whether that's an act of grandeur or of self-effacing irony. For the next few centuries they serve as a hideout for pirates; then the tables are turned and they make for an especially unattractive new penal colony.

And then:

In December, Selim II, sultan of the Ottoman Empire, dies. Named by his loving subjects as Selim the Drunkard, or Selim the Sot, he dies inebriated, clumsily slipping on the wet floor of his harem and falling into the bath. His corpse is kept in ice for twelve days to conceal the fact he's dead and to safeguard the throne until his chosen heir, his son Murad, can reach Istanbul and take power. On arrival, Murad is proclaimed the new sultan, and there is much rejoicing, and hope (as ever) for a new age of enlightenment; that night he has all five of his younger brothers strangled in a somewhat overemphatic attempt to dissuade them from challenging his new authority.

And then:

Andy's hair fell out. It had been a slow process at first. For weeks he'd had to keep picking out stray strands from the solvent, he kept accidentally rubbing them into the picture—Juan Fernández's beard seemed to grow ever bushier, Charles IX died sweating not just blood but fur. And then, one day, it poured out all at once, in thick heavy clumps that rained down on his shoulders—and Andy was fascinated at the amount of it, it seemed he wasn't just losing the hair he already had but all the potential hair he could *ever* have had, the follicles were squeezing the hair out in triple quick time, as if his skull had contained nothing but a whole big ball of the stuff just waiting to be set free. The hairs would bristle out toward the light, thousands of little worms making for the surface, now covering his scalp and chin, now turning his head into a deep plush furry mat—and then, just as soon as the hairs seemed so full and thick and *alive* they'd die, they'd all die, they'd jump off his head like so many lemmings jumping off cliffs—and Andy couldn't help feel a little hurt that all this hair had been born, had looked about, and had been so unimpressed by the shape and texture of the face that was to be their new home they'd chosen to commit mass suicide instead.

And then:

The hair stopped falling, there was simply no hair left to fall. And then—Andy had to sweep it all up; it took him quite a while, there was an awful lot of it, and he resented the time he spent on doing that, this was work time, this was 1574 time. And then and then and then—he forgot he had ever had hair at all, he had no thoughts of hair, his head was an egg and it felt good and proper as an egg, 1574 was all he could think of now, 1574 was all there was, 1574 ran through him and over him and that's what filled his skull now and all that was ever meant to: Huguenots, drunken sultans, the flora and fauna of the Juan Fernández Islands, 1574 for life, 1574 forever.

And then:

↙

And then sometimes she would visit him and he'd have forgotten who she was, and sometimes he would visit her and she'd have forgotten who he was. But most times they remembered, and the memory came on them like a welcome rush. And they might even celebrate; they'd put their work aside, they'd get into the clapped out old elevator, pull the grille doors to, and ascend to the main gallery itself. And they'd walk through the exhibits on display, they'd turn the lights down low so it was more intimate, low enough that to see the art properly they'd have to squint a bit, as if even for just a little while it wasn't the most important thing in the room; they'd walk through the centuries together, but not be overwhelmed by the centuries, they'd walk at such a gentle pace too, they were in no rush, they had all the time in the world; they'd walk hand in hand. And Andy thought they must look such a funny pair, really. Almost identical, really, bald and white and plain—she just a little shorter than him, he a little more flat chested than her. They must have looked funny, yes, but who was there to see? (Who was there to tell?)

He didn't like it when he forgot her. So he wrote down on a piece of paper a reminder, so that whenever he felt lost or confused he could look at it and find new purpose. "Miriam," he wrote. "She's your boss. Works with you here at the gallery. Very good with the varnish. Works too hard, takes herself too seriously, not much of a sense of humour, but you know how to make her smile, just give it time. Not pretty, she looks like she's been newly laid from a hen's backside, but that doesn't matter, she's your friend. She's the only one that knows you, even when she doesn't know herself."

One day Miriam came to find Andy, and he remembered who she was clearly, he remembered her at a glance without the aid of a memo. And he smiled and he got up and took her by the hand, and she said, "No, not today, Andy, this is business." And she looked sad, and maybe a little frightened, and the bits of her face where she'd once had eyebrows seemed to bristle in spite of themselves.

She'd received a missive from the Curator. It had come in an envelope, bulging fat. She hadn't yet opened it.

"I don't see what's to worry about necessarily," said Andy. "Isn't it good that he's taking an interest?"

"This is only the third missive he's ever sent me," said Miriam. "The first one was to appoint me to this gallery, the second one was to appoint you to me. He doesn't care what we get up to here." She handed him the envelope. "This is bad. You read it."

But it didn't seem so bad, not at first. The Curator was very charming. He apologized profusely for giving Miriam and Andy so little attention. He'd been up to his eyes, there was so much to do, a whole universe of things under his thumb, and regretfully the arts just weren't one of his main priorities. But he was going to change all that; he was quite certain that Miriam and Andy had been working so very hard, and he was proud of them, and grateful, and he'd be popping into the gallery any time now to inspect what they'd been up to. No need to worry about it, no need for this to be of any *especial* concern—no need for them to know either when his visit might be. Remember, it was all very informal; remember, he'd rather surprise them unawares; remember, remember—he had eyes and ears everywhere.

That he referred to them both as Miriam and Andy was a cause for some concern.

And he finished by adding a request. A very little request, attached as a P.S.

The Curator said there were two ways of looking at history. One, that it was all just random chance, there was no rhyme or reason to any of it. People lived, people died. Stuff happened in between. This seemed to the Curator rather a cynical interpretation of history, and not a little atheist, didn't Miriam and Andy agree? The second was that there was a destiny to it all, an end resolution that had been determined from the beginning. The story of the world was like the story in a book, all the separate years just chapters building up to an inevitable climax—meaningless if read on their own, and rather unfulfilling too. The entire span of world history only made sense if it was considered within a context offered by that climax—and what a climax it'd been! 2038 really was the Curator's absolute favourite, he had such great memories of it, really, he'd think back on it sometimes and just get lost in the daydream, it was great.

And that's why the Curator wanted to see, in all the years preceding, some hint of the end year to come. He didn't want them to interfere with the art they'd been conserving—no—but, if within that art they saw some little premonition of it, then that'd be good, wouldn't it? Maybe they could *emphasize* his final triumph, they could pick out all the subtle suggestions throughout all time of his ineffable victory and highlight them somehow. The value of art, the Curator said, is that it reflects the world. What value then would any of these years have if they did not reflect their apotheosis? Their preservation would be worthless; no, worse, a lie; no, worse, treason itself. History had to have a pattern. And up to now, Miriam and Andy had been working to conceal that pattern— with diligence, he knew, and hard labour, and love, he could see there'd been lots of love. All that had to stop, right now.

And if they couldn't find any premonitions to highlight, maybe they could just draw some in themselves from scratch?

Miriam said softly, "It goes against everything I've ever done here."

Andy said nothing for a long while. He took her hand. She let him. He squeezed it. She squeezed it back. "But," he then said, and she stopped squeezing, "but if it's what the Curator wants," and her hand went limp, "and since he owns all this art, really . . ." and she took her hand away altogether.

"It's vandalism," she said. "I can't do it, and I don't care if it's treason to refuse. You . . . you, Aidan, whatever your name is . . . you do what you like."

She left him.

He studied 1574. He looked at it all over. He knew it so well, but it was like seeing it with fresh eyes now that he tried to find a part of it to sacrifice. He took out a pen. An ordinary modern biro, something that future conservationists could tell was wrong at a glance, something that wouldn't stain the patina or bleed into the oils underneath. Andy wasn't much of an artist, and so the demon he drew over the battle of Mookerheyde was little more than a stick figure. It looked stupid hovering there so fake above the soldiers and the bloodshed. He didn't even know what a demon looked like, he'd never seen one, he'd imagined that Hell would have been full of the things but they'd always kept to themselves— and so his drawing of a demon was really just the first thing that came to mind. He gave it a little pitchfork. And fangs. And a smiley face.

He wondered if this would be enough to satisfy the Curator, and thought he better not chance it. He drew a second demon over Juan Fernández discovering his islands. The pitchfork was more pointy, the smile more of a leer.

He went to find Miriam. She was crying. He was crying too. And that's why she forgave him.

"I don't want you taken from me," he said, and he held her. "Please."

"I'm sorry. It's a betrayal. I'm sorry. I'm sorry."

"Then I'll do it. Let me do all the betraying. I'll betray enough for both of us."

So they would walk the gallery again, hand in hand through the centuries. But this time, as they reached the end of a picture, Miriam would stop, she'd turn away, she'd close her eyes. And Andy would get out his pen, sometimes just a biro, sometimes a Sharpie if the year was robust enough to take it, and he'd draw in a demon or two. And he was surprised at how much easier it got, these acts of desecration; and his demons were bigger and more confident, sometimes they fitted in to the action superbly, sometimes (he thought secretly) they even improved it. He desecrated 1415, he desecrated 1963, he desecrated each and every one of the years representing the First World War. And it seemed to Andy that he was beginning to see the Curator's point; he'd see there was something foreboding about these years, maybe there *was* something in the design of them all that forecast the apocalypse.

But she wouldn't let him touch 1660. "It's mine," she said.

One night they reached the 1782 room. The Americans were in the throes of revolution, the French were chuntering on toward theirs. Andy thought 1782 had great potential; there were plenty of places where a demon or two would fit the bill. Miriam stood up close to the year. She reached out. She stroked it. When she pulled her hand away, Andy could see that her fingers had been brushing the image of a man in a top hat. His eyes were the most gorgeous blue, and around his mouth played the hint of a flirtatious smile.

Miriam took out the piece of paper from her pocket. She read it. She dropped it to the floor.

"It's the man you loved, isn't it?" said Andy.

"No."

And she reached out again, stroked the face again. This time Andy could see it wasn't done with affection, but with professional enquiry. "I must have worked on this," she said. "Look at the man's face. There was a rip here, from the neck, up to the forehead, look, it took out one of his eyes. I worked on this, I recognize my handiwork. I put his face back together."

And now that he was looking closely, Andy could see she was quite right. The work had been subtle, and so delicately done, but an expert could see the threads that bound the cheek flaps together.

"What I'd written down, it wasn't a memory," said Miriam. "It was an instruction for repair. I never knew this man. I never loved him, and he never loved me. All I ever did was to stitch his face up."

She ran.

By the time Andy caught up with her she was back at her studio. She was painting. Each stroke of her brush was so considered, was so small, you'd have thought that not a single one could have made the slightest difference—but their sum total was extraordinary. On the canvas she had created a demon. And the oils she'd chosen were perfect, they seemed to blend in with the background as if the demon had always been part of 1660; and its eyes bulged, and saliva was dripping from its mouth, its horns were caught in mid-quiver; it looked at the complacent folly of the seventeenth century with naked hunger. And it hung over the shoulders of King Charles II as he celebrated the restoration of the Crown, the spikes of its tail only an inch away from the Merry Monarch's face, if Charles just turned his head a fraction to the right his eye would get punctured. And the demon's presence seemed artistically *right*; it was an ironic comment upon fame and success and the paucity of Man's achievements—yes, the King was on his throne, but time would move on, and the human race would fall, and nobody could stop it, or nobody *would*, at any rate; and all of this, even this little slice of long past history, all would be swept away.

"It's beautiful," said Andy. "At painting, you're. Well. Really good." It sounded quite inadequate. And had Andy not known better, he'd have thought the demon in the picture rolled its eyes.

"I know," said Miriam. But she wouldn't look at him.

☟

They didn't know when the Curator came to visit. Only that another missive was sent one day, and it said that his inspection had been carried out, and that he was well pleased with his subjects.

They hoped that would be the end of it. It wasn't.

☟

The Curator's final missive was simple, and straight to the point. He said that he thought the work of the gallery was important, but that the art on display wasn't; there was only one significant year in world history, the year of his irrevocable triumph over creation—all the bits beforehand he now realized were just a dull protracted preamble before the main event.

He wanted to display 2038. And only 2038. 2038 was big enough, 2038 could fill the entire gallery on its own. All the other years could now be disposed of.

There were jobs going at the gallery, and everyone queued for them, man, woman, and child. And this time everyone was a winner, they *all* got jobs—really, there was so much work to do! The chatter and laughter of a billion souls in gainful employment filled the rooms, and it looked so strange to Andy and to Miriam, that at last the art they had preserved had an audience. They squeezed in—the gallery was packed to capacity—and yes, everyone would stare at the pictures on show, and perhaps in wonder, they'd never seen anything so splendid in all their lives—or maybe they had, maybe they'd lived the exact moments they were ogling, but if so they were long forgotten now, everything was forgotten. They'd stare at the pictures, every single one, and they'd allow a beat of appreciation, of awe—and then they'd tear them down from the walls.

And there were demons too, supervising the operation. So that's what they looked like, and, do you know, they looked just like us! Except for the hair, of course, their long lustrous hair.

The people would rip down the years, and take them outside, and throw them on to the fire. They'd burn all they'd ever been, all they'd experienced. And over the cries of excitement of the mob, you'd have thought you could hear the years scream.

Once they'd destroyed all that had been on view in the public gallery, the people made their way down to the vaults. Miriam stood in her studio, guarding 1660 with a sharpened paintbrush. "You can't have this one." And a demon came forward from the crowd, just a little chap, really, and so unassuming, and he punched her once in the face, and her nose broke, and he punched her hard on the head, and she fell to the ground. She didn't give them any trouble after that.

Andy found her there. She wasn't unconscious as he first thought; she simply hadn't found a reason to get up yet.

"This is all because of you," she said. "You made me fall in love with you, and it drew attention. This is all because of us."

And in spite of that, or because of it, he gave her a smile. And held out his hand for her. And she found her reason.

They went through the back corridors, past the hidden annexes and cubbyholes, all the way to his studio. 1574 was still draped over it higgledy-piggledy, January and December were trailing loose along the ground. Andy had never managed to learn even a fraction of the order Miriam had insisted upon, and for all that her life's work was in ruins, she couldn't help but tut. But seeing 1574 like that, less an old master, more a pet, it was suddenly homely and small, not a proper year, a year in progress—it was a hobby project that Andy liked to tinker on, it had none of the grandeur that the Curator was trying to stamp on and destroy. And for the first time, Miriam surprised herself, she felt a stab of affection for the old thing.

"We can save 1574," he told her.

And she knew it was worthless. That had the Curator sent his thugs to take 1574 from the beginning, she'd have given it up without a second thought. An unnecessary year—but now she helped Andy without a word, he took one corner and she the other, and together they rolled it up. And because it *was* so unnecessary, it rolled up very small indeed, and Andy was able to put it in his pocket.

No one stopped them on the way to the elevator. There was nowhere to go but up. And there was nothing up there. Not anymore.

Andy pulled the grille doors closed. He pressed the highest button that there was, one so high that it didn't even fit upon the panel with all the other buttons, it had to have a panel all of its own. It hadn't been pressed for such a long time, there wasn't much give in it, and when it finally yielded to Andy's finger it did so with a clunk.

The elevator didn't move for a few seconds. "Come on," said Andy, and kicked it.

↓

The lift doors opened out onto the Earth. And there was no air, there was no light, there was no dark. There was no *time*, time had been stripped out and taken down to the art galleries long ago, time had been frittered away then burned.

"We can't stay here," said Miriam. "I love you. I'd love you anywhere. But this isn't anywhere, I can't be with you here."

But Andy took 1574 out from his pocket. And holding out one end of the scroll, he *flung* out the other as far as he could. And the year unrolled and flew off into the distance. And when it had unrolled all that it could, after it had sped over the crags that had once been continents and oceans, when the far end of it could be seen flying back at him from the opposite direction, Andy caught hold of it, and tugged it flat, and fixed the end of December to the beginning of January. And it lay across the Earth, all the lumps and bumps, and yet it was still a perfect fit.

"This won't last. He'll come and get us in the end," said Miriam.

"He will. But not for another four hundred and fifty years." And then Andy kissed her, straight on to the mouth. He hadn't remembered that's how you were supposed to do it, but suddenly it just seemed so logical. And they kissed like that for a while, one mouth welded to the other, as the Middle Ages settled and stilled around them.

↓

They'd bask for a bit in August if they wanted the sun; then, to cool down, they'd pop over to February and dip their toes in the chill. And if they wanted to be alone, away from all the kings and sultans and soldiers and peasants and peoples set upon their paths of religious intolerance, then they'd hide in November—and November on the Juan Fernández Islands, just before Juan Fernández himself arrived on the scene. They spent a lot of time there. Alone was good.

They practised making love. If the mouth on mouth thing had been inspired, it was the tongue in mouth development that was the real breakthrough. They kissed a lot, and each time they did they both felt deep within the stirrings of dormant memories—that if they just kept at it, with diligence and labour, then they'd work out the next step of sex eventually.

"I love you," Andy would tell her, and "I love you," Miriam would reply. And they both wrote these facts down, privately, on pieces of paper, and kept them in their pockets always.

Miriam's nose healed. It didn't quite set straight, but Andy preferred it the new way; the very sight of its off-centre kink as it came up at him would set his heart racing faster. And the bruise where she'd been struck at last faded too. In its place there grew a single, shiny, blonde hair. Miriam felt it pop out of her skull one day and squealed with delight.

"It's all coming back," she said to Andy. "Everything's going to be all right again."

And Andy had seen enough of history to know that one lone random hair didn't necessarily mean much. But he laughed indulgently as she combed it into position, and she laughed at his laughter, and then they both forgot what they'd been laughing at in the first place—but that was all right, that they were happy was all that mattered. And then they started the kissing again, and all they knew and heard and felt was each other, and they ignored the stick figure demon chattering and giggling above their heads.

A JOKE IN FOUR PANELS

Snoopy is dead. They found his body lying on top of his kennel, wearing those World War I fighter pilot goggles he liked, and there must have been a foot of snow on him. Charlie Brown told the reporters, "At first I just thought it was one of his gags. That up out of the mound of snow would float a thought bubble with a punch line in it." He went on to admit that he hadn't cleared the snow off the body for hours, just in case he did something to throw the comic timing. But Snoopy was dead, he was frozen stiff, it's a cold winter and the beagle was really very old. The doctors say it might have been hypothermia, it might have been suffocation, he might even have drowned if enough snow had got into his mouth and melted. Charlie Brown is distraught. "I can't help but think I might be partially responsible." But no one blames Charlie Brown, we all know what Snoopy was like, you couldn't tell Snoopy anything, Snoopy was his own worst enemy.

Everyone's being nice to Charlie Brown. No one's called him a blockhead for days. Lucy van Pelt has offered him free consultations at her psychiatry booth, and the kite-eating tree has passed on its condolences. And all the kids at school, the ones who never get a line to say or a joke of their own, all of them have been passing on their sympathies. You admit, you immediately saw it as an opportunity. That if you went up to Charlie Brown and said something suitably witty, maybe it'd end up printed in the comic strip. You came up with a funny joke, you practised the delivery. You'd find him at recess, maybe, or on that pitcher's mound of his, and you'd say, "It's a dog-gone shame, Charlie Brown!" That's pretty funny. That's *T-shirt* funny. That's funny enough to be put on a lunch box. But when it comes to it, you just can't do it. When you see Charlie's perfectly rounded head, and the expression on it so vacant, so *lost*, it's not just a sidekick who's dead but a family pet—no, you *won't* do it, you have some scruples.—Besides, you can see that all the kids have had the same idea, he's being harangued on all sides by the bit part players of the *Peanuts* franchise, and their gags are better than yours.

Your name is Madalyn Morgan, although none of the readers would know that. Your name has never been printed. You've appeared in quite a few of the cartoons, whenever they need a crowd of kids to watch a baseball game or something. Once you got to be in a cartoon in which Charlie Brown and the gang were queuing up to see a movie, and you were standing just three kids in front! You didn't get to say anything, but you were proud anyway, you cut out the strip from the newspaper, and framed it, and now it hangs on your bedroom wall. You think Madalyn Morgan is a good name. It's better than Patricia Reichardt, she had to change her name to Peppermint Patty just to get the alliteration, and you have the alliteration already, they should have used you in the first place. And Peppermint Patty's friend is called *Marcie*, that's so close to *Maddie*, oh, it's infuriating. Some of the supporting characters have a gimmick, and you've been working on some of your own. Schroeder has a toy piano; you're learning how to play the harp. You think there's room for a harp in the *Peanuts* strip. Linus carries a security blanket everywhere with him and believes in the Great Pumpkin. You've experimented with towels and Mormonism.

You're sorry that Snoopy is dead, of course, but you can't say that you'll miss him. He was a self-obsessed narcissist, that's the truth of it. And all those fantasies he had, that he was fighting the Red Baron on a Sopwith Camel, that he was the world's greatest tennis coach or hockey player or novelist, that by putting on a pair of sunglasses he could be Joe Cool and hit on the girls—is it just you that thinks these delusions aren't charming? But actually the symptoms of a sociopathic mental case? He was only kind to one of the characters, that little yellow bird called Woodstock, and you suspect that's because Woodstock can't speak English, and with no jokes of his own he'd never rival the dog in popularity. Snoopy is dead, and the world is in mourning, and you're *sorry*, but you can't pretend you care. But you admit that without his comic genius, there's a cold wind now blowing through the funny pages.

There's a funeral for Snoopy, but it's only for close friends and stars of the strip. You're not invited. It's quite a big send-off; all over town everyone can hear it. There are fireworks. You like fireworks.

The *Peanuts* franchise has been marketed to the hilt, and it doesn't take you long to track down a full-size Snoopy costume. When you try it on you're pleased that it's so woolly, that'll keep you snug during the cold winter months ahead. Your hair is quite distinctive, and you're worried that the head piece won't cover it up properly, but it's fine, it's better than fine, it pads out all the crevices nicely and helps give Snoopy's head that soft squidgy shape that's so endearing.

You put the supper bowl between your teeth, the way you've seen the real Snoopy do countless times in countless strips. You go up to the front door of Charlie Brown's house. You kick against it three times, loud, insistent.

You know this is a classic opening to many a *Peanuts* strip. Suppertime at the Charlie Brown house, and Snoopy banging on the door, demanding to be fed. And you can already imagine it on the page, this is panel one.

Charlie Brown opens the door. He stares at you. He doesn't say anything. He doesn't know *what* to say. And this is the crucial moment, you know this—if he accepts you, then you're okay, and the strip can continue, but there'll be a million and one reasons why he wouldn't *want* to accept you: for a start, you're some strange kid he doesn't know pretending to be his dead dog. His eyes water. Is he going to cry? You think he might cry. Or will he be angry? Charlie Brown doesn't do anger well, his character is sold on that essential wishy-washiness of his, but if ever a boy is going to get angry, it's now, surely—and you're suddenly aware of just how *obvious* the costume looks, the zips and fasteners exposed for all the world to see, you're some ill-fitting parody of a best friend he only buried last week.

And then his face softens. He has made the decision to play along, you can see it. Or has he been fooled? Is he really that much of a blockhead? "Snoopy, where have you been? We thought you were gone for good!" he says. The speech bubble appears to his side, you can read the words clearly, his response is now official. And that is panel two.

In panel three you're both walking to the kennel. Charlie Brown is now carrying the supper bowl. You're following behind, on hind legs, of course. You wonder whether you should be doing the happy dance, when Snoopy's fed his supper he sometimes does the happy dance, but you think that maybe it's a little ambitious. And it might break the comic focus—if there's one thing you've learned on your long stint on *Peanuts* it's that you mustn't smother the gag with extraneous detail. Always focus on what the story is *about*. This isn't a strip about Snoopy doing a happy dance. It's a strip about Snoopy coming home and Charlie Brown accepting him. Keep it simple. Charlie Brown says, "I threw out all your dog food, all I've got left are these old vegetables . . ."

And he's gone. And you're into panel four. The final panel on a weekday *Peanuts* strip is panel four, and it has a special job—it needs to sum up the world weariness and despair that is the hallmark of the cartoon at its best. To take all the hope that was present in the first three panels and show that it is wanting. To demonstrate that at best, life is an awkward compromise we all just have to buckle down and accept. You don't know how to convey all that. All eyes are on you. You stare down at the awful food in your supper bowl. You roll your eyes. You send up a thought bubble. "Good grief," you think.

And it's a wrap.

The strip is printed in the newspapers the very next day. The world is glad to see that Snoopy is back again, even if he's sporting a zip.

You soon find out, in the absence of a really good punch line, rolling your eyes and thinking "Good grief" tends to work pretty well.

↓

Sometimes the supporting cast come to see you. Linus says, "You are exploiting the grief of someone who is suffering, don't you feel ashamed?" And then quotes some Bible verses at you, and that's so *very* Linus—and you want to say, if you're so smug and sanctimonious, why do you carry a security blanket? No, you don't feel ashamed, because *Snoopy* wouldn't feel ashamed—that was the point of Snoopy, can't they see that, he had no conscience at all. You just lie on the roof of the kennel and let their criticisms wash right over you. Lucy is more direct, as usual; she says she wants to slug you; she says she wants to pound you. The best way to deal with Lucy is to call her "sweetie" and kiss her on the nose, that never fails to infuriate her.

Incidentally, it's hard to sleep on the roof of a kennel, especially one that tapers into such a very sharp point. It took you a week to learn how to do it without falling off. And even now, you haven't found a way of lying there without the pain, it jabs right into your spine, it's agony. Thank God your contorted face is masked beneath that Snoopy head. Thank God your Snoopy head is fixed in that expression of cute self-satisfaction.

Robert Shearman

Woodstock comes by only the once. He jabbers at you, and he's angry, but you've no idea what he's saying, his speech bubbles are full of nothing more than vertical lines. And you tire of him, and you punch him—you thwack him with your paw and it says, "Ka-pow!"—and Woodstock is lying still on the grass for ages, and you wonder whether you've killed him. (And wonder whether it would matter; if the *Peanuts* strip can survive the death of the original Snoopy, who cares about the fate of a little bird that wasn't even given a name for the first twenty years of syndication?) But Woodstock *does* revive. And he flies away. And you never see him again.

The only one you need to keep happy is Charlie Brown. And Charlie Brown is *very* happy; he brings you fresh bowls of dog food every day, and you wolf them down, and dance the happy dance for real. He's the butt of all your jokes, but he has faith in you, and you have faith in him—life will knock the stuffing out of Charlie Brown each and every day, but he rolls with the punches, he keeps coming back for more. It's harder to be a Charlie Brown than a Snoopy. You have to admire him a bit for it.

You try out Snoopy's tried and tested specialty acts. You fly your kennel into World War I, and fight the Germans. The first time you strap on your goggles you think maybe something magical will happen, that you'll really take off into the air, that you'll really have to dodge the bullets of enemy fire. And you feel a bit disappointed at first that it's all pretend—of course it's all pretend, and it always was. But there's a certain thrill to it, that you have a nemesis, the Red Baron, even if it's just a made-up nemesis. And every time he shoots you down you shake your fist up to heaven and curse him, and it's fun, even though you know there's no one up there listening and that no one really cares.

You try to introduce some of your own skills into the act. For a few strips Snoopy begins to play the harp, with hilarious consequences. For a week or two he becomes a Mormon. The last storyline is seen as a noble failure, and is never repeated.

Sometimes you forget you're Madalyn Morgan at all. Sometimes you think you really were born at Daisy Hill Puppy Farm. And when your head itches, and once in a while you're forced to pull off your mask, you see that that hair of yours has just kept on growing, there's so much of it now, and you stare at it in the mirror with horror.

You don't see why a dog would try so hard to be human. Being human doesn't look that remarkable to you.

A kid pretending to be a dog, that's eccentric. But a kid pretending to be a dog pretending to be a kid? To coin a phrase, that's barking mad.

↓

So, you tire of Snoopy and his anthropomorphistic ways. You want to be a real dog.

You try to tell Charlie Brown. But real dogs don't have thought balloons. You bark, you wag your tail in urgent manners. Charlie Brown looks very confused, but then, that's a default setting for Charlie Brown. You find a leash, drop it in front of him on the floor. At last he gets the hint.

He puts your leash on warily. He's waiting for the punch line. He's waiting for your ironic sneer, the little bit of humiliation you'll make him suffer. "Good grief," says Charlie Brown. His hands are shaking.

He takes you out to the park. That's where most people take their dogs, but he's never done it before. Now you're there, he hasn't the faintest idea what to do.

In your mouth you pick up a stick, and offer it to him. He takes it suspiciously.

His hands are still shaking.

You realize he's scared of you. Not scared that you'll bite him, like an ordinary dog might. But that you'll bully him. That you'll point at him and laugh. He was once the star of his own comic strip, and the wacky dog took that away from him, and reduced him to a stooge.

He throws the stick for you.

And, as Snoopy, so many options come into play. You could bring him back the stick, but have already fashioned it into some exciting piece of woodwork—a model boat, maybe, or a pipe rack. You could bring him instead an entire branch, an entire log, an entire tree. You could just roll your eyes, say "Good grief," and walk away. That would be the most hurtful.

You bring him back the stick. And not in your paws, as if you're a human. And not with a little gift bow on top, in sarcastic overenthusiasm. You bring it back properly, as a loyal dog would.

He takes the stick from you. He doesn't trust you. He's still waiting for the joke.

There is no joke. And each time he throws it, you bark, and race after it, and bring it back to your master. And each time, Charlie Brown's face breaks into an ever-larger smile, and the smile is sincere and free, and it's not a smile for the newspaper readers at home, it's a smile for you, just for you, his faithful canine pal.

↙

The supporting cast come back to see you again. Lucy van Pelt says, "What are you doing, you blockhead?", and then she starts on about wanting to slug you again. Linus tells of how selfish it is that you are putting the needs of one above the livelihood of many, and finds some bit of scripture to emphasize the point. The truth is, the *Peanuts* readership is dwindling fast. No one wants to read about Snoopy if Snoopy's just an ordinary dog. No one wants to read about a Charlie Brown who's happy.

It's easy to ignore Lucy and Linus, because you're a dog, and dogs aren't supposed to understand what humans say.

And not everyone minds. All the kids at school, the ones who never got names, the ones who never felt valued—they're free now, they can do whatever they want. Maybe they'll become proper kids now, with real lives, and real futures, and dreams that they have the power to fulfil. Maybe they'll find some other comic strip to knock about in. It's up to them.

And Charlie Brown, one morning, is excited to find something growing on his chin. "Look, boy, it's stubble! I think I'm growing a beard!" He's spent so many years trapped as an eight-year-old, and now even the banalities of aging seem wondrous to him.

You wrap up your storylines. Snoopy the would-be novelist puts aside his typewriter; he finally has to admit that he was never good enough to get published. Snoopy throws away his tennis racquet, his Joe Cool sunglasses, his stash of root beer.

You put on your goggles for the last time, and climb aboard your kennel. It's time you put an end to the Red Baron once and for all. The engines roar into life, and you can feel the Sopwith Camel speeding up into the clouds. Kill the Red Baron, shoot him in cold blood if you need to, and the war will be over. You circle the sky for hours, but you can't find anyone to fight. There's no enemy aircraft up there. Because the First World War was such a long time ago. And the Red Baron, if he even existed, is dead, he's already dead—maybe he was a dachshund, or a German shepherd, and he was a dog in Berlin who used to climb aboard his own kennel and fantasize about being a hero—and by now the poor animal will be long dead; maybe he died of old age, maybe he died peacefully in the arms of some round-headed little German boy all of his own.

↡

Panel one. And you're indoors. And your head is on Charlie Brown's lap. And he's scratching at your ears, and you like that. It makes you feel dizzy, it makes you feel you could just let go of this world altogether and drift off somewhere magical. And Charlie Brown says to you, "It was never what I wanted. I didn't want fame. I didn't know what I was agreeing to. I was just a little kid. What's a little kid to know? And do you sometimes feel that you just want to change, to be a different person, but you can't be? Because you're surrounded by people who know you too well already, and they don't mean to, but they're going to hold you down and keep you in check, there'll be no second chances because you can't escape their expectations of you—and the whole world has expectations of me, they're looking at me and know who I am and how I'll fail at every turn. And then the second chance comes. Impossibly, the second chance is there. I never wanted a dog who was extraordinary. I wanted a dog who was ordinary to the world, but extraordinary to *me*, who'd love me and be my friend. I didn't want a dog like Snoopy. I wanted a dog like you." And this was all far too much to fit inside one speech bubble, but it didn't matter, this is what Charlie Brown said to you.

Panel two. And he's still scratching at your ears. But, no, now he's tugging. He's tugging at your ears. He's tugging at your head. And you want to say, no, Charlie Brown, no, you blockhead! Because he's going to ruin everything. Because Charlie Brown was never supposed to be happy, because this isn't the way it's meant to be—and he should leave your fake dog head alone, the two of you work like this, it's *nice* like this, isn't it? It's neat. And if he pulls your head off and reveals the girl beneath there's no going back, it'll all change forever—and maybe the head won't come off anyway, maybe it isn't a costume anymore, maybe at last you've turned into a real dog—but still he tugs, he just keeps tugging, and there's give, you can feel the weight lift from your shoulders—oh, you want to shout out, tell him to stop, good grief, Charlie Brown!—but you can't speak, a dog can't speak, you can only bark.

Panel three. And the head's off. The head's off. The head's off. And there's your hair everywhere. It's spilled out all over the frame, there's so much of it, how it has grown, how ever did you manage to stuff it all

55

away? And its colour is so vivid, bursting out of a black and white strip like this, it's wrong, it's rude. Rude and red, the brightest red, the reddest red, red hair everywhere. You stare up at Charlie Brown. And he stares down at you. The round-headed kid, and the little red-haired girl.

You stare at each other for a long time.

You wonder whether you'll move on to panel four. What the punch line will be, the thing that'll bring you both crashing down to earth. But there doesn't have to be one. There never has to be.

THAT TINY FLUTTER OF THE HEART I USED TO CALL LOVE

Karen thought of them as her daughters, and tried to love them with all her heart. Because, really, wasn't that the point? They came to her, all frilly dresses, and fine hair, and plastic limbs, and eyes so large and blue and innocent. And she would name them, and tell them she was their mother now; she took them to her bed, and would give them tea parties, and spank them when they were naughty; she promised she would never leave them, or, at least, not until the end.

Her father would bring them home. Her father travelled a lot, and she never knew where he'd been, if she asked he'd just laugh and tap his nose and say it was all hush-hush, but she could sometimes guess from how exotic the daughters were, sometimes the faces were strange and foreign, one or two were nearly mulatto. Karen didn't care, she loved them all anyway, although she wouldn't let the mulatto ones have quite the same nursery privileges. "Here you are, my sweetheart, my angel cake, my baby doll," and from somewhere within Father's great jacket he'd produce a box, and it was usually gift-wrapped, and it usually had a ribbon on it—"This is all for you, my baby doll." She liked him calling her that, although she suspected she was too old for it now, she was very nearly eight years old.

She knew what the daughters were. They were tributes. That was what Nicholas called them. They were tributes paid to her, to make up for the fact that Father was so often away, just like in the very olden days when the Greek heroes would pay tributes to their gods with sacrifices. Nicholas was very keen on Greek heroes, and would tell his sister stories of great battles and wooden horses and heels. She didn't need tributes from Father; she would much rather he didn't have to leave home in the first place. Nicholas would tell her of the tributes Father had once paid Mother—he'd bring her jewellery, and fur coats, and tickets to the opera. Karen couldn't remember Mother very well, but there was that large portrait of her over the staircase, in a way Karen saw Mother more often than she did Father. Mother was wearing a black ball gown, and such a lot of jewels, and there was a small studied smile on her face. Sometimes when Father paid tribute to Karen, she would try and give that same studied smile, but she wasn't sure she'd ever got it right.

Father didn't call Nicholas "angel cake" or "baby doll," he called him "Nicholas," and Nicholas called him "sir." And Father didn't bring Nicholas tributes. Karen felt vaguely guilty about that—that she'd get showered with gifts and her brother would get nothing. Nicholas told her not to be so silly. He wasn't a little girl, he was a man. He was ten years older than Karen, and lean, and strong, and he was attempting to grow a moustache; the hair was a bit too fine for it to be seen in bright light, but it would darken as he got older. Karen knew her brother was a man, and that he wouldn't want toys. But she'd give him a hug sometimes, almost impulsively, when Father came home and seemed to ignore him—and Nicholas never objected when she did.

Eventually Nicholas would say to Karen, "It's time," and she knew what that meant. And she'd feel so sad, but again, wasn't that the point? She'd go and give her daughter a special tea party then, and she'd play with her all day; she'd brush her hair, and let her see the big wide world from out of the top window; she wouldn't get cross even if her daughter got naughty. And she wouldn't try to explain. That would all come after. Karen would go to bed at the usual time, Nanny never suspected a thing. But once Nanny had left the room and turned out the light, Karen would get up and put on her clothes again, nice thick woollen ones, sometimes it was cold out there in the dark. And she'd bundle her daughter up warm as well. And once the house was properly still she'd hear a tap at the door, and there Nicholas would be, looking stern and serious and just a little bit excited. She'd follow him down the stairs and out of the house; they'd usually leave by the tradesmen's entrance, the door was quieter. They wouldn't talk until they were far away, and very nearly into the woods themselves.

That Tiny Flutter of the Heart
I Used to Call Love

He'd always give Karen a few days to get to know her daughters before he came for them. He wanted her to love them as hard as she could. He always seemed to know when it was the right time. With one doll, her very favourite, he had given her only until the weekend—it had been love at first sight, the eyelashes were real hair, and she'd blink when picked up, and if she were cuddled tight she'd say "Mama." Sometimes Nicholas gave them as long as a couple of months; some of the dolls were a fright, and cold to the touch, and it took Karen a while to find any affection for them at all. But Karen was a girl with a big heart. She could love anything, given time and patience. Nicholas must have been carefully watching his sister, just to see when her heart reached its fullest—and she never saw him do it; he usually seemed to ignore her altogether, as if she were still too young and too silly to be worth his attention. But then, "It's time," he would say, and sometimes it wasn't until that very moment that Karen would realize she'd fallen in love at all, and of course he was right, he was always right.

↯

Karen liked playing in the woods by day. By night they seemed strange and unrecognizable, the branches jutted out at peculiar angles as if trying to bar her entrance. But Nicholas wasn't afraid, and he always knew his way. She kept close to him for fear he would rush on ahead and she would be lost. And she knew somehow that if she got lost, she'd be lost forever—and it may turn daylight eventually, but that wouldn't matter, she'd have been trapped by the woods of the night, and the woods of the night would get to keep her.

And at length they came to the clearing. Karen always supposed that the clearing was at the very heart of the woods, she didn't know why. The tight press of trees suddenly lifted, and here there was space—no flowers, nothing, some grass, but even the grass was brown, as if the sunlight couldn't reach it here. And it was as if everything had been cut away to make a perfect circle that was neat and tidy and so empty, and it was as if it had been done especially for them. Karen could never find the clearing in the daytime. But then, she had never tried very hard.

Nicholas would take her daughter, and set her down upon that browning grass. He would ask Karen for her name, and Karen would tell him. Then Nicholas would tell Karen to explain to the daughter what was going to happen here. "Betsy, you have been sentenced to death."

59

And Nicholas would ask Karen upon what charge. "Because I love you too much, and I love my brother more." And Nicholas would ask if the daughter had any final words to offer before sentence was carried out; they never did.

He would salute the condemned then, nice and honourably. And Karen would by now be nearly in tears; she would pull herself together. "You mustn't cry," said Nicholas, "you can't cry, if you cry the death won't be a clean one." She would salute her daughter too.

What happened next would always be different.

When he'd been younger, Nicholas had merely hanged them. He'd put rope around their little necks and take them to the closest tree and let them drop down from the branches, and there they'd swing for a while, their faces still frozen with trusting smiles. As he'd become a man, he'd found more inventive ways to dispatch them. He'd twist off their arms, he'd drown them in buckets of water he'd already prepared, he'd stab them with a fork. He'd say to Karen, "And how much do you love this one?" And if Karen told him she loved her very much, so much the worse for her daughter—he'd torture her a little first, blinding her, cutting off her skin, ripping off her clothes and then toasting with matches the naked stuff beneath. It was always harder to watch these executions because Karen really *had* loved them, and it was agony to see them suffer so. But she couldn't lie to her brother. He would have seen through her like glass.

☇

That last time had been the most savage, though Karen hadn't known it would be the last time, of course—but Nicholas, Nicholas might have had an inkling.

When they'd reached the clearing, he had tied Mary-Lou to the tree with string. Tightly, but not *too* tight—Karen had said she hadn't loved Mary-Lou especially, and Nicholas didn't want to be cruel. He had even wrapped his own handkerchief around her eyes as a blindfold.

Then he'd produced from his knapsack Father's gun.

"You can't use that!" Karen said. "Father will find out! Father will be angry!"

"Phooey to that," said Nicholas. "I'll be going to war soon, and I'll have a gun all of my own. Had you heard that, Carrie? That I'm going to war?" She hadn't heard. Nanny had kept it from her, and Nicholas had wanted it to be a surprise. He looked at the gun. "It's a Webley Mark

IV service revolver," he said. "Crude and old-fashioned, just like Father. What I'll be getting will be much better."

He narrowed his eyes, and aimed the gun, fired. There was an explosion, louder than Karen could ever have dreamed—and she thought Nicholas was shocked too, not only by the noise, but also by the recoil. Birds scattered. Nicholas laughed. The bullet had gone wild. "That was just a warm up," he said.

It was on his fourth try that he hit Mary-Lou. Her leg was blown off.

"Do you want a go?"

"No," said Karen.

"It's just like at a fairground," he said. "Come on."

She took the gun from him, and it burned in her hand, it smelled like burning. He showed her how to hold it, and she liked the way his hand locked around hers as he corrected her aim. "It's all right," he said to his little sister gently, "we'll do it together. There's nothing to be scared of." And really he was the one who pulled the trigger, but she'd been holding on too, so she was a *bit* responsible, and Nicholas gave a whoop of delight and Karen had never heard him so happy before, she wasn't sure she'd *ever* heard him happy. And when they looked back at the tree Mary-Lou had disappeared.

"I'm going across the seas," he said. "I'm going to fight. And every man I kill, listen, I'm killing him for you. Do you understand me? I'll kill them all because of you."

He kissed her then on the lips. It felt warm and wet and the moustache tickled, and it was hard too, as if he were trying to leave an imprint there, as if when he pulled away he wanted to leave a part of him behind.

"I love you," he said.

"I love you too."

"Don't forget me," he said. Which seemed such an odd thing to say— how was she going to forget her own brother?

They'd normally bury the tribute then, but they couldn't find any trace of Mary-Lou's body. Nicholas put the gun back in the knapsack, he offered Karen his hand. She took it. They went home.

↓

They had never found Nicholas' body either; at the funeral his coffin was empty, and Father told Karen it didn't matter, that good form was the thing. Nicholas had been killed in the Dardanelles, and Karen looked for it on the map, and it seemed such a long way to go to die. There were lots of funerals in the town that season, and Father made sure that Nicholas' was the most lavish, no expense was spared.

The family was so small now, and they watched together as the coffin was lowered into the grave. Father looking proud, not sad. And Karen refusing to cry—"Don't cry," she said to the daughter she'd brought with her, "you mustn't cry, or it won't be clean," and yet she dug her fingernails deep into her daughter's body to try to force some tears from it.

↡

Julian hadn't gone to war. He'd been born just too late. And of course he said he was disappointed, felt cheated even, he loved his country and whatever his country might stand for, and he had wanted to demonstrate that love in the very noblest of ways. He said it with proper earnestness, and some days he almost meant it. His two older brothers had gone to fight, and both had returned home, and the younger had brought back some sort of medal with him. The brothers had changed. They had less time for Julian, and Julian felt that was no bad thing. He was no longer worth the effort of bullying. One day he'd asked his eldest brother what it had been like out there on the front. And the brother turned to him in surprise, and Julian was surprised too, what had he been thinking?—and he braced himself for the pinch or Chinese burn that was sure to follow. But instead the brother had just turned away; he'd sucked his cigarette down to the very stub, and sighed, and said it was just as well Julian hadn't been called up, the trenches were a place for real men. The whole war really wouldn't have been his bag at all.

When Julian Morris first met Karen Davison, neither was much impressed. Certainly, Julian was well used to girls finding him unimpressive: he was short, his face was too round and homely, his thighs quickly thinned into legs that looked too spindly to support him. There was an effeminacy about his features that his father had thought might have been cured by a spell fighting against Germans, but Julian didn't know whether it would have helped; he tried to take after his brothers, tried to lower his voice and speak more gruffly, he drank beer, he took up smoking. But even there he'd got it all wrong somehow. The voice, however gruff, always rose in inflection no matter how much he tried to stop it. He sipped at his beer. He held his cigarette too languidly, apparently, and when he puffed out smoke it was always from the side of his mouth and never with a good bold manly blast.

But for Julian to be unimpressed by a girl was a new sensation for him. Girls flummoxed Julian. With their lips and their breasts and their flowing contours. With their bright colours, all that perfume. Even now, if some aged friend of his mother's spoke to him, he'd be reduced to a stammering mess. But Karen Davison did something else to Julian entirely. He looked at her across the ballroom and realized that he rather despised her. It wasn't that she was unattractive; at first glance her figure was pretty enough. But she was so much older than the other girls, in three years of attending dances no man had yet snatched her up—and there was already something middle-aged about that face, something jaded. She looked bored. That was it—she looked bored. And didn't care to hide it.

Once in a while a man would approach her, take pity on her, ask her to dance. She would reject him, and off the suitor would scarper, with barely disguised relief.

Julian had promised his parents that he would at least invite one girl onto the dance floor. It would hardly be his fault if that one girl he chose said no. He could return home, he'd be asked how he had got on, and if he were clever he might even be able to phrase a reply that concealed the fact he'd been rejected. Julian was no good at lying outright, his voice would squeak, and he would turn bright red. But not telling the truth? He'd had to find a way of mastering it.

He approached the old maid. Now that she was close he felt the usual panic rise within him, and he fought it down—look at her, he told himself, look at how *hard* she looks, like stone; she should be *grateful* you ask her to dance. He'd reached her. He opened his mouth to speak, realized his first word would be a stutter, put the word aside, found some new word to replace it, cleared his throat. Only then did the girl bother to look up at him. There was nothing welcoming in that expression, but nothing challenging either—she looked at him with utter indifference.

"A dance?" he said. "Like? Would you?"

And, stupidly, opened his arms wide, as if to remind her what a dance was, as if without her he'd simply manage on his own in dumb show.

She looked him up and down. Judging him, blatantly judging him. Not a smile upon her face. He waited for the refusal.

"Very well," she said then, though without any enthusiasm.

He offered her his hand, and she took it by the fingertips, and rose to her feet. She was an inch or two taller than him. He smelled her perfume, and didn't like it.

He put one hand on her waist, the other was left gently brushing against her glove. They danced. She stared at his face, still quite incuriously, but it was enough to make him blush.

"You dance well," she said.

"Thank you."

"I don't enjoy dancing."

"Then let us, by all means, stop."

He led her back to her chair. He nodded at her stiffly, and prepared to leave. But she gestured toward the chair beside her, and he found himself bending down to sit in it.

"Are you enjoying the ball?" he asked her.

"I don't enjoy talking either."

"I see." And they sat in silence for a few minutes. At one point he felt he should get up and walk away, and he shuffled in his chair to do so— and at that she turned to look at him, and managed a smile, and for that alone he decided to stay a little while longer.

"Can I at least get you a drink?"

She agreed. So he went to fetch her a glass of fizz. Across the room, he watched as another man approached and asked her to dance, and he suddenly felt a stab of jealousy that astonished him. She waved the man away in irritation, and Julian pretended it was for his sake.

He brought her back the fizz.

"There you are," he said.

She sipped at it. He sipped at his the same way.

"If you don't like dancing," he said to her, "and you don't like talking, why do you come?" He already knew the answer, of course, it was the same reason he came, and she didn't bother dignifying him with a reply. He laughed, and hated how girlish it sounded.

At length she said, "Thank you for coming," as if this were *her* ball, as if he were *her* guest, and he realized he was being dismissed. He got to his feet.

"Do you have a card?" she asked.

Julian did. She took it, put it away without reading it. And Julian waited beside her for any further farewell, and when nothing came, he nodded at her once more and left her.

That Tiny Flutter of the Heart
I Used to Call Love

☟

The very next day, Julian received a telephone call from a Mr. Davison, who invited him to have dinner with his daughter at his house that evening. Julian accepted. And because the girl had never bothered to give him her name, it took Julian a fair little time to work out who this Davison fellow might be.

Julian wondered whether the evening would be formal, and so he overdressed, just for safety's sake. He took some flowers. He rang the bell, and some hatchet-faced old woman opened the front door. She showed him in. She told him that Mr. Davison had been called away on business, and would be unable to dine with him that evening. Mistress Karen would receive him in the drawing room. She disappeared with his flowers, and Julian never saw them again, and had no evidence indeed that Mistress Karen would ever see them either.

At the top of the staircase Julian saw there were two portraits. One was a giantess, a bejewelled matriarch sneering down at him, and Julian could recognize in her features the girl he had danced with the night before, and he was terrified of her, and he fervently hoped that Karen would never grow up to be like her mother. The other portrait, much smaller, was of some boy in army uniform.

Karen was waiting for him. She was wearing the same dress she had worn the previous night. "I'm so glad you could come," she intoned.

"I'm glad you invited me."

"Let us eat."

So they went into the dining room, and sat at either end of a long table. The hatchet face served them soup. "Thank you, Nanny," Karen said. Julian tasted the soup. The soup was good.

"It's a very grand house," said Julian.

"Please, there's no need to make conversation."

"All right."

The soup bowls were cleared away. Chicken was served. And, after that, a trifle.

"I like trifle," said Karen, and Julian didn't know whether he was supposed to respond to that, and so he smiled at her, and she smiled back, and that all seemed to work well enough.

Afterwards Julian asked whether he could smoke. Karen said he might. He offered Karen a cigarette, and she hesitated, and then said she would like that. So Julian got up, and went around the table, and lit one for her. Julian tried very hard to smoke in the correct way, but it still kept coming out girlishly. But Karen didn't seem to mind; indeed, she positively imitated him, she puffed smoke from the corner of her mouth and made it all look very pretty.

And even now they didn't talk, and Julian realized he didn't mind. There was no awkwardness to it. It was companionable. It was a shared understanding.

↓

Julian was invited to three more dinners. After the fourth, Mr. Davison called Mr. Morris, and told him that a proposal of marriage to his daughter would not be unacceptable. Mr. Morris was very pleased, and Mrs. Morris took Julian to her bedroom and had him go through her jewellery box to pick out a ring he could give his fiancée, and Julian marvelled; he had never seen such beautiful things.

Julian didn't meet Mr. Davison until the wedding day, whereupon the man clapped him on the back as if they were old friends, and told him he was proud to call him his son. Mr. Morris clapped Julian on the back too; even Julian's brothers were at it. And Julian was suitably impressed at how he had been transformed into a man by dint of a simple service and signed certificate. Neither of his brothers had married yet; he had beaten them to the punch, and was there jealousy in that back clapping? They called Julian a lucky dog, that his bride was quite the catch. And so, Julian felt, she was; on her day of glory she did nothing but beam with smiles, and there was no trace of her customary truculence. She was charming, even witty, and Julian wondered why she had chosen to hide these qualities from him—had she recognized that it would have made him scared of her? Had she been shy and hard just to win his heart? Julian thought this might be so, and in that belief discovered that he did love her, he loved her after all—and maybe, in spite of everything, the marriage might just work out.

For a wedding present, the families had bought them a house in Chelsea. It was small, but perfectly situated, and they could always upgrade when they had children. As an extra present, Mr. Davison had bought his daughter a doll—a bit of a monstrosity, really, about the size of a fat infant, with blonde curly hair and red lips as thick as a darkie's, and wearing its own imitation wedding dress. Karen seemed pleased with it. Julian thought little about it at the time.

That Tiny Flutter of the Heart
I Used to Call Love

⤓

They honeymooned in Venice for two weeks, in a comfortable hotel near the Rialto.

Karen didn't show much interest in Venice. No, that wasn't true; she said she was fascinated by Venice, but she preferred to read about it in her guidebook. Outside there was noise, and people, and stink; she could better experience the city indoors. Julian offered to stay with her, but she told him he was free to do as he liked. So in the daytime he'd leave her, and he'd go and visit St. Mark's Square, climb the basilica, take a gondola ride. In the evening he'd return, and over dinner he'd try to tell her all about it. She'd frown, and say there was no need to explain, she'd already read it all in her Baedeker. Then they would eat in silence.

On the first night, he'd been tired from travel. On the second, from sightseeing. On the third night, Karen told her husband that there were certain manly duties he was expected to perform. Her father was wanting a grandson; for her part, she wanted lots of daughters. Julian said he would do his very best, and drank half a bottle of claret to give him courage. She stripped off, and he found her body interesting, and even attractive, but not in the least arousing. He stripped off too.

"Oh!" she said. "But you have hardly any hair! I've got more hair than you!" And it was true, there was a faint buzz of fur over her skin, and over his next to nothing—just the odd clump where Nature had started work, rethought the matter, given up. Karen laughed, but it was not unkind. She ran her fingers over his body. "It's so *smooth*, how did you get it so smooth?

"Wait a moment," she then said, and hurried to the bathroom. She was excited. Julian had never seen his wife excited. She returned with a razor. "Let's make you perfect," she said.

She soaped him down, and shaved his body bald. She only cut him twice, and that wasn't her fault, that was because he'd moved. She left him only the hairs on his head. And even there, she plucked the eyebrows, and trimmed his fine wavy hair into a neat bob.

"There," she said, and looked over her handiwork proudly, and ran her hands all over him, and this time there was nothing that got in their way.

And at that he tried to kiss her, and she laughed again, and pushed him away.

"No, no," she said. "Your duties can wait until we're in England. We're on holiday."

So he started going out at night as well, with her blessing. He saw how romantic Venice could be by moonlight. He didn't know Italian well, and so could barely understand what the *ragazzi* said to him, but it didn't matter, they were very accommodating. And by the time he returned to his wife's side she was always asleep.

↙

The house in Chelsea had been done up for them, ready for their return. He asked her whether she'd like him to carry her over the threshold. She looked surprised at that, and said he could try. She lay back in his arms, and he was expecting her to be quite heavy, but it went all right really, and he got her through the doorway without doing anything to disgrace himself.

As far as he'd been aware, Karen had never been to the house before. But she knew exactly where to go, walking straight to the study, and to the wooden desk inside, and to the third drawer down. "I have a present for you," she said, and from the drawer she took a gun.

"It was my brother's," she said.

"Oh. Really?"

"It may not have been his. But it's what they gave us anyway."

She handed it to Julian. Julian weighed it in his hands. Like his wife, it was lighter than he'd expected.

"You're the man of the house now," Karen said.

There was no nanny to fetch them dinner. Julian said he didn't mind cooking. He fixed them some eggs. He liked eggs.

After they'd eaten, and Julian had rinsed the plates and left them to dry, Karen said that they should inspect the bedroom. And Julian agreed. They'd inspected the rest of the house; that room, quite deliberately, both had left as yet unexplored.

The first impression that Julian got as he pushed open the door was pink, that everything was pink; the bedroom was unapologetically feminine, it blazed out from the soft pink carpet and the wallpaper of pink rose on pink background. And there was a perfume to it too, the perfume of Karen herself, and he still didn't much care for it.

That was before he saw the bed.

He was startled, and gasped, and then laughed at himself for gasping. The bed was covered with dolls. There were at least a dozen of them, all pale plastic skin and curls and lips that were ruby red, and some were wearing pretty little hats, and some carrying pretty little nosegays, all of them in pretty dresses. In the centre of them, in pride of place, was the doll Karen's father had given as a wedding present—resplendent in her wedding dress, still fat, her facial features smoothed away beneath that fat, sitting amongst the others like a queen. And all of them were smiling. And all of them were looking at him, expectantly, as if they'd been waiting to see who it was they'd heard climb the stairs, as if they'd been waiting for him all this time.

Julian said, "Well! Well. Well, we won't be able to get much sleep with that lot crowding about us!" He chuckled. "I mean, I won't know which is which! Which one is just a doll, and which one my pretty wife!" He chuckled. "Well."

Karen said, "Gifts from my father. I've had some since I was a little girl. Some of them have been hanging about for years."

Julian nodded.

Karen said, "But I'm yours now."

Julian nodded again. He wondered whether he should put his arms around her. He didn't quite like to, not with all the dolls staring.

"I love you," said Karen. "Or rather, I'm trying. I need you to know, I'm trying very hard." And for a moment Julian thought she was going to cry, but then he saw her blink back the tears, her face was hard again. "But I can't love you fully, not whilst I'm loving them. You have to get rid of them for me."

"Well, yes," said Julian. "I mean. If you're sure that's what you want."

Karen nodded grimly. "It's time. And long overdue."

↙

She put on her woollen coat then, she said it would be cold out there in the dark. And she bundled up the dolls too, each and every one of them, and began putting them into Julian's arms. "There's too many," he said, "I'll drop them," but Karen didn't stop, and soon there were arms and legs poking into his chest, he felt the hair of his wife's daughters scratching under his chin. Karen carried just one doll herself, her new doll. She also carried the gun.

It had been a warm summer's evening, not quite yet dark. When they stepped outside it was pitch, only the moonlight providing some small relief, and that grudging. The wind bit. And Chelsea, the city bustle, the pavements, the pedestrians, the traffic—Chelsea had gone, and all that was left was the house. Just the house, and the woods ahead of them.

Julian wanted to run then, but there was nowhere to run to. He tried to drop the dolls. But the dolls refused to let go, they clung on to him, he could feel their little plastic fingers tightening around his coat, his shirt buttons, his skin, his own skin.

"Follow me," said Karen.

The branches stuck out at weird angles, impossible angles, Julian couldn't see any way to climb through them. But Karen knew where to tread and where to duck, and she didn't hesitate, she moved at speed—and Julian followed her every step, he struggled to catch up, he lost sight of her once or twice and thought he was lost for good, but the dolls, the dolls showed him the way.

The clearing was a perfect circle, and the moon shone down upon it like a spotlight on a stage.

"Put them down," said Karen.

He did so.

She arranged the dolls on the browning grass, set them in one long neat line. Julian tried to help—he put the new doll in her wedding dress beside them, and Karen rescued her. "It's not her time yet," she said. "But she needs to see what will one day happen to her."

"And what is going to happen?"

Her reply came as if the daughters themselves had asked. Her voice rang loud, and it had a confidence Julian had never heard before. "Chloe. Barbara. Mary-Sue. Mary-Jo. Suki. Delilah. Wendy. Prue. Annabelle. Mary-Ann. Natasha. Jill. You have been sentenced to death."

"But why?" said Julian. He wanted to grab her, shake her by the shoulders. He wanted to. She was his wife, that's what he was supposed to do. He couldn't even touch her. He couldn't even go near. "Why? What have they done?"

"Love," said Karen. She turned to him. "Oh, yes, *they* know what they've done."

She saluted them. "And you," she said to Julian, "you must salute them too. No. Not like that. That's not a salute. Hand steady. Like me. Yes. Yes."

She gave him the gun. The dolls all had their backs to him, at least he didn't have to see their faces.

He thought of his father. He thought of his brothers. Then, he didn't think of anything.

He fired into the crowd. He'd never fired a gun before, but it was easy, there was nothing to it. He ran out of bullets, so Karen reloaded the gun. He fired into the crowd again. He thought there might be screams. There were no screams. He thought there might be blood . . . and the brown of the grass seemed fresher and wetter and seemed to pool out lazily toward him.

And Karen reloaded his gun. And he fired into the crowd, just once more, please, God, just one last time. Let them be still. Let them stop twitching. The twitching stopped.

"It's over," said Karen.

"Yes," he said. He tried to hand her back the gun, but she wouldn't take it—*it's yours now, you're the man of the house.* "Yes," he said again.

He began to cry. He didn't make a sound.

"Don't," said Karen. "If you cry, the deaths won't be clean."

And he tried to stop, but now the tears found a voice, he bawled like a little girl.

She said, "I will not have you dishonour them."

She left him then. She picked up her one surviving doll, and went, and left him all alone in the woods. He didn't try to follow her. He stared at the bodies in the clearing, wondered if he should clear them up, make things tidier. He didn't. He clutched the gun, waited for it to cool, and eventually it did. And when he thought to turn about he didn't know where to go, he didn't know if he'd be able to find his way back. But the branches parted for him easily, as if ushering him fast on his way, as if they didn't want him either.

↓

"I'm sorry," he said.

He hadn't taken a key. He'd had to ring his own doorbell. When his wife answered, he felt an absurd urge to explain who he was. He'd stopped crying, but his face was still red and puffy. He held out his gun to her, and she hesitated, then at last took it from him.

"Sorry," he said again.

"You did your best," she said. "I'm sorry too. But next time it'll be different."

"Yes," he said. "Next time."

"Won't you come in?" she said politely, and he thanked her, and did.

She took him upstairs. The doll was sitting on the bed, watching. She moved it to the dressing table. She stripped her husband. She ran her fingers over his soft smooth body, she'd kept it neat and shaved.

"I'm sorry," he said one more time; and then, as if it were the same thing, "I love you."

And she said nothing to that, but smiled kindly. And she took him then, and before he knew what he was about he was inside her, and he knew he ought to feel something, and he knew he ought to be doing something to help. He tried to gyrate a little. "No, no," she said, "I'll do it," and so he let her be. He let her do all the work, and he looked up at her face and searched for any sign of passion there, or tenderness, but it was so *hard*—and he turned to the side, and there was the fat doll, and it was smiling, and its eyes were twinkling, and there, there, on that greasy plastic face, there was all the tenderness he could ask for.

Eventually she rolled off. He thought he should hug her. He put his arms around her, felt how strong she was. He felt like crying again. He supposed that would be a bad idea.

"I love you," she said. "I am very patient. I have learned to love you."

She fetched a hairbrush. She played at his hair. "My sweetheart," she said, "my angel cake." She turned him over, spanked his bottom hard with the brush until the cheeks were red as rouge. "My big baby doll."

And this time he *did* cry—it was as if she'd given him permission. And it felt so good.

He looked across at the doll, still smiling at him, and he hated her, and he wanted to hurt her, he wanted to take his gun and shove the barrel right inside her mouth and blast a hole through the back of her head. He wanted to take his gun and bludgeon her with it, blow after blow, and he knew how good that would feel, the skull smashing, the wetness. And this time he wouldn't cry. He would be a real man.

"I love you," she said again. "With all my heart."

She pulled back from him, and looked him in the face, sizing him up, as she had that first time they'd met. She gave him a salute.

He giggled at that, he tried to raise his own arm to salute back, but it wouldn't do it, he was so very silly.

There was a blur of something brown at the foot of the bed; something just out of the corner of his eye, and the blur seemed to still, and the brown looked like a jacket maybe, trousers, a uniform. He tried to cry out—in fear, or at least in surprise?—but there was no air left in him. There was the smell of mud, so much mud. Who'd known mud could smell? And a voice to the blur, a voice in spite of all. "Is it time?"

He didn't see his wife's reaction, nor hear her reply. His head jerked, and he was looking at the doll again, and she was the queen doll, the best doll, so pretty in her wedding dress. She was his queen. And he thought she was smiling even wider, and that she was pleased he was offering her such sweet tribute.

SOUNDING BRASS TINKLING CYMBAL

For his birthday, David Allan was going to get a cake, a big one with chocolate sponge and nuts and fondant icing, and a tongue with which to taste it; he was going to have candles on his cake, one for each year he'd lived, and a tongue that could curl into a little tube through which he could blow air and puff the candles out; he was going to get presents, and a tongue with which he'd say thank you. So many different tonguey tasks! And David might have thought all that required three different tongues, but he was assured that a single tongue could do the lot of them—it was a very versatile piece of flesh. Indeed, it could do all that and more besides, it could do rather adult things. He was too young to be told what they were yet, but he'd find out for himself soon. Very soon now, this year. This year was his time, they were certain.

David was so excited he could barely sleep the night before. Or was he nervous? No, excited, what did he have to be nervous about? He lay in the dark for hours staring upwards at the bedroom ceiling, and he'd put his fingers into his mouth, and feel about inside—and it seemed like such a very small space, what with all the teeth hanging down like stalactites from above and thrusting up like stalagmites from below. He wasn't sure how anything else could be expected to fit in there. He mouthed the words "stalactite and "stalagmite," and tried to visualize how the tongue would help pronounce them just like Mrs. Dempsey had taught him. Mrs. Dempsey had been teaching him lots of long words recently; they wouldn't be easy to say out loud, granted, but this year he really ought to aim to impress. "Throw in a few extra syllables," she'd told him, "and you're going to knock this one right out of the park." Mrs. Dempsey knew what she was doing, she'd helped hundreds of kids get their tongues.

David had a crush on Mrs. Dempsey. Sometimes he imagined he would tell Mrs. Dempsey he loved her. Sometimes he imagined this would be the first thing he'd say when he could speak for himself.

He must have fallen asleep eventually, because his mother and father were shaking him awake, and were standing right over him, and their smiles were so wide and hopeful. "Happy birthday, champ!" said Daddy; "happy birthday, darling!" said Mummy. They enunciated their happy birthday wishes so clearly and precisely, David could see their tongues flicking about with such practised ease. They had presents for him to unwrap. He was given a tongue straightener, and a tongue brush in David's favourite colour (green), and a little box in which David could keep his tongue brush. Mummy laughed; "I know it's a bit premature, but I just know you're going to nail it this year!"—and Daddy laughed; "He certainly is, this is going to be his best birthday ever!" Their tongues wagging away all the while, as if urging David on.

They had him put on his second best suit. They had him wear a tie. No school today, not on his birthday, and maybe never again. Yesterday Mrs. Dempsey had made a special announcement at the end of class, she'd said to everyone that David Allan was turning thirteen tomorrow, and that she had a treat for him. Then she presented him with a good luck card, and she had signed it, and she'd had all the kids sign it too, and inside everyone said that they'd miss him. David was the biggest boy in class by a head, and all the younger children looked up to him. He was going to miss them too. But he thought it'd be embarrassing if he were forced to come back and ever see them again. "Don't you worry, dear," said Mrs. Dempsey, "I'll be there tomorrow night, in the front row, cheering you on!" David rather wished she wouldn't be in the front row, and would have told her so had he been able.

The government buildings were grey concrete, and didn't look as if they housed anything magical at all. Maybe that was the point, David didn't know. The guard at the front desk demanded to see David's birth certificate, and Mummy and Daddy handed it over, and the guard gave it a cursory inspection. "Happy birthday, lad," he said. The guard had a dark, commanding sort of voice; David hoped he'd get a voice like that. He told them to take seats and wait to be called. They sat down with other families, lots of birthday children in their second best suits, and mummies and daddies looking flushed with pride. Some of the children could barely sit still for all the excitement, some of them were still very young. David was old enough now that he could sit still and keep his back straight, he could hide his nerves. "Keep your back straight," Mummy whispered to him, which seemed a little unfair, because it already was.

"David Allan?" And at last there was someone for him, a woman all in black, and wearing small round glasses that made her look like an owl. David thought she might have looked quite friendly if she'd only wanted to try. She asked to look at his birth certificate; it was given another brief inspection. She smiled. "Happy birthday, if you'd like to follow me?" She led the family down some corridors into the very heart of the building. "Is this your first time? If so, there's nothing to be worried about." She must know it wasn't his first time; he was older than all the other kids, perhaps she was being nice. Perhaps it was just something she was paid to say. The narrow corridors opened out into a wide courtyard; the ceiling was a glass dome that let all the light in, and it shone down upon the tongue.

"My, my," said Daddy. "That's a big one, isn't it, champ?"

And so it was. David had never seen a tongue so huge. The one he'd visited on his last birthday must have been half the size, surely? And that one had stood about thirty feet tall, and David had refused to be frightened of it, no matter how much it twisted and coiled, he'd just pretended it was a tree. But this new tongue was more like a thick wall of red meat, David couldn't even see round the trunk of it, and it stabbed up high into the air, the very tip of it was licking at the ceiling. "Some of them do grow pretty big," the woman agreed. "In this job I've seen some that are even bigger!" Mummy told David to stand a little closer to it, and the woman nodded, and Daddy gave his most encouraging smile. David took a couple of steps forward. And as soon as he did so, the tongue seemed to spasm, it thrashed about wildly from side to side, and David saw saliva spray off it as hot steam. "I think it likes you!" said the woman.

A man came up to them, he was wearing a white laboratory coat and carried a clipboard and looked really very scientific. He asked to see the birth certificate; it was shown one last time. "Happy birthday," he said to David. "Now, you want to get up real close, you don't want to be nervous of old Tommy here. Tommy Tongue, do you see, he's the oldest we've got, aren't you, Tommy?" And he actually patted an overarching stump of tongue, and smiled with what looked like affection. "Truth is, Tommy doesn't even know we're here, most like. He can't see, he can't hear, can't smell. As far as we can tell, all he can do is taste. Take a look at him. What a beauty." And David couldn't help but look, could he, he was right up next to it, and Daddy was close behind him, he had his hands firmly on his shoulders. David could see now that the tongue wasn't that red after all—or, if it were red, it was a dead red, there was something lifeless to the hue, something flattened out. But there was blue, there were thin blue veins crisscrossing all over the tongue's surface, and there were motes of speckled white, there was green. It wasn't as smooth as David had supposed either; chunks had been torn out of the flesh, and David thought that probably wasn't natural, that would have been the birthday children who had queued before him. And there was saliva pooling in the holes that had been gouged out, and dripping forth, and down; in fact, now as David watched, he saw that saliva was dripping everywhere.

"You know what to do, right, kid?" And the scientist handed him a knife.

David looked back then, and there was Mummy and Daddy, both looking so proud, and the woman with the owl glasses, she was looking proud too, David couldn't even guess why.

"Reach up, there's a nice bit just above your head," said the scientist. "Yes, reach up," said Mummy, "up on your tiptoes," Daddy said. Some people believed that the higher from the tongue you cut, the more intelligent it would be. But Mrs. Dempsey had told David that that was a nonsense, that he mustn't worry about things like that, it was the man who maketh the tongue and not the other way around. And besides, David had always cut high before, and it had never done him much good.

So this time he bent low, he actually stooped. Daddy protested, but the scientist said, "Each child gets to choose his own tongue. That's the way it's always been." David remembered just the way he'd practised on apples and grapefruit, to make one clean single slice—"You'll have to dig deep, the dermis is a bit thick down there," the scientist said—and David stuck the knife in, and felt all the wetness ooze around the incision, and he pulled the blade down, three jerks of the wrist the way he'd been taught—in, down, and out. And there it was, flapping about in his hands like a fish. "Well done," said the scientist, "well done," said everybody else, and they clapped the birthday boy, and the scientist took the hunk of meat, gave it a slap, and washed the blood off.

"Now, open wide," he said, "as wide as you can go!" And David did his best. He drooped his chin toward the ground and aimed his nose toward the sky, and the strain made his jaw hurt. "I'm coming in!" said the man, and he chuckled, and suddenly David's mouth was full, so full it made his eyes bulge, and there were fingers and there were knuckles and there was tongue and he couldn't tell which was which. "Steady, it's a bit stiff," said the scientist, more sternly now, "it's always a bit stiff with these older kids," and so David rooted himself to the spot; the scientist stuck his own tongue out in concentration as he felt for the right slot. "Got it," he said at last, and there was a snap as the tongue locked into position, and out came the knuckles and out came the fingers. And there was some relief to that, but horror too, because David thought his mouth was still full, the tongue was too big, he'd never be able to breathe, and it was darting about all over the place, dabbing at each of his teeth, dashing at his palate, writhing about and knocking against the small confines of its new prison. And spraying spit everywhere it went. David gagged, he began to choke.

"Looks like we've got a lively one!" said the scientist, and he didn't seem too alarmed, so David tried to force his panic down, maybe he wasn't going to die after all. And then there was a hypodermic needle in the man's hands, quick as a flash, and in a moment the fingers were back inside David's mouth, and other fingers were wrenching the mouth wide, there was no time for niceties now. And they were grasping at the tongue, they'd got it, they'd grabbed hold of the tip, and the back of the tongue lashed about in fury. Something sharp. The smell of something acid. And then the tongue flopped dully down against the jawbone.

"What was that? What the hell was all that?" Mummy was upset, and the woman was doing her best to reassure her, she said she'd seen this happen a hundred times. Mummy said, "You've tranquilized his tongue! You do realize it's got to make a speech tonight?" Of course they realized, everyone knew the importance of it, and Daddy tried to calm her down and put his arms around her. Mummy shook herself free. "Get off me."

"The tongue is fine," said the scientist. "Some at the base can get a bit frisky, that's all. And it's not knocked out, I've just calmed it down a bit, I've shown it who's boss. The boy here can use it right away if he wants to." And it was true, David could feel the tongue flexing again, the extrinsic and intrinsic muscles starting to pull and stretch. It was a little sulky, maybe, but it was quite definitely awake.

"Go on, son," said Daddy. "Give it a trial run."

"Say something," said Mummy.

"Try saying your name," said the woman. "Whenever I don't know what to say, I always give my name a go."

And so David took a deep breath. If he concentrated he could stop the tongue roaming about of its own free will, he could tell it there was work to do. It stopped, stood still, waited for instructions.

"My name," he said slowly, "is David Allan." And he liked the way that felt in his mouth, the parts of the palate the tongue had to tickle to get it sounding right. Every time he had to tell someone who he was, he realized, it would give him a little buzz of pleasure.

The scientist smiled. The woman stepped forward, shook hands with David formally. "We're very pleased to meet you, David Allan," she said. "Speak well, and speak wisely."

Mummy said, "His voice has got lower, did you hear that?" Daddy said, "I suppose that's because his balls have dropped," and Mummy said, "David, did your balls drop?" And David took a deep breath, and concentrated hard, and visualized the word, and said with great precision, "Yes."

↓

He blew out all of his candles, one by one by painstaking one. The tongue took no interest in that, he had to blow them out in the usual way, but David didn't let on. And he ate his birthday cake. It had chocolate sponge and nuts and icing, all as promised. It also had lemon rind, and raw onion, and David was pretty sure the chewy bits were bacon. The tongue recoiled at the lot of it. "I wanted to give you a taste sensation," Mummy explained. "Not just sweet, but salty, and sour, and bitter." David nodded, finished his plate, raised his hand to indicate he really couldn't manage another slice.

He got up to clear the table as normal, but Mummy said, "No, don't do that!" And Daddy said, "Not on your birthday." So he stayed sitting where he was, and they both smiled at him expectantly.

"You're not too worried about this evening, champ?" said Daddy.

"How about a sneak preview?" said Mummy.

David smiled, shook his head.

"Come on," said Mummy. "Just a few sentences. What are you going to talk about?"

"He probably wants to keep it as a surprise," Daddy suggested.

"I don't want a surprise."

"He probably wants to practise on his own."

"No, he can practise in front of us." Mummy took hold of David's hand. "You don't need to be shy with me. I love you. You know that, don't you?"

David took a deep breath, opened his mouth. Closed it again. Nodded.

Mummy let go of his hand. She got up from the table, walked to the sink, slammed her hand against the draining board. "*Christ*," she said.

"It'll be all right," said Daddy. "You'll see. She'll see, won't she, champ?"

"It *won't* be all right. It'll be just the same as last year. David standing up there on stage. Opening his mouth, closing it, opening, closing. Like some bloody goldfish! Not coming out with a bloody word."

"I know," said Daddy gently.

"Not even a bloody syllable! I nearly died. Do you hear me, David? I'm not exaggerating. I actually nearly died of shame."

"He knows, we both know . . ."

"My heart nearly bloody stopped."

"Don't, love," said Daddy. "You're frightening him."

"Am I? Well. Well then. Maybe that's what he needs." And in a moment she was away from the sink, she was back at the table, back grasping on to David's hand, only this time it was much too tight, and she was hissing straight into his face.

"Listen to me," she said. "We can't keep doing this forever. This'll be the last time. This will be the most important thing you ever have to do."

"Love, please . . ."

"So don't fuck it up." At that she let go of him. "What Helen and Nigel make of you, I don't know." Helen was David's younger sister. She'd got to keep her tongue when she was ten, and now she worked at a bank. Nigel was a prodigy, everyone had agreed. He'd won his tongue the very first time, and he'd been only *six*, and that was two years before kids were even supposed to try. But the school had recommended he give it a go and he'd dazzled the audience and been given a standing ovation. Nigel was a barrister now, somewhere in the city, one of the big cities far away; David never saw his little brother much, only at Christmas.

"I know you think I'm being unkind," Mummy said, and her voice was softer now, and David looked up at her, and hoped that the worst was over. He felt dead inside, and his eyes were starting to water, and even his tongue felt limp and ashamed. "I only want what's best for you. I want you to be happy. I want you to go out into the world and be the best that you can be. I don't want you to end up as one of those muteoid cretins. Cleaning streets and stacking supermarket shelves. I want you to have a *life*."

She smiled at him, big and wide, and her tongue touched lightly upon her top lip. She looked at Daddy for support, and Daddy smiled too.

"What do you say?" she asked.

David forced out a word. "Sorry."

Mummy snorted. "You're going to have to do better than that." And she left the kitchen.

Daddy smiled at his son, wider now that Mummy had left, but the smile was embarrassed and sad.

"She shouldn't," he said. "She shouldn't use her tongue to say such things. She used to be nicer. Do you remember? Of course you remember."

David said nothing. Daddy sighed. Daddy seemed to struggle for words, David could see him forcing a deep breath, trying to visualize the words in his head, trying to concentrate.

"The thing is," he said. "She doesn't love me anymore. That's the truth of it. She's met someone else. She's told me she wants out. But she can't leave. Not with you here. Not whilst you're still a child. She can abandon me. She can't abandon her child. Do you see?"

And he smiled. "I think you see."

David nodded.

"So you'll try your best tonight, won't you, champ? For her sake. Because I want her to be happy."

"Yes," said David. It took him some effort, but he got there. "Yes." He repeated it, for good measure. Daddy beamed at him, and stood up, and ruffled David's hair.

"I used to," said Daddy. He stopped, had to start again. But this time it wasn't his tongue that was playing up, it was the eyes. "I used to be able to say such great things to her. I used to make her laugh. I don't know how to do it anymore. I can't find the right words."

David didn't know what to do. He looked away. He looked right down at the table, and didn't look up again until after his father had left.

Now David. All on his own. Except for the tongue.

Stalactite, he mouthed stalactite. His teeth hanging down like stalactites, and the tongue rising to the teeth, glancing over the back row for the first syllable, flicking lightly against the soft palate for the "l," rolling into a ball and hissing loud for the grand finale. "St," is what he said. "St. St. St. St. Stop. *Stop.*"

And out came the tongue, as far as it could stretch, rigid and firm and forming a right angle to his upper lip.

David went to the bathroom to see in the mirror. The very end of the tongue seemed to wiggle at him, a little cheekily.

He tried to remember all the exercises he had been taught to bring the tongue to heel. They didn't work. He tried to roll it up by hand, grabbing it wetly between his fingers. He might as well have been trying to fold an iron bar.

If he could just get it back inside his mouth. That would be a start. Don't worry about it having to speak. Or it having to taste anything. But if it could just stop sticking out like that, it was so rude. *Please*, he thought.

And the tongue screeched.

He stared at it in horror. And yet it screeched—it let out all its frustration and loss and pain. And somewhere, distantly, he could feel it too—the tongue was a part of him now, he could feel how it had been ripped from its home and from its family, and it was now angry and confused and so very, very frightened.

He couldn't see at first where the screech could be coming from. The sound wasn't using David's mouth, or David's breath. And then as the tongue flared, trying to stand as tall as the huge parent out of which it had been sliced, rearing up on its hind tendons like a panicked horse, David could see the underside of it—those blue veins looked thick and were straining now, the white specks seemed to bulge out like rivets, and there was a hole—there was a hole—there was a mouth—and inside it, he could see were little teeth, and there behind the little teeth the tongue had a tongue of its own.

David tried to yell for help, but he couldn't. Tried to clamp his mouth shut but there was no give. Jammed his fingers in his ears so he wouldn't hear the noise but the noise was all in his head now and it wouldn't st st st st stop.

And then the tongue fell limp. It had given up. It had screamed out its misery to the world, and the world didn't care, no one had come to rescue it, no one could do anything. David tentatively opened his mouth wide to let it back in. It pulled inside, almost guiltily.

He closed his mouth. He wasn't sure he'd dare open it again for a while. He wanted that tongue locked away.

And he felt the mouth fill with water, so much water he had to open up anyway to spit it out, and David knew it was just saliva, but somehow he believed that the tongue was crying.

⤓

They had him put on his very best suit now, they gave him a better tie. Daddy looked smart. Mummy looked beautiful, and she seemed quite calm, as if there had been no upset before. She wore dark shadow around her eyes.

The town hall was packed. There must have been over a hundred children there, each of them full of birthday cake, and speeches to recite, and new tongues with which to recite them. And with the children came two parents each, always two parents, and the smell of musk, perfume and aftershave hung in the air like a cloud.

The stage was small, but surely still bigger than it needed to be, it was only children who would be performing tonight. Downstage centre there stood a little lectern, with a microphone in front. At the side of the stage there sat a jury of six. David thought he recognized the scientist. And wasn't that the woman who'd taken them to the tongue, it was hard to tell, she wasn't wearing glasses and her dress was pink and she no longer looked like an owl.

David sat between his parents. His father took his hand, smiled at him. With the other David reached for his mother's hand. She accepted it.

The chairman got to his feet. He addressed them all, and spoke with a tongue that was masterfully assured. "Greetings to you," he said. "And especial greetings to our children, and happy birthday. These children are the voices of our future. All our hopes and dreams lie in what they may achieve. And tonight, for some, that journey will begin. Tonight they will be given an opportunity to speak. And, if they are ready, they will go from here, as adults, to fulfil their destinies. So. Let us hear what the future has to tell us! Speech is a privilege. And to be allowed that privilege, we only ask that our children tonight speak with clarity, and with the same forthright confidence of their parents. That they say something worth listening to. That they are interesting, and original."

"Interesting and original," Daddy whispered to David. "Mummy and me, we were interesting and original once! Can you believe it?"

Since its outburst in the bathroom the tongue had been as good as gold. It was as if it had only wanted one moment of protest, and now it had had its say. It had been a little listless, and David had had to use the straightener on it to improve his diction. But he had managed to practise his speech no less than five times, and each one had been better than the last. It was a speech that expressed a love for speleology he did not feel, but which pronounced "stalactite" and "stalagmite" most impressively.

"We shall begin," said the chairman. "Best of luck to you all. Speak well, and speak wisely!"

The children were called to the stage at random. It had always been done this way.

The first child got up behind the lectern and spoke coherently for three and a half minutes about his love for his country. It was met with a round of applause, and he shone with pride, and he was now a man.

The second child spoke about her love for her country, and good family values.

The third child focused mainly upon family values.

"Do you mention the family at any stage during yours, champ?" asked Daddy. David didn't; he was wondering whether there was a way to crowbar it in.

And for the first hour each child passed. It was easy. David saw that the jury *wanted* them to pass; they wanted more adults in the world. The odd stutter or mumble, that didn't matter; who cared if the speech was boring? If you got rid of all the boring adults, where would the world be? One child got up and spoke for barely two minutes about the battle of Waterloo and his analysis was frustratingly simplistic, and only once did he use a word of more than two syllables, and that was "Waterloo." Still, he was applauded, and was passed.

I'm going to be all right, David told himself. This year, at last, I won't let anyone down.

Then, the first failure.

The little girl was just too young. Anyone could see that. The audience was on her side right from the start, she looked so pretty with all her ribbons and bows, and everyone loves an underdog. The chairman too was positively smitten. He helped her up on to the lectern, and he'd not done that for anyone else. "All right, dear," he said to her kindly, as he adjusted the microphone toward her babyish face, "we're all rooting for you." And she stood there, and she stared out at the crowd, and tears began to roll down her face. "I want my Mummy," she said. "I want to go home." She said it quite clearly, to be fair.

The jury looked so sympathetic. "Never mind, sweetheart," said the chairman. "Next year for sure!" And they took the little girl, and held her down fast, and the red-hot tongs were in her mouth before she even had a chance to scream. The microphone picked up the wet hiss, and there was lots of smoke, and then—yes!—the tongue was yanked right out of her head. It wriggled there on the tongs for a moment, high for all the world to see, and then it was cast down upon the stage, and one of the jury stamped on it. And the little girl was crying still, crying for all she was worth, but David thought it was in relief; she didn't have to be a grown-up yet after all. She could go back home with her Mummy and Daddy and play with her dolls and be tucked into bed at night and be a baby for another whole year. Or maybe she was crying with the pain; they always said the tongs didn't hurt, but they really did.

There were some more rejections after that. Maybe the jury had realized they'd been too lenient, and had let too many children pass already. One boy got up and gave an account of his passion for stamp collecting; the chairman said, "All very pleasant, I'm sure, but so what?" He tried to run, but they caught him, they ripped the voice right out of him. And as the rejections began to outnumber the passes, and the stage was strewn with a whole carpet of spent tongues, David thought he might have missed his chance. He should have been picked first. Then he'd have been safe.

But as the evening wore into its fourth hour, the jury began to get lazy again. They just wanted to go home. All of the audience, they wanted to go home. An end to this.

"David Allan."

And David had almost nodded off. In a flash he felt a surge of adrenalin, he got to his feet, he wished he had time to go to the toilet. He made his way to the stage, the applause by now polite at best, most parents saving their energy for their own kids.

Close up the jury seemed like such very small people. Not great figures of authority at all, just older children in older clothes. The chairman was positively leaking nostril hair. "Speak well and speak wisely," he said to David.

David looked out into the hall. His daddy waved, his mummy waved too. And there in the front row was Mrs. Dempsey, just as she'd said she would be, and she gave him a brave smile.

David leaned into the microphone. "Stalactites," he said. It was a good start, nice and clear and full of hard consonants. He could almost feel the keen anticipation of what the second word might be. Would it be as challenging as his first? The audience seemed to move forward in their seats in eagerness. What about stalactites, what could he tell them?

David gulped. He tried to free his tongue, but it was locked in position. After that first, promising, brilliant word, it had shot up, bolt upright, and was now full vertical in his mouth like a pillar. It had become both stalactite and stalagmite there. And it wasn't prepared to budge.

David stole a look at the jury, who were beginning to frown. Dramatic pauses were allowed, certainly, but they had their limits. He looked at his daddy, whose face was anguished. At his mummy, who looked just as composed as before—she'd known this would happen.

"Yes, son?" said the chairman.

And David could now feel the tongue tip pushing further. As if it were trying to break through the palate. As if it wanted to go straight up, higher into the skull. It pushed with all its might.

David closed his mouth, opened it again, shook his whole head from side to side. He'd have put his fingers into his mouth, but finger contact was expressly forbidden.

It was trying to *drill*. It wanted to drill up into his brain. David could feel the urgency of it. It wanted to lick at his brain; it wanted to tell the brain something vitally important.

"We're going to have to hurry you."

It couldn't do it. Of course not, it wasn't strong enough, for all it strained and battered against the top of David's mouth. But it would get stronger. Would it be strong enough to do it one day?

David thought it might. He could imagine it now, the day it'd break through the bone—and then the tongue would drive upwards like a bullet, past his nose, all the way to the brain, all the way through to the top of his head if it wasn't careful, bursting free through his crown like it were an egg.

The tongue had something to say.

Maybe he should let it.

And even then David knew, that one little boy's tongue couldn't change anything. Not on its own. But maybe other tongues would speak freely because of his. Maybe this would be the first step toward revolution.

You had to start somewhere. David knew this. His tongue did too.

"I'm very sorry," said the chairman. "Better luck next year." And there were sympathetic groans from the audience, some kindly applause.

David relaxed. And the tongue allowed him to speak.

"No," he said, calm, clear. "No. Wait. Listen."

They waited. They listened.

And David thought, all right, you're on your own. And he emptied his mind. He let his brain go blank. His mouth opened, and he wondered what he was going to say.

PAGE TURNER

He called her his *grande dame*, his grand lassie, Miss Grandiosity—and it was sort of a joke, because she was really rather short, when she turned the pages for him the audience could barely see her lurking behind the piano, in some theatres they worried that the rake of the stage would prevent her from reaching the pages at all, in one of them they had to fetch her a box to stand on!—but it also wasn't a joke, because she produced such grand emotion within him, he said he felt his love for her as a roar inside, and so it was; and for all her size she was such a whirlwind, when she was happy, it was infectious and she felt so happy too, and his problems seemed unimportant and the sunshine brighter and the music he played sweeter, even when it wasn't sweet at all; when she was unhappy, he wanted to put his arms around her, wrapping up every little bit of her body, and hold on to her tight, and ward off all the bad things. He called her "kitten" and "darling" and "sweetheart." He called her Mrs. Dimpleface, because when she smiled she produced dimples he thought were just adorable—and he called her Lady High Dimpleface when she was being bossy or stuck up, and that happened sometimes, or when she was cross with him, and that happened a lot—and it never failed, it made her smile, and within moments Lady High would leave the building and she'd be his Mrs. Dimpleface again. He called her his "dearest dear," his "own," his "world." He called her "love."

She called him maestro—but then, everybody called him maestro—but then, she alone really meant it.

Both of them had prayed for this, in their own ways.

Louis had prayed to God to make him a musician. He hadn't even thought about music before the age of fifteen, when he had reluctantly accompanied his mother to a concert, and there he had heard Bach. It was, he later recognized, an indifferent performance at best, but it didn't matter, it was as if a light had been turned on in his head and he wondered how he'd lived so long without realizing his purpose. His mother made discreet enquiries, and all the tutors said he was too old to start if he wanted to do it seriously—it could be a hobby, they suggested, something nice, something fun. But Louis was having none of it, this was now going to be his life, and he was going to be the greatest musician of his age, and he would show his genius before the crowned heads of Europe. His father was having none of it; Louis may have been too old to be a musician, but he was too young to *decide* to be a musician either; at the very reminder of his son's ambitions Father would fly into one of his tempers. "My son wants to be a performing monkey!" he said. He'd planned for him to be in the army, or in the church, or in law. "An entertainer?" he said. "Over my dead body!" And Louis prayed, and over his dead body it was—his father suffered a sudden heart attack during one particularly contemptuous rant against tunemerchants and singsongsmiths and hurdygurdyists, and dropped dead right there on the spot—and Louis went to church and gave thanks to God. He didn't even know what instrument he wanted to play. He tried the violin, the trumpet, even the harp—and he was glad the harp didn't take, because it really was most cumbersome, and a bit effeminate, he never thought he'd find himself a woman while hugging a harp. The piano seemed the natural fit. It was sturdy. It was solid. It wasn't a bit sissyish, not if he banged on the keys hard enough. So a pianist he became.

And Lizbeth too had prayed. She prayed for Louis to notice her. She had been to five of his concerts, each night, one after the other, and she'd sat on the front row, hoping that he would catch her eye. But he looked only at the piano, at his piano and nothing else. And on the sixth night she could bear it no longer. It was his last night in Edinburgh, then the tour would continue to other cities far away, and Lizbeth would never see him again, and she couldn't bear that—she'd never seen a man she had wanted more. Se felt it deep in her belly, a desire, a yearning, an actual yearning, and she'd never felt such things before, she was a little shocked at herself, and she didn't know it was whether he produced such beautiful music or that he looked so very dapper in his coat and tails. Before the performance she found her way backstage. She knocked at his door. He looked a little scandalized to see her, and she liked that—in coat and tails he was intimidating, but now with that shy and awkward face he looked like a little boy. "Mademoiselle," he said, "you should know I am a married man!" Married, yes, she knew that; and twenty years older; and French; and Jewish; oh, Mother would never approve. "I want to be of help to you, sir," she said. "I could be your page turner." He told her he already had a page turner for the night—the theatre supplied one—but she said, "Not tonight, for every night." He looked at the clock. "I have to get ready," he said, lamely. "I'll give you an audition, but we'll have to be quick." He played some Chopin, one of the nocturnes. And she stood so close to him as his fingers slid across the keys, and her heart was beating so fast she thought it might distract him, it might put him off the music— he would say, "Mademoiselle, I cannot play the piano with all that drum accompaniment!"—but she turned the pages, she kept up with him— and she knew the Chopin, it was very famous, and she supposed very pretty, but she'd never properly listened to it before, and it made sense to her now, it wasn't just melody, it was full of life and such sweet passion. She kept pace, turned the pages cleanly, and he never had to pause, the entire piece ran as smooth as could be, she wanted to say, don't let's stop, never stop, let's drag it out to a full symphony! And she didn't tell him she'd lied. Didn't dare tell him until months later. On their wedding night, and she was still afraid he'd be angry at the deception, but he just laughed and kissed her and then they made love once more. She'd lied, she'd never turned pages for other pianists as she'd claimed; she couldn't even read music, the notes on the page were just black smudges to her; she didn't know why it was the right time to turn the page, it just was, it was an answered prayer, it was Louis, it was her, it was the togetherness of them both, they were simpatico. He told her she must now leave the dressing room. He had to perform for his audience. But she would be watching, wouldn't she? She'd be in the front row? And she was, and this time as he played he didn't just look at the piano. And never again in her lifetime did she watch him from the stalls, from this point on she would always stand up there with him, turning his pages, and standing so close with her heart beating—but this was maybe her favourite performance, watching him as he watched her, hearing the nocturne, hearing him make little stumbles when he caught her smiling at him. And from that moment she loved Chopin, and from that moment she loved Louis, and she called him maestro.

He divorced his wife, a fat, atonal, double bass of a woman. And they went on tour, and that tour merged into another tour, and then another; the tours went on for years. And he never played before the crowned heads of Europe, not even one of the minor ones. And he never played to a full auditorium. But he'd never played better either. And sometimes they'd both wonder if they'd prayed for the wrong things. He wondered whether he should have asked God to make him not just a musician, but a *great* musician; she wondered whether she'd held him back, whether her love for him had been a selfish thing that had stunted his talent and stopped him from being the maestro he ought to have been. But then they'd put those thoughts right from their heads. They loved each other. They'd got what they'd prayed for, and so much more. They couldn't complain.

On they toured, and he played Bach, and Brahms, and Mendelssohn, and Schubert, all for the thinning crowds; and when he played Chopin, he played it for her.

The tuberculosis took Lizbeth fast—and she was too young, and that was unfair, no, it was *obscene*—but it took her fast, and there was some mercy to that. It took her fast enough she didn't much suffer, but slowly too so there was time to prepare. She arranged the next touring dates for after she'd gone, when he'd be on his own; she'd always arranged the tours, she was the practical one. She told him to hire a new page turner, and he'd said no, and she'd pressed the point, and he'd said no, adamantly no, the theatres would have to provide, just as in the old days, and on this matter at least he won. And he said to her, "I don't want you to go," and, "I can't bear it if you go," and she'd say, "Oh, love," and she'd say, "Love, I know." And he'd pray that she wouldn't die, and that was too much to ask. And he'd pray that she wouldn't feel any pain, and that too, it was just too much, God didn't answer prayers like that. And he'd pray, at least let us be together, let us always be together. And he had no right to expect an answer to that either, hadn't they been given enough already? But God listened.

One day she woke and she was smiling, and it wasn't one of the brave smiles he'd grown used to, it was a smile broad enough to make her cheeks dimple. She told him that the pain was gone. He could hardly believe it. He began to hope. Though as he looked at her she still seemed so pale and thin, still, he let himself hope. She felt a little numbness on her back, and when he turned her over, he saw that it had turned to wood. A brown, rich wood, he thought it might be mahogany; he knew it was mahogany, he recognized it from the grand piano they owned in the drawing room. He pressed against it gently, she said he could press harder—he asked if she could feel him and she said she could, but he mustn't worry, it was a nice sensation; it seemed somehow *solid*, if a sensation could be solid. He rapped his fingers against her and she smiled—and he kissed her on the wood, and there was something familiar and earthy about that taste, as if the wood had just this day grown out of the soil—and he kissed her again, not on the wood now, on the mouth, and she kissed him too, and he could taste the blood there, and the sickness, and death.

The wood grew. She was such a little woman, and so she remained; the illness made her shrink into herself, if anything. But her back now stood proud and tall, like a great sturdy frame. He stroked it. "Oh, my love," she said. Her feet narrowed, then they doubled, then they turned to brass. She opened her mouth in her widest smile, and her teeth filled an entire keyboard with dazzling white ivory; on her hands her fingernails blackened, and it was a rich black, a deep black, and they smoothed, and they swelled, and they dotted between the ivories as the sharps and flats. "I love you," she told him, and he loved her too; he loved her as her two eyelids merged into one heavier lid altogether, the one that locked the keyboard away and kept it safe; he loved her as her lungs, her kidneys, the heart itself, as they all stretched themselves taut as strings; as one single eye became a knot in the wood just above the rack on which he kept his sheets of music, so now, when he sat at his wife and played on her and had his fingers tease at her and thrilled to the strange music she made, he gazed at the eye and it gazed at him, it wouldn't wink, it wouldn't blink, it held him, so wide, so sure, telling him that it was all right, everything was going to be all right. He played for hours, and no matter the tune, no matter how jaunty or light, each time it made him cry. "I love you," she told him. "I love you, and you're the best of me, and you always have been, and you always will."

And in the drawing room the grand piano softened into a mass of pale and melting flesh, and it coughed blood, hawking thick black gobs of it on to its own chin, and there was pain there, and something rather worse than pain, but it was only a piano, it was only an instrument, it didn't cry out, it didn't complain, it didn't say a word.

And when the doctor came it was the piano he examined, not the wife; Louis thought him rather a fool not to notice; and the doctor shook his head and led Louis away from the piano's earshot and told him to expect the worst. But Louis knew there was no worst, his wife was alive and well and getting so much better, no longer turning the pages of his music but producing all the music herself—he couldn't even pretend it was him any longer, it all came from her, the music flowed straight from her, and when his fingers danced upon her teeth it was just so she could let her genius out. And the piano died, it gave one splutter one morning and just slipped away; and it was the piano they took away, the undertaker and his crew all muttering condolences, and Louis was glad to be rid of it—it looked like a poor faded corpse, like a spent thing, like something broken, something that could never have made music, what music could there be in something so sad? And they buried it. And Louis could hardly stop himself from laughing, but he knew for form's sake he must be seen to grieve—and yet it was a trick, he'd still got Lizbeth, his dearest dear, he'd still got her and would never lose her, and he could tickle her ivories and make her chest thrum, he'd got her, he'd never let her go.

All the stories say that he went back on tour and took his own piano with him. And he performed in his dear wife's memory, and whilst he never found great success, he was happy. But not one can agree on the ending. Here are just a few of those endings.

In one story Louis dies onstage. He's an old man, but he's still performing, and it's his birthday, it's his hundredth birthday—no, that sounds a bit too neat, let's say he's ninety-nine. He bows before the audience and dedicates the evening, as he always does, to Lizbeth—who was the best of him, always has been, always will. And it isn't a full house—even sentiment can only go so far in this tale, he'd never have sold that many tickets, a ninety-nine year old has-been like him! But though it's only of modest size, the crowd is appreciative. It gives him a standing ovation at the end. And Louis cannot stand to acknowledge it, because he's dead, he's had a heart attack, so sudden and so profound he wouldn't have felt a thing, there was one great thrum in his chest and that was it. Louis dies proud. They can't prise his fingers off the piano keys, and they can't prise his foot off the pedal. It's as if he's become fused to the piano itself. There's no join where the piano ends and the man begins—there is ivory as far as his knuckles, brass spread over his foot. And his back has become wood, all the best mahogany. They're buried together, the grand maestro and his grand piano.

And, in another story, the Nazis get him. He lives to be an old man, but it's no good, history catches up with him. The Nazis break down the front door to his house. They find Louis in the drawing room, sitting at the piano. Maybe he's playing. Maybe he's just caressing it, like he does every day—because that's enough now, there's no more performance left in him, but if he caresses the piano and strokes the wood and kisses at the keyboard there's still music of a sort. He doesn't rise for them. He doesn't even turn around. The soldiers jab the old Jew with their guns, and laugh, and tell the music man to play them something good—something patriotic—Deutschland über alles! Louis doesn't play that, of course. Maybe he even tries to, but Lizbeth won't let him. Whatever his fingers tell the keys to do, the piano will only play Chopin. And no matter the shouts of anger, the threats, Louis won't even change the tempo—this is a calm Chopin, something sweet to be savoured, he won't be rushed or panicked. They shoot him. Or maybe they're so overcome by the music's beauty, and the dignity of the old man and his darling piano, maybe they leave him in shame. No, they shoot him, clean, in the back of the head, and then, and then the piano keeps on playing. The Chopin won't stop. The love just won't stop, not for them, not because *they* say so, not because *they* will it, it's more powerful than anything they will ever feel in their uniforms and jackboots, this is his *grande dame* playing, his grand lassie, Miss Grandiosity, in tribute to the man she adored. The piano plays until, in rage, the soldiers chop it into firewood.

Or, in one last story. And this one seems real to me. This one true. Because what more magic can Louis and Lizbeth expect? In a lifetime that has given them such miracles already?

Louis falls in love. He doesn't mean to. Oh, don't blame him, he doesn't want to. He tells the woman this. He says, I can't do this, and she says she'll be patient, and she is, and it's all right.—And he's been lonely enough, surely? Hasn't he had his fill of suffering?

And when she smiles her face doesn't dimple. But her face does entirely new things he couldn't even have guessed at.

On their wedding day he feels as if he's inviting a curse upon his head. But nothing happens. He toasts his new love, and she toasts him, and everyone applauds, and is happy for them as they cut the cake and kiss and dance their first dance as husband and wife.

He doesn't tour again. That part of his life is over, and besides, his new wife doesn't love him for his music. This doesn't make her a bad person. She loves him for other things. But he keeps the piano. He keeps it, and he buries it under a rug, and he locks it away upstairs, and keeps the key hidden.

They have a daughter. He loves his daughter. At this late stage in his life, third time lucky, Louis has at last created a work of art all his own.

He indulges the girl, but he won't spoil her. If she wants to ride a horse, he'll find the money for riding lessons. If she wants a new toy, a new dress, a pet dog, a pet parakeet even, that's all right, she can have them. But he won't let her learn the piano. No more music. Enough.

And one day he hears it. He has been out walking with his darling wife; they've walked hand in hand through the parks of Paris, as they like to do, they've smelled the flowers in bloom, they've kissed. But it begins to rain, and they hurry home.

And though the locked room is right at the very top of the house, really so very far away, he hears it immediately. Fingers bashing at keys, not knowing how hard or light to be, and the notes straining in protest. All that discordant music. All that ugly din.

He races up the stairs as fast as he can. He has never been so angry. He can feel his heart pounding in his chest, and he thinks of his father, and how angry he always was, and he thinks, is this it? Will I kill myself with my anger too? But he keeps running, and below him he hears his wife distraught, Louis, she cries, go easy on her, Louis, come back!

She's beating away at the piano so loudly she doesn't even hear him until he bursts into the room. She's lifted the rug from the piano lid, but most of the piano is still smothered; it looks now like something old and dead—it looks like something embarrassing. And her hands are dirty, he sees, she hasn't even washed them, she'll be smearing her fingerprints all over those gleaming white keys, she hasn't even put on *gloves*—and as she hits the keys, *plink plonk plunk*, in any order, she keeps time by kicking at the wood—sitting on the stool and so short she can't even reach the floor, her legs dangling in mid-air and scuffing the side of the piano as she finds some sort of rhythm.

She turns around now, and she still doesn't know, still doesn't see he's angry. She smiles at him, as if she's been clever, as if she's just uncovered a big secret—there's music in the world! And her smile is so big, and no, the cheeks don't dimple for her either—but that smile certainly has something good about it.

"Papa," she says. "Teach me! Teach me how to do it!"

When he puts his hands on her he still doesn't know what he's going to do. But he lifts her off the stool gently, ever so gently, and she laughs. He sets her down safely on the floor. He pulls the rug off the piano, it comes off in one hard tug, and the piano doesn't look dead anymore, or embarrassing—it's *old*, certainly, but that's all right, he's old too. And he sits down upon the stool. And lifts little Lizbeth up onto his knee. And begins to play for her.

TABOO

Your sister's phone call wakes you. You know it must be your sister even before, fumbling, you pick up the receiver. Who else would call at half past four in the morning?

"Emma?" you say, and you're right, it's Emma.

"For Christ's sake," your wife mutters, and sighs loud and heavy, and you think that Emma must have heard.

"What do you think of camels?" Emma asks.

"Emma, is something wrong, it's the middle of the night . . ."

"No, no. I checked. There's an eight-hour time difference, it's early evening for you now."

"I don't think so."

"Are you sure?" she says. And you can picture her narrowing her eyes, giving you that long hard glare, the way she always does when you contradict her—nothing hostile, not as such, not aggressive, just very forthright. Right from childhood you could never hold that glare, you'd always look away. "Are you sure, because I *checked*."

"Maybe you're right. Are you in London? Is everything okay?"

"Everything's wonderful," Emma says. "I'm in Egypt. It's very hot in Egypt. What's it like in Sydney?"

You don't live in Sydney, you live in Melbourne. "It's hard to tell, it's dark outside . . ."

"Yes, yes, it doesn't matter, listen. Listen, I'm getting married."

"Well," you say. "My God. I mean. Well done."

"Christ," says your wife, and she sighs again, and this time it's so loud that Emma *must* have caught it, and you cradle the phone away defensively. "If your sister is going to be rude enough to wake us up in the middle of the night, when we've both got work in the morning, there's no reason why you should have to *compound* that rudeness by carrying on a conversation with her in the bedroom."

"No, sorry," you say to your wife, and you get up, you take the phone with you. "Sorry," you say to Emma.

You close the bedroom door gently, you open the door to the sitting room, you close that too behind you, gently. You sit down on the sofa. "Right," you say to Emma. "So. Start again."

"I'm getting married," she says.

"Yes, I got that bit."

"I decided to go on holiday. I wanted a little bit of me time, I hadn't had any me time in a long time. Barry never gave me any me time, so when Barry and I broke up, I thought, this is my chance, I went straight to Expedia."

"And Barry is . . . ?"

"Barry is nothing, Barry is history," Emma says. "Keep up. I'm not marrying Barry."

"No."

"I *thought* I was marrying Barry, but Barry wasn't the marrying type, or so it turned out. Forget about Barry, I don't want to hear about Barry again."

"Fair enough."

"Besides, Barry never proposed. I'm marrying Abdul."

"And Abdul is . . . ?"

"I'm getting to that. I wasn't looking for romance, you know, frankly, that's the *last* thing I was looking for. I'd worked it out, men are just shits, I'm better off without them. Well, you'll know. But Abdul and I connected right away. There was just a bolt of electricity, you know, when we first met? It was the same for both of us, I thought, at last, this is the one. And besides, Abdul isn't a man, he's a camel."

"You did," you agree, "say something about camels."

"What do you think about camels?"

"Erm," you say. "I don't think I've ever met one."

"Not even at a zoo?"

"I might have seen one at a zoo," you concede. "I don't think I *met* one at a zoo."

"I haven't told Mum yet," Emma says. "I think Mum will be very angry. I think she's a bit racist. And a bit animalist. In fact, I don't think I'm going to tell her. She'll only try to upset me, and I don't need upset, not in my life, not right now. The only person I'm inviting to the wedding is you."

"Oh, right," you say, and you do actually feel flattered, "thanks."

"Will you give me away?"

"Yes," you say, "yes, of course. Emma. When you say 'camel' . . ."

"Yes?"

"I mean. Are you really happy?"

"I'm very happy," she assures you. "I've never been happier." And you know, you can hear the sincerity in her voice, and it makes you happy too. "Do you think that you can get here for Thursday? The wedding's not 'til Saturday, but there's all sorts of things to prepare, and I could do with a hand."

"Thursday?" you say. "Hang on. Why so soon?"

"Why wait? I tell you, Abdul and I are in *love*."

"Right."

"And anyway, Abdul is nice and heavy at the moment, he's been storing food. Best get it done whilst the weight is in the zone."

"Right. Well. I'll get on and book my flights then."

"Great. I love you."

"I love you too."

"How's your wife . . . ?"

"Kirsten's fine."

"And your daughter . . . ?"

"Tammy's fine."

"Good," she says. "See you soon then." And hangs up.

☟

When you go back to bed your wife is very deliberately pretending to be asleep, and when your alarm wakes you in the morning she's doing the same thing, her eyes are squeezed tight and she's refusing to stir. So it's not until you get home in the evening you can tell her your plans. In your lunch hour you went to the bookshop and bought a guide to Egypt, you think the pictures of the Sphinx and the pyramids will excite her as much as they do you.

"That's so typically selfish of your sister," she says. "How dare she decide when and where we take our holiday!" She points out that she only gets four weeks leave a year, and one of those has to be spent visiting her father in Brisbane, and another her mother in Adelaide, and the two remaining weeks are consequently very precious, and it's up to *her* where she spends them, not your bloody sister. "Going all the way round the world for her wedding, as if. It's not as if she came to our wedding."

The location of your wedding created the need for much negotiation between your family and your wife's—it began like negotiation, anyway, but soon took on the air of a war summit, with demands flying back and forth across the oceans in ever more hectoring language and with ever less room for compromise. And the Australian contingent eventually won, they dug their teeth in and refused to budge, they won the war not with better ammunition but simply by sheer reserves of manpower, it seemed as though Kirsten had unlimited numbers of cousins her family could produce whenever they needed more muscle. The ceremony finally took place in a chapel in Melbourne with a vast army of in-laws in attendance, and none of your own family at all. The concession made in the treaty was that before the wedding you and Kirsten would take a holiday in England, so that the bride-to-be could be met by *your* family; Kirsten said it was like being inspected under a microscope, like being poked at and prodded by a whole gang of slack-jawed drongos who'd never seen an Aussie before. "But you like Emma," you say. "You don't mind Emma." And at this Kirsten snorts in derision, she *hates* Emma, didn't you know?—and you didn't, you knew that Kirsten hated your parents, and Uncle Bill and Aunt Val, and your only surviving nanna, and your cousin Tim, and your cousin Tim's kids—but that she hated your sister as well is news to you. And it makes you feel just a little sad.

"But we've always talked about going to Egypt someday," you point out, "so now seems as good a time as any!" And Emma tells you you've *never* talked about going to Egypt, when on earth have either of you even mentioned Egypt, and on reflection you think maybe she's right, maybe you've never discussed Egypt whatsoever. So.

"If you want to spend your money flying to Egypt, then that's fine," your wife says. "But I'm saving *my* money for *my* holiday." You ask whether you can take Tammy, but Kirsten tells you that taking her out of kindergarten would be disruptive to her emotional wellbeing, she'll take her on holiday herself later in the year. You check the prices to Cairo, and it costs a couple of thousand dollars. When you click on the "buy now!" button on the webpage your heart skips at the expense of it all. You speak to Emma again on the phone; she explains that because of circumstances, circumstances she'll feel more comfortable explaining face to face, she can't offer to put you up—perhaps you could find a hotel? And you do, and that's another thousand dollars gone right there.

Your little girl gets very excited about the idea that you're going to

Egypt. She races around the kitchen shouting that Daddy is going away, and drawing little pyramids everywhere. She's never spent a day without you there since she was born. "You do understand you're not coming with me?" you ask her. "You do understand I can't disrupt your wellbeing?" "Yes, yes!" cries Tammy, and she races around all the more. It's an early flight to Cairo—you have to make your goodbyes to Tammy the night before. "I'll bring you back a present," you promise her, "something nice and Egyptian," and she says, "No worries." You bite your tongue, you do wish she wouldn't say things like that. You don't mind the fact that your daughter will be Australian, you just don't want her to end up like one of the crass ones. When you talk to Tammy, you sometimes feel it's just to cram English accented conversation into her head—Kirsten gets to talk to Tammy lots, she has more time to do so, so you do your very best in the evening to counter that, you'll sit your little daughter on your knee and speak proper English phrases at her. But just recently it's been hard to find things to say.

"You be good for Mummy," you say, and Tammy smiles at you, and she promises she will; "You be good for Mummy too," she says. And at that moment you've never loved your daughter so much or so fiercely, you want to pick her up and hold her close and never let her go and press down kisses hard upon her head, you want to fold her up and stuff her in your suitcase—you can't wait until she's older, what a perfect little woman she is going to be! But you don't do any of these things. You smile back at her, you give the mobile over her head a little push so that Tammy can see all the animals in the zoo twirling gently above, you close her bedroom door.

↓

It's two long flights to Cairo, and by the time you get through customs you're really very jetlagged, and that's why when your sister greets you you don't recognize her at first. That, and the fact she's wearing a black hood over her face.

"It's called a burqa," she says helpfully.

"I thought that was a Muslim thing."

"But I've become a Muslim," she said. "In honour of my husband-to-be."

You hail a taxi. "It's quite a long way," Emma says. "I hope you've got lots of money." You ask Emma whether you can look at her face, and she tells you she's pretty sure only her husband will be allowed to do that, and you assure her that family members are allowed to as well, though really you've no idea—you'd have looked it up in the Egypt guide book if you'd thought it was going to be an issue. So she sort of shrugs, and checks that the taxi driver isn't peeking in the rear-view mirror, and lifts her veil. Her face is a bit fatter than you remember, she looks so happy and she can't stop smiling, it's obvious she's been smiling a lot. She looks beautiful. Being in love suits her. You tell her so. She beams all the more.

"I'm so excited for you," you say. "My big sister, getting married! The Muslim thing's a bit weird, though, isn't it?"

She frowns. "Everyone here's Muslim. Anybody who's anybody, anyway. It's not hard. I've looked in the Qur'an, it's just like being a Christian, it's all about being nice to people, with Eastern bits."

You realize you're far too tired to talk to your sister. She's always easier to deal with after a solid eight-hours sleep; you knew that even when you were children—there was an exact time to leave her and go hide in your bedroom. You've come all this way to see her, and now you suddenly feel shy, and you're annoyed at yourself for that. So you watch the road for a while. You wonder why the taxi driver is going so fast, and how he's able to fit his car into the little gaps in the traffic without crashing, and whether he's ever run anyone down on the pavement. And after only a few minutes' such musing it dawns on you you'd far rather talk to your sister after all—and you manage to wrench your eyes away from the window and the chaos around you and turn back to Emma. But she's done talking now too. She's back behind the burqa, and it seems to have sealed off her face, there can be no conversation through all that cloth. But she sees you're looking at her. And although her expression is of course unreadable, she takes your hand. She squeezes it.

You're not quite sure what to expect from an Egyptian house. You were half expecting it to be some sort of shed, or a wigwam even. But it looks from the outside just as modern as any normal house might be. Bricks, windows, a large garage. The taxi driver jabbers something. He shows you the fare. You don't know if you're supposed to haggle or not, isn't haggling part of what goes on here? And the fare does seem to have a lot of noughts. So you make a half-hearted attempt to haggle, and the driver scowls angrily, and you give him what he asked for in the first place and add a tip. He takes your suitcases out of the boot and bumps them

Taboo

onto the pavement hard, and then drives away. Your sister asks you for the taxi fare that brought her to the airport to pick you up; she borrowed the money, she'll have to pay it back. So you offer her the same amount. "No, more than that," she says.

And you go into her new home. "We'll have to be quiet," she says. "It's family time." She explains that her fiancé is owned by a man called Ali, who rents out camel rides to tourists. Ali has very kindly allowed Emma to stay in a spare room on condition that she does the housework— cleaning, cooking, general chores. In fact, she'd better get back to work: she was given permission to meet you at the airport, but only if she made up the time when she got back, and now she's running a few hours behind.

You stand in the doorway of the sitting room and peer in. Three teenage children are watching television; one of them is listening to an iPod as he does so, so loud that you can identify the song from where you're standing, it's something by Britney Spears. Their mother is watching television too. It looks like a game show, but every so often the children laugh at it uproariously, so maybe it's something entirely different. The mother never laughs, never smiles. "Hello," you say. They ignore you. Neither the mother nor the little girl, you notice, are wearing burqas. Your sister pulls her own burqa down smart, and fetches a vacuum cleaner out of the cupboard. She plugs it in, turns it on, and the cleaner isn't new, it coughs and rasps. Without a word the mother levels the remote control at the television, presses a button, and turns the volume up loud over it. The noise of vacuum cleaner and widescreen high definition TV compete for a moment, but the TV wins—it's very loud, and you wonder whether the neighbours might complain. Your sister cleans the carpet around the sofa, around the coffee table; the little boys lift their feet so she can clean underneath, and the little girl doesn't bother—and every thirty seconds or so they burst into laughter at the antics of the game show host, they laugh and laugh.

"Would you mind doing the dishes?" your sister asks.

So you go into the kitchen, you rinse all the plates and the cutlery, then you stack them all in the dishwasher. You don't turn the dishwasher on. You don't think that should be your job.

And at last the vacuum cleaner is turned off and your sister comes to join you. "Thanks for that!" she says. "Phew!" The television volume stays just as loud, she has to talk quite loudly herself just so you can hear her. The game show ends and segues into something that might be a cop show—whatever it is, there are lots of sirens.

"Emma," you say, "this is all very nice, but I'm very tired, I should be getting to my hotel . . ."

"No, no," she says, "no, I need you to meet Abdul. He'll be getting home from work soon, you'll see."

And sure enough, very soon the door opens. And Emma looks nervous—she adjusts her burqa once more, and she leaves the kitchen to greet the master of the house. This, I take it, must be Ali; his wife and children wear modern clothes, but he has a grey sheet wrapped around his head, he looks like something out of the history books, frankly, he looks like a camel driver, a *peasant*. He pulls his headscarf off and you see that underneath he looks just as western and civilized as anyone else, the costume was a bit of a fraud. The children turn the TV off at last, and they hug him, all smiles. He hugs them back, but he's too tired for smiling. His wife gives him a single nod, and he nods back.

Emma steps forward, and offers him the money you gave her earlier. He counts it slowly, carefully. Then gives her too a nod. "Hello," you say, and he looks at you for the first time, and then *you* get the nod, nod number three—it's not a friendly nod, and again it's without a smile, but it's at least respectful, and it feels like the first proper acknowledgement you've had since you arrived in the country.

"May I?" asks Emma, and Ali says, "Yes." And Emma takes your hand, excited, and Ali frowns at that. And Emma doesn't care, she's already pulling you out of the door, out of the house.

"Where are you taking me?" you say.

"To meet my husband."

She pulls up the garage door. Inside there's a family car, nicely polished, new. And to its side, on a bed of straw, a camel rests, kneeling.

"This is Abdul," Emma says, at last lifting her burqa, and you can see how her face is glowing with pride.

Abdul is very definitely a camel. Now that you're there, face to face, confronted with the full camel bulk of it, there's really no escaping the fact. It isn't a donkey, or some strange humpy shaped horse, this is your actual bona fide ship of the desert—and he's big, and he's hairy, and he looks at you with clear disdain.

"So," says Emma. "Here we all are!"

"Nice to meet you," you say to the camel, but your new brother has already turned away.

"Isn't he wonderful?" enthuses Emma. "Just look at his eyes!" But you can't, Abdul is demonstrating only his arse, it's clear he has eyes only for your sister. "So deep and, and soulful. Oh, I could drown in them. And these long eyelashes, wouldn't you just *die* for eyelashes like that? And he has, you know, three eyelids." She kisses the side of his face, and the camel's breathy groan turns into a harrumph. "Camels are the most beautiful creatures in the world, and Abdul is the most beautiful camel, so."

"That's great," you say, and "How long do camels live for?"

"About forty years."

"Right."

"Abdul's only seven now, so the chances are we'll die about the same time. That's what I'm counting on, I don't want to outlive Abdul. Only seven, he's my toyboy, really!" And she laughs.

"Right."

She nuzzles at his face. He harrumphs again.

"Right. Well, look, I best be getting to bed . . ."

"You can't go yet," says Emma. "Please."

"I'm really very tired."

"You don't understand. This is a Muslim wedding. I'm not allowed to see the groom beforehand unless I'm chaperoned. No one wants to chaperone me. I haven't seen Abdul in *ages*."

And it occurs to you that your sister barely even *knows* this camel she's getting hitched to. And then something else.

"Wait a moment," you say. "Are you telling me you haven't yet . . . you know . . . ?"

"We can't have sex until we're married. Obviously."

"But . . . for God's sake . . . I mean, how can you tell if . . . ?" Before you married Kirsten, she insisted she tried you out in all manner of positions. When she found one you were good at, she allowed you to propose.

"The anticipation," whispers Emma, "is *wonderful*," and she licks her lips.

Abdul harrumphs, but it's a very different sort of harrumph this time, it's directed at you.

"Oh, hello," you say. And you back away a bit.

"Don't worry, he's just wanting to know you better." Abdul gets to his feet, those spindly legs straighten, you think they'll never carry such a bulky lump, but no, he's upright and tall and without so much as a stagger he's bearing down on you. "Keep still," says Emma, so you keep still, and the camel sticks his pointed head right at you, he opens his mouth, out of it pops a red sac that bulges at you querulously. He harrumphs louder, and it's clearly not a happy harrumph, he's agitated now, he's shaking from side to side and that red sac seems to be *pulsating*, "Oh dear," says Emma, and he hawks a sea of spit into your face.

"Quick!" your sister says. "Take off your jacket!"

"But it's my best jacket . . ."

"Take it off!"

And you do, and you hold it out to Abdul, and now he's ripped it from your hand, he's tearing into it, he chews it and spits out patches from it onto the ground, he's jumping on it and destroying that jacket as if it were his mortal enemy.

"I don't think he entirely trusts you," says Emma. "But he'll come to understand in time how much you mean to me."

"I want to go to the hotel now."

The taxi arrives. You don't think it's the same driver, but really, they all look much the same. "Thanks for coming all this way," Emma tells you through the car window as she sees you off.

"You bet."

And she can't help it, she can't keep in the giggle. "I'm getting married! Me! Just think!"

ᴥ

But it isn't marriage, not really. The technical term for it is civil partnership. And yet that still isn't enough for some people, it'd seem—they say that their relationships are not given proper respect by society, that they demand equal rights. They're always going on some demonstration march or another, they'll be asking that their animal spouses get the vote next!—and when you go to work each morning some creaturehugger with a placard is always soliciting for your signature outside the train station at Flinders Square.

You consider yourself a tolerant and open-minded sort of man, but you do wish they'd stop making a fuss. Because they're bloody lucky, really, haven't they got enough? A hundred years ago they'd have been locked up for what they're now allowed to do in public. They ask that their animal loving be treated as something natural and normal—but it isn't natural, it's not normal, you can't say it is, if God had wanted humans to fall in love with animals then the union would be able to produce children. Not that you're religious, but the religious groups are correct on that, at least, surely—and you're not arguing about the *ethics* of bestial relations here, as you say, you're a tolerant and open-minded person, but there's no arguing that it makes any kind of biological sense. And yet when you try to say this in the office you're shouted down as being bestiophobic. It really makes you sick.

But the law now states that sexual relations are permitted between a human and a consenting animal. For a while it was hard to determine what actually proved the animal was consenting—after all, it wasn't as if they could tell us whether they were up for it or not, and if we simply all waited until they were eighteen years of age the vast majority of them would be dead. At last it was agreed that an animal's suitability should be judged on body mass, and that the four-legged bride or groom in question must weigh at least one and a half times the amount of its human counterpart. The theory being that if you try to make love to a horse or a rhino or an elephant, and it's not too happy about the arrangement, it will have the strength to resist—but try to shag a reluctant gerbil, say, and there's really precious little the gerbil can do about it. One and a half times the body weight guarantees a beast's complicity in any carnal act you might share—and if you try it on with a gerbil, no matter how much she might seem up for it, or how flirtatiously she twitched her whiskers, then it's statutory rape, clear and simple.

You suppose your sister is now one of those people who would go on marches. Which is funny, because you can't picture her being the sort who'd want to march about anything.

You've got nothing against creaturehugging per se (so long as it's within the privacy of their own homes, so long as you haven't got to see it, so long as it's not shoved down your throat), you say live and let live, you say they're not hurting anybody (except themselves), you're not a bigot, you're not a bestiophobe, you're tolerant, and you're open minded, and. . . And you're just lucky you're normal, and in a normal relationship, one that is healthy and clean and childbearing. But coming face to face with your sister's fiancé has made you upset, and you don't like that, it's annoying to discover you're just a little bit prejudiced after all. It wouldn't be so bad, you reflect, if she'd found an ordinary animal, something close to home; you can imagine you'd be very accepting if your brother-in-law were a horse of good Anglo Saxon stock. But no—she had to go and find something exotic, some zoo creature—she had to go and fall for some fucking Arab.

⩗

In your hotel room you open up your laptop and fire off a quick email home. "Hello from sunny Egypt! It's very hot! Wish you were here. Miss you loads. Lots of love, give Tammy a hug from Daddy." And then you go on to Google, and type into the search engine "camel sex."

You read about the camel penis, and are shown a diagram that measures its length and breadth. You read how, when aroused, the penis is in a different axis to most mammals, and when erect enters the female from the reverse direction. You find out that the camel's right testicle is slightly bigger than the camel's left testicle.

You break into the mini bar.

You read how a camel in heat is referred to in Arabia as the "hadur," literally, "the braying one." You suppose there's a lot of braying in camel sex. You read that, when he's rutting, the camel will secrete behind the ear a sticky smelly residue. That he'll grind his teeth uncontrollably during copulation. That his mouth will froth, he'll gargle, he'll spit. He'll piss, and he'll swing his tail back and forth through the stream of piss to swish the piss about. That all this water loss, this very deliberate waste of precious fluids, is part of a courtship ritual designed to impress the female. That he'll blow out his soft palate (the dulla) to turn her on the more; that, for his part, he'll sniff at his partner's genitalia, and the smell of urine from a non-pregnant female will excite him to no end.

You drink the mini bar dry.

When at last you sleep you dream of fat, hairy, hooked cocks impregnating your urine-drenched sister, and though she's wearing her burqa, you can somehow tell throughout the whole thing that she's grinning from ear to ear.

⩗

Emma phones you in the morning. She's been given permission to take a whole afternoon off work so you can explore Cairo together. The taxi pulls up outside the hotel, she waves at you to get inside. Once again she is wearing her burqa. She hands another burqa to you. "Put this on," she says.

"What for?"

"I want to show you where Abdul works. Abdul's marvellous at his job! But Ali doesn't like me being there, he says I'll distract him, bless."

And she gives a very dry and very un-Muslim-like chuckle. "I don't want us to be recognized, you're going to have to cover your face like me."

So you put on the burqa. The air conditioning of the taxi makes the cloth ripple across your face, and the sensation is not unpleasant.

You pay the driver, and you and your sister stand and watch Abdul and his master work. Ali is transformed; the surly and serious man you met last night is now all smiles, he wheedles his way around the tourists, he invites them all to inspect his camel, to see what a fine beast it is, to take a ride to the Great Pyramid in such style—and he's so good at it, no one seems able to blank him or walk away, no one, not even the Americans. He's such a good actor. And Abdul is a good actor too, because whenever a foreigner approaches he lowers his head toward them and flutters his eyelashes and even parts his lips into some sort of camel smile, he doesn't seem to mind when the children pull his ears or pick at his coat or dribble ice cream on him, he's the very picture of patience, the very model of Oriental dignity—and amongst all the sphinx snow globes and mummy paperweights and postcards of the pyramids, amongst all these imitations of history made cheap and plastic, he looks like the genuine article, he looks himself like a piece of antiquity, so old and so very wise. And for the first time you understand why your sister could have fallen in love with him. "Hoosh hoosh!" says Ali, and Abdul stoops to let tourists onto his back; "Hoosh!" and he straightens up, and the tourists are raised high in the air, each one of them laughing and crying out in surprise at the sudden speed of it. And you picture your sister up there, mounting her camel husband as much as she wants for the rest of her life.

You watch for a good hour and a half. Emma never gets bored. "Isn't he wonderful?" she'll say. You begin to get tired, and there's a reservoir of sweat pooling at the top of your thighs. You suggest that maybe there's more to see in Cairo than her husband, what would Emma recommend? And she says she doesn't know, she hasn't done any of the tourist stuff. "You never do, do you, when you're at home?" And you resist the urge to remind her she's only been here in Egypt for two weeks.

You go to the Cairo museum, you pay for two tickets. You walk around the exhibits, and the collection is vast. Everywhere there are mummies and canopic jars and little stone pots with heads of jackals. But it seems to you that you've seen it all before, in dozens of other museums all around the world, and you really might as well be in London or Paris or Prague; my God, for a civilization that collapsed thousands of years ago they certainly left an awful lot of stuff behind, didn't they? But Emma is happy. She says to you at one point, "It's beautiful, I'm so proud that my country could produce all this," and she talks a little of Mother Egypt. "I'm so proud you're here," she whispers too, and she takes you by the arm, and the eyes behind the burqa slit are wet with tears, and you can't tell whether she's crying out of awe and admiration for the pharaohs or out of love for you—and then you realize with a start you've spent all this time looking out of a slit too, you forgot to take the burqa off, you've been walking all around the Cairo museum wearing a bloody burqa, you feel like an idiot.

"Come on," you say, and take her to the café. The food there costs a fortune. You buy two coffees, and two sandwiches, and a pastry, you pay for it all. Emma gobbles down her sandwich. She looks so hungry suddenly, and you let her eat your sandwich too.

"You're a good person," she says suddenly. You don't know where that's come from. You then see she's eaten the pastry as well. "You're a good guy. I think you're kind, and I don't think you've got the easiest life, and you put up with a lot. And me. I think you put up with me."

"Oh," you say. "I don't know about that."

"I never found good guys. I always ended up with the other sort of guys. The selfish shit sort of guys. If I'd met someone like you, God, I don't suppose I'd now be marrying a camel."

You blush, and you wish you were still wearing your burqa. She doesn't say anything else for a bit, and you wonder whether she'll do her usual trick, whether now she's let show a little emotion or humanity that she'll sweep it away with some dismissive gesture. But she doesn't. She doesn't.

"I always thought you saw me as a bit of an idiot," you say.

"No."

You don't look at her. "You pulled my hair. You kicked me. I never thought you even liked me very much."

"I haven't pulled your hair."

"Not recently. I mean. But when we were kids."

"Well. You're my little brother." As if that explains everything.

"Are you sure you want . . . Are you sure that . . . Emma?" And you'd like to carry on, but you mustn't ask, and you're still not looking at her, you still don't dare, and even if you did what would be the point, her face would still be veiled, wouldn't it? "I just want you happy," you say, and you leave it like that, and maybe that's just as well.

Taboo

ᵚ

That evening at the hotel you check your email and there's nothing from your wife, so you write to her again. "Hello from sunny Egypt! It's still very hot here! I haven't heard from you, are you all right? Wish you were here. Today I went to the Cairo museum. I think you'd have liked it. I know you like museums, and it was a very big one. Lots of pots everywhere. I wish you'd been here to see them. I miss you. How are you, are you all right? Write soon. Give Tammy a hug from her Daddy."

Then you decide to take a walk. As you leave the hotel the doorman stands to attention and calls you sir. He looks funny dressed up posh like that, like an English gentleman from a hundred years ago, top hat and spats. (He must be baking.) You walk around the streets for an hour. This is Cairo, the real Cairo, isn't it? Your clothes cling to you, damp and sticky, you wonder why anyone would choose to live here. I mean, you know that historically people just settled where they were born, but nowadays, in these days of international travel, why do all of these Egyptians stay? The roads are noisy. The sand is everywhere, it looks like dirt. You go back to the hotel, and the doorman stands to attention once more, once more calls you sir, so efficient—you bet he doesn't even recognize you from last time—and you wish he wouldn't call you sir, you didn't ask him for that, you didn't ask for anything.

In the room you check your email. Still nothing from your wife, but then, you suppose, she's probably asleep. You consider phoning, but you'd only wake her. You'd only make her cross. You write to her once more.

"Me again! I've been thinking. I may extend my visit here, if that's all right. I don't know how long. But I think my sister needs me."

You open the mini bar and it's empty. Not so fucking efficient after all, for all their fancy doormen, for all their top hats, they've let you down. You phone reception, you demand they restock your mini bar at once. A waiter in a red velvet jacket comes up soon after, lines the shelves with little bottles, smiles at you widely, says "Sorry, sorry."

You write another email.

"I don't think it's working out. I don't think I love you anymore."

You drink a whisky. And then think, why not? And send it.

And you think, oh, Tammy. Tammy. You'd have grown into such a beautiful woman. And you try to picture how beautiful, like a model maybe, like a girl on the cover of a glossy magazine, like a pin-up.

You lie on the bed. You turn on the TV. There's some sort of game show on. You can't work out what the rules are, but the host is quite funny, all the audience seem to be laughing at him, what a character.

☟

It's now the day before the wedding, and Emma and Abdul have to be weighed. It's a formality, of course. Your sister is a fat woman, but it's obvious that her camel is big enough to resist her sexual advances should he want to. But everyone has to be weighed regardless, that's the law of the thing.

Ali has booked an early morning appointment for the marriage weigher. He wants Abdul out there at the tourist sites as soon as possible, the groom still has a full day's work ahead of him. The marriage weigher arrives promptly, wearing a suit and carrying all the paperwork. He brings with him a couple of assistants who are responsible for lugging the large set of scales.

The weighing takes place within the garage. Your sister goes first, and she's easy; she strips off completely naked, climbs onto the scales. It seems so strange to see her exposed when, since you've arrived, she's always been smothered in purdah. She stands still for a few seconds, breasts drooping, minge flashing, but nobody is interested in what she looks like, it's the digital reading of her weight that they care about. She comes in at 167 pounds. Even though it's hot and sweaty here, and she doesn't appear to eat much, she's still a big girl.

Abdul is harder work. He simply doesn't want to be weighed. Ali does his best to coax him, he says "Hoosh, hoosh!", he tries smiling, he tugs at the rope running through his nostrils. The weigher's assistants try to push him onto the scales by force, they take one bottom cheek each, but Abdul doesn't like that at all, he harrumphs his misgivings about the matter most insistently. "Let me try," says your sister, "he'll listen to me." And as she approaches Abdul, he does indeed calm down, he stops jerking his head from side to side, he seems to concentrate on the words she breathes into his ear. "Please, darling," she says. "Because without this, we can't get married. We can't be together, and I love you so much." Abdul nods his head a bit. He considers what she says. He trots forward to the scales, contemplates them studiously. Then pisses on them.

Ali sighs, he keeps looking at his watch; at last he gives in, he takes out money, he offers the man in the suit a bribe. The man doesn't seem in the least surprised. He takes the cash, he counts it, it looks very dirty to you, why is Egyptian money so dirty? Then he writes something on a form, he tears off a receipt. It's all over. The bride and groom are deemed compatible.

Whilst your sister is getting dressed, Ali comes up to you. You think he is going to offer some appropriate platitudes about the forthcoming marriage, and indeed you get in first—you smile, and you say, "Don't they make a lovely couple?"

"I do not like your sister," he says.

You don't know how to respond. You know you should defend her. But he's taken you completely by surprise. "Oh," you say. And then, "Hey. Wait a moment. Hey!"

"I do not like it, all these foreigners, coming over here and marrying our camels. Take her home with you. Take her back to England."

"Hey," you say. "Now then. Now, you wait." Because that's just *racist*, isn't it? That's just fucking bigotry, and he should feel *lucky* that an Englishwoman is prepared to marry an Egyptian, what the fuck does he think Egypt is?—it was big once, mate, it was powerful, but the civilization's long gone, the civilization has crumbled to dust, it's ruins and pots and canopic jars from now on for the likes of you, it's canopic jars forever. And all you do is grovel around in the sand trying to fleece tourists, you're in the shadows of something greater than you can ever be, and they're thousands of years old, they were made by *primitives*, you can't reject us, you can't afford to be picky, you fucking *need* us. But what you say is, "I don't live in England now, I live in Australia." And, at this, he shrugs.

Abdul's close by, he's been listening. And you think that even if you can't defend your sister properly, even if you haven't got the guts, he should at least try—it's his *wife*, after all. But Abdul sort of shrugs too, as if in imitation of his master. And then he's led away to start his day's work.

Your sister has heard nothing of this. She looks so excited. "It's all over!" she says. "The forms are signed. I'm getting married tomorrow morning!"

"I know."

"I mean, I was always getting married tomorrow morning. But now I am, officially!"

"I know."

"I'm so happy!"

You tell her you'll be there, how much you're looking forward to it, that you'll give her anything she needs.

"The night before a Muslim wedding all the women get together, they celebrate with song and dance. But I don't know any women here. It's not strictly proper, but would you spend my last evening as a singleton with me?"

☒

You spend the afternoon in the hotel. You don't check your email.

☒

"They call them henna nights," Emma explains. "The bride has her hands and feet dyed with henna on the eve of her wedding."

"Do you have any henna?"

"No."

You didn't bring any henna. You did, though, bring the contents of your mini bar.

"I'm not allowed to drink," says Emma. "I'm a Muslim."

"You're not a Muslim until tomorrow," you point out. So she takes a little bottle of Drambuie and downs it in one. You have a Courvoisier. She has another Drambuie. You have a Smirnoff. She has her third Drambuie. You have your first Drambuie.

"If you've got something to say," Emma pipes up suddenly, "then I think you should just come right out and say it."

"I haven't got anything to say."

"No, come on. Come on. Ever since you got here, no, come on. Look at me. Yes. If you don't like Abdul, I think you should just have the balls to say so."

"All right," you say. "I don't like Abdul."

"There you go."

"I don't think he's good enough for you."

"That wasn't so hard, was it?"

"I don't think you should marry him tomorrow. He stinks and is covered in sand. He stinks of sand."

She has another Drambuie. She's got a real taste for Drambuie. You think maybe she wants to be rescued. Is that what this is? Is that why she brought you to Egypt? She wants you to rescue her?

"He's a camel," you say.

"Yes."

"He's just a camel."

"Yes."

"I mean, he's not even a special looking camel. He's not even some sort of super camel. He looks just like the other camels. And what's this about you being a fucking *Muslim*?"

"If I'm going to be in Egypt, I want to live my life here properly, and it's a very beautiful thing, actually, and I feel that in my soul . . ."

"Don't give me that. You don't believe in anything. You've never believed in anything."

"Just because *you've* never properly assimilated, it doesn't mean I shouldn't."

"Assimilated?"

"Assim. Oh. Is that right, did I get the word right?"

"I think so."

"Fuck," she says, and drinks the last Drambuie. "Because you don't, do you? You don't commit to anything. I mean, how long have you lived in Australia, and you've still got your English accent, you're still holding on to your accent, what's that about?"

"I like my accent the way it is."

"You never commit. You never did. This wife of yours, and that kid, I mean, what do they get out of you?"

"I'm leaving Kirsten," you say. "And my kid."

"Well then."

"You see?"

"I'm sorry to hear that. But don't . . . don't then start in on me about *my* marriage. When you can't even . . ."

"I wasn't . . ."

"When you can't even . . . do it . . . with marriage. Yourself, yes."

"I wasn't. I wasn't saying anything of the sort." You pause. "I don't think you even have a soul."

Since there's no more Drambuie, no matter how hard she looks, she settles for a Bell's whisky.

"You couldn't wait to run off to the other side of the world," she says. "As far away from mother as you could get. You left me alone with her in

London. After what . . . afterwards. I was the one, I have to be the one to visit, to see her every week. Most weeks. Don't you criticize, I do my best, she's not easy. And you took away the right to have an opinion when you ran away, I think so, I really do."

"Well," you say. "Well. Well, and what are you doing?"

"As far away," says Emma, and throws the little glass bottle onto the growing pile, "as far away as I can get."

You both sit there for a while.

You reach out, you put your hand on her shoulder. It feels awkward. It looks awkward. It was meant to be supportive, you think, somehow, or conciliatory, something nice anyway. You think it would be a mistake to move it away.

"So long as you're going to be happy," you say at last. "Because that's all I worry about. Because I do worry, big sis. Because I love you. You know I love you, don't you? I love you." And you squeeze the shoulder a bit, you think with that you've earned the right to move your hand now. You do.

She says nothing to this. Then, "I want to see Abdul."

"I didn't think you were supposed to see the groom before the wedding . . ."

"I'm not." And she flashes you a grin, and you're so grateful for that, and you smile back. "But it's not as if Abdul is going to tell, is he?"

And so you creep out of the room, out of the house. You think you're probably very quiet, all things considered, but you really couldn't swear to it. Out to the garage.

And there is Abdul. And he's shagging another camel, he's riding her doggy style, he's swinging about from side to side like it's some fucking slow dance, they're both braying away like there's no tomorrow.

"Oh my God," says Emma, and she runs out.

And Abdul doesn't even bother to look ashamed, he just turns those big soulful eyes on you, and gives a slow and deliberate blink. And you can bet there's a sticky smelly residue even now being secreted behind his ears—and it occurs to you that this lady camel couldn't have ended up here by accident, Abdul didn't just pick her up drunkenly in a bar, she must have been *brought* here—and my God, those Egyptians must *really* hate your sister.

You walk up to Abdul. Abdul doesn't flinch. Abdul doesn't care. Abdul doesn't even slow down his rutting, the shit, no, Abdul is busy. "Shame on you," you say. "Shame on you." And you spit in his face.

You go outside. She's standing on the pavement. She's shaking. She's wearing the burqa, she's protecting herself. She's smoking a cigarette, though, and every so often she has to raise the burqa to take a puff. You didn't even know she smoked.

"I'm sorry," you say.

"It's what you wanted, isn't it?"

She's angry, she'll say anything. So you stand with her whilst she finishes her cigarette. Whilst she fishes for another one, and she can't get the lighter to work, her hands are all over the place, you help her.

"Thanks."

"Well, I think he's mad," you say.

"Really?"

"Very mad. He's the maddest camel I've ever met. To choose anyone over you." And she smiles at this. "If I were a camel," you say, "I would treat you right. If I were a camel," you say, "I wouldn't be able to keep my hands off you. Paws. Hooves. Whatever camels have."

"Hooves," she agrees.

"Hooves then," you say. And you give her a little kiss on the cheek. She gives another smile, just a small flash of one, a thank you. She takes your hand. She sighs. So you give her another kiss, again just on the cheek, no grander or bolder than the first.

And somehow then you are kissing her properly, and *hungrily*, and she's kissing you too, it isn't just one way, it really isn't. There are lips everywhere, and tongues, and it starts off gently enough, just a little exploratory mission around the gums—and you think, so *this* is what it's like inside my sister's mouth, and it's just like all the other girls' mouths, it's just like Kirsten's mouth. It's nothing special, you know, but nor is it anything *wrong*, it's just a mouth. But it isn't, either, really, is it, and as you kiss something pops into your head about saliva, and that saliva contains your DNA, and that if someone swabbed the inside of Emma's cheek right this second they probably wouldn't be able to tell apart your tongue leavings from hers—and you fight off that thought because it really ought to be putting you off, but it doesn't, strangely, anything but. And you kiss, and you wonder who it was who started the kissing, it must have been Emma, it can't have been you, you'd never have given in to those urges—after all, you never have before.

And you're pulling off your trousers, and you're pulling off her bra, you're right out there on the streets of Cairo and you don't care, out plops breasts, out plops a willy, and there's so much sand on the streets and you hope the sand doesn't get into the cracks, the dirty sand gets everywhere, and you look down at the willy, and it isn't great, but at least it doesn't hook backwards, at least it's *normal*—and the breasts look normal too, so very normal—and the shock appearances of one or other of these really very normal protuberances has an effect—"No," says Emma, "no," and she pushes you away.

"What is it?"

"No," she says, and dashes back inside the house.

You follow her. She's in her room, she's breathing hard, she's staring at the mound of little mini bar bottles as if she's never seen them before and wondering how they got there. You want to take her hand and offer her some comfort. Just comfort, but you don't quite dare.

"It's just wrong," she says.

"For God's sake," you say, and you try not to sound impatient. "After what Abdul's been up to behind *your* back? I think you're entitled, don't you?"

"That's not what I'm talking about," she says.

It takes you a moment. "Oh. Right. Of course."

She picks up one of the empty bottles. She tips it into her mouth, just to see if there's anything inside. She sticks her tongue in the neck, just to reach a few stray drops.

"It's nonsense," you say. "You know full well, give it a few years, having a relationship with your brother will be perfectly acceptable. God, you're allowed to do it with the same sex now, you can do it with animals. Family members are right around the corner. All we are, we're just a bit ahead of our time."

"Is that what you think?" she says, and the voice is curiously flat. "That what is between us is just ordinary?"

"Yeah," you say. "Sex, it's just a little thing, isn't it? It's not worth all the melodrama. It's such a little thing."

She nods, and you think she's agreeing with you, and you're pleased. "I don't want you at the wedding," she says.

"You mean you're still going ahead with the . . . ?"

"And I don't want you there."

"But I brought my suit," you say.

"I'm not sure, actually, if I'm honest," she adds, and there's no anger in it now, that's what makes it so terrible, "that I even want to see you again."

⬇

Kirsten has emailed. She says that you're stupid and you're selfish. But she's worked too long at this marriage of yours to end it so suddenly. So, spend as long as you want in Egypt. She'll be patient. Let her know when you're coming home, she'll pick you up from the airport. You can start all over again, everything will be all right. And then you'll talk, and if you still don't want to be with her, then fair enough, if you still don't love her, fair enough. But think of Tammy, she knows you love Tammy, you've always been such a good father.

And you lie on the bed, and you do indeed think of Tammy. You strip right down, it's so very hot, and there's nothing cold to drink in the mini bar, you strip right down, you lie on the bed naked, you think of Tammy. And how beautiful a woman she'll grow up to be—she'll be a model, she'll be on the cover of glossy magazines, she'll be *perfect*. She'll look a bit like your sister, but younger, fresher, thinner. You can start all over again. Everything's going to be all right, you can start all over.

⬇

The next morning you don't know what to do with yourself.

You check your phone, just in case your sister has called. She hasn't. You check your email. There's something new from your wife, dripping with forgiveness probably, but you don't bother to open it yet.

"Take me somewhere touristy," you say to the taxi driver.

All the camels are lined up, and they're all going to the Great Pyramid of Giza. It's one of the Seven Wonders of the Ancient World. It is, in fact, the only one of the Seven Wonders of the Ancient World that still exists. "This'll do," you say.

"Hoosh, hoosh!" says the camel driver, all smiles, he's such a happy fellow. And you get onto the camel's back, right behind the hump. "Hoosh!" Up you rise, and you dig your heels into the camel's side, hard.

"The Great Pyramids of Giza!" the driver calls. And you're off, a whole train of you, pasty-faced westerners all looking pale and weedy, all looking like children as they giggle and gawp and play at being Arabs. The camel paces forward and you roll with his gait—you feel a bit nauseous, actually, you wonder how long the journey will take, it's like being on a rough sea and you think if there's more than ten minutes of this you might just throw up. But the camel is patient, and calm, and suddenly you feel calm too. And he seems to hold you no grudge for kicking him, maybe under that tough hide he didn't even feel it.

On top of the camel you feel like you're king of the world, you feel like a pharaoh, he's making you feel so special, he's making you feel like you're the only one he's ever had on his back.

And you ride out into the desert, tourists ahead of you, tourists behind you, but you try to ignore them, you pretend you're on your own, that it's just you and the camel. And he's in no rush, and by God, he's *solid* under there, and strong, and confident, the camel's got a confidence you don't think you'll ever have.

At last you reach the pyramid. It's been there on the horizon for ages, of course, but you refuse to look at it seriously until you get close, you want to get the full impact of it—you'd rather look down at the sand, you'd rather look at the camel. But there it is now, finally, unavoidably, it's not going to get any bigger—"There!" says our guide, rather unnecessarily. And yes, it's *different*, but the camel harrumphs a bit, he's seen it all before, he's none too impressed. And from now on you're taking your cue from the camel. As pyramids go you're sure it's one of the biggest—but you know, if it's size that's the issue, there are bigger things out there, you've stayed in bigger hotels, shopped in bigger department stores, parked your car in bigger car parks even. And you say out loud, for the camel's benefit, you suppose, so he'll know you're in accord—"It's just a little thing, isn't it? Really. Just a little thing."

PECKISH

There was never any scandal in the Von Zieten family. The Von Zietens did not approve of scandal. Sieglinde knew that there had been a Von Zieten in the war once and that he had done something very bad—she didn't know which war, and by now it was probably too late to tell—he had either been cowardly when he should have been heroic, or had been heroic when the tide of public opinion had turned against heroism, and discretion would have been the better option. But Captain Von Zieten had made amends by taking his own life, he'd shot himself with his service revolver, and the family had grimly forgiven him.

And sometimes at parties, sometimes if Uncle Otto got drunk, Sieglinde heard muttered tales about an Aunt Ilse who had harboured an amorous fascination for goats. Otherwise, nothing; the Von Zietens were respectable and decent and clean.

And so when the scandal broke around Großmutti Greta everyone was surprised, and privately even a little pleased; it gave them someone new to condemn.

It took Sieglinde a few days to find out what the scandal was. She was still a child, they said, and so everyone's voices dropped when she came into the room. But at last she was told by her mother, on the pretext that it was for her moral education. She was sat down, with all due solemnity—but Sieglinde noticed how excited her mother sounded, how her eyes sparkled and how fast she talked, how much she revelled in Großmutti Greta's wickedness.

And it was this: that after over sixty years of marriage, Greta now wanted a divorce. "Over sixty years!" mother said, and that as far as the Von Zietens could tell, it had been a happy marriage too—certainly the family had never seen reason for complaint. It wasn't as if Greta had anything she could do with her remaining years—she was at least eighty, and in everyone's considered opinion there was precious little point Greta should cause a scandal now for a few last gasps of independence. Greta hadn't given a reason, or, at least, Großvatti Gunther said he'd not been given one; everyone felt a bit sorry for Großvatti Gunther, and that was uncomfortable in itself, Großvatti was a sturdy man of no fixed emotion, feeling sorry for him was just wrong somehow. The family wondered whether Greta had simply gone mad. That would make sense, might even mitigate somewhat in her favour. But surely it would have been better if she'd gone mad quietly without drawing attention to herself.

Sieglinde had been taught to avoid scandal, and had always done her best. Here she was, a few months shy of sixteen, and she still wasn't allowed to see Klaus without a chaperone, even though the family knew the two would one day get married—even though the family had chosen him in the first place! Sieglinde knew she should ask no further questions about her grandmother and her heinous ways. But she liked Großmutti Greta. She was her favourite of all her grandparents, probably—Greta was a little stern, but then, they were all a little stern. And sometimes when Sieglinde went to visit, especially when she'd been a little girl, Greta had made her the most wonderful gingerbread men. Sieglinde had never tasted anything as good as those gingerbread men. Sieglinde never knew what special ingredients there must be in them.

She knew that if she asked her parents whether she could visit her grandmother they would say no. So she didn't ask. One afternoon, when father was in his study, and mother was busy in the kitchen, Sieglinde snuck away. She didn't want to go to her grandmother's empty-handed, and so spent her pocket money at the baker's, buying a bag full of brioches; some of them had chocolate in the middle.

Her grandmother didn't seem surprised to see her. "There you are," she said. "Good. You can help me find a suitcase."

"I brought brioches," said Sieglinde.

"I have eaten my last brioche," said Großmutti Greta.

"Some of them have chocolate inside."

"The same for chocolate," said Großmutti Greta.

"So, it's true, then? You're really leaving?"

"Yes," said Großmutti Greta.

"Are you mad? Everyone thinks you've gone mad."

"I haven't gone mad," said Greta. "Or, if I am mad, I am as mad as I was before. I have just decided to stop pretending. All the pretence, I am so tired of it. I have baked some gingerbread men, my very last batch. We shall eat gingerbread men and talk."

Sieglinde agreed. She hadn't tasted one of her grandmother's gingerbread men for a long time, and had rather assumed she was now too old for them.

"Ach, nonsense," said Greta. "You're the perfect age for my gingerbread men. All the other men you've eaten, that was just practice. Now, at last, you can eat the real thing. But first," she added, "we find my suitcase, yes?"

They went up to the attic. There was no light up there. "Your grandfather," said Greta, "he always said he'd fix the electrics, but he never did, it was always tomorrow, tomorrow, you'll have your light bulbs tomorrow." Sieglinde asked if that was why she was leaving him. "All in good time," said Greta, as she poked around in the dark, and then she said, "Yes, yes, here it is," and she was pulling a suitcase out of the shadows. It was big and brown and had brass buckles on it. "Good," she said. "Now, we talk."

The gingerbread men were fresh from the oven; they smelled moist, they smelt *juicy*, somehow, even though Sieglinde knew there was no juice in gingerbread. She felt her mouth water. Greta picked up the bag of brioches, opened it, recoiled, then dropped it unceremoniously into the swing bin.

"Do you really have to go away, Großmutti?" asked Sieglinde, and tears pricked at her eyes, and that was strange, for she was not a sentimental girl, sentiment was frowned upon in the Von Zieten house.

"Now, now," said Großmutti, and she tapped at Sieglinde's hand sympathetically, and she wasn't used to acts of sentiment either, and she did it too hard and too awkwardly, and it felt like being comforted by a wrinkly bag of onions. "I shall tell you the story, the same as I told my husband. And you shall eat."

Sieglinde bit into the gingerbread man. It tasted good.

ↆ

I came from a poor family, much poorer than yours. I had a brother called Hans, a father who cut wood, and, for a little while, I had a mother. Then the mother died. And my father married again. The stepmother didn't like us much.

(*"Was she a cruel stepmother?" asked Sieglinde.*)

I don't think she was particularly cruel, or any crueller to me than my own mother was. Stepmothers have a bad time of it. It's hard enough to love your own flesh and blood, and I should know. It's almost impossible to love someone else's. Ach, this is not a story about wicked stepmothers.

("All right.")

You're as bad as your grandfather. No more interruptions.

("Sorry.")

Stepmother didn't want us home. She tried to smile when we were there, but Hans and I could see through them, there was effort in those smiles, it was like she had toothache. We played in the forest. Deeper and deeper we'd go, every day, we'd dare ourselves to get to the very heart of it. And one day out playing, Hans said to me, Well, we've done it now, sister, we're well and truly lost. Home could be miles away, and in any direction. We could walk around for the rest of our lives and never find it. Might as well face it, we're going to die out here—if starvation doesn't get us first, the cold and the wolves will. And he had a tear, for my brother was an unnaturally sensitive boy.

We lay down to die, and we were resigned to it, we didn't use to struggle so much against death as people do now. But before we expired we found an old woman was standing over us. I say she was old; she was probably not old; but I was of the age when I thought that anyone with grey hair and missing teeth and pockmarks was old. She said, You poor children, you must be hungry. Let me take you to a place where there is food, all is food. My pantries are filled to bursting, and the bricks of my walls are made of fresh soft bread, the cement is warm chocolate fudge, the roof is thatched with liquorice sticks. Will you come with me? It isn't far.

Hans was my brother; I always did what Hans said; Hans said, Okay. And I wondered whether this woman could be our new mother. I asked for her name, and she said she hadn't got a name, or if she'd had one, she'd lost it. I began to tell her our names, and she stopped me, and she said she didn't think we would have that kind of relationship.

And so it turned out to be. We entered her house, and she locked the door behind us with a big key. I'm so sorry, my dears, she said, and to be fair, she looked very sorry too, and we couldn't be angry with her. She said, As you can see, the bricks are made of brick, the cement is just some cement, the thatch has largely blown away but when it was there it was very far indeed from looking like liquorice. This is a house of food— but the food is you—you are it—by which I mean, I'm going to eat you both up, are you following me? It's inside you, your kidneys and your hearts and your chitterlings, you walk about carrying all that tasty grub wrapped up in thin sausage skin, and it's a waste, and we're going to let it out.

She snapped off one of Hans' fingers, and ate it. Then she snapped off one of mine, chewed at it thoughtfully. Because, as you know, the fingers are the best way of determining whether a child is ripe or not—Not quite ready yet, she said, but not long to go, and what a feast you'll make! And in the meantime, I promise you, I'll be kind to you, and nice, I'll be a mother to you, it's the least I can do. I really am most terribly sorry, but you must understand, I really am most terribly hungry as well.

She had to fatten us up. And that wasn't easy, since there was no food in the house. She would stand us upright in the bathtub, naked, and scrub away at us with a loofah, one of those big loofahs with the hard bristles, do you know? And all the dead skin would come peeling off, and she'd gather it all up, every last wormy strand, and she'd fry it, and tell us to eat—and that skin smelled so good, it was like onions, it'd sizzle so invitingly in the pan. And yet she never ate a morsel, no matter how hungry she got—No, no, she'd say, this is a treat for you kids, don't you worry about me, I'll get my dinner soon enough. But sometimes she would watch us eat and she couldn't help it, the sight of it would make her tummy gurgle, and she would cry. We'd beg her, Eat, please eat. We'd say, Take another of our fingers, snap them off, have them as a snack. One day she did that, and she put them in her mouth, and she winced, and said we still weren't ripe—and we'd caused her to *waste* two perfectly good fingers before they were ready, that was very selfish of us. She was angry, I think, for the only time we knew her, and she sent us to bed without any supper. Which was pretty much par for the course.

One morning, over breakfast, as Hans and I gorged ourselves on the dead skin leftovers, the woman said she couldn't wait any longer. She was starving; she would be dead from starvation within the hour; then where would we all be? She'd have to eat us both right now. And if we weren't ripe enough yet, well, she'd just have to put up with any resultant indigestion. She was too weak to prepare the oven, so Hans and I did it all for her, and we did our very best, but somehow we made a mistake, we ended up cooking her instead of ourselves. I kept saying to Hans, Are you sure we're doing this right, as we folded the woman's arms together and tucked them underneath her belly so she'd fit through the oven door— and he told me not to worry about it. The woman didn't blame us. She said, oh well, either way, here's an end to my suffering—and I suppose it was.

We took the key and opened the front door and went out into the forest, and oh, the air tasted so fresh, it was almost good enough to eat. And we were free. And we set off home.

I don't like that suitcase.

↓

"Sorry?" said Sieglinde. "What about the suitcase?"

"I don't like it," said Großmutti Greta. "All those big brass buckles! Such ostentation! So shameless! Ach, when you're lugging a suitcase about, with nowhere you can call home to take it, you don't need brass buckles weighing you down. No. We go back to the attic. Come on. Back to the attic, we find a better suitcase."

Sieglinde thought that the dark of the attic seemed even darker than before, and that was impossible, surely, but the black made Sieglinde's eyes hurt. "Stay here," said Großmutti Greta, and then she plunged into the blackness, and Sieglinde knew she wouldn't be able to see a thing—Sieglinde's eyes were still young and untainted, how much weaker must Greta's be, ancient as she was! And she heard Greta grunt with effort, as if she were wrestling with something, as if she were wrestling with the dark itself. And Sieglinde felt the sudden certainty that she would never see her grandmother again, that she'd be lost within the dark, that she'd die, and that the only way she could save her would be if she too jumped into the blackness and put herself at the mercy of whatever was inside and begged for her grandmother's life—and she hadn't got the courage, she realized, and what was worse, she hadn't got the *inclination*.

And then Greta emerged, and her hands were tight around another suitcase—this one bigger, greyer, and free of all offending buckles. She looked calm, and matter of fact, as if she hadn't tussled with the monsters in the black, as if she hadn't confronted death itself—and maybe she hadn't. "Some tea," she said, "that's what we need, and you can have another gingerbread man, yes? Come along, come along."

In the kitchen Sieglinde said, "I won't have another gingerbread man, thank you."

Großmutti Greta said, "Why not?"

Sieglinde explained she didn't want to get fat.

Großmutti Greta said, "There was a time when we didn't worry about such stupid things. It was good to be fat. It meant we might survive the winter."

Peckish

Sieglinde said that had been a long time ago, and now it wasn't good to be fat, and that Klaus wouldn't want her if she put on weight, he told her he didn't fancy girls with big thighs.

Greta said, "That Klaus of yours is an idiot," and she said, "And your thighs are not fat, and believe me, I am an expert, I feel they could do with a lot more fattening. Now eat another gingerbread man, or you will offend me, and we shan't part as friends." Sieglinde didn't want that, and besides, she did like the gingerbread men, they really were quite delicious.

"Won't you have one?" asked Sieglinde, as she bit off a leg, and Greta waved the offer aside, and instead clasped hold of her teacup, and Sieglinde noticed that there were indeed fingers missing from Greta's hand, and she'd never seen that before, how strange.

"I liked your story, Granny," said Sieglinde. "But I don't understand why you're leaving Großvatti."

"That's because the story isn't finished yet," said Großmutti Greta. "Now be quiet, blood of my blood, and listen."

↓

I said that the air tasted so fresh that it was good enough to eat. Well, you couldn't. And though Hans and I enjoyed our freedom, and thought we'd escaped certain death at the hands of the old woman, in truth we were still in danger. We walked through the forest as hungry as before, and as lost. We walked for hours, and our feet hurt, and our stomachs hurt, and Hans said, It's no good, my sister, we were better off as we were. At least before there was a *reason* for our deaths; another would have lived through our sacrifice, and she would have buried our bones, and she would have remembered us, and in the darkness of the night when she was all alone she might have patted her belly for company. Hans shed a tear, because, as I say, he was very sensitive.

Still we walked on, and it was with our last remaining strength that we dragged ourselves to a house. And only as we reached the door did we realize we knew this house; we had spent all this time walking in a circle. We had returned to the cottage where we had been imprisoned, and the bricks were not made of bread, and the cement not made of fudge—but nevertheless, something very tasty smelled from the inside. And we opened the door, and there, of course, was the woman—just as we'd left her, and cooked to an absolute tee.

Oh, how my tummy cried out for that meat. We have no choice, said

Hans, and from the oven he took the roast dinner, and broke off one of the woman's arms, and began to gnaw at it. The woman stared at us through eyes that had browned in the heat and looked like fried eggs. At least close them, I said, and Hans did one better, he tore off her face altogether and threw it into the fire—You have to eat, he said, my dear sister, you know we can't afford to be picky with our food now—and I said, Could you find me a piece of meat that isn't *too* meaty, something that won't look too much like it's from a corpse?—and he had a rummage, and then produced something that looked a little like chicken, and I put it in my mouth, and I swallowed.

And oh! It was good. My stomach roared with approval—so much so in fact that at first it sent the meat right back up again, and I had to swallow it once more, more slowly, to prove to it it wasn't dreaming. We had a feast that night. I soon overcame my scruples, what else was there for it, when I had the evidence of my own senses? The body had such a *variety* of tastes: the heart, the lungs, the kidneys, the flesh, not a single one bland, not a single one without subtle flavours all their own, we are meant to be eaten, we are *designed* that way. Pretty soon I even fished the woman's face out of the fire, and we ate that too, and do you know, the eyes did taste a little like eggs, if you closed your own, and pretended.

I said that the food would give us the strength to find our way home the next day, and Hans agreed. And that night we slept with full bellies— so full that we couldn't sleep on them, so full that we kept rolling right off the bellies and onto our sides. And in the morning Hans said, But why leave? This can be our house now. And we can dine on the fruits of the forest. Because the forest is full of children, all the children of the world play here at some time, and most will come too far and too unwisely; there are a million cruel stepmothers to escape from, there are a million, million kindly woodcutters who don't take enough care.

I remember the first child we caught. It looked up at us with such idiot relief. It said, it thought it was going to die alone. Hans said, Not alone—and he broke its jaw fast, because the woman had been right, it was better the child didn't give its name, you didn't want to get too attached to the livestock. We broke off a finger each, and sucked on them, and they seemed ripe enough to us, but what did we know? Then we hung the child upside down and it was bawling all the while, and then it stopped bawling and its sobbing was so quiet, and we slit its throat, and then even the sobbing stopped. Childmeat is the best meat of all, it lifts straight off the bone and melts in your mouth—and it tastes of death, and the taste of death is good. You can *survive* on vegetables but you can't enjoy them, and feasting on death gives even for a moment the sense we have risen above death, we are gods, we will live forever.

And this went on for some years. And we were never cruel to the children, they never suffered unnecessarily—and that was good too, because an unripe child may taste a little sour, but a suffering child tastes sourer still. And we forgot the face of our father. And we didn't care, I thought we didn't care.

One day we found a little girl, sleeping under the bushes. She was just outside the house, no more than a few feet away, it was as if she'd been left there as a gift. At first I thought she was already dead, and there is little worth in a child who is already dead—it's edible, but where's the fun in eating the leftovers of crows and worms? Hans turned it over with his foot, and she opened her eyes, and blinked at us, and smiled. She smiled. Hans said, We are going to eat you. And the girl said, I know the way out of the forest. I know the way home.

I said to Hans, This is it—this is our chance to escape. And Hans said, There is no escape for us. We are what we are, and we can never be anything else. We prey upon the weak and the defenceless, and if that makes us evil, why then, so we are evil, but we do our evil honestly. There is no home out there for us, Greta. And he shed a tear, but by now I was sick of my brother's sentiment. I said, This is not what I wanted my life to be. To eat and pretend what we eat is something else. To shit, and pretend what comes out is not what we have eaten. To fuck, and pretend you're not my brother. There has to be more to life than that. And Hans said, That is all life has *ever* been.

And the child. The child never stopped smiling. I swear to you, if the child had caved in, if it had begun to cry like all the others, if it had struggled or begged for its life, I'd have given into my hunger, and eaten it raw right there on the spot. But it smiled. So what else could I do?

I said to Hans, I'm leaving.

And he said, If you leave, we will never meet again.

And I said, So be it. Will you let us go?

Because he held his knife. And we were starving—it had been a cold winter, and the children had been playing safe. And I thought he might eat the girl regardless. And I thought he might eat me too.

And we stood there for a while, all three of us, my brother, me, and the smiling girl. And then my brother turned around, and went back to the house, and went inside.

Come on, said the girl, and she took my hand. And I held on tight, and I tell you, I was blinking back tears, and I don't know whether it was because someone had rescued me at last, or because I had lost my brother—Come on, she said, I'll get you home.

And we walked right out of the forest. I got a job in a department store, selling hosiery. That is where I met your grandfather. He was working there as an accountant. He took pity on me. He didn't mind my coarse ways. He married me, he smoothed off my rough edges. Ach, he took me to his bed, and I gave him children. One of them was your father.

(Sieglinde asked, "What happened to the little girl?")

And the family accepted me for his sake. Or, if they did not accept me, they tolerated me. They tolerated me to my face. And we lived happily ever after—I never ate another child, I need you to know that. I need you to understand. I never hurt anyone ever again, not after I had left the forest. I paid that price.

("What happened to the little girl?")

This suitcase does not suit! Look at this suitcase. It is too big. What is the use of such big suitcases? Who needs to carry so much?

(And for a moment Sieglinde thought her grandmother was going to ignore her question, and then Großmutti Greta sighed, and looked straight at Sieglinde, and said—)

It was a very large forest.

⭳

Greta offered Sieglinde another gingerbread man, and Sieglinde didn't want one, and her grandmother told her not to be silly. Sieglinde said, "What is the special ingredient?" And Großmutti Greta looked shocked for a moment, and saw that Sieglinde was in earnest, and that she was even shaking, a little, and shaking with fear of all things—and she laughed, and said it was cinnamon, just cinnamon. And Sieglinde bit into the head, and now she knew, of course, it was obvious it was cinnamon, but she couldn't help but taste something fleshy there too. Her grandmother was watching her. Her grandmother would be disappointed if she didn't finish. She didn't want that. She wolfed the whole man down, every last scrap of him.

Peckish

🔽

It was a very large forest. The girl had told me she could find her way out of it, and I don't think that she was lying to me, or if she were, she was lying to herself. We got lost. It was dark. It began to rain. We were hungry. We slept for hours, sometimes complete days, because we were too tired to move. And I said to her, You or I have to eat the other. It's the only way one of us even stands a chance of survival. And I said to the girl, I think you've got a whole life ahead of you, and it's still sweet and untainted, and you haven't made any mistakes yet, or if you have, they weren't of your making. You should be the one who lives. It should be you. I said to her, Eat me.

And the little girl said no. And I told her there was no choice, and I told her it wasn't hard. And I ran my finger down my breasts and down my thighs, and showed her the best meat she could get from them, and how thinly she should slice, and exactly how long over an open flame she should cook for the most appetizing results. I told her there was nothing to it. I told her that I had done it, and so had my brother, and we were nothing special. Not like her. Not like she could be.

And she begged me. She begged me not to make her go through with it.

Eat me, she said. Eat me. Because you know just what to do. You'll enjoy the meat so much more than I will. Don't waste your chitterlings on a palate as weakly sensitized as mine. And she said, Eat me knowing that I give myself to you in full cooperation, I give myself to you as a present; feast on me, and enjoy, and know that I'll be in heaven looking on. Eat me, and let your last meal of child be the best meal of child you've ever had, let me be the apotheosis of all who have gone before, let me be the reason you can stop afterwards, because there'll never be a child as succulent as me.

And I said, All right.

And then she told me her name. Her proper name. And I let her.

(*Sieglinde asked, "What was it?"*)

Ach, what does it matter now?

(*"Did she ask you your name?"*)

Yes.

(*"Did you give it?"*)

No. What good would it have done her? I was about to hang her on a tree upside down and slit her throat. I gave her a name. A made-up name, it was a perfectly good name.

("*Is that what really happened?*")

It's the way that I remember it.

(*Sieglinde said quietly,* "*And was she succulent?*")

Oh yes.

(*The grandmother lent forward, and Sieglinde thought she was going to impart some terrible secret, something that would be so dreadful that it would taint her even to hear it—and she lent forward too, she wanted to hear it, she knew she wanted her innocence destroyed, let it be now, she thought, let it be now. Großmutti Greta smiled. And said, softly,* "*Shall we go up and find that suitcase, once and for all?*")

🗸

The dark of the attic was now solid, like a wall; the light from the staircase touched it and died. "You can't go in there," Sieglinde said to Greta, and Greta agreed: "No, my dear, now it's your turn. You go into the attic, and fetch for me the best suitcase you can." Sieglinde thought it would be impossible—that that solid darkness would knock her back—and she looked at her grandmother's face, and it was so old, and she saw now how close it was to death. Sieglinde stepped forward, and the darkness pooled around her, and all the light was gone, all the light was gone completely.

There were things there, in the dark—things that feed off the dark, that aren't afraid of it, that need the pitch black to survive. She felt something leathery, like a bat, but it was too scaly for a bat; something tickled against her hand, a spider? But it was too large for a spider. And the blackness was thick like syrup, and it was pouring out all over her, into every last corner of her body—a syrup, and she could bite into it if she chose, she could eat it, if she didn't eat it, it would eat her, she knew. But she didn't want to eat it.

She heard her grandmother's voice. There was an echo to it. As if it came from a long way away.

"Don't panic," she said. "Just listen to my voice. Listen to me, and all will be well."

And Sieglinde knew nothing would be well again, that she would never more be able to see, or speak, or feel—because if she opened her mouth to speak the darkness would swim down her throat, if she dared to feel, then the darkness would feel at her right back. But she listened to her grandmother's voice, and to her surprise, it worked—her heart steadied, she stopped shaking, she began to calm.

"You think you now know why I'm leaving your grandfather? Yes? You think it is guilt? It is not guilt.

"Oh, I feel guilt enough. But not for the children I've killed. I feel guilt because I married a man I did not love, and have never loved, not one day in all these sixty years. I feel guilt because I never loved my children. I kept popping them out, just to see whether I'd produce a single one I might feel some affection toward. I didn't. I hate them all. Your father, he's an especially cold fish. He deserves that bitch of a mother of yours. You do know your mother is a bitch, my dear? And that she has never cared for you?"

Sieglinde didn't open her mouth to answer. But, yes, she thought. She hadn't realized it before, and now she did, it didn't much seem to matter.

"I have spent so many years trying to be what I am not. The scent of childmeat clings to me. I taste it on everything I cook. Just a hint, mocking me, telling me that out there is something tastier, richer, better. And I will be dead soon. And I must not waste another day on this little excuse for a life.

"I need to eat the flesh of innocents again. I was wrong. All these years, I was wrong. I should never have left my brother. I will go to him. I will go, and see whether he will take me back. I shall fall into his arms, and apologize, and beg his forgiveness. He may not recognize me. If he doesn't recognize me, he will eat me. But if so, ach, well then, there's an end to this suffering.

"I am so hungry. I am so hungry. I am so hungry.

"Now, get me a suitcase. Come out of the darkness, and bring the best you can find."

Sieglinde thought she would stay in the dark. It might be safer in the dark, after all. But the dark began to drain away from her—and she tried to cling firm to it, she reached her arms out and grabbed—onto the bat, onto the spider—and then she saw she was clutching onto a suitcase, a nice, neat, little suitcase—and the bat leather was its shell, and the spider legs were its straps.

Großmutti Greta took it out of her hands. She looked it over. "Yes," she said. "Yes, good choice." She held it against Sieglinde's body, as if measuring it against her.

And Sieglinde knew. That she was going to be put into the suitcase.

And then her grandmother would take her into the forest, and she would find her brother, and together they would hang Sieglinde upside down and gut her and eat her.

"Please don't kill me," said Sieglinde.

And it was as if Sieglinde had slapped her grandmother. It made her step backwards.

"You think I would eat you?" said Greta. "Oh, my darling. Oh, blood of my blood. I could never hurt you. Because you're like me. You're just like me. All these years, I've been waiting to find someone in this family I could love. And it is you. Don't be afraid. Be afraid of everyone, but never of me."

And Sieglinde saw her grandmother was crying, and realized she was crying too.

"The suitcase," said Greta, "is for you."

"I don't understand," said Sieglinde.

"Ach, you think I need a suitcase? At my time of life? What would I want with a suitcase where I am going? But you. My darling, my blood. You will leave. You will leave this place, thank God, because you cannot stay here, with these people, with these passionless people. And when you do, this suitcase is for you."

She gave it back to her granddaughter.

Sieglinde weighed it in her hand, and it felt right. Not too heavy, the right size, none of those annoying buckles. The strap fitted snugly in her fist.

"There is no forest anymore, Granny," said Sieglinde. "They chopped it down. Father said they chopped it down years ago. There are factories there now."

"I know where my forest is," said Greta. She bent down, kissed Sieglinde on the cheek. It still felt awkward, uncomfortable, like being brushed by a wrinkled bag of onions.

Greta walked into the attic. The darkness swallowed her.

Sieglinde waited to see whether she would come out. She didn't. Sieglinde went home.

⚐

Sieglinde tried to think of an excuse to explain where she'd been. But when she got home, Father was still in the study, Mother was still in the kitchen; they hadn't even noticed she'd gone. They hadn't cared.

Peckish

She phoned Klaus. He wasn't in; she got the answering machine. She told him she had never loved him. She told him she would never see him again.

She took the suitcase up to her bedroom, opened it. It seemed so big inside; you could fit a whole world in there, a whole future. She opened up her wardrobes and closets, worked out what she wanted to take with her. There was nothing. She needed none of it. So she closed up the suitcase again, and carried it down the stairs, and out of the house, and into her new life. She would fill it up along the way.

DUMB LUCY

There was little magic left to those dark times. The world seemed cracked somehow, too weak for the magic to hold; latterly, as he'd performed his tricks, he'd begun to doubt they would work at all, he'd stand before his audience behind his patter and his sheen and a beaming smile that was well-oiled and ready practised, and he'd felt himself starting to sweat, he'd felt the fear take over—the magic wouldn't hold, the magic would fail. Lucy never seemed to notice. Lucy never seemed to get nervous. And he supposed that if Lucy couldn't see how frightened he was, then neither could anybody else. The magic *had* held. Still, it worried him.

They hadn't performed for a month. It would be better, he supposed, when they reached the town. The villagers wanted nothing to do with their conjuring. They had no coins to waste on such a thing. But he had strong arms, they said, he could work alongside them in the fields—and the little girl, she could join the other children, there were always berries that needed picking. Sometimes the coins they earned were enough to buy them shelter for the night, and sometimes not.

And in the meantime they'd keep on walking, trying to keep ahead of the darkness. Because what choice did they have? He pulled the cart behind them. It would have been much quicker without the cart, but then they couldn't have performed their magic. She walked by his side, and matched him step for step, and kept him company, though she never spoke.

"Is this the town?" he said one day, and Lucy of course didn't answer, and he knew already that this couldn't be the town, it wasn't big enough, it was little more than a street with a few houses either side. But maybe it might have grown into a town, one day, had the blackness not come.

One of the houses was marked "Inn." He put down the cart, and beat upon the wooden door with his blistered hands. There was no reply, but he knew that someone was inside, he could hear breathing just an inch away, someone trying very hard to be quiet, someone scared.

"Please," he called. "We mean you no harm. We're two travellers, we just want a room for the night."

"This is no inn," a woman's voice came back. "And the people who called it one are long since gone, or dead most like. There is no room for you here."

"If not for my sake, then for the little girl's." And at that, as if on cue, Lucy lifted her head and flared her dimples, and opened her eyes wide and innocent. It was an expression she could pull at a moment's notice, and it had been a useful trick in the old days, to gather about a sympathetic crowd, to persuade the crowd to part with coins. He saw no signs that anyone inside could see them; there must have been a secret window somewhere, or a crack in the wood, because next time the woman spoke her voice was softer.

"D'ye have money?"

"We are, at present, financially embarrassed," confessed the man, but he puffed out his chest, and his voice became richer—somehow Lucy putting on her pose beside him gave him a little swagger too—"But we propose to pay you with a spectacle of our arts. We are magicians, conjurors, masters of the illusory and the bizarre. We have dazzled the crowned heads of three different empires with our legerdemain, the only limit to how we can surprise you is your own imagination. I am the Great Zinkiewicz, and this, my assistant, Lucy!" And at this he delivered a sweeping bow, directed at where he hoped his audience was watching him.

There was silence for a few seconds.

"You can come in anyway," the woman said.

The inn was dark and dirty, but welcoming for all of that, and warm. The woman showed them both to the fire, and the magicians stood before it, and baked in it, and the man hadn't realized how cold he must have been. But now the heat was on his skin he felt a damp chill inside him it would take more than one night's shelter to rid.

"My cart?" he said.

"It's safe. No one will touch your cart."

"It contains everything we own."

"No one will touch your cart."

The man nodded at that, turned back to the fire, turned back to Lucy. Now that they were at rest, he realized once again what an incongruous couple they made. For all that he spoke like the gentleman, his clothes were ripped and mud-spattered; there were ugly patches in his grey beard and his face was bruised. Burly and broad shouldered, he stood nearly seven feet tall. Lucy, by his side, somehow still looked refined. The mud of the fields had never clung to her quite, and as ruddy as his face was hers was as pale as milk. She seemed dwarfed next to him, she seemed small enough to be folded up and put away in a little box—exactly, in fact, as one of their tricks required.

"There's no food for you," said the woman. "But there's a room upstairs, just for the night, you and your daughter are welcome to it." So, she thought Lucy was his daughter. Perhaps that was for the best.

There was noise on the staircase, and the man looked up, and realized why the woman had taken pity on them. Grinning at them in wonder was a little girl, surely no older than Lucy. And she was a proper little girl too, the man could see that, she had somehow managed to keep her youth, unlike Lucy who just pretended. She was dressed in pink; there was some attempt still to curl her hair.

"My daughter," said the woman, and she said it gruffly enough, but the man could see she was trying to hide her affections, he could sense how she burned with love for the girl, he didn't need his magic arts to tell. He was glad for them. He wondered if there was a father. He knew better than to ask.

Her mother said, "We have guests, make up their bed."

The little girl's eyes widened. "Like in the old days?"

Her mother hesitated. "Yes," she said. "Like in the old days."

The innkeeper and her daughter ate their bread and cheese. The innkeeper wouldn't look at her visitors, but the daughter couldn't help it, she kept stealing glances in their direction. The man knew not to make eye contact yet, not to ask for a single crumb of food. Lucy just stared into the flames, as if fascinated by something she saw there.

"What's your name?" the little girl suddenly asked her.

"She's called Lucy," said the man.

"How old is she?"

"How old are you?"

"I'm seven."

"Then Lucy's seven too."

The little girl liked that. And the magician looked at her directly, and held her gaze, just for a few seconds, and he caused his eyes to twinkle. Lucy never looked up from the fire.

"The magic you perform," said the mother. "It's an entertainment?"

The man nodded gravely. "Madam, many have told us so."

"But it's not *real* magic? I wouldn't have real magic in my house."

"I assure you, it is nothing but tricks and sleight of hand. There is a rational explanation for everything that we do." The woman nodded at that, slowly. "We would be happy to give you a demonstration."

At this the little girl became quite excited. "Oh, please, Mama!"

The woman looked doubtful. "But what good can it do?"

"It cheers the soul somewhat. It amuses the eyes. If nothing else, it makes the night pass that little bit faster."

"Please, Mama!" The little girl was bouncing up and down now. "I do so want the night to go faster!"

"No magic," promised the man. "Just a little trick. So simple, your child will see through it. I give you my word."

Words counted for nothing in those days, but the woman chose to forget that. "All right, if it's just the one." And then she smiled wide, and the man could see how beautiful she was when she did that, and how much younger she looked, and how she wasn't that much older than her daughter, not really, nor so very different either.

Lucy rose from the fireplace, stood as if to attention. The man said, "We'll get changed into our costumes." The woman told him there was no need for that. The man said, "Please, madam, you must allow us to present ourselves properly, presentation is what it's all about!"

The magicians went outside to the cart. They changed into costume. No one was in the street to see, and besides, there was no moon that night, it was pitch black.

When they went back to the inn, the little girl clapped her hands at the sight of them, and her mother's smile widened even further. What a pair they looked! The Great Zinkiewicz wasn't a tramp, how ever could they have thought him so!—he was a lord in a long black evening coat, and his blistered hands were hidden beneath white gloves, and the top hat made him taller still, my, he towered over the room! And he looked smoother, softer, he was charming. Lucy was in a dress of a thousand sequins, and when she moved even the slightest muscle the sequins seemed to ripple in the firelight.

"The Great Zinkiewicz will ask his beautiful assistant to give him a pack of playing cards." His beautiful assistant did that very thing. Zinkiewicz held the pack between his thumb and forefinger. "I shall now ask a member of the audience to confirm these are just ordinary playing cards. You, little madam? Would you do me the honour? Would you be so kind? Would you tell everyone, we have never met before?"

The little girl giggled. She inspected the cards. She confirmed they were very ordinary indeed.

"I shall now ask you to pick a card. But don't let me see it. Don't let my assistant see it. Trust neither of us, keep it secret from us. Yes? Good. That's good. Now, put it back in the pack. Anywhere you like, good."

He handed the pack to Lucy. Lucy fanned the cards in her hand, held them out. The Great Zinkiewicz produced a wand, and tapped at the deck once, twice, three times. "Abracadabra," he said.

"What does that mean?" asked the girl.

"I'm glad you asked me that. I don't know. No one knows. That's what's makes it magic."

"All right," said the girl. She seemed unconvinced by that, so he winked at her.

He took back the cards from Lucy. He shuffled them. He removed one. "Now," he said. "Is this your card?"

"No."

"Oh." Zinkiewicz pulled a face. He looked at Lucy. Lucy pulled a face back. It was so perfect an imitation, and was so unexpected, those blank passive features suddenly contorting like that, really, you had to smile. "Oh. Well. I'll try again. Hmph. Is *this* your card?"

"No!"

"This one, then?"

"No!"

"Then this one!"

"No!" She laughed, she could see something good was coming.

"Well then," said Zinkiewicz. "Well, I'm stumped. Lucy, do you have any idea?"

And Lucy sighed, a big mock sigh, why was she saddled with such a dunce for a partner? She walked up to the little girl. She reached behind the girl's ear. She seemed to tug at it, gave a little grunt of exertion. And then out she pulled a piece of card, and it was all rolled up tight like a straw. She opened it, presented it to Zinkiewicz.

And, as if taking credit for the magic himself, Zinkiewicz then presented it to the little girl, with a bow and a flourish.

"Yes! Yes, that's the one!" She clapped, so did her mother.

There were a few more tricks performed, for as long as it took for the fire to burn out. And, at length, the innkeeper offered the magicians some bread and cheese. Zinkiewicz thanked her, and they ate.

"I know how you did the trick," said the little girl.

"Oho! Do you, indeed?"

"Yes."

"Well, we have to keep these things secret. You better whisper it in my ear."

The little girl laughed, looked at her mother for permission, and the mother nodded, laughed too. So the man got down on his knees, and the girl bent close, putting her lips right up to his ear, and whispering softly, and covering her mouth with her hand so no one could see. She told him the secret, and the man rolled his eyes, slow and despairing.

"You've seen right through me!" he wailed. "You'll become a magician too, I'll be bound, like my Lucy!"

But the little girl had got it wrong. The man had broken his promise. There had been real magic tonight, he had felt it flow right through him, he had felt the old confidence back, and it had been good. There had been no fear at all; it had been so very good. And the innkeeper and her daughter need never know. Lucy would know, but she'd never say.

"Does she ever say anything?" said the woman suddenly. "Is it just part of the act, or . . . ?"

The man shook his head, put his finger to his lips, as if it were something mysterious he wasn't allowed to divulge. But the truth was, he had no idea.

↙

They sat up late that night, into the small hours, the magician and the innkeeper. The children had gone to bed. The woman fetched an old bottle of Madeira wine, she said she'd been saving it for a special occasion. Maybe this was one.

He said to her, "Aren't you going to run away?" And then he blushed bright red, because he supposed that would sound like an invitation to accompany him, her and her kid, and he didn't want that.

"We're going to stay," she said. "We've decided. We're happy here. There's nowhere out there that's better. And maybe, maybe they'll leave us be."

The man nodded, and finished his glass, and went to bed.

↯

In the morning, the magicians left. The woman gave them some bread for their journey. The little girl gave Lucy a hug, and Lucy didn't quite know what to do with it, but the girl didn't seem to mind she wasn't hugged back.

They never saw the innkeeper or her daughter again. In the weeks to come, as the blackness overtook them, the man would suppose they were dead.

↯

For there was little magic left to those times, since the demons and angels had gone to war. No one had seen a demon and lived. And yet some said they were monsters, giants, dreadful to look upon, so terrible that if you so much as glimpsed one your heart would stop in terror. And others said they looked just like us. They looked just like us, except if you got close you'd find out their eyes were sharper than ours, and redder too, maybe; and they had little bumps on their head, just small, not quite horns, but maybe, no, horns, small—they could be hidden beneath hair, or a big hat; and when they spoke sometimes fire and brimstone would come out their mouths. But they looked just like us. No one had seen an angel either, but they were just as deadly, and they looked just like us too, like every stranger coming into town, like everyone you do not recognize. There were no wings, nothing so easy or giveaway, no holy trumpets playing to herald their arrival. Some had halos, but they were very ordinary halos, a little grey, a little rusted. The angels and the demons, they could be everywhere, anywhere, all about us. And yet no one had ever seen one. Not seen one, at any rate, and lived.

No one could guess why the demons and angels were at war. But it wasn't about us. They didn't care about us. And wherever they met in battle a blackness would descend, and it would engulf everything, and nothing could escape it, and it was spreading across the land.

The world seemed cracked, somehow, too weak for any magic to hold; or happiness; or faith; or love.

Still, he pulled his cart onwards, and sometimes he faltered, and Lucy never faltered.

One week away they found a road sign directing them toward the town, and it wasn't even damaged, it was in one piece, and the man felt his spirits lift.

Four days away they found the old road itself, and there were some holes in it, and it wasn't strictly straight, but it was still easier going for the cart.

One day they arrived at the town. There were bridges and churches and statues and shops. The road was choked with old discarded vehicles. There was litter. There was a theatre. They went into the theatre. It was big and imposing and the roof was still on.

The man took Lucy's hands, and he made her look at him, directly, into his eyes. And he said, "Listen. We don't have to stop. We can keep going. We can just outrun the blackness. We can keep going."

And Lucy didn't even shake her head. She pulled free, began to unpack the cart.

It was all in good condition, considering. The Sword of a Thousand Cuts had rusted, but that could be put right with a good dose of varnish. A trick mirror had fractured, but just a little, it needn't spoil the illusion too much. The Cabinet of Vanishments was soaked with rainwater, and one of the doors had warped slightly with the wet, and they sat it upside-down on the stage to let it dry out. But it didn't matter. It didn't matter, they didn't use the Cabinet anymore. They only kept the Cabinet for show.

The man unrolled the pack of posters. He walked over the town, stuck his posters up against the sides of buildings, walls, the disused telegraph poles that stuck out of the ground like dead tree stumps. Really, he stuck them up against anything that was still standing. He didn't see anyone, but they saw him, he knew; he knew that once he'd moved away the people would come out from their hiding places and see what he had to sell. They were old posters, he'd stuck them up and pulled them down from any number of towns upon his tours—he looked younger in them, photographed in his full costume, in days when he filled out his clothes better and his smile was more fluent—"The Great Zinkiewicz Entertains!" it said, and beneath, "With His Glamorous Assistant, Lucy!"—but this was the *old* Lucy, the Lucy from before, buxom and beaming, almost as tall as he was, standing proud in her sequined gown and her feather headdress, gesturing toward him in the picture in a display of pride and awe. His assistant, his best friend, his wife, back before he'd lost her, and the blackness had swallowed her soul. How he missed her.

By the time he got back to the theatre the sun was already starting to set, and he could sense that the townsfolk were on the move; in spite of themselves they wanted to be dazzled and entertained. Little Lucy was already in her dress. He put on his white shirt, black trousers, white gloves, black hat. He stood with Lucy in the wings as he heard the auditorium fill, and he felt a sudden sickness in his stomach, performer's nerves. And he wanted to run away, and he wanted too to do what he was born for, and stand in front of the crowd, with all those eyes on him, all expectant, all hungry, all making him the centre of their diminished worlds for a couple of brief hours.

"Break a leg," he muttered to Lucy, and together they stepped out into the lights.

The lights shone in his eyes, he couldn't see his audience, couldn't see how large they were, how apprehensive. He gave his smoothest smile and hoped it passed as confident. He spread his arms out wide, as if inviting everybody in for a special hug.

"I am the Great Zinkiewicz," he cried, as if challenging anyone out there to deny it. No one did.

The patter went well. He felt he had a real rapport with Lucy that night; their little rehearsal at the inn those weeks ago had sharpened them both. He was garrulous, the bigger the tricks he performed the more grandiose the metaphors he used to describe them, he'd never use one syllable when five would do. And beside him Lucy in all her blessed muteness struck such a comic contrast; she'd never open her mouth, she'd talk to the audience in her own way, she'd roll her eyes, she'd shrug, she'd flop her arms once in a while as if to demonstrate the physical heaviness of having to work with such a braggart. The audience began to chuckle. This was one way in which little Lucy always scored over her glamorous original; his wife had often tried to top his jokes, and she'd never been a funny woman, it had never worked.

So they chuckled, then they laughed outright. At some of the tricks there were even admiring gasps, and there was lots and lots of applause.

There was no real magic. Not tonight, it seemed. But that didn't matter.

And at some point the mood shifted. The applause seemed thicker somehow, not crisp like clapping should be, but thick like syrup; the laughter . . . what, more ironic? Crueller, even? He didn't know what had caused it. Had it been him? It might have been him. Because the fear was back. Everything had been going so well, and he couldn't believe the signs as the fear first stole over him—a coldness in his heart, a slight loosening in his bowels—no, he thought to himself, why now? He heard his jokes for what they were, and they were just words, pointless words; he felt how forced his smile was, could feel just how far it stretched across his face and no further; he began to shake, and sweat. He could see himself, one man caught in the lights, pretending that there was still something magical to the world when all about him was darkness.

The darkness, the darkness had come. The proper darkness, solid, weighty, and it lumbered across the theatre toward him. And he could hear his audience die, every one of them, and the demons came in, or was it the angels, or was it *both*, were they both here together, had they put aside their differences and stopped their war and come to see the show? His audience were lost; the angels and demons were in their seats now, crushing down their corpses. And the darkness, all the darkness, all about, unyielding, and pure, and the only light left in the world shone down upon him and Lucy.

His patter dried. He stumbled over his words. Stumbled over his feet. He panted, he licked his lips.

From the void came a voice, a single voice, and it was sharp like gravel, and he didn't think there was anything human in it at all.

"Give us a good trick, magic man. And maybe we'll spare your life."

⬇

It was in just such a theatre that the Great Zinkiewicz had first seen the darkness. It had not been a good show. The audience weren't attentive, he thought some of them were drunk. And Lucy was talking too much again, in spite of what he'd said to her the night before: it was all in the rhythm, he kept explaining to her, gently, the act could work only in a very exact *rhythm*. "I just feel there's more I can offer," she'd said. "I just stand about looking decorative, and getting sawn in half, and stuff. I'm worth more than that." And he had promised he'd try to find a better way to include her in the show, and they'd kissed, and then made love. And, do you know, he thought he'd probably even meant it.

As they'd trudged toward the grand finale, he'd given her the signal, and she'd nodded, gone into the wings. And out she had wheeled the Cabinet of Vanishments.

"Behold," said Zinkiewicz. "The Cabinet of Vanishments! Now, my wife will vanish before your eyes. When she gets locked up in my special box, and I tap upon the door, and say the magic word—yes, you all know it, abracadabra! I don't know what it means, no one knows what it means, if we knew it wouldn't be magic—I'll say the word, and my wife will be gone!"

He'd felt at last a flutter of interest from the audience.

His wife had said, perkily, whilst wagging her finger at him, "And just you make sure I get back in time for tea!" Audience death once more. Jesus.

He closed the door on her, and he felt a relief that she was out of sight. And a sense of something else, deep inside, some new confidence. Or power.

He tapped on the door three times with his wand. "Abracadabra," he said.

He opened the door. She'd gone. There was some half-hearted applause.

He closed the door again. "Now to bring her back," he said. "I suppose!" And there was some laughter at that, and he thought to himself, you see, Lucy, one *can* improvise comedy, but only if one's a professional.

"Abracadabra," he said. He opened the door. The cabinet was empty.

He closed the door. He turned to the audience, smiled, but he felt it was a sick smile, and he could feel himself beginning to sweat.

"I'll try again," he promised them. "Abracadabra!"

Still nothing—but no, really *nothing*—and this time it seemed to Zinkiewicz the cabinet was not merely empty, it somehow seemed to have no inside at all. Black, just black, a darkness. That would spill out into the world unless. Unless he slammed the door shut.

He did. He held the door closed. He felt it, he felt something beat against it, thrum against his fingers. He didn't dare let go. He didn't dare hold on either, he didn't dare stand so close, because he knew that for all its fancy design and name the cabinet was just a bit of plywood a few inches thick, it wouldn't be enough to contain what was growing within. And at the thought of it he pulled away, as if he had been burned—and for a moment he thought he had, and he stared down at his fingers, expecting them to be charred and black. They weren't. They weren't, but he stared at them anyway—and for too long, he could hear behind his back the audience stir from stultified silence and begin to heckle.

He turned back to them. He didn't know what to say. His tongue felt heavy, sick, and yes, his fingers, they still *burned*. "I'm sorry," is what he came out with. "I'm sorry."

And behind him he heard it, and he knew now he wasn't imagining it: there was a knocking from within the cabinet, something impatient to be released. And then there was a voice to it—"Hey!" Muffled, but still sounding perky, so annoyingly perky. "Hey, let me out! Is it time for my tea yet?"

There was some polite laughter, they thought it was part of the act. He opened the door. There was Lucy. He took her hand to help her out, she had to bow so her feather headdress wouldn't get caught, and her sequins sparkled as they came out from the dark. They made their bows together. They went for two bows, although the applause didn't really warrant it.

That night in their digs they had argued. She told him this wasn't what she had expected from their marriage. It wasn't just the act anymore, it was the entire *marriage*. She was bored with the constant travelling. It wasn't as exciting as she'd expected. She thought they'd be on television by now. "Do you still love me?" he'd asked. She'd thought about it. "I don't know," she'd replied.

She turned away from him in the bed, and he wanted to reach out towards her, but he was too proud, or too frightened he'd be rebuffed. And he lay there in the darkness, and it seemed to him that it was a darkness so profound, and he wished they'd left the bathroom light on, or had the curtains open, anything, the darkness was beginning to hurt his eyes. And he felt that surge of power inside him again, and he knew she was right, he should be better than this, it was all supposed to be better.

He didn't know her anymore. He didn't know her. Their magic was gone.

And he realized all the darkness in the room was her, it was her, it was coming from her. He could feel it now, it was pouring out of her. With every breath she made she was spitting more of it out, and it lay heavy on her, and it lay heavy on him, and it was going to suffocate him unless he stopped it. He'd lost her. He'd lost her. She'd been swallowed up whole.

He got up. She didn't stir.

He packed the truck with all the props he needed for his magic act, his costume, the takings from the last three weeks of performance. He drove off into the night.

Within a few days the truck ran out of petrol. There hadn't been a petrol station. There was barely even a road anymore. He abandoned the truck. He found a horse cart amongst the rubble that lay about, so much rubble, things thrown away and no longer wanted. He loaded the cart. He picked up the handle. It was so heavy. He had to be strong. He walked.

The world was cracked, and the darkness was pursuing him, and he had to outrun it. And in some towns there was talk of war.

He did a few tricks for coins and food. Most of his tricks didn't work without an assistant.

Some nights, if the ground was dry, he slept underneath the cart. He could pull the canvas covering down for added warmth or shelter. One morning he woke to find a little girl was curled up, at his feet, like a dozing cat.

"Oi!" he said. "Wake up!" The girl did, stretched, looked at him without shame or curiosity. "Who are you?" he demanded. "Where have you come from?"

She didn't answer.

And he didn't ask again, because he felt somehow if he did she would go away.

When he pulled the cart along, she walked beside him. And the next town he reached, he played his act, and she was there. She knew the tricks just as well as he did. And she had her own sequined dress, it fitted perfectly.

The distance between towns seemed greater and greater. Sometimes they'd walk for weeks before they'd reach a new one. And when they did the people were hostile, or hid from them altogether. The paths were hard to walk, the ground rough, chewed up even, and no matter how much it rained the mud beneath their feet seemed so hard and sharp and unyielding. "I can't go on," he'd say to the girl, "I don't see why we're going on," and he might cry, and then the girl wouldn't look at him, as if she were embarrassed. One day he dropped the handle of the cart. "I've had enough," he said, "if we must walk, I'm not carrying this anymore!" Without missing a beat she went to the cart, tried to lift it herself, tried to drag it behind her. She was such a little thing, but she managed it; he could see her grit her teeth with the effort, and then force one foot on in front of the other, so slowly, too slow—she was going to pull the cart no matter how long it took. Shamed, he went back, relieved her. She smiled at him then, just a little smile, and it was of triumph, but it was not unkind. On he walked. On she walked, always keeping pace.

He called her Lucy; it was what it said on the posters. And sometimes as she slept beside him he thought he could see something of his wife in her face. Sometimes he liked to pretend this was his wife, but small, and silent, from the years before he'd met her. And sometimes he didn't need to pretend, he knew it was true.

Dumb Lucy

"Give us a good trick, magic man. And maybe we'll spare your life. You, and that brat of yours."

He tried his best. But the cards kept slipping through fingers damp with sweat.

"Haven't you got anything better?"

He pulled a rabbit out of his hat. He pulled a hat out of a rabbit.

"Last chance, magic man."

He didn't know what to do. He looked at Lucy for help.

Lucy didn't seem afraid. She seemed as blandly unaffected by this as she was by everything else. And for a second the man rather envied her. And for a second he was rather frightened of her too.

She held his gaze for a moment, then turned, and left the stage.

He thought she'd abandoned him. And he couldn't blame her.

But she came back, and when she did, she was wheeling on the Cabinet of Vanishments.

"No," he said to her. "No."

She shook her head at that. She set it down centre stage. She presented it to the audience. And so, he went on with the act. He cleared his throat.

"I shall say the magic word, abracadabra. I . . . I don't know what it means. No one does. What it means, I." His voice cracked. "Maybe that's why it's magic."

There was laughter. Real laughter, or were they mocking him?

He opened the cabinet. There was no darkness in there, the darkness had all got out long ago.

And Lucy gestured that *he* should step inside.

"No, I'm the magician," he said.

She ignored that. With a bow, with a flourish, she once more waved him toward the box.

"No," he said. And this time he was quite firm.

She stared him down for a little while. Then she leaned forward, and he thought she was going to speak at last, he thought she was going to whisper something in his ear. He bent down to listen. She kissed him lightly on the cheek.

"Get on with it," came the voice from the audience.

They got on with it. Lucy climbed inside the cabinet. She looked so tiny there suddenly, you could have fitted five Lucys inside, more maybe.

147

He closed the doors on her. One didn't shut properly, the rainwater, the warping—and there was laughter again, and this time they were definitely mocking him. He had to hold the door to keep it flush.

"Goodbye," he said to her. And he liked to imagine that inside she mouthed a goodbye to him too.

He tapped on the box three times with his wand. "Abracadabra," he said. He stepped away from the box, the warped door swung open and revealed that the cabinet was now empty.

"Can you bring her back?"

"Yes," he said.

"Bring her back."

"No," he said. "I'm not bringing her back. Not to this place."

They came up onto the stage then, and took him by his arms, and bent him over backwards so his spine hurt, and held him tight. He saw that they were demons and angels, both—that they had little lumps for horns, and lapsed haloes, both.

"Bring her back," they said.

And he felt such a power surging through him, the magic was back, even in a world as cracked as this. And he thanked them, sincerely—he thanked them that they had helped him give his best performance, that they had made his act at last mean something. The fear had gone. The fear had gone forever, and they could now do what they liked to him.

⬇

They bit him, and punched him, and pulled at his skin and hair. And he didn't cry out, he laughed, he barely felt a thing, he was so full of magic now, he was invincible. This enraged them still further. They shut him inside his box, and they set fire to it, and he didn't cry out, not once, and he looked deep into the flames and fancied he saw in them what Lucy had found so fascinating, and it didn't hurt, not very much, right up until the end.

⬇

And Lucy turned about, and opened her eyes, and there was noise, and people, and the buildings stood intact, and the smell in the air may not have been clean but at least wasn't sulphur.

Her sequined dress was ripped, and spattered with mud.

There was a pack of playing cards in her hand.

There was a tongue in her head.

She began to speak, and the more she said the better she got, and the better she got the louder she became.

She fanned out the playing cards to the world.

"Roll up, roll up," she said. "Prepare to be dazzled by the Great Zinkiewicz!"

For a while no one paid any attention. But then, even in a world so cracked, the magic began to hold.

72 VIRGINS

Michael Bell died, and went to heaven, and was told by the man at the front desk where he could collect his seventy-two virgins. "Oh," said Michael, much surprised, "I don't think I'm entitled to . . . There's been a mistake . . . I mean, I'm not a Muslim," and the man at the desk looked cross and said that if Michael had any complaints could he please take them up with someone else, it was a busy day, and he had a lot of corpses to process. So Michael apologized, signed the register, took his room key, and set forth into the afterlife.

He had been assigned his own apartment. They called it an apartment, but it was more like a mansion, really: there was a garden with a swimming pool in it, and a billiard room, and a study, and a kitchen full of all the latest mod cons, and a basement with a swimming pool in it. It would have been far too big for Michael all by himself, so at first he was rather pleased there were seventy-two virgins to help fill it.

Some of the seventy-two virgins were useless. He could see that in an instant. Eleven of them were babies. Eighteen of them were men. Four of them weren't even human: he'd been given two virgin cats, one virgin goldfish, and a virgin grey squirrel. But that still left him with thirty-nine virginal women—young (mostly), ripe (he supposed), and his for the taking. "Hello," he said to the throng, a little shyly, "my name's Michael, but, uh, why not call me Mike?" He asked them their names. "Goodness," said Michael, "I'll never remember all those. Maybe you should all wear name badges?" So, for a while, they did.

He told them they should feel free to use all the facilities. The swimming pools were at their disposal, and if anyone ever wanted to join him in a game of billiards, all they had to do was ask. None of the virgins liked swimming, apparently. And no one fancied billiards. They would instead crowd into the sitting room around the widescreen television set. They would squabble for space on the single sofa that was there, and shush each other when the ad breaks came to an end. Michael sometimes watched TV with them, but they never seemed to want to watch any of the programs he liked, and besides, he was never fast enough to get a spot on the sofa. Sometimes he'd hang out in the kitchen and make himself toast. He couldn't work out how to use most of the mod cons, but the toaster was nice and easy. Or he'd go to the billiard room, and he'd roll all the balls from one end of the table to the other, and then walk to the other side, and roll them all back again.

↓

He got to know Eliza quite well. Eliza was fond of toast, and would sometimes come into the kitchen when Michael was making some. She wouldn't say much, but her fingers and his fingers might collide taking slices of bread out of the breadbasket.

Michael began to think about Eliza a lot. He wondered if she ever thought of him too. One day he asked her why she didn't watch TV with all the other virgins, and she blushed, and said she didn't like TV much, and that besides, she'd rather be with him. She wasn't especially pretty, but she looked as if she were in her teens, and Michael was pushing seventy, and he felt guilty for flirting with her until she told him she'd died of scarlet fever in the 1860s and was therefore older than his grandmother.

He asked her whether she'd like to be his girlfriend, and steeled himself for a rejection, and she kissed him gently on the cheek and said that that'd be quite all right.

He was intimidated by his own bedroom. Sweet incense and crushed silks and pillows that were fleshy—he couldn't sleep like that. He'd kicked the pillows onto the floor. Before they got into bed together, Eliza stacked the pillows high again.

She said, "I'm scared. Is that silly?"

He said, "Of course it's not silly."

She said, "You won't hurt me?"

He said, "I promise."

"Tell me," she said. "What it was like. Your first time. Were you scared?"

"No," he said, wanting to be brave for her sake, but he had been terrified. He could remember the circumstances now, and the basic sequence of events that had got the girl from the dance floor to the car seat, but there were events missing, the bits that linked A to B to C. He remembered now only the urgency, the desperate urgency, the need to be a man and abandon his childhood as fast as could be, and that he wasn't sure during the whole thing whether he was in the right hole or not, the girl seemed to have grown holes all over the place, was she going to laugh at him?—and then afterwards the dull realisation that the world hadn't changed, everything was just the same, he may now be a man but nobody cared.

"But it was nice?" she said.

"It was very nice," he said.

They had sex then, and it had been so long since he'd done it with Barbara that frankly he felt just like a virgin too.

And after he was out of breath and sweaty and his heart was going like the clappers, and he wondered whether he might be having a heart attack but supposed he couldn't die twice. He stroked at Eliza's hair, kissed her softly. He asked her if her first time had been all right.

"It was very nice."

He fell asleep then, with Eliza in his arms, and he dreamed of Barbara, and he hadn't dreamed of Barbara in ages, really not much since the divorce at all. And there were some bad things in the dream, inevitably, but it wasn't quite bad enough to be a nightmare.

When he woke in the morning Eliza wasn't there. He thought she might be making some toast. She wasn't.

He asked the other virgins if they had seen her. They were watching *The Jeremy Kyle Show*, they didn't want to be disturbed.

Michael went back to the man at the front desk. He explained the situation. The man didn't look very sympathetic, he spoke to Michael as if he were an idiot. "You get seventy-two *virgins*," he said. "She's not a virgin now, is she? She's gone." Michael could see the logic of that. But he asked whether he could have Eliza's address. Even if they couldn't be anything more, and why should she want to be, with an old man like him, he'd be a fool even to think it—even so, he hoped they could still be friends. He'd like to see her still, as a friend. The man rolled his eyes. "When I say gone, I mean *gone*. That's it. One bang, and she's gone forever."

☟

From the remaining seventy-one virgins there came one morning a deputation of ambassadors to his bedroom. "We want you to get rid of Cheryl," they said.

Cheryl was big and blousy and so fat she took up space for two upon the sofa. She talked too loud during the programs and had an annoying laugh and would fight for the remote control, and, moreover, was an utter bitch.

They brought Cheryl to his bedroom later that evening. There was a sack upon her head. There was some evidence of a struggle: her legs were bleeding, and she had had to be dragged to him. But she was quiet now, accepting. They pushed her into Michael's arms, and shut the door on them.

Michael pulled the sack off her, asked her to sit down, tried to be as nice as he could. "It's all right," he said. "We don't have to do this, you know."

"No," she said. "I suppose I'm going to have to pop my cherry sooner or later, may as well be with you."

They both got undressed in silence. He tried not to look at her, all drooping bust and tummy. She had no such qualms. She stared at him, grimly, as if staring at an execution block.

"I'm sorry," he said. "I know I'm not much to look at."

She shook her head.

"So, what?" she said. "You get killed in a war, or something?"

"Me? No."

"To get all us virgins."

"No."

"But you did something heroic, right?"

"No." Michael's death hadn't been especially heroic. Up to the end in that hospital pleading for even one more day of life, and all of the nurses trying to reassure him that it was going to be all right—and he'd felt, he really had felt, that they had never seen this happen before, that he was the very first man in the world who was going to die, that he was special. "I didn't go to war. There wasn't any war on."

Cheryl sniffed. "There's always some war on somewhere, if you just look."

"I suppose I was too scared."

She nodded at that, seemed to accept it. She got into bed. She seemed resigned now, not too nervous, neither of the loss of her virginity, nor of the oblivion that would happen afterwards.

She kissed him on the lips, almost by way of experiment. He kissed back. It was nice. She kissed at his neck then, and he nibbled at her ear, and he'd never thought to be a nibbler before, not ever, not even when he and Barbara had been happy. She moaned a bit, and he was worried for her, but she said it was a good moan.

"You're wonderful, Cheryl," he told her. "Do you know that? You're wonderful."

And she smiled at him, and she cried a little.

"I'm going to make the very best love to you that I possibly can," he said, and she thanked him, and true to his word he did his best.

↙

He tried to remember the last time he and Barbara had slept with each other, but there hadn't been a last time, not as such, but then, there had to have been a last, surely? But it had been nothing momentous. It hadn't been so bad that it had caused either one of them to be banished to the spare bedroom, there had been no tears or anger. One night he and his wife had had sex, and, as it turned out, they'd never bothered to try it again.

In the same way, nothing specific had ever caused the divorce. Looking back, he couldn't even decide which one of them had brought the matter up.—No, it had been her, definitely her. Still.

One night as he dreamed of Barbara he realized he'd given her Cheryl's face. And try as he might, he couldn't recall what Barbara had looked like. And one night, while he dreamed, he realized he couldn't recall Cheryl's face either.

↙

He killed Eunice quite by accident. She'd suggested they just fool around for a bit, and Michael had never been much good at foreplay, he just told her he'd follow her lead. They didn't do anything worse than kiss and squeeze at the other's genitals, and yet in the morning she was gone, and there was no way of getting her back.

And Natalie was unhappy, she had attempted suicide any number of times, she had tried drowning herself in the swimming pools, she had stuck a fork into the toaster. Nothing had worked. Before she impaled herself upon him, Michael asked her what she was so upset about, and the poor woman had burst into tears. "It's my babies, I miss my little babies." Michael asked her why she had ever been given to him, she wasn't a virgin at all then, surely? And Natalie shrugged, she really wasn't

154

interested in discussing the finer points of her employment contract, not now—and she flung herself upon him, all lactating breasts and crude stretch marks, and she was gone.

The other virgins kept their distance. Michael didn't blame them. It wasn't that they were afraid of death, it was simply that they didn't like him very much. Even the squirrel gave him a wide berth.

And in the summer the eighteen young men lay out in the garden and sunbathed, and they bronzed there naked, and their muscled limbs gleamed golden in the heat, and their tackle looked thick and firm like barbecued meat, and Michael thought he had never looked as good as that, not when he'd been young, not his entire life.

One day he came up from the billiard room to find all the virgins were having an orgy. To be fair, they asked him if he wanted to join in, but he could see they were just being polite. There was a lot of sucking and suckling and squelching, everybody was trying to find ways of inserting themselves into another so that they became some writhing wall of flesh, even the goldfish was throwing herself into it—and as they did so the virgins began to break apart and pop like soap bubbles. Michael went and hid in his room for a while. When he came out later, he was entirely alone.

ᛣ

Michael didn't see anyone for quite a while. He ran out of bread to toast, and so moved on to cereal.

ᛣ

They came for him one night, put a sack over his head. They said, "You've been reassigned, handsome."

He was taken with seventy-one other virgins to a new, bigger apartment. They called it an apartment, but really, it was more like a palace, it had everything: Jacuzzis and saunas and an entire beauty salon. The virgins were mostly young men, but there were a few girls thrown in, and some babies, and half a dozen squirrels. Michael said, "There's been a mistake . . . I mean, I have had sex, really." They told him to shut up.

And Barbara arrived, and inspected her entourage, and seemed pleased by the young men, and bemused by the squirrels—and when she reached Michael in the line she just stopped, and stared, and swore. "I'm sorry," said Michael. "Just keep away from me," she hissed, "and I'm sure it'll be fine."

Michael could never get a seat on the sofa, let alone get close to the remote control. But Barbara cut a swathe through her virgins, showing a sexual voracity now she was dead she'd never hinted at when she'd been alive. She got through all the boys, then the girls, then the babies, then the squirrels, and didn't even spare a glance at her ex-husband. Michael was a little hurt, but soon enough he was able to stretch out wide and comfy upon the sofa and watch whichever channels he liked.

↓

They muddled along amiably for a while. They'd potter about in separate rooms during the day, in the evening they'd sit together silently and watch television. Then they'd say goodnight, and go to different bedrooms. It was very safe, very familiar.

One evening Barbara turned off the television. Michael looked up at her in surprise. It had been *Coronation Street*, it was one of her favourites. She went without a word to the kitchen, returned with two glasses and a bottle of rose wine.

"We're going to have sex," she said. She poured two glasses, both to the very brim. "Whatever it takes."

They drank three bottles before Barbara was in the mood. She fell off the sofa flat onto her arse, which she found hugely funny. "Sod it," she said. "Too much wine. I'll know better tomorrow."

The next day they drank only the one bottle, Barbara was strict about that. They drank it very slowly, and Barbara said they would have to wait for it to take full effect. Some half an hour after the last dregs were drained, Barbara nodded primly, said, "It's time," pulled Michael up from the sofa, pulled him into the bedroom.

The sex was quite nice, and their bodies sort of fitted together in all the right places, and Michael wondered why they'd ever stopped doing it all those years ago.

Afterwards she looked at him intently, and Michael wondered whether she wanted to say something loving. Then realized she was just waiting to see if he would pop.

"How do you feel?" she said.

"Fine."

"No, I mean, how do you . . . ?"

"No, I know, fine, fine."

"Okay."

They lay there for a bit. He said, "Would you like some toast?" She nodded. He got out of bed. She watched him carefully, as if to see whether his weight upon the carpet would be too much for him, whether at last his structural integrity would break. It didn't. He brought her in some toast. He'd buttered it thick, the way she'd always liked it. She munched upon it gratefully.

"What are you going to do today, then?" he asked her. She didn't know.

They got up eventually. He sat down on the sofa, watched afternoon television. She stared at him for a bit, then went off to the kitchen to wash up his breakfast things, clear up the mess he always made.

She went out shopping later. Before she went she kissed him on the cheek, said goodbye, just in case he wasn't there when she got home. When she returned she looked annoyed by his continued existence—but as Michael helped her put away the groceries, he noticed she'd bought ready meals for two.

That evening they watched television. And she sighed, and said, "One more try. Okay?"

"Okay," he agreed.

She fetched the wine. She seemed somewhat impatient this time; they barely had more than a glass each.

They got undressed. This time they watched each other. They'd not bothered before—either they'd been too drunk, or too disinterested, or both.

He said to her, "I'm going to make the very best love to you I possibly can." And at those words a faint memory of Cheryl stirred, it's true. But Barbara didn't know.

"I'm going to miss you," Barbara said.

They made love very gently this time, hoping against hope they wouldn't damage the other.

"Are you done?" Michael asked her, and she smiled, and said yes. He didn't pull out. He thought he'd wait.

And he felt something for her that was a little like love—but it wasn't love, was it? It was relief. And it soared inside, he felt it fill his body up, he filled up like a balloon. He looked at her, and she was still smiling, and he could see that she felt the very same thing. And they both held on to each other, and waited, to see which of them would burst first.

STATIC

When Ernest went into his sitting room that morning, he found that his television set had been bleeding.

Of course, it could all have been much worse. What if he hadn't gone into the room until the afternoon? What if he hadn't gone into it at *all*? He didn't always feel like the sitting room. It had too many memories, none of them unhappy, but you don't always want memories crowding in on you, even the happy ones. Besides, it seemed silly to have a room just for *sitting*, if he wanted to sit there was always the kitchen, there was a perfectly good chair in there, and the stove made the place warm.

But he *did* go into the sitting room, and he was alarmed. "Oh dear," he said. He might easily have come out with a swear word, so great was this alarm, but he always rationed his swearing for really special occasions. "Oh dear," he said again.

Not to overstate the problem: it wasn't a *puddle* of blood. It didn't look as if anyone had been butchered on the carpet. But you'd have been hard pushed to have written it off as anything as trivial as a speck either. It sat there, bright but un-dramatic, probably no more than three centimetres in diameter, already drying into the faded taupe with which Lizzie had chosen to furnish the room so many years ago. With a heave that hurt his joints, Ernest bent down and looked at the underside of the television. He couldn't see where the blood had spilled from, and it might only have been a little cut—certainly it didn't seem to be bleeding anymore. Better to be safe than sorry, though. He fetched a Tupperware bowl from the kitchen, and stood it on the red patch so it could collect any more drops. And then he thought for a bit, removed the bowl, and scrubbed at the red patch hard with a wet flannel and soap. All he succeeded in doing was in making the patch a little pinker and a lot bigger. He sat the Tupperware back down in the middle of it, and had another think. And he went for the telephone.

Static

The repair shop said they didn't like to make home visits—couldn't be bring the television in? And Ernest explained that he was elderly and had a bad hip. Then the repair shop said that they'd send someone out, would Thursday afternoon be any good for him? And Ernest said that it was really terribly urgent, his television set was *bleeding*; admittedly, the blood had stopped now, but there *had* been blood, and that couldn't be good, could it? And the repair shop went silent. Then said they'd send someone round right away.

That said, the repairman was a disappointment. "I can't repair it."

"Oh dear," said Ernest. And, "Why not?"

"Well, look at it," said the repairman. And gestured, as if it were obvious. "Look how *old* it is. That must be twenty years old, that must."

"It's forty-eight years old," said Ernest. He knew exactly when he bought it. It was in that month just after he'd married Lizzie.

"Forty-eight?" The repairman was incredulous. "My parents aren't that old! You've got a TV older than my parents!" And he laughed with the gusto of the very young who cannot conceive that the world in any way predates them. Ernest smiled politely. He wondered if the repairman, with his young parents and his stud earring and his blond apology for a beard, thought he was an adult. He probably did.

"Is it blood?" asked Ernest. "I thought it might be oil."

"TVs don't run on oil," explained the repairman. "That doesn't make any sense." Ernest wondered whether the blood made any *more* sense, but didn't say anything. "They're not cars," the man went on, almost sneering. "You don't put *petrol* in them. That's not the way they work, is it?"

Ernest said he supposed not. "What should I do with it now?"

"We can sell you a new TV."

"I don't want a new TV."

"I don't mean *new*. I mean, second-hand. But very good, you know. Cheap."

"I'd rather you fixed this one."

The repairman sighed. "Look, even if I could . . . and I can't, you know, it's the parts, they won't make the parts anymore. It'd be very expensive, you'd be better off starting from scratch . . . I mean, I'm amazed it still works at all. It does work, does it?"

Ernest didn't watch television very often. It hadn't picked up ITV in years, but that didn't matter, neither he nor Lizzie had ever watched anything on the commercial channel. BBC1 had recently become something of a snowstorm—you could see that *something* was there, but it was hard to hear what over the gale of fuzzy spots. BBC2 still worked, though. Most of the time.

The repairman made another offer—he could give Ernest a bit of a discount. They had lots of TVs in stock, he explained, they were a TV shop. Had a whole raft of new features, too, like plug-in aerials and remote controls and this new thing called colour, Ernest wouldn't believe he'd lived without them. And Ernest was very polite, said no thank you, and steered the man to the front door. He paid the call-out charge, said goodbye, then went back to the sitting room.

"Well, that didn't do much good, did it?" Ernest had never spoken to his television before, and even as he did so he told himself he shouldn't make a habit of it. But it seemed somehow appropriate. "Oh dear!" he said, still not swearing. "You're bleeding again!" And so the TV was. Three spots of blood now lay in the bowl, small but very red and unarguably *there*.

Ernest wondered whether it'd been his fault. Maybe he'd used the television too much, he'd exhausted it. And then he reasoned that he hadn't watched it in days, that couldn't be it. Then he worried himself all over again—maybe he'd not used it enough? Maybe it was because he'd neglected it. He stood in front of it, aching with indecision. "Sorry about this, old boy," he said. "Hope this doesn't hurt." And he turned it on with a click.

It took a few seconds for the screen to warm up. BBC1 was still there—well, as there as it ever was. It seemed to be some sort of garden program. Or maybe it was a western. He turned the knob, and found himself BBC2. It wasn't crystal clear, but then, it was never crystal clear. The snooker was playing, and Ernest always enjoyed the snooker. He thought he should keep watching for a bit, try to ascertain whether or not the picture had got worse since he'd last watched it. And to see whether that snooker chap could pot the pink. As he sat down in the armchair he idly wondered whether it was Ray Reardon—but then, he supposed Ray Reardon had probably retired, which was a shame as he'd always liked Ray Reardon. The man who may or may not have been, but on balance probably wasn't, Ray Reardon did indeed sink the pink, but came unstuck on the black—and Ernest never did find out what his name was, or whether he won the game at all, because he soon dozed off.

He woke to the telephone ringing. And felt immediately guilty.

Dozing off in front of the television! That's what Lizzie used to do—he used to laugh at her a lot for that. Always affectionately, she knew that, she'd always laugh back. Her mouth would be open, and she'd be snoring, drowning out whatever was being broadcast. And Blackie, she'd be cuddled up to her mummy, seeing Lizzie on her favourite armchair was a red rag to a bull, Blackie could never resist,—she'd have to cuddle up, and she'd put her paws over her face as if she felt ashamed to be caught dozing like that, and she'd be snoring too, it was like a little whinny. With Lizzie snoring and Blackie snoring you really couldn't hear a thing, and Ernest would laugh at them, and they'd laugh at him too—well, Lizzie would, anyway. And here he was, doing the same thing! The shock of the phone, and the rush of the memories, made his head spin for a moment.

"Dad? Are you all right?"

"Yes. Yes, I'm fine."

"Are you sure?"

"Why wouldn't I be?"

"You took a long time answering the phone. I had to ring off, try again."

"I was asleep," said Ernest, and immediately regretted it. Now Billy would think something *was* wrong.

"But it's two o'clock, Dad."

"I know," said Ernest, who didn't, in fact.

"In the afternoon. You shouldn't sleep in the afternoon. You know what the doctor said."

"No," said Ernest. "What did the doctor say?"

"He said you shouldn't sleep in the afternoon."

"What is it you want, Billy?" asked Ernest, hoping it came out kindly.

"We haven't seen you in a while. The family. We thought we might pop over." And see if I'm all right, Ernest supposed. "And see if you're all right," added Billy.

"I'm all right, I'm always all right," said Ernest. "Have you been speaking to anyone? Has anyone said I'm not?" Ernest thought hurriedly. "That repairman. You've been speaking to him, haven't you? Did you phone him? Or did he phone you?" Ernest couldn't work out what was worse—that his son would be employing a repairman to spy on him, or that a repairman would be spying on him and telling his son by his own volition.

"I don't know what you're talking about, Dad. What repairman?" So

Ernest told his son the whole story. It just spilled out, and even as he told him he knew he should shut up, keep it all to himself, it'd only be more reason for Billy to come over.

"Bleeding?"

"That's right," said Ernest. "It's not bleeding much," he added hastily, but the damage was done, he knew that.

"That doesn't sound right, Dad. Televisions shouldn't be doing that sort of thing. How's the video? Is that still playing all right?"

Billy had given his parents a video recorder for Christmas a couple of years back. Well, as Billy had said at the time, it wasn't *really* a present—it was just an old cast-off, the family were upgrading their own, and rather than just sling it out he thought that Mum and Dad should have it. They'd never used the video recorder. It was in a box in a cupboard somewhere, Lizzie had packed it away, she took care of things like that. She had taken a look, and said that the television was too old—it wouldn't have the right lead sockets or what-have-yous, but that they mustn't tell Billy, it had been such a kind gesture. Ernest agreed, but he hadn't thought it was a *particularly* kind gesture: it wasn't as if they had any videotapes to play on it anyway.

Ernest thought for a moment about all the things Lizzie had put in cupboards—he wouldn't have said they had that many cupboards, but Lizzie had certainly put away a lot of things over the years, so they must be bigger than they looked. He'd have to go through them one of these days, see what was there. The thought gave him a sick feeling in his stomach, and he was almost pleased to realize his son was still talking nonsense down the phone at him. If he listened to Billy for a bit, it might distract him. "What?" he said.

"I said it sounds like it's broken. You should sling it out, Dad. Just sling it out."

Ernest said he didn't want to sling it out; there was far too much slinging out going on these days. What with Blackie and with Lizzie and with, what was her name, Jane, yes, Billy's own wife, Jane, you can't keep slinging out everything when it gets broken, what about trying to mend things for a change? And Billy started to argue, and Ernest said he was sorry, and he *was* sorry, it was none of his business, of course. And he looked around desperately, trying to find something urgent that could end this phone call, get him free—and that's when he saw the television actually *leak* blood, no longer dripping in red but spattering out thick and black, and Ernest hung up on his still protesting son.

Static

The blood lay in the bowl, warm, sticky like tar. Again, Ernest wondered whether it really *was* blood, but when he put his fingers to it they came away with the same tell-tale coppery smell. BBC2 was still playing snooker, but there was interference now; the picture kept strobing, as if it were in distress. Ernest quickly turned the knob to off, and then looked at the ailing set uncertainly.

He wished Lizzie were there. He often wished Lizzie were there, of course—but never quite as fiercely as he did now. She would know what to do.

On the shelves in the bathroom were a whole array of medical bits and pieces, most of them bought by Lizzie, so probably now out of date. Ointments, tablets in all different colours, painkillers that should be taken with food, some to be taken after food, and others to be taken as far away from food as possible. These were all useless, of course; if his television didn't have the right socket for a video recorder it clearly wouldn't have one for paracetamol either . . . And for just a second Ernest wondered whether his thoughts were altogether rational, but then he found a whole box full of plasters and put the worry out of his head.

Lying beneath the television set, Ernest struggled with the sticky covering of the bandages, trying to pull them from first one finger then another. He still couldn't see where the TV's wound was, but the greater quantity of blood at least gave him a better clue, and he liberally pasted all possible areas with Elastoplast Extra. He felt a growl in his hip, and he crawled out onto the carpet, caught his breath.

Lizzie would have been so *good* at this. She was never fazed by the sight of blood, not hers nor anybody else's. He remembered that evening when Blackie had started coughing. She'd been dozing on the armchair as usual, making her little whinny snore—she'd been dozing and whinnying rather a lot recently. At first they had both laughed, because the coughing had woken her up, and the expression on Blackie's face had been so scandalized—she'd always been a haughty dog, and that such an ugly sound could have disturbed her, and, even worse, that the ugliness had come from *her*, clearly appalled her. When they'd seen, though, that she'd been bringing up gobbets of black, and Ernest had begun to panic—what was going on, what should they do?—it had been Lizzie who had taken charge.

"Go and get a towel," she'd said. "Go on." And she'd cradled Blackie's head, wiped the glop from the mouth without a qualm, comforted her.

"Is it blood?"

"It's bile. And bring me the phone. I'll need to call the vet."

They'd stroked Blackie to calm her down, but she'd clearly been in some distress. And whenever they thought the coughing had stopped, that their dog had miraculously been restored to full health, off she'd start again. "I've made an appointment, first thing tomorrow morning," said Lizzie. "We'll have to keep Blackie in the kitchen tonight, close the door so she can't get out."

"Why?" asked Ernest.

"It'll be easier to clean up the bile if we keep her off the carpets." He'd carried Blackie down the stairs in his arms—such a big dog, such a dead weight. Normally Blackie would have cried and scratched to have been shut in the kitchen—she'd both cry and scratch merely to be shut away from her rightful place, at the foot of her mistress' bed. But she didn't make a sound of complaint as he'd closed the door on her, leaving her her favourite rug and her favourite cushion and her favourite squeaky toy. In the morning Ernest had opened the door, and Blackie didn't appear to have moved from where he'd put her. Just for a moment he had a horrid thrill that she might have died in the night, just unexpectedly, she might have saved them the bother of having to . . .—but no, when he'd called her name she'd raised her head slowly and incuriously. By the side he'd seen further traces of brown black gunk.

"It's the kidneys," the vet had said. "There's really not a lot you can do."

"Oh dear," Ernest had replied. His wife hadn't said anything, her mouth set in hard decision.

"Can't you fix her?" Ernest had gone on. "I mean, I know there are kidney transplants and things . . ."

"Not for dogs," the vet had said. "Blackie could struggle on for a while longer, I can give some medicine. But the quality of her life would be drastically reduced, and she'd never be comfortable. I think you should strongly consider putting her to sleep."

Ernest had made to protest, but "Do it," Lizzie had said suddenly, and he'd shut up.

The vet shaved Blackie's foreleg, and the whole while Lizzie and Ernest had stroked Blackie's head, reassuring her. "It'll all be all right soon," Lizzie had promised her, "no more pain soon." There was a syringe, it was in and out, and before Ernest could change his mind, before he could say, no, wait, this is wrong, we're not trying *hard* enough, Blackie seemed to stiffen then slouch, and her eyes grew harder. And greyer. And wetter, or maybe that was just Ernest's.

"They didn't have the parts," he said to himself now, as he put a fresh Tupperware bowl underneath his poor sick television. "They didn't have the parts, you see."

The next morning the plasters had come off. The blood had seeped through, made them sodden, and they'd fallen into the Tupperware with the rest of the matter. At first Ernest was heartened to see that the blood was red rather than the thick black he had been dreading—red seemed so much healthier somehow—but to counter that, there was rather a lot of it. When he'd gone to bed, the bowl had had no more than a few specks in it. Now it was lapping at the rim.

Ernest found a bigger bowl—one from Lizzie's brief but fondly remembered cake-baking exploits. And he was washing out the older one when the doorbell rang. He was still in his pyjamas and wasn't expecting anyone.

"What do you want?" he asked Billy. And it wasn't just Billy either—there was his wife, and those two children.

"I told you I was coming today, Dad," said Billy. "Don't you remember?" He stepped past him into the hallway. Billy looked frail and a little feminine, and not unlike his mother. It hurt Ernest to be reminded of how she'd once looked; it hurt him even more to see her features cut off, rearranged, and pasted so inaccurately upon this ineffectual man standing there. Standing so awkwardly, as if he were a stranger, as if he wasn't even his son. "You're in your pyjamas," Billy pointed out.

"I know."

"Yes. Right."

And after him trailed the two kids, barely concealing their disinterest, and then the wife. Oh, no, she wasn't the wife, was she? That was the other one, before he'd got the divorce.

"Hello," he said to the children, wishing he could remember their names. "Hello," he said to the woman who wasn't the wife, and therefore wasn't called Jane, he mustn't do that again.

"We've brought you presents, Dad," said Billy. And indeed, the two children were each laden down with a cardboard box. "Put them down here, kids. That's it."

"Would you like a cup of tea?" asked Ernest.

"I'll make some tea," said the woman, and disappeared into the kitchen. This left Ernest with nothing to do but be drawn back to the cardboard box, which, he supposed, was the idea.

"What is it?" he asked, when Billy opened the first one and took out some gadget or another.

"It's an answering machine," said Billy. "You know, for the phone."

"Why would I want one of those? Nobody phones me anyway."

"That's not true, Dad," Billy said patiently. "*I* phone. I phoned yesterday, and you didn't answer, I had to phone again. And it would make me feel much happier, if that happens again, that I could leave you some sort of message. No, don't do that," he said to the children. Ernest didn't want to see what they'd been doing.

"If it makes you happier," said Ernest, not, he felt, unreasonably, "then it's more a present for you than it is for me."

"If you say so, Dad," said Billy with a sigh. The woman emerged from the kitchen with tea. "Shall we go to the sitting room?" he suggested.

"When can we go home?" one of the children asked its mother, as it flopped into Lizzie's favourite armchair.

"Ssh," she said, "not yet."

"But I'm bored," said the child.

Ernest stole a look of worry at the television set in the corner. He supposed it was resting, and if it were sick, it needed all the rest it could get. He didn't want its peace disturbed.

"And here's your other present," said Billy, with just a hint of playfulness. "Ta-dah! . . . There you are, you see."

It was another television. Newer, shinier, smaller, and a damn sight more plasticky than Ernest's own.

"I don't want it," he said.

"Come on, Dad," said Billy.

"I already have a television set," said Ernest.

Billy laughed. "This old thing?" he said. "You had that when I was a kid!"

"Forty-eight years," said Ernest. "I bought it the month after I married your mother." It had been one of those little peculiarities in her that he had never got used to. Most of the time she'd been so practical, so careful with money. But once in a while, right up to the end, she could surprise him, could indulge in a bit of a "splurge," as she'd called it. The honeymoon had worked out cheaper than either of them had expected. Both of them supposed that the sensible thing would be to put the leftover in the bank, but Lizzie had grinned at him a little wickedly and said, "Well, we *could* be sensible. Or we could just splurge out and buy ourselves a television set." He'd laughed, but she'd been serious, and so that's what they'd done.

He supposed it was the thing that had kept their marriage fresh. All those little surprises. "I've got cancer," she told him one day.

"Oh," Ernest had said. "Oh dear."

"I don't know what can be done, my darling. I don't know, I'm sorry." And she'd kissed him with so much tenderness, and he'd hugged on to her. He hadn't wanted to cry, he had to be the strong one—and, looking back, he supposed she'd felt exactly the same thing.

A few nights later he had been lying next to her in bed. After that hug they hadn't mentioned the cancer again. As if ignoring it would make it go away. "You know I'm dying," she'd said to him in the dark.

"I don't want to think about it."

"I know, darling. I know you don't. But it's there." And she had held him close. "I'm not going to get better, you know. I'm only going to get worse. I've been reading up on it in the library."

"You think you know everything," Ernest had said to her, not without spite. "But you don't."

"It would be easier, it seems to me," she'd said there, in that thick darkness, and it had seemed to Ernest to get thicker, to make his head swim, "if we just stopped it now. You could, you know. You could give me a kiss. Say goodbye. And put a pillow over my face. And that'd be an end to it."

Ernest couldn't, and wouldn't, he said he couldn't and wouldn't . . .

"I know, darling," Lizzie had said, perfectly placidly. "I know." His poor Lizzie, who'd never even smoked, dying of lung cancer.

"I'm popping into the garden for a cigarette," said the woman who wasn't married to his son.

Billy waved her on with a smile. One of the kids ran out after her. The other was too busy wrecking the armchair. Billy moved toward the old television, sick and neglected in the corner, and no doubt trying to sleep through all the noise. "What are you doing?" asked Ernest. "No."

"I'll unplug this one, put the new one in. My God, it's ancient. You said yourself, it was broken."

"I said it was bleeding," said Ernest. "Not broken. Look at the bowl underneath." But, of course, he'd just changed bowls, this one was fresh and clean. "I said, don't!" he said, more sharply, and pushed his son back. Billy looked at him in surprise. "I bought that with your mother," he said. "I bought it with her."

Billy stared at his father for a few seconds. "I miss her too," he said at last.

"You have no idea," Ernest almost spat. "You have no idea. You had your wife, what was her name . . . ?"

"Jane."

"Jane. That's it. And then you threw her away. Her and the grandchildren, you threw her away. And now you're here with another woman, and children who aren't even your own. It's all fucked up."

"Dad, Graham's still here, he can hear you . . ."

"It broke your mother's heart. It did. She said to me, why'd he sling her out, Ernie, why'd people just sling things out? She never forgave you, you know. Not ever. Not even when she died. The last thing she said to me, and I was there when she died, I stood over her, she said, I'll never forgive Billy, never."

Billy breathed long and hard through his nose. Ernest wasn't sure if the boy was going to cry or punch him. One or the other, he thought, do get on with it. This kid of his, this kid who had kids of his own, and kids that weren't *even* his own, what sense did that make? This kid of his, who looked like Lizzie reassembled by an idiot.

But the Lizzie look-alike didn't cry or punch; he finished that funny breathing thing, then bent down, back toward the television. "We'll just swap these over," he muttered. "Then we'll get out of your way."

"Don't touch it," said Ernest. "You'll hurt it. It's sick. If you must give me a television, for God's sake, put it in the kitchen."

Billy straightened up. "You don't want a TV in the kitchen, Dad. This would be much more comfortable. With your nice chair, look . . ."

"There's a perfectly nice chair in the kitchen. I want it in the kitchen. Leave my old set alone. Put the new one in the kitchen."

"William, just put it in the kitchen, if that's what your father wants." So said the non-wife, stepping back through the door.

"Right," said Billy. "Of course. Fine." And he picked the new TV up, carried it downstairs without another word.

There was silence in the sitting room as Billy worked away. "Thank you, Jane," said Ernest at last. The woman ignored him.

"Mummy, I'm bored," said a child, who may or may not have been the one called Graham.

"I know. We'll be going soon."

And indeed they were. "That's the answering machine plugged in," said Billy. "And the TV. Shall I show you how to . . ."

"No," said Ernest. And he closed the door behind them.

Ernest all but ran upstairs to the sitting room, as fast as his hip would allow. "I'm sorry," he said to the television. "We're alone now, I'm sorry." There was still no blood in the Tupperware bowl, and for a moment Ernest thought his poor patient had come to no further harm.

But when he turned it on, he saw that the snowy fuzz that was BBC1 was no longer just grey. It was red too. And getting redder. All the dots of static fizzing in a frenzy, punching themselves against the screen, punch punch. And Ernest watched with horror as the screen began to bulge out under the pressure of them all, and a hairline fracture traced its way from one diagonal to the other, and then . . .

. . . Out gushed the blood. Red and black, thick and coppery. It exploded out, over the room, over Ernest. "Oh dear!" he cried, and then, because he'd let it out anyway, so why not?—"This is fucked up, this is so fucked up." It felt good to say that, to admit that truth at last after so many months of pretending everything *wasn't* fucked up, he felt so much better as he stood in the centre of his sitting room, his pyjamas dripping with the blood of an elderly television set. He even allowed himself a smile.

Ernest waded over to the TV. "Do you feel better now too?" he asked, putting his arms around it soothingly. "There, there," he assured it, "better out than in. It'll be all right now."

He felt he should dry himself off, but knew too that it would be heartless to abandon his poor television when it was suffering so badly. How would it look, he being so perfectly well and happy, to be worried about his personal *cleanliness* of all things? And it wasn't unpleasant, this sensation of blood, on his hands, in his hair, even in his mouth: it warmed him, calmed him. So he stayed in the room. The blood could wait, all this mess, the gunk over him, over the new answering machine (was it?), over Lizzie's favourite armchair . . . He wouldn't abandon the invalid now.

He remembered how, near the end, Lizzie had begun to cough blood. "Never mind," she would say, as she would dab at her mouth as pertly as if she'd been eating chicken, "never mind." But, of course, he *did* mind, how could he not mind? Sometimes in the night he'd wake next to her, find her pillow drenched in the stuff. She'd asked him to move to the spare room so she wouldn't disturb him, but he'd refused—he'd wanted to take care of her. And he'd only relented when she'd said it was for her sake,

God, please, Ernie, it was for her, it was for *her*.

She'd come to his room one night. Stood at the doorway, silhouetted against the landing light. "What is it?" he'd said. "Are you ill?" Which was, even looking back, a pretty stupid thing to say.

"I don't want to go back to the hospital tomorrow," she'd told him. "I'm sick of it. If I go in," she'd said, "I'll never come out again. This isn't how I want to go."

"No, Lizzie," Ernest had said, and then cried. "I can't do it. I can't do to you . . . what we did to Blackie. I can't."

She'd climbed into bed next to him. "No," she'd said. "We could just go, though, couldn't we? Just get in the car, and go."

"Go where?" he'd asked, sniffing away his tears.

"Somewhere else. Anywhere else. And never come back. No more hospitals. We've got lots of money saved, we could have a splurge, couldn't we? We could splurge it all out."

"It'd kill you," he'd said.

"Yes," she'd said. And she'd said no more, but spent that night with him after all. And the next morning he'd taken her to the hospital, just as they'd always planned. And Lizzie had been right—she had never come out again. He wasn't there when she'd died a few days later. He'd wanted to say goodbye, be beside her bed when it happened. But you can't be there all the time, can you?

Ernest woke up, found he'd been dozing again. His television was on, but the static behind the split glass looked reassuringly grey and normal. His stomach growled. "I'm going to get some lunch," he told the television. "But I shan't be long. I promise."

In the kitchen he found some bread and some butter. Ideal for a sandwich. He also found the new television set. He'd forgotten it was there. "Ugly little thing," he told it.

He picked up the remote control, turned it over in his hand. And then—and he didn't think he'd pressed any of the buttons, but he supposed he must have—the television sprang to life. It was clear and it was sharp and it was *colourful*, my God, there was more colour on that screen than you got in real life, but principally it was *loud*. "Shut up," he told it in alarm. He stabbed at all the buttons he could find. He didn't hit the one to turn it off, but he did succeed in turning down the volume. "Keep quiet," he hissed at it angrily. "There's a sick television up there, and it's better than you. And I don't want it getting any funny ideas that you're its replacement. That wouldn't be nice, would it?"

And then he fell silent. Stared at the screen, his sandwich forgotten.

It was BBC2, and it was the snooker. The table was green—oh, it was such a green, you could imagine this was a snooker table only played upon by angels! Someone was lining up a shot, and with the perfect clarity of the image Ernest could see it wasn't Ray Reardon, this man was young and short and scruffy even in his dinner jacket.

But it was the *balls*. The white and the black and the pink and the . . . so many reds, so many, all like the apple the Wicked Queen gave Snow White in that film, but nine of them, so plump and shiny and red you could *bite* them. He looked at the red on his arms and clothes, the blood from upstairs, and it wasn't nearly so impressive.

The snooker player sank a red. And then a brown. Everyone applauded. Ernest had to sit down.

All these years, with his black and white television, he'd never been able to tell the red and the brown apart. It had caused some confusion. But Ernest knew that you could work out which was which, so long as you were patient, so long as you used your brain. The brown was put back up on the table, but the red, once potted, stayed down. Not knowing whether the player had miscued as he cannoned into the ball in question lent an extra soupcon of suspense to the game that Ernest knew he wouldn't have experienced seeing the game live—his snooker, in all its monochrome ambiguity, was *better*. And here was this new television. This colour television. Making it all so *easy*. Explaining everything. As if its viewers were children. Idiots. To be patronized. Ernest looked around the kitchen, considered the rows of Tupperware bowls he'd been using. No, he'd need something heavier. The saucepan, that would do. He drove it hard into the television screen. Into all its colour and clarity and condescension. It fizzed and popped and banged.

When he went back upstairs, he saw that the snooker was playing on his black and white set as well. Though he hadn't changed channels, as far as he could remember. But it was a different game—look, this time it was Ray Reardon. That was good. Ernest preferred Ray Reardon.

"Hello, Ernie," said Ray Reardon.

"Hello, Ray," Ernest replied.

"I'm in such pain, Ernie," said Ray. "So why don't you take that saucepan of yours, and smash my snooker-playing face in? Put me out of my misery."

"All right," said Ernest. And he lined up the saucepan, as if swinging a golf club. Come on, Ray gestured, come on, it'll be all right. And then frowned as Ernest lowered his arms.

"I can't," said Ernest.

"Why not? You murdered that TV downstairs."

"I know," said Ernest. "But I can't. I can't let you down the way I did Blackie. Or the way I did Lizzie, either. I suppose," he added, a little embarrassed, "I love you, Ray. I suppose that's what it is."

Ray stuck out his bottom lip, then rubbed his eyes, making boo-hoo gestures. Then he winked to show he was only kidding. And his face faded back into the snowstorm.

"Bye, Ray," said Ernest.

He dropped the saucepan. He knew he wouldn't be needing it. And he went close to the television, knelt before it. He put his arms around it the best he could, gave a squeeze to its unyielding bulk. "I love you," he said once more. And he slept happily, a man who feared he'd never love again.

He was woken once more by the sound of the telephone. He stretched his arms painfully, surprised he'd slept in so uncomfortable a position that soundly. He decided to ignore the ringing, cuddle back next to the television, and snuggle. But the answering machine kicked in.

"Hello, Dad? It's me. Look, I . . . I'm sorry about yesterday. I wasn't in the best of moods, I think, the kids were driving me mad, and I . . . I'm sorry I snapped at you. It was silly. Look, I don't know but . . . I thought I'd come over again. Just me this time. Would that be okay? Just the two of us. We haven't talked, not really, I thought we could talk. About Mum, I miss her, you know, I know you do too . . . well, obviously. And I can show you how your new TV works. Hope it's okay, it's not new or anything, just an old cast-off, didn't want to sling it out. And I'll take away that old one for you . . . I love you, Dad. Don't say that enough. Must say it more, I think. Love you."

And the voice clicked off.

"Shit," said Ernest. He looked at the room, all the blood, all the mess. "Shit," he said again. And then, "Come on, we haven't much time."

The television set wasn't as heavy as he'd expected. But as for all the leads and plugs—it was like spaghetti back there! Ernest didn't have time to work out which wire connected to what, just pulled out as many as would set the television free, and hoped for the best. With a grunt, both arms stretched as far around the box as they could go, he took it from the table on which it had sat so many years. And puffing, ignoring the pain in his hands, in his back, the *screaming* pain in his hip, he edged toward the stairs. One foot shuffled forward, then the other. It looked as if he were dancing.

When he reached the top of the steps he was able to balance the television on the banister rail, catch his breath. It reminded him of having to carry Blackie to the kitchen all those years ago. "But I'm not taking you to the vet's," he promised the set. "You'll see."

Halfway down, the doorbell rang. Ernest froze. Peering through the banisters he saw the face of his son fractured and misshapen through the frosted glass.

"I'm not letting them take you now," whispered Ernest.

Billy had parked out front. But it was all right. It was fine. Because Ernest's car was in the garage. And he could get into the garage by the side door, and if he were quick, Billy would never notice. His muscles protested—they couldn't *go* any quicker. But Ernest insisted. No one else was going to be slung out. There was going to be an end to all slinging.

"Dad?" he heard, as Billy knocked against the door. "Dad, are you in there?"

But Ernest had reached the car. He had to set the television down for a moment as he fumbled for his keys—he marvelled at his thin fingers, how bruised and squashed they now looked. But he didn't feel anything, not a thing. With a final heave, he lifted the television into the passenger seat. Smiled at it. And then, with a sudden wave of concern, he pulled the seatbelt across it. "Got to keep you safe," he said, as he climbed in next to it.

"Where are we going?" the television didn't ask.

"Somewhere else," said Ernest. "Anywhere else." He turned the ignition, the car pulled out of the garage. He thought he caught sight of Billy's surprised face at the front door, but he couldn't be sure—he was travelling *so* fast, after all, so very fast, never faster. "And we'll never come back," he said, as he put his foot flat on the accelerator, and sped away onward to freedom.

THE CONSTANTINOPLE ARCHIVES

i

We can speculate, and we can speculate, but the probability is that few of the silent movies made during the siege of Constantinople in 1453 were very much good. And there are clear reasons for this, both political and cultural.

On the one hand, we have to bear in mind the extremely trying circumstances under which the movies were being filmed. In attacking Constantinople, the Ottoman Turks were also attacking the last bastion of the Roman Empire (if only in symbolic form), a direct line of power that stretched back some two thousand years. It was also the seat of the Orthodox Christian Church, a force equal and opposite to the Catholic Church in Rome. Expansionist wars were two a penny in the fifteenth century, but this was no run of the mill example, it was already rife with meaning, and no doubt the Byzantines under threat would have been only too aware of that. Besides which, on a purely practical level, the constant cannoning of the city walls must surely have been a distraction. Even making silent movies, surely, some peace and quiet is required for concentration's sake.

On the other hand, and perhaps more pertinently, Byzantine art had always defined itself by a certain flat austerity. Their mosaics and paintings that we can study today are colourful, but there's a grim functionality to all that colour: the lines are severely drawn and make the characters depicted seem two-dimensional and un-dramatic. It would be foolish to expect that in the creation of an entire new art form several centuries of engrained Byzantine culture would be abandoned overnight. It is unfair to imagine that the clowns who pratfalled and danced and poked each other in the eyes in Constantinople cinema were other Chaplins, or Keatons, even other Fatty Arbuckles. The conditions were wrong. Their genius could not have flowered.

And yet, of course, we remain fascinated by those movies from the Byzantine age. And again, partly this will be because they were the pioneers, the history of cinema begins here with these shadowy figures by the Bosphorus doomed to be killed or enslaved by the Muslim potentate. But I hope our fascination is not purely academic. That we honour not merely the historical significance of what was invented, but that, with care and study, and an open mind, we try to appreciate the art on its own terms.

ii

No entire print of a Byzantine movie survives, and that is to be expected. When the sultan Mahomet II appealed to the Byzantines to surrender, with the promise that their lives would be spared, his terms were rejected. The Byzantine emperor, Constantine XI Palaiologos, said that the city could not be yielded, for it was no single man's possession to yield. And with these brave words he sealed the fate of the fifty thousand inhabitants of Constantinople, and, more importantly, the fate of those few precious cans of film kept within. The Turks had besieged Constantinople for fifty-five days. They were tired and angry. When they broke the defences, as was the custom, the soldiers had permission to ransack and pillage the city for three whole days, taking plunder, razing buildings to the ground, and raping and slaughtering the populace. These were not conditions in which a fledgling film industry was ever likely to prosper.

And yet, we are lucky. In spite of all, some sequences of film are extant. They are fragments only, most no more than a few seconds long, but they still afford us a tantalizing impression of early cinematography, and what those Byzantine audiences must have enjoyed. One man tries to sit down upon a stool, and a second pulls it away, so he falls to the ground with his legs splayed in the air. A farmer waters his crops with a bucket of water, but a prankster holds it upright; when the farmer pours the bucket over his head to see what's wrong, he gets soaked. It is not sophisticated comedy, granted, but there is a spirit of mocking fun to it;

yes, it plays upon the weak and the vulnerable, but no one gets hurt, no one gets savaged, and certainly no one experiences the sort of carnage that is awaiting them at the end of the siege. Some historians have tried to read a political subtext into the extracts, but I think that can be exaggerated. One of the more (justly) admired sequences is of a beggar, or tramp, who at dinner sticks a knife into two vegetables and proceeds to do a puppet dance with them. In siege times food was scarce, and this flagrant disregard for its value can be seen as something deliberately provocative, a renunciation of the very crisis that would have caused the food shortage in the first place, and thus a renunciation of war. But what attracts us to the film is not its message, but its simple beauty: there is such elegance to the dance, and to the comic conceit of it, and for the duration the tramp smiles out at the viewer in childlike innocence.

One might have expected that there would have been a pronounced propagandist element to the films. But the Ottoman Turks are never referenced, and instead what is offered to us is cheap comedy and heightened melodrama. The longest extant extract—and, sadly, one of the most tedious—is a case in point. A moustachioed villain, sniggering silently to camera, ties a damsel in distress to a set of railway tracks. The damsel is left there for no fewer than six minutes of static inaction, as we wait for a train to come and flatten her; however, since we are many centuries shy of the invention of a locomotive engine, it is unclear how much jeopardy the girl can really be in. The tracks are not the important part; it is the villain. Wearing a gabardine common in fashion at the time, he looks like an everyday Byzantine. He's not given a turban, or a Muslim beard, or shifty Oriental eyes. It's the ideal opportunity for the filmmaker to identify and feed off a common threat to the audience, but it refuses to do so; even in its monsters, Byzantine cinema remains stubbornly domestic.

Many eyewitnesses recorded the siege of Constantinople for posterity, and the most celebrated is George Sphrantzes. Sphrantzes recounts the conflict from a mostly militaristic perspective, and pays depressingly little heed to the day-to-day to and fro of the thriving visual arts scene. Nevertheless, he does record in his diary how, one evening, shortly after the siege had been raised, he was ushered into a big hall alongside some other hundreds of citizens. There he took a seat, and the windows were covered with sacks, and the room was cast into darkness. He describes an expectation in the audience, something apprehensive, like fear, but more pleasurable than fear. And then, at the end of the room, facing them all, a large piece of white cloth was illuminated. He writes: "At first I thought there was a stain upon it, and then the stain enlarged, as if by magick." It was no stain; it was the image of a horse and cart, and its approach toward the camera. George Sphrantzes describes the awe and wonder as the "moving painting" flickered upon the makeshift screen—and then the rising panic as it became clear that the horse and cart were coming directly at them. People rose from their seats; they stumbled toward the exit; they fell over in the darkness—if they didn't escape, within *minutes* the cart would reach them and there might be an irritating bump. Sphrantzes records how the authorities arrested the man in charge of the exhibition for disturbing the peace.

No name of any actor has survived the fall of Constantinople. But the name of that man *has* survived, and he must be regarded as the first maverick genius of cinema. His name was Matthew Tozer.

iii

It is all too easy to be seduced by images of the Byzantine Empire as a thing of great glory. That was true at its zenith, but its zenith was centuries past. By the time the Ottoman Turks lay siege to Constantinople, the empire had shrunk to little more than a city state, and the population within were a random ragtag of different nationalities from different backgrounds. Matthew Tozer (or Toza, or Tusa) was probably a Greek Cypriot, but his name is peculiar and no one can say for sure. There is no physical description of the man. There is no record of his beliefs, or anything he stood for—save his obvious love for the cinematic medium.

It is not even clear what Tozer's part in the craze was, merely that he was at the very centre of it. Had he invented the principle of moving photography himself? Was he instead the director of the films, exploiting someone else's discoveries? It is possible that he merely ran the cinema in which the movies were shown. Scientist, artist, entrepreneur—scholars argue which of them he may have been. Maybe there is no single Matthew Tozer. This essay does not purport to take any great interest in specious biography. For simplicity's sake we shall assume Tozer is all three rolled into one: not so much a man, but a personification of a new art form. We can never know Tozer the individual; let us instead study Tozer the wave of revolution.

The earliest account we have of Tozer is what we now refer to as the "Horse and Cart Debacle." Punishment in the middle ages was typically severe, especially in times of military crisis. But within days Tozer has been freed, and moreover, is showing new films, we can only suppose with the blessing of the authorities. Sphrantzes writes again, after a turgid account of a day setting up the city's defences, and his concerns of a maritime engagement with the Turkish fleet: "And, in the evening, to the picture house, there to see a comedic play about three men and a mule. Silly stuff. Amiable."

Sphrantzes might dismiss it as silly stuff, but it is clear that Tozer was doing something right. He set up a cinema just a stone's throw from the Hagia Sofia, and there he'd show the latest movie releases—and the people of Constantinople began to flock to them in droves. It is important to remember what siege conditions were like in the fifteenth century. They were frightening, yes, and they were desperate, and they were hungry, but mostly they were very *boring*. With the Ottoman Turks on one side, and a naval blockade upon the other, there was really very little for the Byzantine folk to go and do in the evenings. However silly the movies on offer may have been, the distractions they provided were hugely popular, and tickets became highly prized; one anonymous commentator writes that to get in to see one particular blockbuster, a family bartered a week's supply of precious bread. Tozer was forced to put on more and more screenings, sometimes letting his cinema run all night until dawn. He employed janissary bands to accompany the films with the music of harp, lyre, and zither; he employed young girls to serve sweet snacks in the intervals.

And what Tozer was accomplishing was not merely artistic, but also sociological. Because if these citizens of a dying empire were merely desperate stragglers with no real identity, here, at least, they could find something that unified them. They could sit in the dark together and laugh and cry as one collective. Is it too much to hope that at last they discovered that they had more in common with their fellow man than they had realized—that the same stunts thrilled them, the same custard pie fights kept them amused? Is this the irony of the end of the Byzantines, that only in their final days they became a proper people?

As for Tozer, he appears to have worked tirelessly. With almost superhuman energy he released several new movies a week, filming them during the day and presenting the results on screen once the sun went down. To satisfy the appetite of a citizenry starved of entertainment, he produced an oeuvre that makes Steven Spielberg look like some dilettante hobbyist. And with the introduction of a new art form, inevitably the people are inspired; they are no longer content to be mere spectators, they want to take part in the art form too. Sphrantzes complains, but when does Sphrantzes not complain? He writes that the most pressing concern the Byzantine population faced was the Muslim hordes outside the gates, and that work should be done repairing those gates, building new walls, training all able bodied men to fight. Instead everybody wanted to be an actor, to star in the movies, to see themselves flicker on the white cloth screens, to be famous, to be adored.

The greatest tragedy of the fall of Constantinople is that not one frame of Matthew Tozer's masterpiece, *The Ten Commandments*, survives. A true epic, it ran for nearly six hours, and used over a thousand extras. It was a gamble on Tozer's part; to find time to make it he had to close the cinema for three full days, and there was civil unrest and small-scale rioting whilst the people were left starved of their fix. But the gamble paid off. It is a testament not only to Tozer's vaulting ambition but to his commercial canniness—even if you weren't in the movie yourself you knew someone who was, and if you saw only one movie that season it had to be *The Ten Commandments*! The sets, by all reports, were sumptuous. The cast were on peak form. And the special effects were remarkable: to achieve the parting of the Red Sea, Tozer had used up a half of the besieged city's water supply.

It was Tozer's greatest achievement. Emperor Constantine XI Palaiologos took time off being the champion of the Orthodox Church to attend the premiere, and had even taken a cameo role as a burning bush. Could Tozer have suspected that it was all downhill from here? And that all that ambition would prove his undoing?

iv

On 29th May 1453, the Ottoman Turks broke through the walls of Constantinople. Their troops numbered some one hundred thousand to the Byzantines' seven thousand. The Turkish flag was flown from the battlements, and many of the Christian defenders lost heart. Emperor Constantine XI Palaiologos himself declared, "The city is fallen and I am still alive," and he tore off his purple cloak of majesty, and entered the fray as a common soldier. His body was never found. The Byzantine people fought bravely, but with a certain dispassion perhaps, a certain defeatism.

The talkie movies had not been a success.

Matthew Tozer had been experimenting with sound for a little while now. He would have the orchestra time their drum beats to the exact moment an explosion appeared on screen, to give the impression that the bang had come from the movie itself. It was witty, but it was a gimmick, and the audience enjoyed it as a gimmick. When at the end of May Tozer announced the premiere of the first proper talking picture, with full dialogue and a pre-recorded score, the people were incredulous, then doubtful, then baffled.

Some extracts survive. As film historians it is impossible not to appreciate what Tozer is attempting. But in practice, as casual viewers, we would have to judge it doesn't work. Tozer has not found a way to make the sound sync accurately to the image; it is rarely more than a second or two out, but that jarring second makes everything seem imprecise and unreal, even eerie. And the voices of the actors are not what we might expect. We see the tramp again. In the silent movies he demonstrates a charm that is both winning and humane. In the sound rushes, he reveals he has a high-pitched voice like a strangled dolphin. The charm is gone. So, too, is the illusion.

As the Turks invade, so Tozer's picture house is burned to the ground. It is not clear whether the Turks or the Byzantines are to blame.

V

Matthew Tozer's fate is unknown. Many people fled the city, and there is every chance that he too might have escaped. But if he did, there is no record of his attempting to make any more films. Either Tozer becomes like Emperor Constantine, one of those anonymous casualties who were lost in the battle—or he survives, in exile, disillusioned, thinking himself a failure and his art form a failure, rejecting his talents and never returning to them for as long as he lives.

Is it wrong to hope that he was butchered by Turks? Is it wrong to wish for him that one little mercy?

Historical opinion has turned against Tozer in recent years. The argument is that without his interference the population would not have been distracted, and would have been better prepared to repel the Ottoman conquest. Professor Kettering has even published his theories that Tozer was a Turkish spy, deliberately undermining the morale of the Byzantines from within with his dreadful movies; it is a theory that I find at once both absurd and heinous, though nothing Kettering says anymore should surprise me.

What is harder to dispute is Tozer's legacy. Sadly, it is negligible. The footage of Tozer's movies was only discovered in a basement in Ankara in the 1920s. By the time Tozer's advances came to light, the motion picture industry was already in full swing. The great filmmakers of the 1890s, Lumière, Michon, Méliès, all reinvented cinema without ever realizing Matthew Tozer had been there first. Mack Sennett produced his movies without Tozer's influence; David O. Selznick, head of production at RKO Pictures, famously viewed the recovered prints of Tozer's films, shrugged, and asked what all the fuss was about: "It's already been done."

And yet surely we cannot write off Matthew Tozer as a failure. We must not.

When we see the history of the world put before us, it's easy to think it's just a catalogue of wars and genocidal atrocities. Of peoples conquering peoples, and then getting conquered in turn. That the development of Mankind has been nothing more than an exercise in studying new acts of brutality to be turned against still larger sizes of population. That, in effect, all Mankind's inspirations are directed toward evil.

But what then of Matthew Tozer? What then of that spark to *create*, to produce art for art's sake, if only because it wasn't in existence before? To take a population and want not to decimate it or enslave it, but instead crowd it together, into one room, into the dark, and make it laugh? And maybe with Matthew Tozer the spark didn't die. Maybe the spark lasted out the centuries, just waiting for the right conditions in which to take fire. Maybe, in spite of all, Matthew Tozer and the better impulse will win out.

We can speculate. And, oh, we can speculate, we can imagine, we can dream. Sometimes I think that's the true gift Matthew Tozer left us.

YOUR LONG, LOVING ARMS

In the end it was the afternoons that were killing him. The evenings were fine. The evenings he could cope with. He wasn't working in the evenings, it was true, but that was okay, lots of people didn't work in the evenings. He'd play with Ben a bit, like a normal dad, might read him a bedside story if Ben fancied it. Like a normal dad, and in a normal family too, he'd cuddle up with Cheryl on the sofa and they'd watch a spot of telly, and at last Cheryl would say that she'd best get to bed, she had to be up early in the morning. And he'd go with her, though he didn't have to be up early, not anymore. And mornings were okay. He could ignore the mornings. At quarter past seven the alarm would wake them both, and Cheryl would kiss him on the head, and tell him she loved him, and get up to rouse Ben. At first he'd get up when she did, but she said there was no need— Steve, she'd say, why not lie in? Steve, you may as well lie in. And so he'd lie in, and shortly after eight he'd hear Cheryl and Ben leave the house and close the front door behind them. For the first few weeks he'd doze until nine-ish, then nine thirty. Recently though he'd crossed the line; as he lay buried in the darkness he'd tell himself that so long as he was up by noon it'd be all right, that'd still mean he wasn't sleeping the entire morning. He wouldn't need to feel guilty, he'd still be normal. But now he was finding he wasn't opening the curtains 'til as late as twelve fifteen, even twelve twenty once. And as he'd blink out into the sunlight, he'd see that the world outside hadn't ended, the world had continued without him, and he was now firmly stuck in the afternoon, and it weighed down his very soul.

Yeah, in the end, it was the afternoons that did it for him. That and the conversation he'd had after dinner one evening. Steve had asked Ben what he'd been up to at school that day, and he enjoyed doing that, Ben was always full of stories of new games he'd learned and new friends he'd made. But Ben just looked at him curiously and said, "What did *you* do today, Daddy?" And he didn't have to justify himself to Ben, and Ben didn't even *want* to be justified to, he didn't really care, an hour before bed on the Xbox his grandparents had bought him would keep him happy. But Cheryl had just said, "Yes, Ben, ask your Daddy what he's been up to today." And there was nothing accusing in it, it was as calm as you like, he couldn't even see Cheryl's face, her back was turned as she did the washing up. Steve hadn't answered, and there was an awkward silence— well, awkward to Steve, Ben didn't seem bothered, and Cheryl, Cheryl was still giving fierce attention to the dinner plates. Then Cheryl said something else, it didn't matter what, and it was just as neutral, and the subject was changed. They didn't mention it again; he didn't apologize for being out of work, and she didn't apologize for making him feel bad about it; they cuddled on the sofa, watched TV, then went to bed when Cheryl said it was time.

That weekend he went for a drink with Ray. Ray had been laid off the same time he was. He hadn't seen Ray for a while; at first they'd meet for a pint every few days, and they both took some comfort from that, in shared anecdotes and shared recriminations. But that was back when his unemployment had seemed like a temporary inconvenience, when deep down Steve believed the management would phone him up one day to say sorry and offer him his job back. "Why not give Ray a call, see if he's up for the pub?" Cheryl would say sometimes, and she'd take a tenner from her purse and hold it out for him. And he knew it was his money too, really, some of that was his dole, but it felt like pocket money. Besides, he found Ray hard to face these days. He feared Ray was coping better with his redundancy than he was. But that weekend Cheryl had pressed him, maybe she felt bad about the dinner incident, "Go on," she said, "have a treat," and waved the tenner in front of him. So he phoned Ray. Ray got in the first round, and he told Ray what he'd been planning. "You must be joking," said Ray. "We're skilled labourers. We're engineers. You wouldn't catch me working in a fucking *garden*." And Steve didn't dare tell Ray that garden shifts came later if you were lucky, they started you off in public parks and forests. During the second pint, Ray said, "What you're forgetting is. That it's not our fault we were let go. It's not our fault." During the third pint, Ray asked how much the Tree Scheme would bring in, and then said, "Christ, we'll get more than that staying on the dole." And Steve said that it wasn't about the money, it wasn't about fault, it was the afternoons, the afternoons were just getting longer, didn't Ray find the afternoons were getting longer and longer and there was no end to them? And Ray finished his pint, and said he'd go along to the training with him. You know, just to see what it was like.

Training lasted a day. "Surprised you need a day," said Ray. "After all, all we do is just stand about, isn't it?" No one wanted to sit in the first few rows of the seminar room, but the place was soon packed, and the latecomers had no choice. Free refreshments were available at the back, and dutifully Steve took his plastic cup of orange squash like all the others. At last a man in a suit stood up in front of them all. "A lot of you here today," he said. "But not many of you will make the grade. You probably think there's nothing to this job. Some of you will think you're too good for it. But there's more to the tree than you think. Regulating the carbon dioxide intake, drawing nutrients from the soil with its roots. The tree is a very complex animal." Steve spoke up and said surely it was a plant, not an animal, and Ray sniggered at this, and there was a tittering around the room, but Steve hadn't meant it as a heckle, not really. The man up front pursed his lips. "Yeah, there's always some clever bugger who thinks he knows it all."

Then the man turned on his overhead projector, and outlined on a whiteboard the differences between some of the major trees: those that were fruit bearing, those that were not. He produced graphs of climate change, how an average tree might be affected by differences in rainfall. Then he said he was proud to introduce someone who'd been working as a tree nigh on fifty years, and a grizzled gentleman got up and tried to explain some of the practicalities of the job. He told stories that weren't very interesting and gave tips that were rather confusing, all with a grimness of tone that suggested he was imparting dark secrets of nuclear science. He stressed again that the tree was a complex animal. Then it was lunch: more orange squash, and some cheese sandwiches. "Now it's time to get some experience in the field," said the man, "as it were," and they all filed out of the seminar room, down the stairs, and into the private gardens of the company offices. "We're going to start you off on sycamores. Sycamores are easy. Any fool can do a sycamore." So everyone gave their best stab at a sycamore, and the man walked through the little forest that had sprung up, appraising their efforts. "Good, good, keep steady, good, a little too feral, good." Once in a while he'd take out a stick of white chalk and mark their sides with a little cross. Steve tried so very hard to be a tree; when the man looked him up and down it seemed to take forever, but Steve thought of Cheryl, and of Ben, and he didn't waver, he stayed rooted to the spot. Then, at last, "Good," came the grunt, and Steve was marked with a cross. "We have your details," the man announced to them all at the end of the day. "If we want you, we'll be in touch." And then Steve went home.

And for once Cheryl was waiting for *him* when he got home from work. She threw her arms around him, "I'm so proud of you," she said, and kissed him on the lips, "I love you." She'd made him his favourite meal, a treat for her working man. Even Ben was excited, and he raced around the house, shouting, "Daddy Daddy Daddy!" And although Steve was tired, he really had to laugh at the little feller, "Daddy Daddy!" He half hoped that Ben would ask him over dinner what he'd done that day, but really was relieved he didn't, because he didn't know how to explain that he'd been a big hunk of wood. So they ate their spag bol to Ben's chatter, and Steve and Cheryl hardly said a word, but once in a while Cheryl would prod Steve with her foot under the table and give him a private smile. And for dessert they had ice cream, everyone's favourite. After Ben went to bed, they cuddled on the sofa as always, but they didn't give the telly much attention. Steve tried to explain that it had only been a training day, that there was no guarantee that there'd be a job at the end of it, and Cheryl said, "I know you did your best. It'll all work out. I *believe* in you," and they made love right there and then, and they hadn't done that for ages. It suddenly didn't matter to Steve whether he heard back from the Tree Scheme at all.

But he did. The very next morning he was woken by a phone call. He answered it blearily. "Did I get you up?" said the man on the end sternly. Steve checked the time, and saw that it was nearly half past ten, and assured the man he'd been out of bed for hours. "I'm glad to hear it," said the man. "Now, listen. I want to offer you a job." Steve thanked him. "Don't thank me. This is a probationary period, all right? To see whether you have the right aptitude. So the pay will reflect that, you'll be on the probationary pay, all right?" Steve said it was all right, and thanked him again. "Don't thank me." Steve wasn't sure whether he should phone Ray, if Ray hadn't heard anything he didn't want to crow, but it was okay, Ray phoned him. "You get the job too? Probationary pay. I nearly told them I had a bloody degree, I nearly told them to stuff it." That evening he was nervous, and Cheryl told him that was to be expected. "Tomorrow's a big day for you," she said. "For all of us." She told him to take a bath, and he did, though logically he knew cleanliness really wasn't what the job was about. And at quarter past four the next morning he woke to the alarm, he was the one who kissed Cheryl and told her he loved her, he was the one who let her sleep in whilst he got ready for work.

Everyone had been told to meet outside the office at half past five sharp. Ray was there too, so were a few others Steve remembered from the training day. They too looked anxious, and were trying to hide it by horsing about and being noisy. "That's it," said their supervisor, "get rid of all your energy now, whilst you still have the chance." Then he bundled them all into the back of a van, and drove them to Clapham Common. "When you've got more experience, you can choose where you want to stand," the supervisor told them, "but for now, leave that up to me." He planted Steve far away from Ray, and away from the lad he'd said hello to in the van, and for a while Steve felt a bit lonely, and then reasoned there wouldn't be much chatting anyway. There were two breaks scheduled during the day: as his first, Steve picked the eleven o'clock slot, and Ray did too. As the trees gathered around, forming an impromptu copse, stretching their limbs and smoking their fags, Ray said, "Christ, this job's boring, isn't it?"

And it was boring, of course it was. But Steve soon realized that being bored wasn't so bad. On that first day the sky was overcast, and so the common didn't get many visitors, but perhaps that was just as well. It meant that Steve could concentrate on not wobbling. Not wobbling, he quickly discovered, was the key. Once he had the not wobbling sorted, he'd have the job down pat. And he learned that the odd wobble was fine, so long as you didn't fight it—lean into the breeze, and you could turn it into a *sway*. The second day the sun came out, and with it the lunchtime workers with their thermos flasks and their sandwiches. One of them sheltered in Steve's shade, and Steve expected he'd be jealous of him, this man in a suit, having a proper job, doing something respectable. But he wasn't. He actually wasn't: he peered down at the man's face, and saw it creased with stress; he was just trying to grab a quick bite in peace, but his mobile phone kept on ringing, it rang no less than three times, and each time the man would put his sandwich down and take the call, and each time Steve heard him pleading to someone on the other end, yes, the contract would be ready by Tuesday, yes, the contract would be ready by the end of the day, please bear with him, please bear with him, please. And Steve felt sorry for the man, he wanted to protect him, and to shield him as best he could with his branches. It was funny—after an hour or so you didn't feel the stiffness in your arms. First they numbed, then felt like something detached from the body altogether. And when the breeze fluttered his leaves, Steve thrilled to it—the wind just teasing them, they didn't seem so much blown about as stroked. He'd zone out, and sometimes he'd think of the common, and how many different shades of green there were, no patch of grass the same. And sometimes he'd think of his family. That if he was moved off probationary pay that maybe they could have another baby, he knew Cheryl would like that, and Ben deserved a little playmate, someone he could look after. Maybe Cheryl and he could even get married at last. And sometimes he'd think nothing at all.

By the end of the second week Ray had had enough. "To hell with this!" he shouted, and Steve was sure the whole common must have heard him. "I'm out of here!" The supervisor told Ray that was fine with him, he was no use anyway, he didn't have the aptitude, he just didn't have the aptitude. But for now he'd have to finish the shift, if he wanted any pay at all he'd bloody well get back to work. "Christ," said Ray, but did as he was told, dragging all his roots behind him and back into position. On the way back in the van Ray wouldn't shut up about it all. "You're being exploited," he told the other trees. "This is the worst job in the world. I'd rather work for McDonald's." The other trees looked uncomfortable and didn't say much. "You don't have to rush off, do you, Steve, you've time for a pint?" But Steve told Ray that he'd best get back home, his family were waiting. Some other time maybe. "Yeah," said Ray, "maybe," and he went. Steve felt rather relieved that Ray wouldn't be on the common with him anymore. He liked Ray and all, but he let the side down. He was a troublemaker.

That evening Steve told Cheryl what Ray had said. Cheryl was quiet for a while, and then asked, a little uncomfortably, whether maybe Ray was right. "You gave the job a go," she said. "Darling, there's no need to stick it out if you don't want to." And Steve assured her he was fine. He liked the job. He did, really! Couldn't Cheryl see that? Isn't that what he'd been telling Cheryl every night as they cuddled? "Well, yes," said Cheryl. "But I'd always thought you were just putting a brave face on it. It all sounds horrendous." No, no, Steve said. He was really getting to grips with it. "Oh," said Cheryl.

And besides, Ray had been exaggerating. It wasn't all just hard graft; there were lighter moments too, lots of them. For example, there was that time with the two teenagers. They sat under Steve's branches, and they told each other that they loved each other, and they snogged. And both the declarations of love and the snogs that punctuated them were so forceful that Steve suspected this was the first time for them both; they were so so young, they'd not used the "love" word before. Steve rather liked them. They were sweet. "I love you," said the boy, "and I'm going to prove it." And he got out a Swiss Army knife from his jacket, pulled out the blade, and Steve was alarmed, he thought the boy was going to do something terrible to himself, or to her: he wondered whether he should break character and call for help, but that was strictly forbidden. But it was all right, the boy just wanted to carve their initials into the bark, and Steve felt relieved—right up to the point that he remembered the bark was *him*. "What happened to you?" said Cheryl that night, and he told her the whole story, and they had a good laugh about it. "And what's that around the initials, is that supposed to be a heart?" Steve supposed that it was. Cheryl said, "Oh dear!" and laughed again, and wondered whether it could all be removed by laser surgery. And Steve pointed out that it wasn't a tattoo, that wasn't the way it worked. "Oh dear!" laughed Cheryl. And then, "But what a romantic gesture." And Steve hit upon an idea, and he told Cheryl that she should carve their names into his bark. "No," said Cheryl. ". . . Do you really think I should? Won't it hurt?" Steve said it wouldn't much, and she said he was being brave, and he said he wasn't really, and she said, no, she liked it when he was brave. "Okay," said Cheryl, and grinned, and looked so excited, and went to fetch a knife. "Whereabouts should I do it?" And Steve told her that she should carve her heart higher than the teenagers' heart—this was *proper* love they felt, not some school crush. Their heart should take precedence. "Here goes," she said, and began to chip out a heart: high up like he'd said, just below his throat. Cut deep, Steve said, unless she wanted the bark to grow over. So she cut deep. And she cut an arrow through the centre of the heart, and then carved their names either side. Their full names, not just their initials, if it was worth doing it was worth doing properly, and Steve was secretly relieved his name only had five letters. Then she laughed at her handiwork, and Steve couldn't see properly, so had to go and take a look for himself in the mirror, and he laughed too, and said she'd done a great job. And then they kissed. And then Cheryl cleaned the knife of the sap and the little smear of blood.

Pretty soon Steve stopped taking his scheduled breaks at eleven o'clock. He preferred to work through, he didn't want to break his rhythm. For a while he was still obliged to take the one at half past four, because by then he'd be bursting for a pee—but he then learned that with just a little concentration he could convert all his waste matter into chlorophyll and pump it out into his foliage. It wasn't necessarily textbook stuff, but hey, it worked. In the van to and from work he didn't talk much to the other trees, and they didn't talk much to him; he couldn't tell whether they just wanted to maintain their focus as he did, or just didn't like him. And he honestly didn't care either way. One day the supervisor came to Steve and told him that he'd noticed his common or garden sycamore was now showing signs of becoming a *variegated* sycamore; Steve wasn't sure whether this was a good thing or not, but the supervisor said that the extra effort was appreciated, and gave him a friendly slap on his trunk. And only a few days after that, the supervisor asked Steve if he could have a private word with him away from all the other trees. He asked Steve if he fancied being an oak. "One of the oaks in St. James's Park has gone sick. Don't know what, some sort of fungus, doesn't matter. Would you be my new oak?" Steve was surprised and flattered and just a bit scared; he wasn't sure he had what it took, to be an oak was every sycamore's dream. "You've got what it takes," said the supervisor. "I don't want you, you know, to get above yourself. But I'll tell you, you're the most promising oak I've seen in years."

After his shift Steve went home and told his family the news. Ben didn't say much, he never said much anymore. "Will there be any extra money?" asked Cheryl. Steve said he didn't know. He'd only be a probationary oak after all, they couldn't expect much. But that was hardly the point. He'd be in St. James's Park! That was just an acorn's throw from Buckingham Palace itself, some days the Queen would look out of her window, and guess what she'd be looking at, Ben? She'd be looking at his daddy! What did Ben think of that? Ben very politely asked if he could be excused from the dinner table, he had homework to do. Steve expressed surprise that Ben was doing homework—he was too young, surely? Cheryl said, "He's been doing homework for weeks now. I don't think you remember. I don't think you listen." She washed up in silence for a while. And then Steve told her that he was even being allowed to choose which oak he wanted to be, there were so many different types of oak, you know. They trusted him with that decision all by himself. He thought he might go for a sessile oak, partly because he admired the way that its acorns weren't carried on stalks but directly on the outer twigs, and partly because he just liked the name. Cheryl coolly said that it sounded like he'd already reached his decision, and Steve said, no, no, he'd welcome her input, she'd every right to help choose what sort of oak tree her husband was going to be. She banged the plates down in the sink and left the kitchen.

The other oaks were set in their ways and standoffish. Sod them, Steve thought, and put his efforts into being the best sessile oak he could. He liked the park; he sheltered a better quality of picnicker there. He loved all the tourists, and all their different accents, and that they were always so excited by everything, and took photos all the time, and he liked to imagine they'd flown all around the world from their own countries just to visit him, they were there to see him. He knew it wasn't true, not necessarily, but it sent a warmth of pride from the tips of his upper branches right down to the furthest ends of his roots. And in the evenings at home he'd study, he'd pore over gardening books and encyclopaedias and the latest academic dissertations about oak care theory. Just so he could be expert. Daddy was doing his homework whilst Ben was doing his!—and he'd tell Ben that, and he thought Ben would find that amusing, he couldn't quite be sure. He'd explain to Ben why the oak was the best tree in the world. There was a reason it had been adopted as a national emblem in England and France and Germany and the USA and Poland and Latvia and Estonia. And he'd tell Cheryl that after that time of unemployment all he'd wanted was to be a normal man again. But he now believed he was actually *good* at this, special, she was living with a man that was special. He loved his afternoons now, they were long and rich and full of sunshine and birdsong . . . "Don't you care," asked Cheryl, "that your own son is scared of you? He's *scared* of you. Doesn't that bother you at all?" That pulled Steve up short. He'd never hurt Ben, he never would, he loved Ben, this was all for Ben, for them both, he loved them both. "He doesn't know what you are anymore. He thinks you're a monster." With all his talk of trees, that's all Steve would talk about anymore, just bloody trees—and Steve didn't raise his voice, he pointed out to Cheryl as gently as he could that he *was* a bloody tree, what did she bloody expect? "We came to see you this afternoon," said Cheryl. "Ben wanted to see where his daddy worked. We came to see you in the park." Silence. "You didn't even know he was there."

She told Steve she didn't love him anymore. She'd tried, but she'd given up trying, she had to give up now. She was so sorry. And she gave him a sudden hug, and held onto him fiercely, buried her head against his hard mottled chest, and began to cry. Steve looked down at her, and thought she looked so small, and she couldn't reach her arms round him of course, it was almost funny—she was so small he could barely feel her.

"I don't want to lose you," she said. She kept on saying that, over and over again. They went to bed, and she sobbed, facing away from him. And he wanted to comfort her, to protect her, but he didn't know how. He reached out for her, he brushed her skin, and he wasn't sure she'd want that, he thought she might tell him to stop, but she didn't tell him to stop, and she didn't stop sobbing either. And he held her in his arms, his long strong arms, and she accepted them gratefully. That's how she fell asleep at last, gripping onto him, her fingernails cutting thin little slits into his bark. When the alarm woke them the next morning she smiled at him, and kissed at him, and for a moment Steve thought everything might be all right. And she asked him to move out.

Sometimes in the park a family would approach him, and the father would say, "Do you want to play in the tree?" and the little boy would say, "Yes! Yes!" and the mother would smile nervously and say, "Now, be careful," and the father would lift the boy into Steve's branches, and the boy would squeal with joy, and Steve would hold him tightly in those branches to keep him safe, and he'd think, Ben, he'd think, it should be Ben I'm holding, I should be holding my own son. And then the thought would be lost upon the breeze.

He tried phoning Ray once. Ray wasn't in. He didn't try again.

One day he was alarmed to find a ridge running across his midriff, over where the navel used to be, right around his body and back again. He was quite certain there'd been no trace of it the day before. He hadn't felt anything even approaching alarm for quite a while now, and wasn't quite sure what to do with it. So at the end of the shift he told his supervisor. "Oh, that's a ring!" said the supervisor. "All trees get those. That means you've been doing this job a whole year. Congratulations!" Steve thanked him. "Don't thank me. A whole year, hey, that must mean you've got a holiday due. Have you taken a holiday yet? You're owed a holiday." Steve informed the supervisor that he hadn't taken a holiday. "Well, you must then. No arguments!" Steve asked him what sort of holiday he ought to take. "God, I don't know, I'm not a travel agent," said the supervisor. "Somewhere sunny. I don't know. With a beach." So Steve dutifully went to the travel agent's, and an excitable young assistant there told him that yes, there were *lots* of sunny holidays she could recommend, and *plenty* of them came with beaches. And she booked him one right there and then to prove it. "Just the single passenger, is it, sir?" she asked.

The aeroplane was full of noisy families. Steve usually liked noisy families, but now he wasn't there to shade them and they made him feel awkward and somehow sad. Once he'd cleared immigration a shuttle coach took him and the noisy families to a noisy hotel. "I hope you like your room, sir," said the bellboy, and Steve said that he did, even though the bed was too soft and too too small, and whenever he turned on the TV something Spanish came out. He sat on the bed to have a think, but no thoughts came to mind. So he got changed into his T-shirt, his shorts, and his sandals, he put on sunglasses and sun lotion. In the mirror he looked at the heart that Cheryl had carved into his skin, and on a whim he covered it up. Then he went for a walk on the sand. He left strange footprints behind him.

He'd walked for a couple of hours, maybe three. The sun was beginning to set. He stopped at last, and stared out to sea for a good few minutes, unmoving, unthinking. Then he turned to the nearest palm tree he could see, and told her that he admired her fronds.

The palm tree didn't reply.

Steve didn't do a lot of talking anymore, so he wasn't sure he'd got it right. Maybe he just thought he'd spoken. Maybe the words hadn't actually come out. He found that happened sometimes. So he told the palm tree again that he admired her fronds.

"I heard you the first time," said the palm tree. "We're not supposed to fraternize." Steve apologized. And then said that he didn't know whether she'd be interested, but maybe Steve could buy her a drink? He was staying at a hotel. Somewhere, back there, he didn't know where exactly, but they served drinks, he was sure of it. Maybe he could buy her one.

The palm tree didn't say anything, and for a moment Steve thought he'd have to come right out and say all that again, and that would be such an effort. But he was just summoning up the breath to do so anyway, when the palm said, "Are you married?"

Steve had to think about this for a while.

"Yes," he said, at last.

The palm tree seemed to shrug. "All right, señor. One drink. Just the one. At your hotel." Steve thanked her. "Don't thank me," she said. "But only after my shift, okay? I've got to finish my shift first."

"I can wait," said Steve. And he sat down beneath her shade, rested his head against her bark, and closed his eyes. And let the crash of the waves against the shore lull him to sleep.

BRAND NEW SHINY SHINY

Richard Marklew had a skull that was cracked across the top, forming a gash that ran from the roof of the scalp right down to the middle of the forehead. In the right light the crack seemed to yawn open most invitingly, and Marklew took pains to enhance this effect, always positioning the skull near candlelight or flickering lamp. And sometimes when Marklew hosted a dinner party (and, sometimes, when he merely attended someone else's), he would present his skull at the table after the meal was done, and he'd dare the ladies to put their fingers into the crack, deep down, as deep as they could go.

Most of the ladies shrank away, of course, but he could usually persuade one or two to give it a try. These bolder women weren't necessarily the most attractive, but that didn't matter; to Marklew, beauty was rarely skin deep.

That night the first woman to accept the challenge was Mrs. Alice Powell, and she was a somewhat unlikely candidate—Marklew had written her off as too mousey, too timid, to be of any interest to him. She too seemed surprised at her own daring, and now that she was standing up seemed only to want to sit straight back down again—but everyone's eyes were upon her, and she wavered, uncertain what would frighten her the most: to touch Marklew's skull, or to suffer the humiliation of changing her mind. She looked back to her husband, but Mr. Powell was no help at all—he nodded and smiled, he actively seemed to be encouraging her. "It won't bite," said Marklew, kindly enough, he thought—and there was a ripple of laughter, and Mrs. Alice Powell blushed bright red. She stretched out one finger, daintily, and let it brush against the skull—not at the crack, nowhere near the crack. And because that was clearly not enough, she touched it again, gave it an actual prod this time, and she shuddered, and laughed as she shuddered.

"But, Mr. Marklew," she said. "How can you ever sleep, with such a fearful thing in the house?" And her eyes were big and round, and Marklew knew she wouldn't be sharing his bed that night.

"I want to try," said Lady Constance suddenly, and rose from her chair, and there was nothing for it but for Mrs. Powell to retreat to her own, dismissed. Lady Constance was the sort of woman that could be termed handsome. Marklew thought there was something bovine about her, as if her blue-blooded ancestors had bred with cattle.

"How old did you say this was?" she asked, and Marklew hadn't, and told her it was not so very old, it dated back maybe to the sixteenth century. Lady Constance nodded at that, as if that were an answer she approved of, as if she had been checking the skull had a decent vintage. And then she plunged her fingers into the crack.

There was silence for a few seconds as she began to explore.

Then one of the husbands said, with a slightly embarrassed cough, "And how many of these skulls have you collected, Marklew?" But Marklew ignored that, it was a typical question from the gentry: how many, how big, how much is it worth? Another man asked what had caused the crack, had it been in battle? And Marklew said, yes, in battle, or perhaps in ritual sacrifice—although of course it was a battle wound, but he liked talking of ritual sacrifice, the women always thrilled to it, it gave them such a frisson. All the time Marklew looked only at Lady Constance, into the crack now up to her knuckles. And she said, softly, "Do you give the skull a name?"

"I do not," said Marklew. "But you can correct my omission. You can name the skull for me." He thought she would like that. She did.

"Very well," she said. "Then I shall name him Oswald."

And there was some amusement at that. It was an open secret that Lady Constance was having an affair with Oswald Lutyens, the artist, and the rumours were that she was tiring of him.

"Oswald it is," said Marklew.

"It's all so smooth," she said. "Do you think we're all so smooth, beneath the skin?" Marklew said, very probably; he knew the reason the bone was so smooth was that he had the servants polish it each week with linseed oil.

"And to think," Lady Constance breathed, her eyes no longer on the skull, eyes only on Marklew, but her fingers were still stroking at the bone, stroking away. "That this man lived hundreds of years ago. He lived, and he died, and now you *own* him. He's *yours*, and you have the power to do whatever you like to him. He cannot resist. He has no rights. He's like your personal dead slave."

"Yes," said Marklew.

And at this the maids brought in liqueurs, and Lady Constance returned to her chair, and the conversation was changed. And Marklew put Oswald away—Oswald, or James, or Sylvester; the skull had been at so many dinner parties, and had been given so many names.

After his other guests had retired for the evening, Marklew took Lady Constance on a private tour of his collection of *memento mori*. He showed her fully articulated skeleton puppets operated by gossamer-thin strings; they stood ten feet tall and came from Mexico. There were canopic jars from ancient Egypt, death masks from Renaissance Europe; there were iron markers from children's graves, dug up in Austria a hundred years before. Lady Constance cooed over the beauty of the jewelled clasps he had collected, and he told her that each of them had been worn by grieving widows and contained locks of hair from their dead husbands' heads. And there were more skulls, of course there were; he had skulls from Saxon times, from Norman times, he had skulls from Africa and Asia and the most obscure island tribes in the South Pacific. And they all looked the same to Lady Constance. But Richard Marklew knew the differences between each and every one of them, and he loved them all.

He showed her an erotic portrait of two cavorting corpses, and Lady Constance reached for his hand and squeezed it.

"What a display!" she said. "Well, well. You must feel you have triumphed over death!" But that wasn't it at all.

As he showed her all the pieces he had, gathered over so many years, the little memorabilia, the nick-knacks, the shards of bone and cartilage, Marklew felt a growing pride. And she seemed still to regard it all as some flirtatious game, as the exotic hobby of a wealthy man who had nothing better to do with his time. Something flippant, something trivial—with every fresh objet d'art he expected less and less from her reaction, and he really rather hated her for that.

He took her finally to his bedroom. He showed her the bed.

"Is it something wickedly sinister?" she asked. "Has it been constructed from the skeletal remains of torture victims?"

"No," he said.

He pushed her onto the bed, and he fucked her. They fucked twice, and then he was tired, and he suggested she should return to her own room so that he might sleep.

↓

Marklew did not expect to be understood by Lady Constance and her ilk; and, truth be told, he wouldn't have much wanted to have been. They saw at best a random assemblage of curios—interesting, certainly, maybe even a little macabre, but without proper form or intent. Whereas Marklew knew that each item he owned had been specifically hand picked, that the entire collection was a single piece of art, that it was a summation of something—that it was a summation of *him*. Yes, it was an expression of self, and by now, at the age of fifty-five, he knew himself quite perfectly, everything he set his mind to accomplish, he did; and everything he did was something he had set out to do, quite deliberately. And whilst the collection grew each year, he also edited out earlier acquisitions—pieces he felt now symbolized a younger man he no longer was and did not want to be again; he would throw out skulls that he judged to be naive, entire skeletons that he'd once loved but in his maturity had outgrown. Had Lady Constance seen his collection for what it was he would have been irked, maybe even a little frightened; what man wants to be so easily decoded, his real and complex self to be exposed? Richard Marklew thought he was deep.—Richard Marklew *knew* he was deep. He was a man who had depths all over him; he alone could guess how many depths he had.

No, if Marklew wanted appreciation for his life's work, he would find it at the convention. The convention was attended by the like-minded: enthusiasts, scholars, and collectors of the arcane. Membership was offered by invitation only, and was reassuringly rigid in its selection: you could not apply for it, or ask others to make applications on your behalf, and any member found colluding in any such practice would face summary expulsion. Membership was also, needless to say, extremely expensive.

Marklew remembered the first time he had received an invitation. It had arrived by some special delivery: the envelope was small and plain and had no stamps upon it. Inside had been a card informing Marklew of the location of that year's convention, and that his attendance would be permitted. It had not said so, but Marklew had known instinctively that had he turned the invitation down, no more would ever be forthcoming. Marklew had then been only twenty-four, and his collection was only small, and, by his later standards, mostly worthless; certainly, by the time he'd reached his forties, he had disposed of the majority of it. He had heard that such a convention existed, of course. Sometimes the dealers he bought from would allude to it—but only in jokes, as if it were a myth none of them quite believed in. Marklew did not know how the convention had heard of him. He never asked.

That year it had been in Istanbul. He later learned that the convention was never held in the same place twice, and that Istanbul was amongst the least exotic of the hosting cities. But this had been in the days of the Great War, and Turkey had not only got itself caught up in the middle of the damned thing, but had ended up on the wrong side. To go to the convention would have all but bankrupted Marklew; he had never been a poor man, but these were still the days in which he could hardly have been described as rich. Nevertheless, he went.

To be in the company of other men who explored so fully the passions he was only starting to feel—that itself made the adventure worthwhile. Marklew had tried to talk to these men, and they'd accepted his drinks, they had even been polite, but they had never encouraged any friendly intimacy. Now, so many years later, Marklew himself understood why—and it sometimes made him wince to think of his younger self, still wet behind the ears and knowing nothing, worth nothing, wanting to impose his presence upon others. He marvelled in retrospect at the senior members' patience with him. He wouldn't have shown any. Indeed, if Marklew was now approached by any such novice he refused even to acknowledge him—there were always new members every year, and it was something the old crowd may have to tolerate, but didn't need to indulge.

If you wanted to be invited back to the convention, you quickly learned: these men were closer to you than family, but that didn't mean they were your friends. To be amongst your peers, the only people to whom you would never have to explain yourself—that was enough.

Richard Marklew liked to hold a dinner party on the eve of a convention. The contrast amused him.

By the time he awoke in the morning, Lady Constance and her chattering friends had gone. He was taken by cab to a private airfield; from there, by chartered plane he flew to Bogota. Marklew didn't know Bogota. By the end of the weekend he still wouldn't; he was met at the airfield by an arranged driver who took him to the hotel in a limousine with windows so black he could barely see out of them. The hotel was maybe a two hour drive away; it was small and anonymous. It could have been anywhere in the world—which Marklew always supposed was entirely the point. He was shown to his room. It was spotlessly clean and luxuriously appointed. The bed was large and hard, as to his stated preference.

He unpacked. It did not take long. There was little that he'd needed to bring. And then he went downstairs to the bar, where the other members of the convention had started to gather. He sat down in an armchair, at a table on his own, ordered an Old Fashioned, and pretended to read a newspaper. He allowed himself to be seen.

↓

The centrepiece of the weekend's events was the auction on the Sunday afternoon. It was always fully attended, although Marklew knew that there were never more than the same dozen serious bidders. There was someone from China, someone from France, someone from one of the Indies, Marklew didn't know which, it may even have been India itself. Several Americans, of course, no doubt trying to seize hold of a history they had never had. The majority were British, which was as it should be.

Marklew knew the names of his rivals, and over the years had learned something of their reputations. Most were reserved to the point of fanaticism and would not speak to one another at all—it was as if the auction were some grand poker game, and revealing any part of themselves would be a strategic weakness. Marklew could understand the sense of that, although he didn't take it so very seriously. He wouldn't talk to the other bidders either, but mostly because he didn't like them very much.

None of the lots were ever announced in advance; it was accepted that any expert in the room should understand their significance without preparation. And Marklew preferred that. He enjoyed the palpable excitement it lent the proceedings; there were usually a few real surprises to look forward to. He had learned one golden rule: whenever a fresh lot was introduced, he made a snap judgment upon whether it would enhance his collection or not. If it wouldn't, no matter how interesting a piece it might be on its own terms, no matter whether it might be a bargain, he would let it go. And if he *did* want it, he would automatically decide upon an upper limit he would be prepared to pay. That, and not a penny more. It wasn't a question of what he could *afford*—he could afford so very many things. It was instead what he would be *seen* to pay. People mustn't think he overestimated the value of anything, offering ten thousand pounds for an Etruscan skeleton when it was really worth no more than eight. He had a reputation to uphold.

The auction at Bogota offered, it must be said, slim pickings. Lots usually came from deceased members, collections lovingly assembled over a lifetime now broken up and divvied out piecemeal; or, maybe, new discoveries would be presented from fresh archaeological excavations. In the year before Bogota no one had died—or no one, at least, of any great significance; there had been excavations aplenty, but little of interest had been found. There had evidently been lots to tell us about how the Sumerians had lived, but precious little about how they'd died.

So, Richard Marklew bid upon a pair of guillotine blades used in the French Revolution, and an entire coffin lacquered with real bone—and he did indeed actively want them for his collection, and won them both at a reasonable price—but moments after the bidding was over he felt a tinge of regret that he'd even bothered, he knew that they already bored him. Not every year could be successful. It didn't matter. Marklew resigned himself to classifying Bogota as an honourable failure. And then the auctioneer announced the final lot.

There was some laughter, naturally—from the younger members, probably, who knew no better. Mostly there were tuts of exasperation, angry mutterings. The auction was not a joke; a sense of humour was not appreciated. But the auctioneer remained deadpan, there was not even the hint of a smile upon his face.

Some wag asked about the lot's provenance, and still the man refused to smile. He stood tall, presented himself proud. "The provenance is me," he said. "Self-evidently. I cannot talk of the mother, I did not know her well. But the boy has my looks. Now," he said again, louder, "may we start the bidding, please, upon the skull of my son?"

For the first time Marklew looked at the auctioneer, properly examined him. He'd never really thought to look at any of the auctioneers over the years, what they were presenting was far more important. The man was some Colombian, Marklew thought, with some surprise—he'd have assumed the convention would have flown some expert in, that they wouldn't have got some local. The man spoke well enough, it was true. He even looked quite dapper in his suit. But Marklew could now see something too dark in the man's face, too swarthy, too foreign.

Another voice—cooler, stiffer: "May we see the lot?"

At this the auctioneer gave a nod. And onto the stage stepped a little boy, no more than four feet tall. Marklew had never spent much time around children, but he supposed the specimen might be about six or seven years old. There was indeed, as the auctioneer had said, a family resemblance: a thick-set swarthiness that made the boy's face hang heavy and look older than it was.

If the boy seemed alarmed or surprised that his father was preparing to sell him, he did not show it—Marklew wondered whether he might have been drugged. "I say once more, gentlemen, I offer this boy's skull. After he is dead, the flesh will be stripped, and the skull boiled and bleached, and it will be packed up nicely in a box and sent to you. I cannot tell when that death may occur exactly, but if you look at him, you can see he doesn't look well, it cannot be long."

That cool, stiff voice once more: "Just the skull?"

"The skull alone, down to the top of his cervical vertebrae. Everything beneath, that belongs to me. May I start the bidding? Do I hear five hundred pounds?"

For a moment, silence. The threat of renewed laughter, even. And then, that stiff voice: "Five hundred then."

"Six hundred," said Marklew.

He hadn't intended to make a bid. Maybe he was intrigued. Maybe there was something about that little child's face he imagined would fit neatly into his collection at Richmond Park. Or maybe it was something about the voice of his rival bidder, something in it that felt out of place at the convention and that he wanted to challenge.

If the auctioneer were surprised he'd attracted a single bid at all he didn't show it; he waited expectantly to see if there would be a counter offer. And at Marklew's bid the little boy's face had come to life. He beamed happily out at the audience, at Marklew specifically. He clapped his hands, just the once, in joy.

"Any more bids?" asked the auctioneer, at length. "For this fine piece by my side." And the little boy loved that, he clapped his hands again, he began to jiggle about in excitement.

"Seven hundred pounds," said the stiff man.

"One thousand," said Marklew, and right then and there he decided that he'd reached the upper limit he'd pay; what was this anyway, what was it for, he collected skulls of antiquity, not skulls of dago stock, this was just an anecdote to impress the ladies at dinner—no, one thousand pounds, and no more, no more surely?

"One thousand five hundred," returned the stiff man promptly, and at last Marklew turned in his seat to find him. There he was, to the side, a few rows behind; as Marklew had suspected, he didn't recognize him, he must be one of those new members, those nouveau riche upstarts who didn't yet know there were rules to this place, that a certain respect should be accorded the practice of auction, a certain respect should be accorded *him*; but no, he didn't look like a young man at all—no, pale, thin, with a face so bland it seemed that all expression had been smoothed out deliberately, and wearing a suit, an undistinguished sort of suit, the suit a solicitor might wear—this man wasn't even a member Marklew realized, he was here as an *agent* for someone else, and didn't that contravene the rules of the convention? If not, it should! If not, it was at least highly irregular!

And he turned back, and he realized that all eyes were upon him, waiting to see whether he would make a higher bid. The auctioneer waited patiently; less patiently, the son, he was now almost frenzied with anticipation, he was shaking and jumping about on the spot. He was sticking out his tongue. He was *stretching* out his tongue, and licking at his face, he was sliding great gobs of saliva over his chin as if to make it look shinier.

"Two thousand," said Marklew. He didn't dare turn to look behind at the solicitor—somehow he didn't want to see that man angry, somehow he couldn't bear the idea of that, what such anger might be. But when the rival bid came, seconds later, it was done without emotion, nothing but cool calculating self-assurance: "Three thousand."

And at this the boy could no longer contain himself. He broke rank altogether, he began to *dance*, he waved his arms high above his head, fingers pointing downwards—it's me, this is me, hear how much I'm worth! If the auctioneer was annoyed by his son's antics he didn't show it. And then, so suddenly, the boy was off the stage—he jumped high, higher than should have been possible, and Marklew could only think in that moment of a frog, or maybe a grasshopper—and the boy landed nimbly and soundlessly upon his feet.

Then rushing toward Marklew, as if to a new prospective father, so eager he was clambering over chairs to get to him—and he was squealing with excitement, the squeals so shrill, and the tongue was still out, and still licking away, but it was so fast now, and so *long*—it stretched down past the chin, it reached up high to tickle his nose, and higher—slathering away, with spit as thick as soup, and with such force it seemed as if he were trying to strip the flesh off to expose what was beneath, and where he slathered it did indeed seem to leave a sheen behind, it did indeed allow Marklew to picture that head as a skull with all the skin removed, just white gleaming bone, just bone, displayed in pride of place in his collection.

"Fifty thousand," said Marklew. He spoke softly—for a wonderful moment he thought it was so soft no one had heard him—but it was out of his mouth, and at the sound of it the hushed room fell more hushed still. It was done now, it was done. "Fifty thousand pounds," he said again, louder now, because why not? If he'd already made the bid, do it with pride! Trying to put into his quavering voice the self-confidence for which he was renowned.

The hush held. And the solicitor stirred. Marklew could see him out of the corner of his eye, he half-turned in his seat—and he didn't want him to make a rival bid, but oh, he so wanted him to make a rival bid—this cool stiff man could win the living skull and Marklew would bid no higher, and there would be an end to this nonsense, Marklew would be off scot free with his integrity intact. He thought he saw the solicitor open his mouth. But no, maybe he was just setting his jaw. The solicitor got to his feet, carelessly smoothed down his cheap suit; he turned, and unhurriedly walked out of the hall.

Marklew turned back to the auctioneer. There he was, banging down his gavel. And there, next to him, stood his son—calm, as if he'd never left the stage—still, slumped, as if he were already close to death.

In the bar afterwards Richard Marklew was the centre of attention. All the young men gathering around, pressing drinks into his hand, even slapping him on the back as if he'd given them the most wonderful sport. As if he'd perpetrated a joke—and all for their especial amusement! Not one of them asked about the guillotine blades he had bought. He soon made his excuses, and retired for the night.

↓

He did not sleep well. He usually found the hardness of a bed reassuring, but now it jabbed and prodded at him accusingly. It seemed to him he woke every other hour or so. One time he awoke and became convinced there was a figure sitting in the chair by the dressing table. His heart lurched terribly at that, and then he realized he'd left his clothes there, his jacket and waistcoat on the chair back, the trouser legs drooping down toward the floor. He even laughed at himself.

Then the figure said, "If you're awake, Mr. Marklew, then may we discuss business?"

Marklew was at the bedside lamp in an instant. The solicitor was still cool, still stiff. There was not even the pretence of apology in that too bland face for breaking into Marklew's room and watching him as he'd slept.

Marklew wanted to shout at him, demand to know what the hell the man was playing at—and yet the self-composure that had defined him for so long kicked into play. Forcing down the fear in his stomach, forcing his face into a mask of non-committal reserve, Marklew heard himself ask, "What may I do for you?"

The man said, "That last item you won. My client has instructed me to make you a further offer."

Over the years many buyers had approached him once he'd made a win. Sometimes the money they offered was fully twice what Marklew himself had just paid. He always refused to negotiate. He'd say that he was a collector, not a shopkeeper. And even now, with this strange man in his bedroom, making him feel suddenly so very vulnerable and defenceless, Marklew had to consider the principle of the matter. But the truth was, he didn't *want* the boy's skull. Fifty thousand pounds was by no means the most expensive purchase he had ever made at auction, but this was surely the most unjustifiable. He had heard tell of stories of even the shrewdest collectors who had made, at some points in their careers, hideous misjudgements—their honed instincts deserting them momentarily, buying fakes, damaged goods, art of no skill or value, even in one apocryphal anecdote a Dark Ages skeleton fashioned largely from plastic. Marklew did not think he had made as much a fool of himself as all that—not quite—no, not nearly. But he regretted the whole enterprise and wanted to put it behind him. If his rival was prepared to buy the skull, then he felt he could move on with his dignity intact. He might even make a little profit.

Marklew said, ironically, "If we are to talk business, may I at least get dressed?" And the solicitor gestured slightly with his hand that Marklew may do as he liked. But the solicitor made no movement to leave, and

Marklew stayed exactly where he was.

"My client wants you to understand that this will be a one-time offer. The agreement we come to will be reached here and now, or not at all. And no mention of this conversation shall ever be made again once our business is concluded." Marklew nodded at that, that was all the better.

"My client further wants to state that the skull has no intrinsic worth, to him or to anyone else. But it interests him nonetheless, and accordingly he is prepared to offer you a generous sum as a gesture of good faith. In return, you will give up all rights to the skull in perpetuity, and all prospects for the future acquisition of the skull will transfer to him."

"Yes, yes," said Marklew. "And what is this sum?"

"Ten pounds."

"Ten pounds?"

"As a gesture of good faith."

Marklew laughed. "I paid fifty thousand for it."

"Indeed."

"I don't think you've quite worked out how these negotiations are supposed to work."

"May I have your answer?" asked the solicitor.

Marklew stopped laughing.

The solicitor went on, "My client is not a sentimental man. But he would have the skull. The boy, you see, is one of ours."

Marklew did not pretend to understand that. He licked his lips. "If your client would be prepared to reimburse me the fifty thousand pounds I have already spent," he said, "and offer me some little extra for the sake of honour. Then. Then, I think, we would have something to talk about."

The solicitor stared at him. His face did not even flicker with a reaction. Then he said, "You are rejecting my client's offer?"

"Wait, now. Look here. Even just a small token. Even just ten pounds."

"You are rejecting my client's offer."

"Or even. Damn it. You bid how much at auction? Three thousand, I think? Then offer me that three thousand. Forget the fifty, you just offer me the three."

"No."

And Marklew said, "Why not?" And he sounded like a little boy, and he was ashamed of himself for that.

"My client's offer is, as I say, to be accepted, or not at all. If you do not give my client the skull now, we will not be prepared to take it from you later. It will belong to you forever. You will never be able to be rid of it. You will never be able to sell it, never able even to give it away. This is your final chance. We need offer you nothing. Instead, we offer you ten pounds."

"As a gesture of good faith," said Marklew, feebly.

The man didn't even bother to agree.

The bed seemed cold to Marklew now. The sheets were rough. The bedside lamp was too bright, the glare seemed to sear into his head, it made him feel nauseous. "Not for ten pounds," said Marklew. "You must understand. I can't. I can't. I can't."

There was a moment's pause, and then the man got to his feet. If he were disappointed, he didn't reveal it. And Marklew wondered whether even now it was too late, whether he could change his mind, accept the insulting offer, or at least reopen negotiations—but any little animation the solicitor's face had shown had faded away, there was nothing there now but the cool and the stiff.

And then, an afterthought. The solicitor turned back to Marklew.

"A question, Mr. Marklew? Why do you do it? Why do you surround yourself with the trappings of the dead?"

Richard Marklew said nothing.

"My client instructs me to say he takes no interest in the matter himself. I ask merely to satisfy my personal curiosity."

"Get out," said Marklew quietly. Then, shouting now, "Out! Out!" And stupidly, childishly, he threw his pillow at the solicitor. It bounced off him. The solicitor didn't seem to mind.

"Goodbye, Mr. Marklew," said the solicitor. And he was gone.

Marklew had to get out of bed to retrieve his pillow. There was a draft in the room; he shivered in his pyjamas.

He flew home to London the next day. The day following, he took receipt of two guillotine blades and a coffin lacquered with bone. Of the skull, of course, there was as yet no sign.

$$\downarrow$$

The next year the convention was in Marrakech. It was a better convention. One of the senior members had died, everyone was delighted. At auction Marklew won a collection of shrunken heads, and a mummified body from the Chimu people of fourteenth century Peru. The mummy looked like it was made of faded newspaper, and when Marklew got close to it he thought it smelled sweet like toffee. He looked for the solicitor, but he was not in attendance.

The year after that, the convention was in Leningrad. It was a reasonable convention. At auction Marklew bought an authenticated tooth from the head of Tsar Nicholas. He asked if anyone had seen the solicitor, but no one had; no one admitted even to knowing whom he was talking about.

The year after that, the convention was in Tehran.

Later that year, his eldest son died. Most of the time Marklew forgot he had any sons at all. They had gone away years ago to live with his wife in Italy. Some of the time Marklew forgot he had a wife either. She had a lover there, and they shared a house on the banks of Lake Como. Marklew's wife let him keep the house in Richmond, and granted him an annual pension.

He flew to Italy to attend his son's funeral. He couldn't remember when he had last seen his wife; she had always been petite, but now she had put on weight as if she wanted to look like a plump Italian mama. Husband and wife stood by the side of the grave, threw in clumps of earth that sounded too faint against the coffin. It turned out that the son had died fighting some war. Marklew hadn't known his son had been a soldier. He hadn't actually known there was a war on, wasn't that all over by now? "There's always a war going on somewhere," said his wife. She asked him how he was, and he said he was doing well. She reintroduced him to their younger son, who wore his hair foppishly long and looked to Marklew like a homosexual. He stayed the night with his wife and his wife's lover at their house in Bellagio. The décor was charming, but he thought the room was too cold.

When he returned to London there was a parcel waiting for him. It looked like a hatbox, although he knew he hadn't purchased a hat; he picked the box up, and with a cold thrill he knew what it must be. He took it into his study and opened it immediately.

Inside there was a rock. Presumably it had been put in there to weigh the box down. He lifted the rock, and he supposed that yes, it was about the same basic shape as a young boy's skull. Underneath the rock there was a sealed envelope. Inside, a simple, typed message:

"Not Dead Yet. But Coming Soon."

The following year the convention was in Johannesburg. It was a disappointing convention. At auction Marklew bought some bones, some skeletal fragments, a jar of pickled skin. In the bar on the Sunday night he asked whether anyone had seen the solicitor. He did so, evidently, with increasing volume. It was eventually requested that he retire quietly to his room.

Some months later his wife died. It had either been murder or a suicide pact, it was hard to be sure. Whatever the details, both she and her Italian lover were dead, shot in the head at point blank range, and maybe it didn't really matter which one had pulled the trigger. Marklew was not invited to the funeral. On the day his wife's body was laid to rest, he received another hatbox at his house. Once again it weighed like a skull. Once again there was no skull inside, just a rock. The rock was wet to the touch, and Marklew fancied it was covered with bubbles of solid spit. The bubbles wouldn't burst when he pressed down on them. The message inside the envelope, too, was the same. Maybe it was the type size, or maybe the font, but it seemed a sadder message this time: "Not Dead Yet," it apologized ruefully. And then, brighter, a cheery promise: "But Coming Soon!"

Marklew by rights inherited his wife's estate, but there was some little legal difficulty about it: her Italian family were claiming a substantial share. Marklew knew that the matter would resolve itself in his favour eventually, but in the meantime was obliged to let several of his staff go.

He still liked to hold dinner parties before going to a convention. He didn't attract as many guests as he once had, and the ladies seemed much more reluctant to fuck him. Still, he would show them his favourite skull, he'd talk to them of ritual sacrifice, and he'd invite them all to put their fingers between the cracks. The night before he flew to Buenos Aires he gave a dinner party and no one wanted to touch his cracks at all. And he was telling them some anecdote or another that seemed to be heading toward no discernible ending, when his one remaining maid interrupted him to say there was a young man at the front door to see him.

"I am not expecting any more guests," said Marklew.

"He says he is your son."

Marklew asked that he be shown into the drawing room.

His son was pale and shivering, but Marklew was pleased to see he had at least availed himself of a haircut. Marklew asked what he wanted. The boy helped himself to a brandy without even asking; his hand was shaking as he poured it. "I'm sorry," he said. "I'm sorry. I don't know who else to turn to."

Marklew told him at least to sit down.

"Oh God," the boy said. "Do you ever feel that someone is watching you? I mean, all the time. It's there in the shadows, waiting for me. Oh, not just in the shadows, oh God. It's there when I wake up, I wake up so frightened I think I'll have a heart attack. Do you feel this? Does anyone else feel this? Is it just me?"

Marklew asked his son if he were taking any drugs. The son said he was, a bit. Marklew suggested he should stop.

And suddenly angry, getting to his feet: "What is all this bloody stuff? Why do you want this bloody stuff?" And he was at the shelves now, he'd picked up one of the skulls, he was grimacing at it as if the very touch appalled him. "What do you want with all this *death*?" And he raised it high, he raised it so he could smash it down upon the floor.

"Put that down," said Marklew. "Put that down, very, very gently."

His son froze, and he was like a little boy again, and Marklew suddenly had a memory of him, of them playing together, or having a picnic, how old would his son have been, six or seven? "I'm sorry," said the boy. "Really." And he put the skull back on the shelf. And he burst into tears.

"If it can take me whenever it likes," he sobbed, "what's it waiting for?"

Marklew wanted to get back to his guests. He told his son he was flying to Argentina the next morning, and he had no time to deal with this right now. The boy asked if he could stay in the house whilst his father was away. Marklew pretended to consider, but he knew he couldn't have his son there, he couldn't trust him around all his fragile things. Did he have any money? He could give him some money for a hotel. The boy said he didn't want money, he already had money. "Here, take some money," said Marklew, and his son did.

"Well," said Marklew.

"Well," said Marklew's son.

"You'll be all right," said Marklew.

"Can I see you once you're back home?" asked his son.

"Yes," said Marklew. "Maybe. In time. Once you've straightened yourself out."

"I'll do that then," said his son. "I'll straighten myself out."

The convention in Buenos Aires was dreadful. At auction Marklew didn't buy anything at all.

On his return he found his maid had left the hatbox in the study. The rock inside was wet again, and perhaps just a little sticky. The note was very enthusiastic. "Not Dead Yet. But Coming Soon!!!!!!!"

There was also a message from the police, asking him to get in contact immediately. They had tried to reach him abroad, but the maid had given them a hotel name that was untraceable. Marklew's son had committed suicide, and had hanged himself with such force that he'd been virtually decapitated. The police expressed sympathy for his loss, and Marklew thanked them, but told them that he hadn't known his son well.

The following year Marklew didn't receive an invitation to the convention. It would usually come in the autumn; this year the leaves turned brown and fell from the trees, and then there was the cold; and then, snow.

↓

Richard Marklew rented a four-room flat in Lambeth. A bedroom, a kitchen, a bathroom, and one room left to do with whatever he pleased! Some days he even quite liked the flat. His landlady was called Mrs. Gascoyne. She never smiled much, or said anything very nice, but she had a heart of gold. Mrs. Gascoyne didn't like him moving in with all his dead things, she said it was unnatural. But she agreed to turn a blind eye if she upped Marklew's rent, and refused ever to do any of the cleaning. Marklew agreed, and a happy bargain had been made.

Of course, there wasn't room for all of his collection. He had to get rid of the gossamer wire puppets from Mexico, and his coffin lacquered with bone. He might have got a good price for them at auction, but the convention had never invited him again. As it was, he was able to donate some pieces to the British Museum. A lot had to be binned.

Marklew filled all the wardrobes and cupboards with what artefacts he had left. There wasn't much room left for clothes, but Marklew didn't need many clothes. Two complete skeletons lay spread out in his bath, one balanced on top of the other, and sometimes it seemed to Marklew that they were making love, and sometimes that made him laugh. On good days he'd open up all the cupboards and pull open all the drawers, and he could see his collection all around him. This expression of who he was, somewhat diminished, and in borrowed circumstances.

If the weather were fine he might take the omnibus into the city. He'd walk by the Thames, by St. Paul's, sit in Green Park. If the weather were bad, he'd stay at home.

At night he would lie in bed, and stare into the shadows, and fancy that they rippled.

Dear Mrs. Gascoyne had no choice but to raise the rent again. He wrote to the six biggest collectors of *memento mori* in Britain, men he had shared drinks with at the conventions, men who were very nearly old friends. Two of them replied. Between them they bought his shrunken heads, his canopic jars and death masks, his skulls. They paid so much that he could now pay the rent for four whole months, and he treated himself to a steak dinner too. No one wanted the cracked skull, though; they said it was damaged.

Most of all Marklew liked getting the omnibus to Waterloo Bridge. It was his favourite bridge. He liked to stand at the midpoint; he'd paced the length of it to find out precisely where the midpoint was. And he would tilt his body over the rails, as far as it would go, and stare straight down into the Thames. He could stare into the Thames for hours. Sometimes he saw shadows moving in there. He wondered whether they were the same shadows from his bedroom.

One day he took his cracked skull on an expedition into London. "You'll enjoy this," he told it on the bus—only a whisper, he didn't want people thinking he was mad! He took it to the midpoint of Waterloo Bridge, and dropped it over the side. He thought it would make a bigger splash. It somewhat disappointed him. The skull went straight down, it didn't even struggle for air. He watched for ages to see if it might float back to the surface, and then it began to rain, so he gave up, and went home.

The shadows in his bedroom reached out some nights and stroked him, and their touch was so very soft.

↓

And one day he was on the omnibus, and it was very crowded, but nevertheless Marklew managed to get a seat, people always gave up their seats when he came near—and for the life of him he couldn't remember whether he was going to Waterloo bridge or was coming back from it, and that was funny, but he was sure he'd work out which one when he got there!—and suddenly, by the doors, he saw him.

He had never expected he'd be able to recognize the man. There had never been anything remotely distinguished about his features, nothing that Marklew could ever recall to mind. But there was no question. He looked no older. But still cool, still stiff, his face a pose of professional blandness. Wearing a suit that was smart but not dear, not tailored but practical.

And just as soon as he'd seen him, the doors were opening, and the solicitor was getting off the bus. "Hey!" called Marklew. "Hey!" But the crowd was surging forward to fill up the little space that the solicitor's body had taken, and the bus was starting to move. "Hey! No, stop!" He was pushing his way through the other passengers now, and they were pushing back, they were angry. And he was pulling at the door, but the door wouldn't open, and then the driver brought the bus to an abrupt stop, and the doors freed, and Marklew hurled himself forward and tumbled out onto the street.

The crowds were no easier here than they had been on the bus, it seemed the whole world was out in London that day. "Hey! Stop! Stop!" called Marklew, but he wasn't even sure whom he was calling at anymore. And then—and then he saw him, the solicitor was maybe twenty feet further down the pavement, and he was moving fast, how could he move so fast in all this crush? "No, please!", and Marklew was running too. "Please!" Elbowing people away, waving his arms, breaking into little sprints on the spot when he got blocked and could advance no further. Marklew jumped off the pavement. Horns. Screams. The screech of tires. He was running down the road. He was catching the solicitor up.

And he reached him at last, and he grabbed him by the shoulder, and he didn't know what to expect when he touched him: he half expected his fingers would go straight through, or that he'd feel cold to the touch, or burn like fire—but no, no, he felt like an ordinary man. Swinging him around so they were face to face. And that face wasn't so bland now, it was frightened! He'd lost that cool, that stiff poise was gone for good. Now he had him. Although there was a beard, and there hadn't been a beard before—and this man's hair was grey, and he was old, and he was shorter than Marklew had remembered.

"Help me!" Marklew begged him. "You know me! Do you know me?"

"Please let me go!"

"You know me! You know who I am!"

"I don't know who you are, please!"

Marklew let go of the man, and he thought he didn't look much like a solicitor at all, not in that cheap brown coat, Marklew thought the man was probably in trade. "Please help me," said Marklew.

And the man hesitated. As if unsure whether to run, or whether to call the police. And then he said, "Go home. Go home, Mr. Marklew. It's waiting for you."

The hatbox was sitting outside on the pavement, where anyone might have stolen it. Still, no one had.

Richard Marklew picked it up, and it felt no heavier and no lighter than the boxes he had been sent before. He tucked it under his arm as he struggled with the keys to his flat, and it suddenly felt like such a disrespectful thing to do to a dead little boy, and he hoped that the front of the skull was at least pointing away from his armpit. He went indoors. He set the box down in the middle of the floor. Gently, carefully. He sat on the floor beside it. He looked at it.

He decided he wouldn't open the box.

He opened the box.

He saw only the top of the scalp, whiter and shinier than he had ever thought a scalp could be. He prodded it, daintily, with his finger. It was warm. It was cold.

He reached into the box so he could lift the skull out; with one hand he grabbed it by the back of the head, with the other he fingered the eye sockets. The skull was free, but he wouldn't look at the skull, not for the moment, he looked instead to see if there were another envelope to read, some special message to announce the long awaited arrival. Maybe even a receipt!—There wasn't. There wasn't, and all there was was the skull, and he was still holding it, it was in his hands, warm, cold, and he was looking at it at last, he was daring to look.

His heart beat so fast and he wondered if he were going to die. But he didn't, he just sat there on the floor, and the skull sat in his hands, and they were both touching each other, and yet neither had anything to say. To be honest, it was more than a little awkward.

The skull was perfect. It had not a single blemish. No browning discolouration around the temporal bones, as was common—the mandibles were in immaculate condition. The eyes were two round holes that seemed wide open in innocent surprise, the jaw was intact and allowed the mouth a reassuring smile.

And now Richard Marklew knew why he'd spent his lifetime building up a collection of the dead. He thought he'd known before, what the urge was, why he had to satisfy it, why he had *never* satisfied it, not 'til now. But he'd been wrong, and now he knew the truth, and the truth made him cry. He was crying with happiness. Was it happiness? Yes, probably.

He didn't want to let the skull go. He wasn't sure if he even could have. He got to his feet and his old bones cracked with the effort, but he didn't care. He held the skull tight, and he swayed a bit because he felt so giddy now, and it seemed to him they were dancing. He went to lie down upon his bed. He was still wearing his clothes. He couldn't get undressed without putting the skull down, so that was all right, he wouldn't get undressed again. It was simple.

He thought maybe he dozed a little, and when he awoke the little boy in his hands was watching over him. He felt comforted, he dozed some more. It got dark. It didn't matter. Some little light streamed in from the window, a streetlamp maybe, or the moon.

The shadows moved around them both, but he didn't need to look at them any longer.

And there was the crack—just the one crack, running horizontally from side to side, just above the chin. It wasn't damage, it was a beautiful crack, wide and inviting, and it was studded with bright white teeth like smooth pebbles, not a single tooth was missing. He dared himself to touch the crack. Would he touch the crack? He would. He pulled the crack closer to his face, right against his very lips, and he pushed his tongue inside, past the pebble teeth and onwards, deeper, he pushed his tongue into the smiling crack as deep as it could go.

PATCHES

Mother seemed cheerful about it, but then Mother was cheerful by default. Father was wary, though. "If it seems too good to be true," he'd say, "then it usually is." He said he'd go over the house with a fine-toothed comb, although the little girl thought he was probably exaggerating. He didn't find any dry rot, or damp rot, or rot of any persuasion; the plaster wasn't crumbling, the foundations were sound. Still, Father was wary. He was a man of the world, a man of business—a *man*, at least, at any rate. He was nobody's fool.

Mother and Father would ask the little girl what she thought, but they'd never wait long enough to hear her reply. But maybe this time that didn't matter. The little girl didn't know *what* to think. Mother said she'd make new friends at the new school, and the little girl shrugged; it wasn't as if she'd made any at the old school, so what did she care? And Father promised there'd be more room in the new house for all of her toys and games and books. But the little girl couldn't help but worry a bit, when her parents packed away her things for the removal men, that somehow putting them into cardboard boxes would mean that her toys and games and books would always seem *old* to her from now on, that when she took them out of the boxes at the other end she wouldn't want them anymore. And a new house would mean new creaks on the floorboards to navigate, and new places she'd have to discover when she wanted to hide.

The removal men came a little after nine o'clock, and that was very nearly punctual. Father said the family should follow on in the car an hour later: "We don't want to overtake them," he said, "we don't want to get there before all our belongings, what would that be like?" Mother was cheerful in the car, and Father pretended to be cheerful too, he even let Mother sing that song that was all about the green bottles, he even joined in a bit. They stopped off at a service station along the way, and Father let them all buy travel sweets. Pretty soon it began to rain, and Father had to turn on the windscreen wipers, and the screeching noise they made against the glass acted as background accompaniment to Mother's bottle singing—"Could you stop that now, please?" asked Father. By the time they reached their new town, and then their new street, it was pouring down, and the little girl wondered to herself why they were moving somewhere that was so wet. And there, at the bottom of a cul-de-sac, was *their* house; the little girl had been there several times before, of course, whenever Father had made one of his toothcomb inspections, but back then it had just been a house, and now it was a home, and that felt weird. The rain fell on all the other houses, but theirs was left dry, they were lucky, overhead there wasn't a single cloud. "It's an omen," said Mother. "We're all going to be so happy here!" And it meant that they could unpack the car without getting soaked to the skin.

There were so many cardboard boxes waiting for them, it seemed far more than had been taken from their old house that morning. And the little girl wondered how they would ever find the time to open them all, and yet she still marvelled that their entire lives had been crammed into such a small space. "We'll open them tomorrow," said Father, "Tomorrow!" said Mother, but they nevertheless rescued from one of the bigger boxes a saucepan and some plates. Mother made them scrambled eggs on toast. By now the rain had caught up with them, it battered against the windows as if it were trying to get in, and it sounded different from the old rain the little girl was used to. "It's a fresh start!" said Mother, with a smile. And, at Mother's suggestion, they also retrieved from one of the boxes the little girl's teddy bear. The little girl wasn't sure she wanted it, not yet; but she found, to her relief, that the teddy bear hadn't changed in transit, it was just the same bear it had been that morning. And she cuddled it in her new bed. But some time after midnight, in the pitch black, in the unusual pitch black, she realized the teddy bear now smelled a bit boxy and a bit cardboardy, and that made her feel sick. And she had to turn on the lights, and open up all the cupboards—and inside one there was an old blanket that must have been left behind by the house's previous owners. And the little girl wrapped the teddy in the blanket, and threw it right to the back of the cupboard—she knew that she was safe from the teddy now, she'd never touch it again, because to do so would mean she'd have to touch the blanket as well, and the blanket was even *worse*. And only then could she sleep—and the rain continued to fall hard all around the house, and hard on top of it.

↓

The little girl's new bedroom was right at the top of the house. It was an attic, really, with a bed put in it. The very roof was her ceiling, and the walls caved in on her in an inverted V, giving the room a triangular shape. And all the shelves for her toys and games and books buckled out at her at strange angles. The little girl wasn't sure whether she liked the shelves doing that at first, and then decided she *did* like it, she liked it very much, even if she no longer liked any of the toys and games and books that sat on them. The walls were painted a pure and gleaming white. And set into the ceiling was a small skylight, and it let the sunshine in every morning and protected her from the rain and the wind. The little girl liked this best of all, and she stared up at the skylight when she lay on her bed, she didn't need toys to play with or books to read. She was actually very happy—even if the rest of the house disturbed her, even if she couldn't get used to its new smells and colours and shapes, and the way it seemed so very very still in the middle of the night. If that still bothered her, if it woke her up, she'd just look straight upwards, through the skylight, and out at the sky beyond, and she'd be fine.

↓

"It's a fresh start," said Mother. "Everything's going to be different from now on." And the little girl agreed, it was already *very* different, and Father and Mother were now not talking to each other in rooms where the furniture was facing altogether new directions.

Father was still wary. The house had been too cheap, it had all been too easy, they had been taken for a ride. He wouldn't rest until he found out what was wrong with it. Mother asked, really very gently, why he'd agreed to buy the house in the first place if he wasn't satisfied—and Father just flared up, and said he'd been left little bloody choice, had he? But he was nobody's fool. He'd get to the bottom of it. He'd get to the bottom of everything. And it took him a few weeks, but at last, he succeeded. He called out his family into the front garden so he could show them.

"Look," he said. "It's obvious once you know." He pointed straight upwards.

"I don't see anything," said Mother, and Father clucked his tongue in irritation.

And it seemed ridiculous, but the little girl then thought she understood. "It's the sky," she said. The patch of sky above their house was unlike the patches of sky above the other houses. The skies were all blue, but theirs was a more muted blue, as if it had faded in the wash. And there was white creeping into the blue, and grey. The sun was shining down on them, but not very forcefully, really rather limply, as if it couldn't quite make the effort, as if it weren't quite up to the multitasking of producing both light *and* warmth.

"We've bought ourselves a defective sky," said Father.

It all made sense to him now. Why the house had been on the market at all. That sometimes the rain, or the wind, or the sunshine, seemed to be lagging as much as half an hour behind those of his neighbours'. That, sometimes, when he left for work, dawn had broken over the rest of the street, but not over *their* house, it made it difficult for him to find his car keys in the dark.

"What do you think is wrong with it?" asked Mother.

"Just old age," said Father. "It's wearing down. It's dying."

"What are those up there?" asked the little girl. She'd seen the specks before, peeking out behind the clouds, just little brown smears in the air. She hadn't thought they were anything unusual before. Now it was clear only their sky had them, no one else's did.

"Liver spots, I expect," said Father. "I don't know."

"What can we do?" said Mother.

"We'll probably have to replace it altogether," said Father. "We'll have to rip it out, and start all over. God knows how much that'll cost. God. This sky's had it. It's probably years old. Probably hundreds."

"Just think," said Mother, cheerfully, and it was mostly addressed to the little girl, "just think of all the things it must have seen!"

"It hasn't *seen* anything," snapped Father. "It doesn't have eyes. It's a sky. It breathes wind, and eats sunlight, and, and shits clouds, that's what skies do." He glowered up at it. "But not this one. Not well enough for my liking."

He went indoors, got straight on to the estate agent. He shouted at him down the telephone. Father was triumphant; he'd been right all this while. And although that first conversation with the estate agent proved inconclusive, each day he'd call the estate agent back, it became like a little hobby, and he'd threaten him with lawyers and courts and things. Father seemed so much happier now. He'd smile at Mother and the little girl over breakfast and over dinner—it was a bitter sort of smile, but a smile all the same. The little girl hoped he'd stay happy for a long time.

"It's a fresh start," Mother would say to the little girl. The little girl would nod, but nodding didn't always seem to be enough; Mother would add, so earnestly, "I need you to believe that, I need you to believe all of this is going to work." And then she'd cry, well, usually; but even if she cried she'd be laughing, even then she'd stay cheerful through the tears, and the little girl just didn't know what to make of that at all.

↓

The little girl went to her new school. And pretty soon she was invited to the birthday party of another little girl; she hadn't been around long enough for any of her classmates to realize they didn't like her yet. The other little girl had a big house, with a big garden and swimming pool; most of the children played in the pool, but our little girl didn't like water, and stayed on the side, and on her own. And looked up at the sky. It was brighter and bluer than her sky, and had been especially polished for the occasion. There were balloons and fairy lights attached to the sky, some hanging off white puffy clouds in the shapes of elephants and sweets, and someone had rearranged the stars so that they twinkled in the daylight and spelled out "Happy Birthday Trudy," which just happened to be the other little girl's name. Our little girl knew this sky was nicer than her sky, but preferred her sky nonetheless. When it was time to go home, she was given a goodie bag; the other little girls had got inside it, and torn up the slice of birthday cake, and broken the toy, and had written on the napkin, "Turdmuncher." There was an apple, and the little girl didn't dare eat it, she thought it might have been licked, or spat on, or worse; but there was also a bar of Milky Way, and the wrapping didn't seem to have been interfered with, it had been squashed a little but the chocolate inside was untouched. So she ate that.

↓

The skylight got dusty. And looking up through it on her bed, the little girl couldn't tell what was dirt on the glass and what were liver spots in the air.

The little girl was really too little to reach the skylight. Mother would have to clean it for her. But Mother would sometimes get distracted, she might sit downstairs in the kitchen all day and drink and smoke. Mother went through a lot of these distracted phases. And the little girl found she could get to the skylight—so long as she was standing on tiptoe, and standing on her bed, and standing on some of those fatter books to lend her those few extra inches she needed. She wiped away the dust. She gave the glass a push. It moved within its frame. She realized that the skylight could *open!*—and she fumbled at the catch, it was stiff, she had to tug at it hard and the effort made her fall off her tower of encyclopaedias, she had to build it all up again and start over. She opened the skylight. She expected that straight away the sky would simply come flooding in. It didn't.

If she pulled herself up with all her strength, the little girl could poke her head through the skylight. If she scrunched all her limbs together, really very tight, and thought about how very small she wanted to be, she could squeeze her shoulders through too. But her stomach was too big. So she began to leave her dessert. And, when that didn't make her stomach shrink fast enough, she stopped eating her dinner as well, and her lunch, and her breakfast. She'd put the food in the bin when her parents weren't watching. And very occasionally they did take notice of her, very occasionally she *had* to eat—but she didn't keep the food inside for long, she'd go back up to her bedroom, cough it all up, wrap it in the old blanket and hide it in her cupboard forever.

One day she managed it—she was thin enough to climb up through the skylight. She almost wasn't strong enough to do it, she felt so lightheaded and woozy, but she was a very determined little girl—she pulled herself out and into the moonlight, and the corners of the skylight cut into her sides as she did so, but she knew from now on it'd always be easier, she'd done it once and she could do it again, and it'd be easy, she'd just have to make herself a little bit thinner still. She sat on the tip of the roof, legs over both sides, and panted for breath, and tried to pretend that her body wasn't hurting so much.

The sky was above her. Very close. She lifted her hand up to it, but it was still too far away. Now she could see how livid those liver spots really were. Now she could hear the sky breathing—and it wasn't just the wind as she'd thought, that was just big puffs of breath, this was something softer and closer and private.

"Hello, sky," she said. She didn't know what to say, really. She didn't like speaking to *anyone* very much. But the sky, of course, didn't talk back—it couldn't, because skies can't talk—and that made the little girl feel a bit less self-conscious about the whole thing.

"You're very old," said the little girl. "Does it hurt to get so old?"

She thought about this for a while.

"I don't want to get as old as you," said the little girl. "To be as old and ugly as you. I don't think that would be nice at all."

The little girl thought about this too. And decided that maybe she'd been rude. "Sorry," she said. "No offence."

If the sky had taken offence, it seemed to forgive her. It wafted some light breezes at her, the little girl liked them, they were refreshing; she closed her eyes and opened her mouth and sucked them in, and she smiled. She stayed up there on the roof for a good hour or so.

"I'd better get back inside," she said, at last, reluctantly. "I've got school tomorrow. You don't have to go to school, do you? You're lucky." She shimmied her way back to the skylight, swung her legs over the side, hoped with all those puffs of breeze she'd inhaled she hadn't put on too much weight to squeeze back through. She looked back up at the sky. She gave it a wave. "Night night," she said. "I'll see you again tomorrow."

And, each night, the sky would be there, waiting for her.

Often she wouldn't talk to the sky at all. She'd sit up on the roof, and pretend she was all on her own, on her own like normal—but then, once in a while, she'd look bolt upwards, and smile, as if to let the sky know that her shyness was really nothing personal. And at other times she'd chat, she'd spill her guts—that's exactly what it would *feel* like too, that she was just letting rip, and everything in her head would just pour out; she wasn't very good at expressing herself, she hadn't much practice, so it'd all be higgledy-piggledy, her confusions, her fears—but the sky wouldn't mind. It'd just listen patiently. It never interrupted. It never tried to walk away.

She told the sky her name. Not the name her parents called her— her *real* name, the one she shared with no one, the one that she carried secretly within her heart and never let out.

Sometimes she'd get angry at the sky. "You're so big and powerful, but you won't do anything to help me!" She wouldn't raise her voice, she didn't want her parents to hear, but her whispered fury was sharp and cut through the clouds. Sometimes she'd simply say, "You're my only friend."

She realized that for all the years she'd lived in her old house, she'd never once spoken to the sky there, or thought about it, or wondered if it were all right. It made her feel very guilty.

She'd count the liver spots day by day, and see how they'd begun to outnumber the stars.

Patches

When she was bold she tried to stand on the roof. Her feet slid upon the slates, and she knew that if she fell it'd be straight to the ground, and she'd be lost for good. But even standing, she couldn't reach the sky. And so when she was bolder still, she tried to stand on tiptoe. These were the times when she didn't mind much whether she fell to her death. But strain as she might, the sky was always out of her grasp.

"I love you," she said one night, and she blushed hard at the admission, and felt so embarrassed that she had to crawl back through the skylight and she couldn't even wave goodbye to the sky and she didn't dare talk to it again for three whole days.

"I need you," she said shortly after that, and that seemed so much like a greater confession.

"Help me, please," she said one evening. And she got to her feet—wobbled a bit, because she was nervous, perhaps, or because the roof tiles were slippery after a typically sluggish spell of rainfall. She got onto her tiptoes. She raised her arms up high above her head. If only she were taller—but then, to be that, she'd have to eat more, and then she wouldn't be able to get through the skylight, would she? "Please," she said again, and then she *jumped*, as high as she could—and it wasn't that high at all, it was hard to get a stable platform to leap from—she fell back again, and her feet nearly gave way, but she was all right, she steadied herself. And so she jumped again, arms still up, her hands clasping and unclasping, trying to get a purchase on *something* . . . And she jumped once more, and by now she was crying, and she didn't care how she landed, she didn't care if she fell, "Please," she said, "I need you, didn't I say I *need* you?"

And her hand grabbed hold of the underbelly of the sky.

She was so surprised she nearly let go again.

She clung on for all she was worth. The sky had bent down for her, as far as it could go, but now it relaxed, it heaved itself back into position—and the little girl was swept up further into the air, maybe ten feet from the roof. She hung there, still crying, and she wasn't sure whether it was out of fear, or relief, or whether they were just those tears of thwarted effort she didn't need anymore but still had to come out.

The little girl dangled in the moonlit night. The moon didn't shine as brightly in this patch of sky as it did in all the others. But the little girl just thought it was the most beautiful thing she had ever seen.

She nuzzled into the sky. She was surprised to find it was furry. She began to stroke the fur with her spare hand. The sky began to purr.

She felt she could have hung like that forever. She wished she could. "I've got school in the morning," she told the sky. "Double maths, and a spelling test. Bleurgh."

So the sky lowered her back toward the roof.

And as the little girl dropped back down, oh, she couldn't help it, she fell awkwardly, maybe it was just that she didn't want to let go? In her fist she took a clump of sky with her, fur ripped from its skin. A gash was left in its belly. Just a little gash, but the sky was really so very old, and very weak. And the fur in the girl's hand crumbled into flakes. And from the gash poured flakes too, raining down on her, she thought it was the sky's lifeblood, "No, please no," she said. But the flakes fell down anyway, and twisted gently in the breeze—and the sky was responsible for the breeze too, wasn't she, was she sighing? was she gasping in pain? Like snow, but the flakes weren't cold, they were warm as breath, and they weren't white, they were the colour of twilight. "I'm sorry," said the little girl, and she cried, "I didn't want to hurt you, I just wanted to touch, I'll never do it again!"

And at last the gash healed over, and the sky stopped shedding, it was over, the sky was still alive—and it gave a low rumble, maybe of relief, maybe of despair. "I don't want you to die," said the little girl. "Please don't ever leave me."

↯

One day Father came home from work and he was happy, truly happy. He'd been given a raise and a promotion. "It'll be a lot more money," he said. He gave Mother a piece of jewellery, and the little girl some new toy or other. "I know things haven't been great recently," he said, "and I'm sorry. But this will be a fresh start. From now on, everything's going to be different. You'll see!"

He bought a better sofa for the sitting room, one made out of leather, and so deep the little girl thought she could sink within it and be lost forever. He bought a new dishwasher for the kitchen. And he looked up at the sky, and said, "Time to put paid to you too."

By this stage the sky really wasn't very well at all. It was shedding its flakes regularly now. Every morning Father would have to clear all the clumps of dead sky from off his car before he could go to work, he didn't like the extra effort that required one little bit. He said the neighbours were laughing at him, although Mother quietly pointed out he'd never once even said hello to the neighbours, how would he know?—and Father retorted, "Well, now I'll be able to face them if we get ourselves a brand new sky!" And then he smiled, because he was happy now, and this was a fresh start—sometimes he forgot about all that.

The man from the sky installations service came round at the weekend. He looked up at the sky, whistled through his teeth, and grimaced. "Some cowboy's put that in," he said. How long had they had it? Father said the sky had been there when they moved in. The man whistled through his teeth a bit more, and said he couldn't install a new sky until the old one had been removed. "And you need to do it fast," he said. "Nothing damages property quicker than a clapped-out old sky." Father asked him whether he could remove the sky for them, and the sky installation engineer said that was a specialist's job; he wasn't authorized to handle a sky as clapped-out as that one. Luckily, though, he had a brother in the business, and his brother had a skill with old skies that was almost crafty. He'd give his brother a call, he'd sort it out. And the brother came over the next day.

"It's dying," said the brother, "no doubt about that." Father had kept some of the sky flakes to show him, but the brother didn't give them that much attention. "It's dying, but skies are stubborn bastards, it could malinger on for years. We'll have to give it a helping hand." And so, twice a week, the man brought around to the house a pump and a nozzle, and sprayed acid up into the air. "It's my own formula," he said, "you can't get this in the shops." He told the family that the acid would work its magic, it'd burn the sky inside out. He advised them to take care of the side effects, the clouds might soak it up and start dripping acid rain. After his first enthusiastic bout with the spray gun, the man looked up at the sky, put on his rubber waterproof hat, and listened to it squawk with satisfaction. "Give it a few weeks," he said, "and it'll be toast."

Every night the little girl went on to the roof. "I'm sorry," she said, "I'm so very sorry." And she cried. And sometimes the sky would cry too, and if it did, the little girl put up her umbrella to keep safe.

And every night too, Father went out into the garden. He'd stare up at the sky, study his handiwork. It was easier to see the damage against the blackness. To see the cracks, the burn red boils so ripe and ready to pop.

One night the little girl followed him outside. She didn't like speaking to her father. He made her nervous, and made her stammer.

"Please don't hurt her," she said. "Please stop hurting her."

She said it so softly she thought at first her father hadn't heard, at first he didn't seem to react at all. But then he looked away from the sky, and looked down at his daughter, and the little girl couldn't read his expression. And perhaps that was because it was dark, but perhaps there was simply no expression to read.

"I love her," said the little girl in a whisper.

"You think I don't?" said Father. And his jaw moved, as if for other words to come out, but they didn't, not immediately. "You think," he said at last, "you think I *want* to hurt her?"

The little girl said she didn't know.

"I never wanted to hurt her," said Father.

The little girl dared to hope. Deep inside. That maybe this meant he'd stop spraying her with acid.

"I wanted this to be a fresh start," said Father. He wasn't looking at her now, he was looking anywhere else, he was looking up at the sky. "I tried. You've no idea how much I tried. A new town, a new house. But you can't run away from who you are. Wherever you go, you take yourself with you. Wherever you go, you're always there. You're too young to understand."

They both stood there silently for a while, in the garden, father and daughter.

"I could do it with you," said Father. "If it were just you. I'm sure I could. I know it. We could run away, just the two of us, and everything would be different. What do you say?"

"No," said the little girl, and went back indoors.

Later that night the little girl climbed out onto the roof for the last time. The cracks in the sky's side were weeping something thick and gloopy. "I asked you never to leave me," she said. "But I was wrong. I love you. I love you very much. And I need you to go whilst you still can."

The next morning the sky was gone. What it left behind was nothing, really, nothing at all.

Father was delighted. He called the sky installation engineer. The man arrived and looked upwards, and frowned. "What's been going on here?"

"The sky's gone."

"Dismantling a sky is a careful process, mate. This one has just been ripped out. Look at that. It's an eyesore, that is. It's just . . . it's just *void*.'"

"So when can my new sky be fitted?"

"You're not listening, sunshine. You can't have a new sky. Not now.

There's nothing there to fasten a sky onto. The whole thing's ruined."

Father got cross. And then began to plead. Surely there was something that could be done? And the man whistled through his teeth, and it was the most dismissive whistle of them all. "I take patches of sky and fix them to the heavens," he said, "I don't work miracles." He jerked his thumb straight up. "You're stuck with that, mate."

Father raged around the house. He smashed plates. He overturned tables. The little girl and her mother had to lock themselves in the little girl's bedroom. They didn't come out, no matter how much Father demanded, no matter how much he beat upon the door with his fists and called them both bitches. And, at last, in the night, they dared to open up, they turned the key and pushed the door ajar quietly, so quietly— there seemed to be peace, the beast was sleeping.

"Come with me," said the little girl. Mother shook her head. "I can't just abandon him, I can't." And she gave her daughter a big cheerful smile. "Don't you see? I *chose* him." "I didn't," said the little girl, and she took her rucksack, filled it with food, and left.

↓

The little girl went looking for her sky. She didn't know in which direction it had fled, nor how fast a sky could run. She just had to hope she was going the right way, and her little girl feet could catch up with it. And she walked with her head straight up, and that hurt her neck a bit, and meant the blood kept rushing from her brain, and she kept bumping into things.

Within a few days the food in her rucksack ran out. She got hungry. Sometimes people took pity on her and offered her something to eat. But the little girl had read enough fairy tales to know you must never accept gifts of food, you could be trapped in the underworld forever. So she always refused. She had to steal her food instead. She got good at running. The sky, her patch of sky, that must have been good at running, she could never overtake it, but she, she got good at running too—and as she ran, as she dodged the security guards at the supermarket and *ran*, she hoped that somehow the sky was looking down on her and was proud.

She'd sleep on park benches, in shop doorways, underneath bushes. In the summer it would be warm, it'd almost be comfortable, but then other people would sleep in the same places, and she didn't like that, she didn't want to be around other people. In the winter it would be cold, sometimes freezing, sometimes she'd cry against the frost of the night. But at least she'd be alone.

Presently she came across a deep forest.

She'd heard once that dying animals hide themselves away, as far from their pack as they can get. She wondered if that was true for skies as well.

The deeper into the forest she went the darker it became, and the denser the crush of trees blocking her path. She looked above her and all she could see were thick branches and treetops, she couldn't be sure there was any sky there at all. All there was to eat were berries; but the berries here had never been picked by human hand, never been threatened by another living thing, they grew large and unchecked, they were the kings of the forest—ugly and oozing and the size of the little girl's fists—and as she snapped their stems and put slices of them into her mouth, she was afraid that the surviving berries would marshal their forces, that they would bite back.

And, one day, just as she thought the trees were so tightly compacted her little body wouldn't squeeze through, and that the berries were so wild that they had grown arms and legs—one day, suddenly, she found herself in a clearing. And there, in the middle of it, was her sky.

It was very sick. Most of it wasn't in the air at all now. Most of it was draped listlessly across the grass. Its boils were now sunken like old tomatoes. Its liver spots now merged into one.

It gave a faint rumble, like distant thunder, when she approached.

"I just wanted to say goodbye," said the little girl.

And she was really so very tired. So she wrapped the folds of the sky around her as a blanket. The fur was so very threadbare now she could barely feel it at all, it was as if she were hugging onto thin air. And she made the sky her pillow too, she pressed her ear right against it, and she heard its heartbeat, so thin and hesitant, and it seemed to chime with the hesitancy of her own.

It smelled wrong. The sky smelled all boxy and cardboardy. And she wondered whether this patch of sky was really her patch of sky after all. And then she decided that didn't matter. She loved it anyway, and she'd stay with it, and care for it as long as it needed her. She kissed it. And she went to sleep.

When she woke the next morning she was cold. The sky around her was dead. She cried for a little bit, and then resolved never to cry for it again.

Patches

She'd have liked to bury it, but that was silly, how can you bury the sky? So she gave it a final hug, and she walked on. She didn't know in which direction, deeper into the forest or not, she reasoned that even the deepest forest had to come to an end eventually. And so it did.

↓

You're worried about the little girl. She was fine. She was fine. Don't worry.

The little girl grew up, as all little girls do. As most little girls do.

And she found happiness. Oh, she was lonely for a while—but we're all lonely, aren't we, for a while? And she softened her heart enough that she fell in love. In fact, she fell in love several times. Not all these men and women were worthy of her love, and some of the break-ups were hard and messy. But somehow the experience of every single one of these loves left her better off, and better equipped to deal with the next. She had a little girl of her own, and she loved her too, and the little girl loved her back, it was very uncomplicated, that.

She travelled. Staying in one place too long made her uncomfortable. She'd come to rest under many different patches of sky. And she never loved any of them. Because, at the end of the day, loving the sky is a last resort. We'd all rather settle for anything else. Even if they don't smell right, or they're the wrong shape, even if they say bad things and hurt us sometimes. Even if we sometimes doubt they ever really love us at all. Still better than sky. Really, loving the sky, that smacks of desperation.

The little woman held hands with her lovers, on beaches, on bridges, on towers so tall they scraped the sky's belly. And she'd kiss them, and she'd swear undying love to them, even if she didn't believe it, and they might swear right back, even so. And, happy, or unhappy too, either way—she'd never look up, she'd never do that, she held on tight to what was in front of her. She'd never look up, and above her head the skies swam, and danced, and died.

THE
SIXTEENTH STEP

So, was the house haunted? Probably not; but it certainly had some peculiar quirks, and Mrs. Gallagher always felt obliged to tell her guests of them. She'd warn those taking the box room that they might be able to hear weird whispering sounds in the night—but there was no doubt it was simply an effect of the wind coming in off the North Bay, sometimes in the winter the wind off the coast could be pretty fierce. There was a spot in the breakfast room, she said, upon which if you stood for too long you'd get a chill right down to your very marrow; I never found that spot, although I looked hard enough, I might have felt a chill in any number of different places but never anything that touched my marrow even closely.

And there was the staircase, and that was harder to explain. There were fifteen steps leading up to the first floor, the first nine straight up, the tenth curving around to the left as you ascended. They were covered with a thin shag carpet, and supported by wooden bannisters. Fifteen steps in all—but if you went downstairs in the dark, there, at the bottom, you would find a sixteenth.

It only happened in the dark. If you put the lights on to count, there'd always be the fifteen, looking perfectly ordinary. If you took a candle downstairs with you, the sixteenth couldn't be found, and nor on nights when the moonlight was pouring in neither. But if it were pitch black, if when you looked down you couldn't see your feet or where they might be leading, then that extra step would be waiting for you. And only as you went downwards, never on the way up.

It was a strange thing, but not especially unnerving. Mrs. Gallagher told her guests of it only so they wouldn't stumble, not so they should feel spooked or scared. Especially in the holiday season, she said, when the arcades were open late, and the sea was warm enough for night time paddling, guests might come back once she'd gone to bed, and she didn't want anyone waking her if they tripped. They'd be fine if they went straight to bed themselves, of course; it would be if they came down afterwards for a glass of water, say, that they might run into problems.

You'd get guests trying it out, of course. Especially the young ones: newlywed husbands trying to show off to their wives, squaddies on leave egging each other on. We could tell the sort. We could tell that, first chance they'd get, they'd brave it for themselves. We were smart. We'd encourage them to get it out of the way on the first night, we'd do it before anyone had gone to bed so it wouldn't disturb. We'd turn out all the lights and pull the curtains and let them have their fun. Down they'd come, counting off the stairs as they did so, maybe laughing a bit, maybe trying to scare each other. They'd reach the sixteenth step, they'd laugh a bit more, they might even kick at it to make sure it was real. We'd give them a minute or two, and then they'd lose interest, and we could turn the lights back on and get on with more important matters. It wasn't as if the extra step *did* anything once you'd found it; it was just a step, after all.

George and I tried it too, the first night we arrived. Mrs. Gallagher asked whether she should turn off the lights so we could check for ourselves, and George smiled in that charming way he sometimes had and said he was quite sure he didn't need to put her out. Even I was fooled, I assumed he wasn't interested. But late that night, once he'd had his business with me, and we were lying in the dark, he said that we should go down the stairs and see what this extra step palaver was all about. I couldn't sleep either, the waves were noisy; in years to come I'd realize there was no more reassuring sound in all this world, but I wasn't used to it yet. I was a bit afraid, and I told George so, but he pooh-poohed that; he said it would all be nonsense anyway.

George was in his pyjamas, I was in my nightie, and I remember neither of us wore slippers. He held onto my hand, and told me to count the stairs off with him. I was frightened, yes, but it wasn't a bad frightened, and I told myself it was like all those things at the funfair on the beach, this was the dodgems and the ghost train, all rolled into one. George was even whispering jokes at me, and he had a nice voice when he whispered. We reached the fifteenth step, and George said, "Shall we go on?" And I was going to say no, let's not, let's turn back and go to bed, but he was only teasing, of course we went on; he took another step downwards, and he pulled me after him. We stood on the impossible step. "It has to be a trick," said George, and he sounded a bit angry, the way he did when he thought the foreman was cheating him. My bare feet were cold. The carpet had run out at the fifteenth step—this one beneath seemed to be made of stone. But then, no, not stone, because it wasn't so hard as all that, and it was getting smoother, like it was old mud breaking under our combined weight or even loosening to our body heat, it was getting softer, even liquid now, and I was sinking into it, and yet it was still so very *cold*.

I tried to pull away, but George was still holding me. So I pulled harder, I wrenched myself out of his grip, and that's when I stumbled. I felt myself beginning to fall and I couldn't stop myself, and all I could see was the black and I didn't know how far away the ground might be.

It was just a few feet, of course, and I was more shocked than hurt. And there was suddenly light, and there was the landlady, holding a candle, and leaning over the bannister down at us. "Are you all right?" she asked.

"Yes," I said. "Sorry."

"I did warn you. Please go back to bed."

She stayed on the stairs so she could light our way. As we passed she didn't bother to hide her disapproval. "Sorry," I said again. George didn't say a word.

George was cross with me that night. I told him about the cold step, but he said he'd felt only carpet, just like on all the other steps, and that I was being stupid.

↓

You asked me for the truth. And this is the truth as I understand it.

George was not a good man, but he was not a bad man either, not entirely. Mrs. Gallagher would say I was justifying again. She said I did a lot of justifying, and I suppose she was right. But I know what's fair, and I want to be fair to George. I've known some bad men. There's no tenderness to bad men, and George, he could sometimes be tender.

He said what we did wasn't theft. We'd come into town, and would stay at a little hotel, a bed and breakfast maybe, nothing grand. And then when it was time to move on, we'd sneak away without paying. He said that proper theft would have been if we'd taken the silver with us as we went, but we never did that, George had too much pride. But the idea was there in his head, wasn't it? He'd spoken it out loud. With George, I knew, if it was in his head, if that little seed of an idea was planted, it was the beginning of everything.

The Sixteenth Step

But for the time being it wasn't theft, not really—we would come to a town, and George would spend the days out looking for work. He'd go to the factories, he'd go to the warehouses. He said that as soon as he got a job he'd return to the bed and breakfasts, every single one, and he'd pay them back. I'm sure at the start he even meant that.

George would come back to the hotels and tell me there was no work to be found—but he'd heard talk of work a few miles away, the next town along, just over the hill, just across the moors, wherever. And off we'd go chasing it. I hated it when we had to move on, but George always looked so much happier, he'd suddenly beam with hope, and that made up for it. He might carry my bags as we walked; he might even sing.

One day we reached the coast. And there was nowhere farther for us to go, not unless we changed direction.

"I could be a fisherman," George said. "I would enjoy catching fish all day long. Good honest work. It's all going to work out. You'll see." As far as I knew, George hadn't been inside a boat his whole life, but it was wiser not to say anything.

There were lots of bed and breakfasts to choose from. It was a holiday town, but off-season, everything was empty. I don't know what brought us to Mrs. Gallagher's. Fate, I suppose. Who knows why things happen, they just do.

George rang the doorbell, and doffed his hat, and gave that smile he was good at. I did my best to look like the respectable housewife on holiday that I always wanted to be.

Most landladies would ask for a deposit. We had to hand over the deposit without appearing to mind, as if there were plenty more where that came from. Sometimes it was the hardest bit of acting I had to do. Mrs. Gallagher didn't want a deposit.

"No deposit?" said George. "Well, well." And he smiled wider, but he also frowned, as if suspecting he was being conned.

"No deposit," agreed Mrs. Gallagher. "All my guests pay when they leave."

She told us about the whispering in the box room, but the hotel was empty, we could pick any room we wanted, and I was glad George allowed us a room that wouldn't scare me. She told us about the strange chill in the breakfast room. She told us about the step you could find only in the dark.

↓

In the morning she served us breakfast. She didn't mention the night's disturbance, and nor did we. She asked us how we wanted our eggs. "Fried and runny," said George. I told her I'd like mine poached. She gave a curt nod, then went into the kitchen.

She brought us out plates of sausage and bacon and fried bread. I had a poached egg. "Where's my egg?" George demanded to know. Mrs. Gallagher said she had only one egg, and apologized.

George glowered. He managed a few bites of sausage, then pushed his plate away. I knew how hungry he must be, but he had such pride. He lit a cigarette, stared at me through an ever-thickening cloud of smoke. I pretended not to notice. I wanted to eat as much of my breakfast as I could. I hoped that, if I ate fast enough, he wouldn't say anything until I'd finished.

"You enjoying that?" he said too soon, softly, dangerously softly.

I knew there was no right answer. I looked at him. I tried to keep my expression as neutral as possible.

He took my plate. He held it up, as if to inspect it closely, as if to ensure it was fit enough for his queen. He spat on it. Then he put the plate back down on the table, and ground out his cigarette in the middle of the food, in the middle of the egg.

"I'll be back later," he muttered, got up, and left.

I was still so hungry. But I didn't want to eat from my plate, even though the spit was only my husband's, and I loved my husband. And I didn't want to eat from his, in case he came back.

Mrs. Gallagher took away the plates, and if she was surprised they were still heavy with food, she didn't comment.

I stayed the day in the bedroom.

That evening George came back and he was all smiles. He said maybe he'd found a job after all—a fisherman had said he would take George out on his boat in the morning, try him out for size. He'd brought back a couple of bottles of beer, I don't know where he'd got them, and he let me have a little bit. When that night he did his business, he was kind and quick.

The next morning he left early. I got to eat my breakfast on my own. It was delicious.

That same night George came back to the hotel angry. The fisherman hadn't waited for him. It had all been some bloody big joke. I asked him where he'd been all day, and that was a mistake. Later that night he apologized. He said the fisherman had waited for him, he'd gone out in the boat. But the waters had been very rough, and he hadn't been well. The fisherman found it funny. He supposed it was funny, come to that. I mean, he'd get used to the sea if he had to, but in the meantime, it was funny. Didn't I think it was funny? It was all right, he said, he didn't mind if I did, we could laugh at it together, like we used to laugh at things. I gave him a kiss, and that made him feel better.

He said he'd try his luck again. Maybe another fisherman would take him out. Maybe the first fisherman wouldn't have told all the others. We had breakfast together. Mrs. Gallagher asked how we wanted our eggs. He said he wanted his fried, but runny. I said I'd have mine poached. She brought me a plate of sausage, bacon, and a poached egg. She brought George a plate of fried eggs, and nothing but fried eggs, the yolks all broken and pooling thickly into one another. George stared at the plate, and didn't say a word.

↓

Mrs. Gallagher asked me my name. I hesitated, and she saw I hesitated—but then I told her my name anyway, the real one, not the one George liked me to use.

"Mine is Nathalie," she said.

"Natalie?"

"Nathalie. It's French." She didn't look very French. Her arms were big and thick, her face rough like sand; in years to come I'd think that sand must have blown off the beach and got stuck deep in her skin and she hadn't been able to scrub it out. Not my idea of French at all; George's mother had shown me some fashion magazine, back in the days we were allowed to visit, and there were French women inside, and Nathalie Gallagher was nothing like them. "You're in trouble," Nathalie Gallagher said.

"No, I'm all right."

"You're in trouble. I could help you. You could stay here with me. I can run this place alone if I have to do, but I could use an extra pair of hands. I couldn't pay much, but you'd get bed and board."

"And George?" I said.

She didn't say anything to that.

"George wouldn't like it," I said. I knew all he wanted to do was get his

233

own job and be able to look after me.

"I had a disappointing husband too," said Mrs. Gallagher. She told me that her husband had brought her back to England after the war. She didn't say which war, and I presumed it was the last one, but it was so hard to tell how old she might be. I didn't like to ask. "He said he had some property, I thought he must be a duke or something. Turned out he owned a hotel. I had to spend my days learning how to make full English breakfasts. Yes, he was a disappointment."

"Where is your husband?" I asked. "Is he dead?" The words seemed so blunt, I could have bitten my tongue.

Mrs. Gallagher didn't seem offended though. Indeed, she gave my question some thought. "No, I don't think so," she said at last. "He's probably still alive."

I kept the job offer in my head, turned it over and gave it a good prod whenever things were bad. Things were bad a lot that week. I thought I would tell George when he was in a good mood, maybe he'd see the value in it, even if it were just short term, even if it could just tide us over awhile and give us some sort of *home*—but George was never in a good mood, there was no work out there, and the mood just got worse and worse, so I decided I'd just have to tell him quickly and get it over with and trust to luck.

He didn't shout, that was good. He turned from me, and lit a cigarette, and stared out of the window down upon the cliffs and the sea, as if in deep thought, as if giving it actual consideration.

"It's time we left," he said.

"So soon?"

"There's nothing for us here. We'll go tonight."

We packed our stuff, waited until it was dark. Past midnight I said to George that we should get going, but he shook his head impatiently, it wasn't time yet, he had a feeling for these things. We sat there on the bed, side by side, in silence, and George listened for noise. At last he took my hand, and squeezed it, and that was the signal, and I think it was done in affection too.

It was pitch black. George carried the bags, he told me to walk ahead of him. I clung to the bannister rail. I counted the steps downwards, one, two, three, four, and at five the staircase curled around toward the final descent to the front door. Now, we both knew about the extra step that was waiting down there, and neither of us mentioned it, and I dare say we'd both factored it into our calculations, sixteen stops until we reached the bottom. But now I was in the dark I thought of it only with dread—and I mean that, a hard, heavy dread—I didn't want my feet to touch that step—I didn't want any part of my body to come into contact with something so cold and so inexplicable—and here I was, inching farther toward it, another step down, then another, then another, as if I were falling somehow, as if I were falling and there was no way to climb back up, I couldn't change my mind, I couldn't turn around, my husband was behind me blocking my way and he would never let me free. And another step, and another—and I wondered if I'd miscounted already, were there two steps to go, or three? Three before . . . ? I didn't want to reach that step but I didn't want to get past it either—and it sounds silly but it suddenly seemed to me that step was a dividing line between all of my sorry past and all the future before me—and if I got past the step, then that was it, the future waiting there in the darkness was just more of the same, just more of the same. Two steps. One. I *had* miscounted, but there was no delaying it now, that step in front of me had to be the extra one. And then there was light from up above, and the darkness was spoiled, so there was no extra step at all, and the relief I felt was so overwhelming that it took me a moment to realize we must have been discovered.

The candle didn't give much light, but it was enough. Mrs. Gallagher stared down at us.

George said, "We're leaving. We don't want any trouble."

Mrs. Gallagher said nothing.

George said, "We're not going to give you any trouble. We'll just leave, and be on our way."

Still nothing.

He said, "When I get a job, I'll come back. I'll pay you then. I'm not thieving."

Mrs. Gallagher said, "Just go. But don't you ever come back."

"Well then," said George. "Well! Then I won't. You bet I won't." And he actually grinned at her, and doffed his hat.

I wanted to say I was sorry. I couldn't find the words, as easy as they were. I tried to smile at her, something, but she didn't look at me, not the whole while. That's what hurt.

George opened the front door, and we stepped out into the wind, the night, our future together.

🔽

I thought maybe he wouldn't come looking, maybe he just wouldn't care, and would let me be. I thought maybe he might even be relieved, one less mouth to feed, I wouldn't slow him down anymore. But still I'd keep checking behind me as I walked on, still I'd keep off the main roads, hide sometimes in bushes—because whether he wanted me or not, of course he'd come looking. He had his pride. That's all he had.

I didn't even know which direction I was headed in. And so I shouldn't have been surprised when I reached the coast, but I was. I thought we'd travelled so much farther than that, that the coast was weeks behind us. But there it was, the cliffs at my back, the sea in front, and I trudged my way along the beach squashed between the pair of them.

I certainly hadn't expected to find Mrs. Gallagher again. If I had looked for her house I'm sure I wouldn't have found it. But I gazed up, and there it was ahead of me, it was the only place in miles that seemed to give off any light, maybe, I fancied, the only place in the world.

I knocked at the door.

"I'm sorry," I said. "I'm sorry, I'm sorry."

"You're in trouble," said Mrs. Gallagher. And at last I understood what she meant. Because I was in trouble, and I hadn't quite dared believe it until then—but of course I've known, that's why I'd run away, wasn't it? Because it was all right, my being trapped with George for the rest of my life. Maybe that's all I deserved. But not my child. Not my child. Never.

"You'd better come in," Mrs. Gallagher said.

🔽

I arrived just before the holiday season, and there was a lot to learn.

I learned how to make beds, not in the ordinary way, but in the hotel way.

I learned how to clean a room quickly, so that you could give the impression everything was spick and span on the surface, and not draw attention to the real dirt underneath.

I learned how to make a proper cooked English breakfast. I got quite good at them, but Mrs. Gallagher was always better, so she stayed in charge of the kitchen. "My husband taught me, said he cooked the best fry-ups in Yorkshire," she said. "His only promise that was worth a damn."

I was given a room on the ground floor, and at first I was happy about that, it meant I didn't have to use the staircase at night. But I was never very comfortable there. The little window looked out onto the street, you could hardly tell we were by the sea at all. And sometimes in the night, I could hear noises under the floorboards—like distant footsteps, shuffling about beneath the ground. I told Mrs. Gallagher about them, but she just shrugged, said she'd never heard of that before. But she moved me upstairs to the box room. There was that whispering sound in the box room, but it was just the wind and the ocean spray, and I liked it, and soon I found the strange echo it made in the darkness very comforting, like the elements were trying to send me to sleep.

When the hotel packed out, and it did most of July and August, even the box room had to be let. Then I would share a bed with Mrs. Gallagher. It was a large bed, and quite comfortable, and there was plenty of room—and I was a little afraid at first that a big woman like Mrs. Gallagher would snore, George snored something chronic and he wasn't half her size. But she slept so still, sometimes it was though she was hardly beside me at all.

I want you to know nothing untoward ever happened between me and Mrs. Gallagher. And when August was over somehow I just didn't move out from the room, and I just stayed with her. It meant there was one less bed to make.

And when the pregnancy was full on and I couldn't do much work, Mrs. Gallagher never minded. She said I could stay in bed, or sit downstairs, whatever made me most comfortable, and she'd bring me cups of tea, and slices of cake, anything I wanted. "It's nearly time," she said to me one day, and I asked whether I should go to the hospital. "You don't need a hospital," she said, "I can do this. Do you trust me?" And I did trust her, and I was glad, I hadn't wanted to leave.

She fetched hot water and towels, and you came out, and it was easy, I think your birth was the easiest thing I had ever done. You were the simplest, most natural thing in my entire life. "It's a boy," said Mrs. Gallagher, and she looked happy, but I think she may have been a little disappointed. She helped me name you. Did you know that? Do you like your name? It was Mrs. Gallagher who picked it.

She told me that I shouldn't call her Mrs. Gallagher, I should call her Nathalie. And I did so, from time to time, just to make her smile. But I thought of her as Mrs. Gallagher, and I liked her that way—not formal, you understand, but protective, and strong, and better than me.

I started in my sleep, I couldn't breathe. I opened my eyes and saw a figure was standing over the bed, and I was held down, there was a hand tight across my mouth. I couldn't call out.

"Hello," whispered George, genially enough.

I opened my eyes wide, and blinked, in what I hoped he'd take as a fond greeting.

I didn't know how he'd found me, and I never did know. I suppose he might have broken into all the bed and breakfast establishments across the country until he'd got the right one. That seems quite likely.

He said to me, "I've got a job! It's all going to be all right. I've got lots of money, and it's all going to be as it was, and you can come back with me now, and you'll never be hurt again!" That sounded fine, but his hand was still on my mouth, and pressing down hard, and his fingernails had curved round and were digging painfully into my face.

You started to cry. You didn't care about being quiet, I don't know whether you were disturbed by the intruder, or just hungry—I'm guessing it was hungry, you were always hungry. George hasn't even seen the cot, I think; now he whirled around, and he let me go.

"He's yours," I whispered.

"Mine," he said. And he sounded amused, he seemed to like the sound of that. "You're both mine," he said. And he wasn't bothering to whisper anymore, and that was bad, it meant he didn't feel the need to be secret anymore.

Mrs. Gallagher didn't stir. "Is she dead?" George asked bluntly, and laughed.

"No," I said.

"I want to talk to her."

Mrs. Gallagher's eyes opened at that. She was already awake.

"I didn't steal from you," George said. "I didn't steal from *you*."

Mrs. Gallagher didn't say anything to that. Neither did I. George considered.

"Get up," he said. "Both of you."

"I'll come with you, George," I said. "But you don't need her, let's just go."

He slapped me around the face then, and it wasn't especially hard, but I hadn't been slapped for a long while and it hurt.

"We're all going outside," he said.

238

The Sixteenth Step

"What are you going to do with her, George?"

"I don't know," said George, "I don't know." And he sounded genuinely worried about that. I thought he was going to cuff me again, but he didn't bother.

Mrs. Gallagher got out of bed. She struck a match, and lit a candle. And it was brighter than I expected, too bright, surely; and I saw two things that startled me. One was George himself—his clothes were torn, and he had a ragged beard that seemed in the flickering light a scar across his face. And I realized he had no pride in anything anymore. And the second thing—that was the ugly little knife he was carrying.

"Get moving," he said.

We walked down the stairs ahead of him. Both of us were in our night dresses, and I thought how cold it would be out there in the dark, and that maybe that was the least of our concerns; the shag carpet was at my bare feet; and you were in my arms, and bless you, you'd gone back to sleep, you weren't scared of anything, you were with mummy and you felt safe.

I asked George once again what he was going to do, and I tried to find the right things to say that had always made him feel better, the ones that calmed his rages—but it'd been too long, I couldn't remember any. George didn't reply, and that was just as well, because it meant I heard Mrs. Gallagher plainly when she hissed at me: "Jump."

We were in sudden pitch black. She must have blown out the candle.

And I felt her then leap into that black, and I didn't know how far off the ground we were, I couldn't judge it at all—I couldn't tell how many steps there might be, or what was waiting for us at the bottom. And I didn't care, I leaped too.

George gave a cry of—what? Surprise? Anger? Probably a mixture of both, and he started down the stairs after us, and then he shouted out again, and this time it was fear.

Mrs. Gallagher struck another match. She lit the candle. The glow seemed to take an agonizingly long time to reveal anything.

George had hit the sixteenth step. And then had carried on going downwards. He had found a seventeenth, maybe an eighteenth too. The floor was up just around his knees. It looked as if his legs had been severed, and he was balancing his body on two un-bloodied stumps; no, it looked like the downstairs floor had become a lake, and he had sunk below the surface. And Mrs. Gallagher and me, we, we were walking impossibly upon water.

"Help me," he said. The light seemed to give him some courage, he even dared show impatience. "Get me out of this."

He grunted, tried to turn himself about, but there was nowhere for his body to go—nowhere but onwards. And so doing, he took another step.

For a moment I thought his body was in free-fall, but it came to a stop, the line of the floor was now across his chest. He looked so frightened. He grunted again, his face contorted with effort, and he pulled one of his arms free and waved it at us. At me.

"I'm sorry," he said. "Please. Help me. Please." He reached out to me. And I think I would have gone had it been for my sake alone. I would have pulled him out. Or he would have pulled me in, more likely, in and under, just as he had done over and over for all those years. I loved him. But there was more than my love to think about now.

He saw that I wasn't going to help. And I thought he might threaten me. I thought he'd tell me he'd kill me. I think that would have been better. But his face just fell, that's all, and he looked so very sad.

He tried to pull up his second arm. He couldn't. He put his free hand flat upon the ground, tried to use it to prise himself out. It was no good.

One more step forward. And now only his head was peeking out, and he had to tilt his face toward the ceiling so he could speak. He said, so softly, as if in awed wonder—"The steps are so steep. Oh God. Oh God. They're so *steep*."

Mrs. Gallagher stepped out. He looked at her with such hope. He thought she might want to save him, even now, in spite of all. I knew she wouldn't.

She stood right beside his head. If he'd wanted to, he could have bitten her feet. If he'd wanted to. He looked up at her, and she looked down on him, and she didn't gloat.

He opened his mouth to say something, and she shook her head, and he closed it again.

She blew out the candle.

⤓

When the guests came we'd tell them of the noises in the attic, and the cold chill in the breakfast room, and of the extra step the staircase would grow in the dark. We didn't talk of the strange footsteps under the house, the ones you could hear just sometimes, when the sea was quiet and the wind was at a lull. They didn't need to know everything.

↯

I said that nothing untoward ever happened between me and Mrs. Gallagher, and nor it did. But I wouldn't have minded.

I told her too late. She was dying, and fading so fast—she'd started the holiday season with the same no-nonsense energy as always, but then she'd got so slow, and so tired, and eventually we just asked our guests to leave and closed the doors on them. She lay in the bed and I gave her all the space I could, I'd have moved to another room, but she told me she wanted me to stay by her in the night. I said that I loved her. I said that I had loved her for so long, and wanted to show her, wanted to do anything to her that would make her happy.

She smiled at me. She said, "That would have been nice."

And I kissed her. I kissed her sand-studded cheeks, her skin was so coarse beneath my lips and there was nothing I could do to make it soft.

Still she never snored, still she slept so peacefully that some nights I woke up thinking she might already be dead. And there was that one night I woke, and she wasn't there beside me. She hadn't moved from the bed for over a week, she hadn't the strength, and I was so frightened, I thought maybe she'd died and her body had simply melted away. I left the bedroom, went out into the darkness of the house, I lit a candle, I called for her. There I found her, down the staircase, on the bottom step, and she was stamping down on it weakly, without stopping, as if she couldn't stop, not until I spoke to her. She turned up to me, up to the light. "I can't get through," she said. "Why won't it let me through?" It was the only time I ever saw her cry.

She died only a few days later. I wasn't there for the very end, but I don't think it would have mattered much to her, she didn't know where she even was by then, and if she called out a name it would be Thomas. Her missing husband, maybe? Even a son? Who knows? At the end of the day there was still so little I knew about her.

We found her body, you and I. You weren't scared at all. You are still so young, and so fearless. You don't even remember, do you?

I know you don't remember Mrs. Gallagher. My Nathalie. My own. But she was good to you. I wish you'd ask about her, and not about your father.

You know most of the rest of it.

Mrs. Gallagher had left the house to me in her will. I had no idea, she had never discussed it with me. But I was not a blood relative, of course, and certainly could not have been considered a spouse, and after the death duties were paid there was no way I could afford to keep it. I sold it on.

Bed and breakfasts were all I knew now, that and the sea. I didn't want to stay in the town, too many people seemed to know about me and my relationship with Mrs. Gallagher, and I had no shame of it, but I wanted nothing to do with them. That's why I moved us to the south coast, so far away, and bought our little hotel here. The sea here is warmer, the wind not as fierce, but I don't mind, I'm getting old too.

I want you to understand this. You are not your father.

Your father was not a good man, though he wasn't a bad man entirely. And you, I know there is good in you. I know you are better than he was. You must try to be better. The path you are treading, it isn't the way. You have been caught stealing once, and we were lucky that charges were not pressed, and I know that if you've been caught once you've got away with it a dozen times before. And I know your business with the girls downtown too, you think I don't hear? Mary Suffolk, and that Annie girl. And I don't judge. But you mustn't be cruel to them. Please, not cruel.

And you despise my hotel, and you despise me, and you want to leave, and I understand that. And all you want to know about is your father.

I have told you what I know.

And in the night sometimes, in the pitch black, I have gone down the stairs, and counted them off. I know you have heard me. I know that you have heard, but don't like to ask. I shall tell you anyway. Because Mrs. Gallagher told me. That when all those years ago she lost her husband. Thomas, or whatever his name was, when he found that extra step, and all those steps leading downwards from it, ever on downwards with no bottom most likely. She told me that it wasn't in that house that she'd lost him. She moved away, and bought another hotel, right at the edge of the land, where she felt she could be free of him. And the extra step had followed her. Her husband had followed.

Because maybe we can't just bury our mistakes and move on. Maybe we carry them around with us, regardless. Maybe I'll never be free of

George. That seems right. That seems just. He's had his punishment, I'll take mine.

I go down the stairs. And there are twenty-one steps in the daytime. I can feel a twenty-second in the night.

You're not your father, and you're young, and you need to make your own mistakes. So go make them. But don't make too many. I have come too far, and sacrificed too much. I will not tolerate it.

I want to make sure you never have to join your father.

You've complained about sounds beneath the floorboards in your bedroom. Stamp your feet hard, that'll usually shut the bastard up.

OUR
FALLEN SONS

The king had won another war, and wanted the victory commemorated, and decreed that a statue of himself on horseback leading his troops into battle should be designed, carved, and copied, and erected throughout the land in every single city, town, municipality, and all villages containing a population of more than five hundred souls. The village of K_ had nearly six hundred souls in it. And so it was that the court engineers came and set a statue down right in the middle of the square. It was made of grey stone—it was said that marble had been reserved for the cities alone—and was some twenty feet tall; the horse stood up ready to charge, and balancing upon its hind legs looked for all the world as if it were on tiptoes; and on its back the king raised a sword high, or maybe it was a cutlass, and his mouth was wide open, presumably in the act of shouting out some heroic order or other. The king's nostrils were flared; so were the horse's. The people of K_ quite liked the statue, really; it was a talking point, and it was something to shelter beneath when the sun was hot. And then, one day, not very long after, the king decided it was time to go to war again, and that he would need all the young men to fight alongside him. And in a trice the young men left, and the population of K_ dipped far below five hundred, and really they no longer qualified for a statue at all.

A year passed, and the young men never came home, and it became clear they never would. The burgomaster went to see the stonemason. He proposed that the statue be turned into a memorial to all those from K_ who had died and would not return; at the top of the plinth the stonemason could engrave the words OUR GLORIOUS DEAD, and beneath that, in smaller writing but very neat, the names of all the young heroes. "Do you like 'Our Glorious Dead'?" said the burgomaster.

"I was also toying with 'Our Fallen Sons.'" The stonemason told him he could have both, if he were paid a couple more coins for the effort, and the burgomaster readily agreed. The burgomaster produced a list of all the names that needed to be carved into the stone, there were exactly a hundred of them, and the stonemason decided that if he carved one name every morning, and one name every afternoon, then that would be two names carved a day, and the job would take fifty days to complete.

And so it was. It was another warm summer, but the stonemason was in the best possible place in the whole of K_, working in the cool shadow of the statue. In the morning he would carve a name upon one side of the plinth; in the afternoon, when the sun had moved, he would carve a name upon the other side. There was no order to the names, he would engrave them at random, he looked down the list to see whichever name caught that day's fancy. And the people of K_ would come and see how he was progressing, and when the day came that he would choose the name of one of *their* dead sons, they would get so excited, and read the name out loud in wonder, and press their fingers into the inscriptions and marvel at the weird shapes of the letters, and weep for joy that at last their sacrifice had been acknowledged.

One evening Mr. and Mrs. Klein came to see the stonemason. Mr. and Mrs. Klein had no children. The stonemason couldn't guess what they might possibly want.

They stood there in his cottage and looked nervous.

"We would like you to engrave the name of our son," Mr. Klein said.

"We have money," said Mrs. Klein.

"You don't have a son," pointed out the stonemason.

"But not for want of trying," said Mr. Klein, and he blushed bright red, and Mrs. Klein looked down to the ground. "We wanted a son so very much. But we were never so blessed."

The stonemason had put in a long day's engraving, he had chosen a name that afternoon that had four whole syllables to it, and he was tired. "You'll have to leave," he said. "I don't see how I can help you."

Mrs. Klein said, "If we had had a boy, he would have been taken from us. He would have gone to fight in the war. And we would have lost him, just as assuredly as all the others. We would have had a hero too. It's not our fault. It's not our fault I was never strong enough to bear one."

"Please," said Mr. Klein. "Honour our fallen son. We only want what's right."

"We have money," said Mrs. Klein again.

The stonemason said, "What name did you want?"

"Raphael."

"Raphael? Really?"

"It is what," said the Kleins, "we would certainly have called him."

The stonemason felt shamed by the new commission, but he didn't know why. He knew he couldn't engrave the name on the statue with all the village there to see. So, sleepy as he was, he lit a candle, and went out then and there, he took up his chisel and he tapped out this latest child who had been lost in war. The moon hid behind the clouds, and the mason's arms were weak, and it took hours to complete the job. For the sake of the real martyrs, he made sure that Raphael Klein's name was slightly smaller than theirs.

He had barely had an hour's sleep when he was woken by someone thumping at his front door.

The burgomaster was furious. "Don't you understand?" he cried. "How this discredits the tragedy of the lads who so bravely died for us? The lads who actually *existed*?"

The mason stood his ground. When confronted by any extremity of emotion, he always chose to imitate the stone he worked with and understood so well: his face became impassive, his shoulders slumped hard as granite. "I just follow orders," he said.

"Indeed!" said the burgomaster. "But not for nothing, I'll bet. How much were you paid?"

"Two silver coins."

"Two silver coins! So, that's the price of our town's integrity!"

A couple of hours later the burgomaster returned.

"Two silver coins," he scoffed. "Look here. I've brought you five *gold* coins. And for them I want you to give me two sons. One is called Peter, the other is called Pyotr. They were good boys, strong boys. Identical, born in the very same hour, you couldn't have told them apart—but I could, I could. Twins, and always the best of friends. They were the world to me. And they marched off to war together, and first they slapped me on the back, they said to me, Papa, if we never meet again, it'll be for a higher cause—and they laughed, because they were *men*, do you see? And I laughed too. They gave me the courage to laugh. Pyotr joined the cavalry, Peter the infantry. And they died together, at the exact same time. Peter was stabbed through the heart in the midst of battle; elsewhere on the field, Pyotr's horse was blown up by a mortar shell. They died at the very same instant, inseparable even at the end—and they never knew. They never even knew." And the burgomaster cried. The stonemason knew that the burgomaster had sent four sons off to war already; with the twins, that made it a tidy half dozen.

The villagers of K_ came to the stonemason with all the money they could afford. They bought dead sons. Some bought an entire platoon of dead sons. Some only wanted one son, a single son, a handsome son, kinder and more honourable and just plain better than the one they had spent years bringing up and had sent away shaking and weeping and scared to die. And the villagers would tell the stonemason the stories of their new sons' deaths, and most often they had died saving the king himself, or if not, the whole army, there had been such meaning to the deaths, they had died so that hundreds more could live—and always they'd done so with a hardy smile or a witty quip, it was never in pain or filth or puke, it was never screaming for their mummy and daddy to save them, why wouldn't their parents save them? And it was easier to part with these sons, because they'd been born at the end of a chisel just so they could be killed. And it was harder to part with them, too, because they were perfect. And as the villagers told the stonemason the stories, oh, there were tears of great pride, and tears of loss, a loss all the greater for being for something never actually won in the first place. The stonemason listened politely, but he wished once they'd paid him the money they'd just shut up and leave. He had a lot of work to do.

Pretty soon there wasn't room on the plinth for all the names. If the burgomaster had chosen between OUR GLORIOUS DEAD and OUR FALLEN SONS, then a few more might have been squeezed on, but there it was, he'd just had to be indecisive. The names soon snaked up the horse's legs, onto the horse's flank, right across the horse's arse. And onto the king himself; the king's face was tattooed with the names of all the boys he had killed, or would have killed, if the boys had been foolish enough to let themselves be born in the first place.

The stonemason always did these special names at night. He was no longer ashamed. But the darkness felt the right place for all the never-was-es and should've-beens. He continued to work on engraving the real dead in the daytime, but he was tired, and frequently he made spelling mistakes. No one seemed to mind.

And the stonemason became very rich.

⩗

And once, when he was dozing, he dreamed that the statue fell on him. He hadn't even seen it start to topple, it must have all been very quick—one moment he was condemning another boy to death, the next he was sprawled out flat, pinned fast by the king's buttocks. And he knew that the statue must weigh several tons, by rights he should be squashed to a pulp, but he understood stone, stone ran through him like lifeblood, stone would never hurt him. It was the dead. It was the dead who'd done it. He'd burdened the stone with too many dead, and it had made the stone top heavy—and it hadn't been fair on the stone, it was just unfeeling stone, why should the stone be made to care for them? He knew he could push the statue off, set it back onto its plinth, and they'd both be right as rain—but it was all the dead standing on top of it, they made it impossible, the dead all stomping down with their little army boots, he couldn't budge it an inch. They stared down at him, and he knew they weren't doing it deliberately, they didn't know *what* they were doing, they were just stupid corpses. And there were just too many. There was just *one* too many. One fewer corpse in the world, and he could have set himself free.

When he awoke, he was drenched with sweat. He steadied his breathing. He got up. He went to his coffers.

And went out, into the night.

The house of Mr. and Mrs. Klein was all dark, like mourning. They had only ever asked him for that one son, the first son, Raphael. After that they had avoided the stonemason, turned away from him at the market, or in church, and he had never known why. Maybe they had realized Raphael's inscription was smaller than the others, and more discreetly hidden. Maybe they thought he would tempt them to create and then murder another child.

Underneath their door he slid two silver coins.

He went back home, and to bed, and his conscience never troubled him again.

⩗

One evening, when the moon was its brightest, the dead came back. Not the dead who had ever lived, but the dead who had never been.

Into the town they marched, right to the square, right to the statue itself. And Raphael Klein was at the front, he was their leader. And everyone could tell it was Raphael Klein, even though no one had ever seen him before, because he had just his father's mouth and just his mother's eyes, he did his parents proud.

He announced that they had all been granted a furlough. Just one night, to visit their families. Just one night, and then back to war. And that was good, because war was good, all the camaraderie and all the honour, and they were *winning*, didn't their parents feel proud? And the soldier boys read the inscriptions on the memorial, and how they laughed. They weren't dead, they were well and fit and happy, couldn't Father see how well, didn't Mother feel proud they looked so well in their smart uniforms? And the villagers of K_ *were* proud, and no one wanted to point out that some of them were missing limbs, or parts of their body, or parts of their head; not for all the world did they want to hurt their children's feelings.

There were cakes and ale, and dancing, and games, and no one slept that night.

The stonemason stayed at home. He had never carved a name upon the statue for himself. He had been tempted. Of course he had been tempted.

When the knock sounded at the door, slow and heavy, the stonemason refused to open up. "Go away!" he said.

More knocking, so slow, heavier still, and it was not the knock of a dashing young hussar, it was the knock of a simpleton, from the lowest dregs of the regiment, standing behind the closed front door there was no one better than cannon fodder—"I don't want you!" he shouted at it.

For a moment the knocking stopped. But then, as before, no more insistent, but just as mindless, thump, thump, thump.

And outside he could hear his neighbours celebrating what never was and could never have been.

"I never wanted a child!" he shouted. "Do you hear? I never wanted you!"

And there was silence. And he thought he had chased his son away. And that was a relief. And then, so suddenly, it was such a dreadful thing.

"Are you still there?" he said.

No answer.

"Are you there?"

Still nothing.

The stonemason said, "I never had a child. To have a child, I would

249

have had to love someone. I would have had . . . to make someone love me. And, do you hear? Do you hear me? I never even came close."

Still nothing, but the sound of villagers at play, mocking him.

"Please?" And he opened the door.

There he was, waiting for him. Unnamed. And featureless. His face a fracture of rock and chalk.

"My son," he breathed. And he put his arms around him, and the statue cut at his skin, and made him bleed, and he didn't care.

THE ALL-NEW ADVENTURES OF ROBIN HOOD

My son Paul is in the same class at school as Robin Hood. Not *the* Robin Hood, of course, that would be ridiculous, he's a semi-mythical hero from the twelfth century. No, this Robin Hood would be his son.

Paul brought home a couple of kids from school one day, and one of them was Robin Hood. At first, I'll be honest, he didn't seem much to look at—I wouldn't have given him a second glance in the street. Short, square-jawed, a little meanness around the eyes—but they all look mean at that age, don't you think? But I looked again, and I don't know, I suppose I could see something of the celebrity in him. And he had a stud in his ear, but not in the lobe, stuck into that bony bit at the top, that'd be more painful, wouldn't it? I didn't know whether to shake him by the hand or not. I didn't.

I said to the other kid, "What about you, you got a famous dad too?" I was only joking. The kid said, "No."

Paul said they were all working together on a school project. I asked what the project was about, and they said it was heroes. Each group had to pick a hero from history, and the best essays would be read out at Speech Day. I said, "Can I help?" Janet had told me I should take a greater interest in what Paul was up to, but they said that they weren't allowed to get external assistance from a parent, this was something they had to do on their own. I asked them which hero they had chosen, and they said Winston Churchill.

"Well, can I get you boys anything to eat?"—but Paul said they were all right. So I left them to work on the kitchen table, and they helped themselves to snacks from the fridge: cola and ice cream and peanut butter sandwiches.

A couple of hours later the boys went home. Robin Hood didn't come and say goodbye, but why should he have done, really? I waited until the coast was clear and then went into the kitchen. I asked Paul whether I should fix something for his supper, but he said he wasn't hungry anymore.

"Winston Churchill," I said. "Well. So, what's your favourite thing about Winston Churchill?", and Paul sort of shrugged.

I said it was nice he had made some new friends, and at that he just rolled his eyes. They weren't friends, they'd all been put into groups by the teacher, Paul Hiscock was next to Robin Hood in the register. "I don't even like Robin Hood," he said. "Robin Hood's a spaz."

☟

In my defence, it hadn't been anything serious, and I'd never meant to hurt anyone. If I had thought anyone would have got hurt, I wouldn't have ever got involved. That was implicit from the fact she was married, I'd have thought. If you have a fling with a married woman, it should be pretty clear it's only temporary.

So when the husband came over, and he was a lot bigger than me, I thought he was going to hit me, and I suppose I might have deserved that—when he came over and he said, "You stole my wife!" my first thought was that it hadn't been *theft*, I was only borrowing her for a bit. I didn't say that, though. And the husband didn't hit me; in fact, he just burst into tears, and the fight went out of him, and I felt very sorry for him and didn't know what to do.

Janet left me. She said if I was going to cheat on her, the least I could do would be to show a little discretion. Sleeping with the next-door neighbour had been rubbing her nose in it rather. It was my own fault, I'm not saying it wasn't, I don't think I come out of this story well at all. But Janet works long hours, and travels a lot, I don't think she'd even met the neighbours very often, what difference did it being the neighbour make?

She takes Paul at the weekends, I get him for the school days. I work pretty locally, so it makes much more sense that way. I gave her a call. I told her that Paul had made new friends. I knew she'd been concerned,

Paul had been so withdrawn since the break-up and her moving out and the lawyers and things.

"That's good," she said.

"You'll never guess who his friend is. His name's Robin Hood! You know, the son of the actual Robin Hood."

Janet said she was pleased, and she sounded pleased, but would it have killed her to have sounded more interested? Excited, even? She said, "They're thinking of cutting back on my overseas contracts, I should be based in the city much more come the spring. I think I should take custody of Paul when I do."

I told her it was funny that our son was hobnobbing with famous people! Who would have thought it? And Janet laughed, I'll give her that. And she said she'd once been at school with a girl whose sister was a backing singer for Dexys Midnight Runners. I told her that wasn't the same thing at all.

I asked her how she was, and she said she was all right, working too hard of course, but that was as per usual, wasn't it? She laughed again. She asked me how I was doing, I said I missed her. I said again that I was sorry.

I see the woman from next door sometimes, of course, but I'm not allowed to speak to her. I promised Janet I wouldn't. I don't think she's allowed to speak to me either, she's still with her husband, I think there were conditions to that. We don't speak, but I want her to know it's nothing personal, so if she's out in the garden I'll raise my hand and give her a sort of half-wave. She half-waves back, mostly.

↙

Speech Day came. They said that Paul's Winston Churchill project was one of the best of his year, and it was selected to be read out in front of the entire school. I was very proud, and told Paul so, and he seemed to believe me for once, he grinned from ear to ear.

I didn't go, though. Janet was supposed to be out of the country on business, but at the last minute her trip was cancelled, and she phoned up and asked if she could go and see Paul instead. She felt it'd be important for their relationship. To be fair to her, she didn't insist, she said she'd quite understand if that inconvenienced me too much—she'd be bitterly disappointed, but there it was. I said that we could both go, it would be all right; she wouldn't even need to see me, I could sit at the back. But Janet thought she wasn't quite ready for that yet. "Maybe next year," she said.

I found out after that Robin Hood had been there as a special guest, and had given out the sixth form prizes! I called Janet, asked her how the evening had gone. She said Robin Hood had been quite charming, and he'd given a little speech, and told the kids that stealing was a bad thing and not to follow his example, and that besides what he'd done hadn't been *stealing*, he had taken from the rich to give to the poor, it had been a political act, he called it "re-appropriation." I asked Janet if he had been dressed in Lincoln green. She said no.

I told Paul I was sorry to have missed him. I told him he could perform the Winston Churchill speech to me, if he liked, privately, in our front room. He said he hadn't performed it at all. He'd written the essay, and that other lad had read it out, that's how they'd divided up the work. Robin had barely been involved in the project at all, Robin had skived off as usual. I told Paul to perform it for me anyway, I wanted to hear it. And Paul huffed a bit, but said all right. At the end I gave him a round of applause and told him I was proud, but Paul didn't look too pleased. "You already said," he told me. But I was proud, I meant it. It was a good essay, there was more to Winston Churchill than I had realized, like Robin Hood he'd been a proper hero.

↓

Mr. and Mrs. Hood had the pleasure of inviting my son to young Robin's birthday party. Paul said it was nothing to get excited about, everyone in his class had got an invitation—but it had come in the post, and it was nicely done, and it asked us to RSVP. It told Paul to bring swimming trunks, so that meant Robin Hood had a pool! I asked Paul whether he thought it would be a fancy dress party, and Paul said, "Why the hell would it be fancy dress?" and I didn't know, I just thought it might have been.

Before the big day I asked Paul whether he was going to get his friend a present. He said no. I told him he had at least to buy a card. The card Paul bought wasn't good enough, I had to go out and buy another. I told him to write something nice inside. I hope he did, he wouldn't let me see.

We drove all the way to the Hood house, the other side of town. I suppose I had expected a castle or something, maybe a mansion. It was just a semi-detached. But it was on a quiet street, the front garden was well tended and a little bigger than ours, no, it was nice, it was nice. Paul looked quite smart; I looked smart too, I'd put on my best jacket even though it was rather a warm day. A harassed man opened the front door to us. "Hello, Mr. Hood," I said, and I put my hand out. It wasn't Mr. Hood at all, it turned out he was just one of the other parents dropping his own kid off; they were all out the back, he said, and then pushed past us and made his escape. I was glad he hadn't been Robin Hood, he hadn't been how I'd pictured him at all.

In the sitting room all the furniture had been pushed against the walls to create a larger play area. On the patio outside there was a barbecue going, and there were the drinks, and there on the lawn was the swimming pool. It wasn't a proper pool. It was quite big, I suppose, but it was still made of plastic, at the end of the day you could drain it and flatten it and roll it up and put it away. I was a little disappointed.

There were lots of kids everywhere, all shapes and sizes, and I just think it would have been nicer if someone had thought to make it a fancy dress party—they could have been Robin Hood's Merry Men, you could have had Friar Tucks and Will Scarlets and Little Johns (the tall kids could have been Little Johns). I can't see why someone hadn't thought of that.

There were a few parents milling around too, all of them obviously hoping to catch a glimpse of the famous man himself. "He's not home," a woman told me when I asked, and she sighed, because she'd obviously been asked a few dozen times already. I told her I supposed she was Maid Marian. "I'm Stacey," she said, "Marian is the ex."

She suggested that the adults should go, and return to collect their children at six o'clock. I asked if I could stay. "I told you, he's not here, and he won't be back 'til late." I told Mrs. Hood I didn't care.

Some of the kids had smuggled in cans of beer, and Mrs. Hood and I had to keep going around confiscating them. We'd take them indoors and drink them in the kitchen, and when we'd finished, we'd go outside and confiscate some more. Every once in a while one of us would pop out anyway to check no one had got burned on the barbecue or drowned in the paddling pool.

Robin Hood's house had a big widescreen TV and off-road parking. I told Mrs. Hood it wasn't as grand as I'd expected, and I supposed Robin must have given to the poor and not kept much back for himself. She found that very funny. She laughed a lot. I decided to laugh too, so it'd look as if I'd been witty on purpose.

About half past five the parents started arriving for their kids, and I'd go out into the garden to help find them. I'd ask for the kids' names, and I'd stand in the middle of the lawn, and start calling. It was funny how they all looked the same.

And eventually Paul was the only kid left. A thought occurred to me: "But where's little Robin? Where's the birthday boy?" Robin had left the party ages ago, apparently, he'd gone downtown with his mates. I asked Paul to thank Mrs. Hood, and he did, very politely, and I thanked her too. We had to get a taxi home, I was a little over the limit. I asked Paul whether he had enjoyed the party, and he said he had, very much; he thanked me for making him go even though he hadn't wanted to; he said he was sorry, he said he hadn't been nice to me lately, he loved me, he said. He was very good, he wasn't sick in the taxi, he waited until we were safely home.

I went back the next day to pick up my car. All the balloons and streamers had been taken down out front, Robin Hood's house looked like any other. I supposed Robin Hood was inside, he'd probably come home by now, and I waited for a bit, but I didn't see him.

↡

I was asked to come into the school and see the deputy headmistress. I waited outside her office on a little plastic chair, and I felt nervous, as if I were the one in trouble!

She was very stern. She told me that Paul was a very promising student. She said that his take on Winston Churchill had been good, the words she used were "spirited" and "rousing." But, she said, Paul was mixing with the wrong sort of company. He'd been seen in a gang. There'd been lots of complaints about this gang, they'd hang about the shopping precinct, and drink, and be noisy, and play with traffic cones. They hadn't done anything illegal yet, no one said they'd stolen anything, but it was only a matter of time.

She told me the ringleader was Robin Hood, and advised me to keep Paul away from him. "Don't let Paul give up on his future," she said. She told me she knew he was going through a difficult time, that there were domestic problems, and that she was sympathetic. But the school couldn't condone anti-social behaviour. "How do you think it's going," she asked me, "the relationship you have with your son?" I didn't want to discuss relationships. I didn't want the school to know about my problems with Janet, what had Paul been saying about me?

I spoke to Paul that evening. He told me that the gang didn't have a leader, it wasn't that sort of a gang, and that if the gang did have a leader it'd be Nicky Culshaw, it wouldn't be Robin Hood, Robin Hood just hung out and did shit the same as everybody else. I told Paul that maybe Robin Hood was a bad influence all the same; could I rely on him, could I trust him, that if he went out with his mates downtown to play and Robin tagged along, could Paul make his excuses and come home? "Sure," said Paul.

In retrospect I felt angry, and ashamed, and I phoned the deputy headmistress the next day. I told her that whatever "relationship" my son and I enjoyed was none of her business, her business was to teach him, that was all. And besides, it was all a storm in a teacup, the gang wasn't doing anything wrong, they were just kids having fun. What was wrong with having fun if no one got hurt? Couldn't she remember being young once? She didn't answer. Maybe she couldn't.

It was in the local paper—a cat had been shot with an arrow. The owners found it in the morning when they were taking their kids to school; the cat had dragged its way to the house and tried to get in through the cat flap, but with an arrow sticking out of its side it had got stuck, and it'd spent the night half inside and half out. The arrow was in its flank, just above the hind legs. Miraculously, the cat had survived, the arrow hadn't gone in too deep, that was one lucky animal. Though, mind you, it had to have one of the legs amputated, there was a photo in the paper, nasty.

A few days later a dog was found, and this one was dead, chained up to a kennel, an arrow through its neck. This one had been a more expert kill, and the only consolation the owners could find in the interviews they gave—because by this time the national press had got hold of it, it was even on the telly, in the evening news—was that at least the kill had been quick and the dog wouldn't have suffered. The police urged people to keep their pets indoors and safe, although they were certain whoever was responsible would be caught soon and there was no need for panic. It was odd seeing pictures of our town on the television; I know those streets, but they looked bigger on the screen somehow, and all the signposts and wheelie bins looked like movie props.

Young Robin Hood confessed the very next day. It's said that he didn't offer any explanation or show of remorse; he just went up to a policeman and said, "I did the pets," and as proof showed his bow and his quiver. "I Did The Pets" was one of the headlines the next day; others used "The

Face Of A Monster," alongside a photograph of Robin. He looked calm and insolent, and that meanness around his eyes was plain for all to see.

He wasn't sent to prison the way the public demanded on chat shows; he was too young for that. He was expelled by the school, of course. And he gave a statement to the papers that said he was bitterly regretful of all the distress he had caused, and that he blamed temporary insanity—it was only a written statement, the press weren't allowed to interview the lad. They tried to track down his father for comment, but the family had gone into hiding—the one time they got him on camera he kept silent and tight-lipped, pushing his way through the reporters toward his car, and I was surprised at how ordinary Robin Hood looked, really, how thin, how old.

↓

I didn't see Stacey again after that. I suppose we both used the scandal to put an end to things, but in truth it was on its way out already. The last time she'd come to my house she'd asked me where I thought our relationship was headed.

"Is it a relationship?" I asked. "I didn't know we'd got that far!" I was only joking, I was only trying to make her laugh.

"I just don't know what it is we're doing," she said. I didn't know what to say, and she sighed, and got out of bed, and got dressed.

And I said to her, that she was lonely, and that I was lonely, and that there was nothing so evil in two lonely people meeting up every so often to make themselves feel better. What was wrong in having fun?

"But I'm married," I went on. "And I love my wife, and one day we'll get back together. And you love your husband, don't you? And it's not as if you love me."

She just said, "I don't know what we're doing if it's never going to mean anything."

We'd only ever met up at my place. Saturday afternoons, when Paul was safely with his mother. I thought that was simpler, and she'd agreed. Better that our sons didn't know we were seeing each other, after all our sons were close friends. But there was more to it than that. I just didn't fancy going to the great Robin Hood's house and having sex with his wife in his own bed. I suppose you could say there's a moral ambiguity surrounding Robin Hood and the way he pursued a life of crime for a greater good, but whichever side of the argument you come down on,

Robin Hood as folk hero or as social menace, surely the man deserves better treatment than that.

⚹

Paul brought me the bow and the remaining arrows. He'd taken them from the Hood house, but insisted he hadn't stolen them. There were so many bows and arrows just lying about there, how could it be stealing if no one would notice they were gone?

He didn't know why Robin had confessed. He told me that if Robin hadn't confessed, he would have done so. In fact, he'd just been on his way to confess, and then Robin had got in, just ahead of him.

"He doesn't even like archery," he said. "Any of that stuff his dad was into, he thought it was all bollocks."

Paul was sorry about the cat. He hadn't meant to hurt anything. He was just mucking about, he never thought he'd actually manage to hit the thing. "What about the dog?" I asked. He didn't say anything to that.

"Are you going to tell the police?" he asked.

And he stared at me, and he seemed frightened. Or maybe it was just another sort of defiance, one I wasn't used to.

"I don't think we should even tell your mother," I said.

I took the bow and the arrows. I said I'd get rid of them, I'd dispose of the evidence. I put them upstairs, nicely under my bed.

I asked Paul if he wanted any supper. Normally he'd say no, he'd go out with his mates. That night he agreed to stay in.

Neither of us quite knew what to say as we ate.

"I'm sorry," I said. "This is all my fault."

He looked genuinely surprised by that. "Is it?"

"I just wish," I said. "I don't know. I've always wished. You'd be the sort of son who'd want to take after his father. That I'd done something, achieved something, worth taking after."

He said nothing, just toyed with his apple crumble. That was probably the kindest thing.

After supper Paul asked if he could be excused from the table. That was polite of him. So I said yes.

⚹

The next evening when Paul came home from school, I asked him if he wanted any supper. "No," he said. "I'm going out."

There was still a gang, but no one pretended that Robin Hood was in charge of it anymore.

I had rather hoped Paul might stay in, that the two of us could do something together. I told him this. And he said we'd do something soon, yeah. But he had to go out, he'd promised, and the others wouldn't know what to do without him.

I watched some television. I went upstairs, from under the bed I took my bow and arrow. I wondered whether Robin Hood had ever killed anyone with them. I wondered whether he'd ever killed anyone famous, like King John, or one of the sheriffs of Nottingham. I texted Stacey. She didn't reply.

↓

On Thursday night Janet called and told me she wouldn't be able to fit Paul in this weekend, she'd be at an impromptu conference in Frankfurt instead. I said I'd tell him.

On Friday morning I broke the news to Paul. If he felt rejected, he didn't show it. I asked him whether he had any plans for Saturday. I knew he wouldn't have had time to make any—that got him.

On Saturday I showed Paul what I'd found.

From the attic I'd brought down whole boxes of my past, I'd been through them to find all the best bits. There were photographs, of me as a child, me with my parents, the brother I hadn't spoken to for years. My wedding day. Janet looked so beautiful. I looked a bit fat.

And things I had forgotten. My Cub Scout badges, one for orienteering, one for knots, one for helping the old folk cross the road. A little medal I'd won at school for swimming. Certificates proving I was a qualified chartered accountant. A prize-winning essay about the great hero Sir Francis Drake. Valentine's cards.

"This is who I am," I said to Paul.

"Right."

"No bows and arrows! Ha! Nothing as exciting as Robin Hood could show his son. Ha!"

"No."

"I'm no one special. But. Maybe there's something here that might inspire you."

Paul didn't look very convinced. I sort of smiled at him, encouragingly.

He sort of smiled back. He put his hands deep into one of the boxes, as if it were a lucky dip, and he pulled out some old postcards from somewhere or other.

"I'll leave you to it," I said.

"This is all shit," he said. Not even unkindly.

"I'll leave you to it," I said again. And I walked out of the room. And I closed the door. And I locked it.

"Hey!" said Paul. "Let me out!" He banged his fists on the door. They were heavy fists; Paul was already so strong, stronger than me. But I thought the door would hold.

I went upstairs to my bedroom. I decided I wouldn't free Paul for a while. It was tempting, he'd be so angry when he got out. But if I wanted this relationship to work, I had to believe in it, give it a fighting chance.

I pulled the string from the bow, and I broke all the arrows, I snapped them in two.

I went to sleep for a while. I don't know how long.

And at last I went back downstairs. I trod softly, I didn't want to disturb my son. He had stopped shouting and banging at the door, I hadn't heard a sound from him for ages. I stooped, I peered through the keyhole. It was hard to see properly, and I could only guess at the expression on his face, but he was holding that swimming medal to his chest, hugging onto it tight, and I thought it might have been with pride and with awe and with love.

MEMORIES OF CRAVING LONG GONE

No one ever saw her smile. But hers was a face you wouldn't want to smile—something as hard and as sour as that wasn't made for smiling, and the contorted effort of it would surely have been too much, it would have given nightmares to the children. The children were already frightened of her, she was what parents threatened them with to get them to behave: "You calm down, or we'll take you to Frau Loecherbach. We'll give you to Frau Loecherbach, and she'll make sausages of you!" But it was a *good* fear; the children followed her around market and sniggered; they'd call her a witch, a troll, they'd say she was in league with the Devil—but never to her face, always out of earshot, only in fun, just fun. A good fear, a healthy and exciting fear, full of adventure and the possibility of magic.

She wasn't the public face of the restaurant. Charm, clearly, was not her thing. Her husband Alois served the tables, and he was amiable enough, he would joke with the guests as he took their orders and recommended the specials of the day. And her three sons, Franz, Hans, and little Johann, they would help out too, they would bring out the food from the kitchens—great steaming plates of it, of Knödel and Schweinshaxe and roasted Rindswurst. Frau Loecherbach would stick to the kitchens. No one doubted the genius of her culinary skills. But that didn't mean anyone wanted to look at her.

When you ate one of Frau Loecherbach's meals, you somehow didn't want to like it all that much. Because the cook was so displeasing a human being, you wanted her pancakes and her borscht to reflect that. But it wasn't possible to resist. The food was good. She could do miraculous tricks with a chicken, she could make it fizz with flavour, no matter how dubious the quality of your average chicken to be found on sale in that market square. Her breads tasted light as air. Her soups were rich and thick like steak, and spiced with something you couldn't quite identify but seemed as familiar as nostalgia itself. To eat at Loecherbach's was expensive. And these were hard times, and the townsfolk resented the expense. They resented the expense, and they resented Julia Loecherbach, strutting around the town with her hard face and her tight bosom as if she owned the place. But still they came back. And still they wanted not to like her food quite so much that they paid for it dearly. And still they couldn't help themselves.

No one knew how she had managed to snare herself a husband like Alois. And people wondered why her three sons didn't leave home. They weren't exactly handsome lads, Franz, Hans, and little Johann, but they were strong, the girls of the town could net themselves worse; no one quite understood why they didn't cut themselves free of their ugly mother's apron strings and set out to find futures of their own. But Julia Loecherbach kept her men close. The gossip said she must have put a spell on them. It wasn't just the children who thought there was a spot of devilry to her.

↓

By the time the news reached the town that they were at war, the war was nearly over. Still, the garrisons demanded that every man fit enough to wave a sword must join their number. The army would continue its march toward the front the next morning; the towns were expected to give up their men to them then. It didn't look much like an army. The soldiers seemed like children wearing adult clothes, all baring their teeth with adult disdain, smoking and spitting and swearing the way adults do; there were old men too, squeezed into uniforms too small for them, their white beards now tapered toward sharp martial points. They carried mostly cudgels and sticks. But they were very insistent—they *were* an army, really they were—and the leading officer carried some sort of seal, and said that it gave him authority direct from the emperor of Austria himself, so that was that.

Franz, Hans, and little Johann prepared to go to war. They put their favourite belongings into knapsacks; little Johann took a toy boat his father had carved out of wood for him when he was a child. They all seemed very excited. Alois prepared for war too. He took out the greatcoat his father had worn the day *he* had been called to war; Alois now mostly wore it when the weather turned fierce in the winter, and sometimes killed the chickens in it—but nevertheless it had been part of a uniform, and his father's uniform at that, and Alois was rightly proud of it. Julia watched her men busy themselves with men's things, how they laughed, how they swaggered, how they jabbed at each other with sticks and pretended to kill and pretended to die. And she said not a word. And went to the kitchen to prepare dinner.

Frau Loecherbach let it be known that there would be a special dinner at her restaurant that night, and all were invited. People need only pay what they wanted. This was to be a celebration feast. There would be room for all—there would be tables lined up the streets, everyone would be able to eat at Loecherbach, man, woman, child. And, as one, the town came. Because though no one liked her very much, and she never smiled, and she was a witch, still her food was to die for.

"Do you want me to wait tables, liebchen?" asked Alois. And Alois was standing in his greatcoat, and already stroking at the places where he imagined his medals might hang. And his wife told him no; no, tonight he too would be a customer, tonight he would be able to sit back in their restaurant and relax and eat his fill. And the same was true for her sons; tonight would be a busy night, the busiest night of her life thus far, but still she would manage all by herself.

There was no menu. And there was no wine. Instead, the town took their seats and waited, hungry and sober, for dinner to be served. And there was palpable disappointment when at last Frau Loecherbach brought forth nothing more spectacular than a single tureen full of stew, and began ladling it into bowls. There were catcalls. Some men beat against the tables, and they were laughing, but it was an angry laughter, they were soldiers already and feeling warlike and oh so fierce. "Hush," said Frau Loecherbach, and she didn't raise her voice, but the sound carried to all of the tables, and everyone fell silent. "You shall eat what you are given, and no more," she told them, "and you will like it."

The stew looked unappealing. Thin and watery, and a little bit brown; it seemed to have been made from the dregs of whatever had been in the Loecherbach larder. In one bowl there might float a discoloured lettuce leaf; in another, a chunk of carrot seemed to have considered its stewy surroundings, found them wanting, then chosen to drown itself deep in despair. And here was Frau Loecherbach splashing the liquid into the bowls, still not smiling, still so sour, and warning the townsfolk not to eat until everyone was ready. It all quite took people's appetites away. No one much wanted to like Frau Loecherbach's food, and tonight this was going to be easy.

"Now, eat," she said, and they did.

And they tasted their childhoods.

They might taste the memory of the first pie they had ever eaten, the balance between pastry and meat being just right that first and only time. They might taste the apples they had scrumped when they were teenagers, then lying back on the grass on long summer days that seemed to stretch out before them and promised, faithlessly, never to end. They might taste sauerkraut, or stollen, or schnitzel, they might taste Butterkuchen the way they remembered their mothers making it. They ate not only their favourite meals. They ate the recollections of their favourite meals, the best they had ever been, better than they had ever been, the happiest they had ever felt—when, in spite of all, the world had been so full of possibility; when, in spite of all, they had been in *love*. Long married couples, grown bored and resentful of each other, tasted again their own wedding cakes, and how sweet it had been, and how it had crumbled upon their tongues—and how afterwards they had kissed each other, now husband and wife, now so proud and so grown-up, and had gone to bed, and how together they had made those tongues dance.

They were the best meals, and they were as good as they had ever been, and they were better than they had ever been. Spicier, sweeter, and the portions so much bigger.

Customers begged Frau Loecherbach for seconds. "Fill our bowls again!" they pleaded. She refused: "What you are given, and no more," she said. She asked them all to settle the bill. And the townsfolk paid all the money they had.

Tonight the women take their husbands to bed, and they make love. And their lovemaking is as sweet as memory too. And, for now, their bellies are full, and warm, and they hold each other all night, and they feel as one—and nothing can separate them, not time, not space, not war certainly—and there is a recognition that if there had once been better times, then there can be better times again. Surely. Surely that makes sense. Surely that is *just*. And when at last they fall asleep there lingers the taste of knipp on their lips and spargel on their breaths and the salt sweat of honest passion on their skin. And the next morning the men get up and go to war.

🜂

A few weeks later an army came to town. It was a different army, and the schoolboys and old men wore uniforms of a different colour.

The commander was one of the old men, and on his cheek was a deep scar that he displayed with pride a little too obviously. He told the town that the war was over. There were still pockets of resistance, of course, one must expect that, but the resistance would be quelled, the war was over as far as they need be concerned. They had all been liberated from the rule of a tyrannical emperor who did not love them, and they were now under the rule of another sort of emperor altogether. They were part of Prussia, as they should always have been.

He said too that his soldiers would be billeted at the houses of the conquered townsfolk. And that, in respect of his position, he himself would be billeted at the wealthiest of those houses. That house, of course, belonged to Frau Loecherbach.

Away from the crowds, away from the soldiers protecting him with muskets and swords, the commander looked younger and more awkward. He politely told Frau Loecherbach that he regretted the inconvenience he was putting her through, and that he would do his level best not to get in her way. And he fingered at that scar of his nervously.

"Do you have anyone in the war?" he asked.

Frau Loecherbach told him that indeed she had four men in the army: one husband and three sons, all fighting for their country.

The commander attempted a consolatory smile. "God speed an ending to this damned war," he said, "and that your family will be restored to you, and then we can all live in peace."

Frau Loecherbach didn't smile back. Frau Loecherbach didn't ever smile. Instead Frau Loecherbach gave a nod, just the one. She then said that she was prepared to let the commander stay in her house, and did so with great gravity and after much consideration. But she said that she would not be cooking for him.

"I understand," said the commander.

The commander issued instructions to his troops moreover that they must treat the women whose houses they were occupying with all respect and civility, and any reports of lewd behaviour, up to and including rape, would be punished with all severity. And he was a good commander, and his men listened to him, and most of them even obeyed.

It was believed that because the commander was staying with Frau

Loecherbach that she must be living in luxury. On the days she went to market the people wouldn't look at her. Under their breaths they muttered the word "traitor."

The commander would buy a chicken each week and roast it on the Sunday. Frau Loecherbach could tell from the smell coming from her kitchen that he had found a way to render it devoid of all juice or flavour. But she kept to her room away from him.

When the first snap of winter came on the commander went outside, wearing his greatcoat for warmth, and chopped wood. From the sound Julia could almost believe that Alois had returned to her—or that Franz, Hans, or even little Johann were making logs for the fire. She asked the commander to stop, but he laughed amiably and told her that the exercise alone kept him warm! That it was his pleasure, and his privilege, to make the house a comfort to them both, to do what he could for her. And when Frau Loecherbach went to market that week, her neighbours called her whore and spat at her.

"You don't ask me my name," said the commander one night, as they sat by the fire.

"I don't need to know your name," she said.

"You should ask me something," he said. "It would be polite. You don't ask if I have a wife."

"Do you have a wife?"

"Yes," he said. "Yes, I do. And I miss her."

The winter wore on. The snow began to fall. Log chopping was no longer so much fun, and the commander ordered his soldiers to the task instead. Many of them had been chopping logs for *their* women, but the commander was having none of that, they would chop for Frau Loecherbach or no one at all. Frau Loecherbach stopped going to market altogether. And the commander sent his men to market, and they brought back only the best food.

The commander asked if he could cook for Frau Loecherbach. Frau Loecherbach was surprised. No one had cooked for her since she was a child.

He served her a red wine that he'd been saving for a special occasion. He said tonight was the special occasion. He said that the wine was the emperor's favourite. He said that he hoped it was special to her, that this was all special to him, and he fingered at that scar of his a lot. Frau Loecherbach accepted that the wine was better than the stuff she had served in the days she had run a restaurant, but she still had the power to make hers taste richer, fruitier, darker. He served her Knödel, and Schweinshaxe, and roasted Rindswurst in a wine sauce.

"Do you like it?" he asked. Still touching at that scar.

"Your food is terrible," said Frau Loecherbach.

"Oh."

"It's the worst I have ever tasted."

"Oh."

"You do not care about the food. You do not bother to find anything *inside* the food that is good or special or dear. To you it's not food, it's just something to chew, then swallow, then shit."

"Oh." And then the commander said, and he sounded confused, "Well, what else should food be?"

And so she got up, went to the kitchen, and showed him.

It was a harsh night, and the fire in the hearth made no impression upon the freezing cold, and the snow outside was falling so thick and so fast that it felt to Frau Loecherbach as if the house would be lost, buried behind walls of white forever, and the world would never be able to get in and see them and judge them.

"I love you," he said. "I don't know why."

"No," she said. "I don't know why either."

And he suggested he take her to his bed. And when she refused he nodded sadly. And she told him that she'd take him to *her* bed instead, and his face lit up in surprise and he no longer looked like an old man at all but a delighted little boy.

"We will marry one day," the commander said to her. "My wife will die. She'll die eventually. And your husband too, maybe he'll never come back from the war."

And Julia lay in his arms, and it was she fingering his scar with the tips of her fingers, so lightly, and she said nothing to that at all.

↓

With the spring came the news that the fighting was done. The fighting was done, there would be no more death, and peace would last forever more. The soldiers were no longer soldiers, and the townsfolk no longer hostiles under martial law; they were men, and they were women, let them be friends, let them be one people, one nation united. And in announcement of this, a dozen engagements were announced on the spot.

No one seemed to wonder where the men from the town had got to, or whether they would be home soon. They all *had* men, didn't they, *new* men? Who needed the old?

Frau Loecherbach suggested that maybe the commander could now return to his wife. The commander said his wife was a world away, his wife was in Prussia of all places. Frau Loecherbach asked, but weren't they in Prussia too now, wasn't all the world a Prussia? And the commander glowered and said he didn't care.

"I love you," he said. "You have bewitched me."

And he told her that Alois wouldn't be coming home. Neither would her sons. Neither would any man from the town. That only a week after they had left for war they had been routed by the Prussian army, and they had all been executed. All of them, and little Johann too. "I was waiting for the right time to tell you," said the commander. "When we were no longer enemies, and can just be lovers."

Frau Loecherbach complimented him on his delicacy.

"I'm sorry about your children. But I'm still strong, and you're young enough, I think we can have children of our own. This poor town, and all it has suffered, it needs to move on now, we need to forget the past, what good will the past do us? We need to live, and to love, and can't you hear it? Can't you hear all that love out there? And so soon, I promise you, this war will be forgotten, and the town will be full of babies, the sound of all our babies crying in joy."

It sounded sincere enough. It sounded like a reason for celebration. Frau Loecherbach let it be known that there would be a special dinner that night at her restaurant, and all were invited.

Tables were once more set out on the street. And women sat with their soldier lovers, holding their hands, gazing into their eyes—who had conquered not only their land but their very hearts—and they were all so *hungry*, they wanted this meal so badly, they wanted that after all this time of bitter war and bitter cold there could be now some reason to go on together, some reminder that at the end of the day they were all just people with appetites, and what was wrong with that, what could be the harm? And the commander asked if he could help Julia, and she said no, tonight he too could be a customer, tonight he could sit back and eat his fill.

She brought out the stew. The winter had been hard, and there weren't many dregs in Julia's larder to fill it. No discoloured lettuce, not a suicidal carrot to be seen.

They ate. And they tasted their memories.

And the women cried for the loved ones they had lost, the sons they had weaned for no bloody purpose now, the husbands with whom they had promised to share a life, a whole life, an entire life.

And the men cried, because they thought of their mothers, and that they would have been ashamed to see what they had become.

It was the best food they had ever tasted.

"Fill our bowls again!" they both pleaded, the men and the women. "Just a little more!" begged the commander, who had not been able to stop the tears from the moment the spoon had entered his mouth.

"Oh, as much as you like," said Julia. "As much as your bellies can take."

And they were eating more—eating their first sweets, fed to them by hand by indulgent parents, and how they'd laughed to see their child's eyes bulge at all that *taste*, and how the child had laughed too without even knowing why, but the child knew it was a good thing, it was good to hear Mummy and Daddy happy. And they were eating with their baby teeth, and they were so much softer than their adult ones, and they remembered how different everything seemed when your little teeth wobbled so, little teeth in little heads, little heads on little bodies, such very little bodies. And then they were sucking at their mothers' breasts, all that milk and they could never have too much, and oh my God, mother, long since dead, or maybe just dying, or maybe just old and ignored—does she still love us, could she possibly love us now we've grown so old and hard and cold, and so unlike the little babies guzzling away like animals, all innocent, not knowing anything, not remembering anything, because there's nothing to remember, nothing's happened yet, you're at the beginning, you're back at the very beginning.

Julia steps through the crowd of babies and goes into the kitchen for her knife.

And she bends to pick up the commander. No longer in a position to command anything, looking faintly surprised to be sitting in this pool of clothes, the uniform of a man he could surely never dream of becoming. Eyes wide and so blue, smooth skin, smooth lips, looking at Julia in utter trust as she scoops him up into her arms.

Julia holds the knife to his throat. The commander blinks. Then smiles at her.

And then she does something that only the baby ever sees. She smiles back. She smiles. And there's a magic in that smile—and maybe that's where all her magic ever came from and no one ever saw it to know. Or maybe it came from somewhere else entirely, who can tell, who can ever really tell.

She doesn't kill him.

Into his cheek she traces his scar. It's quick, it's as if she's cutting up a chicken, it's no more cruel than that. And the commander is too surprised to howl out in pain. One quick gulp then that's it. And she has forgiven him.

She kisses him on the cheek, and her lips come away red, but the wound is already healing, and now the bleeding has stopped, look.

The other babies look around at each other in some confusion—what do they do now? Where do they go from here? But that's up to them, that's not Julia Loecherbach's problem. And the commander is so light in her arms, like bread, like her freshly baked bread, and he's no weight at all, and she can walk on with him forever, and she walks straight out of the town.

MOND

She says she'll devise a whole new language, just for the both of you. And you smile and nod. You don't know what she means, but it sounds very sweet. It comes out of nowhere. You've just had a nice conversation about the weather, nothing gripping, but thorough and accurate. And you've finished your main course, and you are studying the dessert menu, and you are expressing some interest in a New York cheesecake. Frankly, you were rather expecting the next words she said to be in acknowledgement of cheesecake, or weighing in with some counterargument for a dessert preference of her own.

"I'll devise a whole new language, something only we can use," she says, and she smiles at you. "I think you might be special." And she brushes at your hand with her fingertips, just for a second. And you put the menu down so you can take her hand, but it's too late, she's got a menu of her own now.

"The New York cheesecake sounds good," she says. "Yum yum!"

It's only the second date, and you weren't even sure you would get this far. The first date was fine. The first date was perfectly fine. You went to the cinema, and that meant you didn't get much time to talk, a quick hello, exchange of pleasantries, an offer to buy her some popcorn. At the end of the movie you asked her whether she'd like to get something to eat—you had always factored a meal into both the time and money budgeted for the evening—and she looked at you very seriously, and said that maybe on the next date you could try speaking. She would see, she said, whether the right words would fit. And then she'd pulled you to her, and kissed you very softly upon the mouth. And that took you aback, because for the whole date she hadn't touched you once, no arms rubbing against each other on the rests, no hands colliding in the popcorn box. The first date was perfectly fine, but inconclusive, and in your experience inconclusive dates rarely got followed up, and you'd been really rather surprised when she'd phoned you up the very next day asking whether she could see you again. Surprised, and pleased. And you wondered whether it had anything to do with that little kiss, whether it had been that which had sealed the deal.

You rather hope there'll be another kiss tonight. You rather hope that may be possible. And this time you won't be so startled. This time you'll move your lips a little too, make it last a bit longer, really become an active participant in the whole kissing experience.

This, then, has been your date for words, and there have been so many of them. She has asked you about your childhood, about your job, about any aspirations you might still have. You've told her what you think about art and music and sports. You've listed for her all the countries you've ever visited, and given a brief account of the differing impressions they made upon you. She hasn't said much. She hasn't said anything at all, really. And you're dimly aware that you're talking too much and being a bit of a bore. And you determine that at any moment you'll stop, you can rescue this, you'll ask about her, you'll even *listen*, maybe over the cheesecake. But she doesn't seem irritated by you. She smiles at your jokes. She maintains eye contact. She hangs on each and every word.

You eat the cheesecake and don't ask about her after all; instead you entertain her with your take on religion and politics. To describe them there are words you'd never use, some with many syllables, words like "hierarchy and "libertarian" and "diocese." You feel like they're being sucked from your brain. From a long forgotten dictionary in it. And it makes you feel a little tired, and you yawn, and you apologize.

You pay for both meals, and she accepts that, she says that next time dinner will be on her. And you stand outside with her on the pavement, and you know she'll be going home now, and you wonder whether there's any way to follow. You thank her for a lovely evening. You say you hope you can do something like it again. "No, better," she says, "next time it'll be better. Oh, the language we shall share!" And she pulls you toward her again, and this time you're ready for it. Your lips meet. And your mouth opens just a little. And something is pushed in, and you think it might be her tongue. And it's the last thing you remember for a while.

�ↆ

You wake up, and it's dark, and it's so quiet, and you don't know where you are. And you try to move, but you can't. Your hands and feet can do no more than jerk a few inches. And you wonder whether this is some sort of a paralysis, have you had an accident, are you in hospital? (A very dark hospital, a very quiet hospital?) And you're lying on your back, and you hate sleeping on your back, and your body tries to turn, and it can't, and something cuts into your wrists and your ankles. And there's a smell in the air, it's like warm bread, or something sweeter, it's soft, and it does nothing to reassure you. You cry out. "Help!" you say. "Help!"

And now there's a chink of light, and a door has opened, and you can't see properly but at least this means you aren't *blind* as well. And it's her, surely it's her. It takes a moment for you to remember her name, and you flush with embarrassment, and you're glad it's so dark so she can't see. "Help, Tracey!" you say. "Ssh," she replies, and she comes to you, stands over you big and tall, she seems such a big mass there in the blackness, and she strokes your forehead. "Ssh," and that's the only word she'll use, and it's not even a word. Then she gets up and leaves, and closes the door behind her, and the world turns blind again.

You don't think you'll sleep, not when you're on your back, not when you're so afraid, frankly—but you must do, because you wake up again, and this time there's light, and there she is again, smiling down. "Help," you say again. And you try to move, and of course you can't, because you see you're tied to the bed by wire cord. And she tells you that this is the last time you will ever hear her speak English to you. It's not a threat, it sounds like a promise. The new language will start right now, and she thinks you'll like it—she's got such a lovely assortment of nouns and adjectives for you both to play with!—oh, she can't wait to get started, her enthusiasm feels so cheap to her like this, expressed in a language that is so very old and banal and is shared with so many strangers. You ask her to release you, and she just shakes her head. You beg her by name, and she says that Tracey isn't her name any longer; she doesn't know what her new name shall be yet, you'll both find one together. You don't have a name either. Choosing you a name will be a pleasure she will reserve for herself alone. "I'm going to leave you now, and you can get some more rest," she says. "And the next time I come through that door, no more English, just our language, just for the two of us." "Help!" you cry out, and she tells you that from now on the word isn't "help," it's "handbag." "Handbag!" you say, hoping that might do the trick, that she'll cut your bonds and set you free. "Ssh," she says again, kisses you upon the lips, just once but on the lips—and goes.

That first week you work on elementary vocabulary.

She brings in a bowl of fruit. Your stomach growls at the sight of it, that cheesecake seems a very long time ago. She smiles expectantly at you. "Let me out of here!" you shout. And without a word she turns, and leaves, and takes the fruit with her.

She leaves you alone for hours.

She brings in a bowl of fruit. She smiles expectantly at you, as if this is the first time she has brought it in, that this is the first expectant smile too. "Please," you say. And without a word she turns, and leaves, and takes the fruit with her.

She brings in a bowl of fruit. And smiles. And it's expectant. "Please," you say, and it's only a whisper, it's just a little whisper. But she looks so sad at that, and clearly disappointed. She turns, she leaves, she takes the fruit with her.

She brings in a bowl of fruit. She smiles. Not expecting anything much this time, but it's hopeful. Full of hope, and has she been crying? You think she may have been crying just a little, and the smile is a brave smile, this is hard on her as well. And your heart goes out to her, in spite of the hunger, and the rage, and the fear. You don't say a word. You won't say a word. She takes from the bowl an apple. She holds it up. "Lampshade," she says. You stay silent. She nods at you, encouragingly. "Lampshade," she says again. You glare at her. She tries to smile again, but the smile wobbles. "Lampshade," she says. "Lampshade. Lampshade. Lampshade. Lampshade."

And at last, sadly, she gets up. Puts the lampshade back in the bowl. Turns. Walks to the door.

"Lampshade," you say, quietly.

She turns back.

"Lampshade," you say again.

She nods. She takes the lampshade once more from the bowl. "Lampshade," she says. "Lampshade," you say. "Lampshade," she says. "Lampshade," you say. "Lampshade?" she asks. "Lampshade," you dutifully admit. She takes out a banana. "Caterpillar," she says. "Caterpillar," you agree. "Caterpillar." "Caterpillar." She takes out a strawberry. Holds it deliberately between thumb and forefinger, and it looks so red and juicy. "Plinge," she says. "Plinge," you say. And she feeds you your plinge as a reward, she holds it to your lips and you suck at it greedily. "Plinge," you say again, and she smiles, nods, she gives you another plinge. "Caterpillar," you say, and she unpeels a caterpillar for you. "Lampshade," you say, and she patiently holds the lampshade straight as you bite into it, bite deep to the very core. You don't know what a core is. You gesture to it with your nose. It takes a while for her to work out what you want. Then she has a think, this is one word she's not translated yet. "Basket," she decides. "Basket," you say, and she laughs, and she balances the basket upright on her palm, and you gnaw away at it, you suck the last juice from that basket, you suck at her fingers too.

She brings in picture books. Together you rename the animal kingdom. She calls a camel a passport, a cow a fork. She accepts some of your suggestions. You name a hippopotamus a divot, and there's something so right about that, something so divot-ish about the hippo, and you feel proud.

She doesn't feed you only fruit. She brings you meals of hedgerows and hedgehogs, of wannabes, of steaming sleet with equanimity on the side.

And sometimes she'll reward you with a kiss. Just a little one, for being a good boy. You try to name a kiss. You call it "tabletop," you call it "tennisball." You call it "moist." None of them seem quite to fit, and whenever you want to ask for one, she doesn't seem to know what you're talking about. "Moist!" you'll say, begging, wheedling, when all you want is just one little bit of touch, something sweet to keep you going through the night. "Moist!" And she'll just shake her head and frown.

Verbs are easy in your new language. There are no tenses. "To eat" is "horserace." But there's no "will horserace" or "have horseraced," there's no future and no past. When you eat, you eat. You live in the present, and that's all you need.

And one day you learn pronouns. "I" is "James." "You" is "Ian." "We" is the most important of all, and the most complex, isn't all of this about "we"? "We" can be "Mary" when it's just as standard, but it can be "Margaret" if there's a hint of something sweeter, "Moira" if there's real togetherness to it, it's "Maud" when it's passionate, "Molly" when it's red hot.

There is no "he" or "she." Not yet. Not until there's a need for one. There will never be a "they."

They say the Eskimos have a hundred different words for snow. And you have a hundred different words for the shade of the wallpaper, for the crack on the ceiling, for the sound the door makes when it opens and it's her and she's there and you're with her again.

You name her "Buttercup." You think it's a pretty name. And she gets angry. And she makes you understand why. You're using an English word, you're taking the meaning of an old dead language and ascribing it to her. She is so upset she leaves you alone for a whole day, and you feel hungry and lonely and ever so sorry. When she returns, at last, you can see her face is red from tears. You try out a new name on her. So tentatively, because this feels like the most important gift you have ever offered. You like the way the syllables play off each other, the teasing hiss of the "x," the lips-together warmness of the "m," the reassuring solidity of that final unshakeable "nt." You like the way the word stretches your mouth: "Excrement," you call her "Excrement," and Excrement tries it out for size, she plays with it for a while, and it makes her smile, and that night she undresses you, she strokes at your sandwich, she tickles at your torpor, she climbs on top of you and holds you firm between her soapstains and rides you like the double glazing that you are.

One morning you wake to discover that the wire cords have been replaced by silk rope. And one morning, not so long after, you wake and find the ropes have gone too. You stretch, and it hurts, and it's a good hurt. You get to your feet. You hold onto the wall. You work your way toward the door.

And at any moment you feel it's a trick, that she'll be behind you, coming at you with her kisses and feeding you lampshades. But you're in the hallway, and you've never been out here before, she didn't let you get this deep into the house even on your birthday when she let you out of your room and let you into the kitchen and tied you to the chair and she'd made you cheesecake, oh God, love her. You're in the hallway, and you're at the front door, and you're fumbling at the lock, and the door is moving! And you're moving! And you're outside! And there's such fresh air! The fresh air is spattered with bits of water, and you lift up your head high to catch the pimp (rain?) and it feels cold and carpet (wet?) against your skin, and you don't mind you suddenly feel turtle (—?). And you realize you've been standing in the garden for minutes now, and if you want to escape, you'd better move on.

And you walk, you *lurch*, you try to remember how to put one foot in front of the other without falling down. And there are words all around you, silly words, like "car" and "park," like "launderette," like the combination of "pizza" to "hut," and the world no longer seems fresh, you miss the warm bready sweetness of your home—and all around you there is only babble, people are speaking so *fast*, and you have to concentrate hard to figure out what they're saying, the old language seems so very far away now—and ugly too, it's like random words have been rammed together with no thought to the poetry or music of how that might sound, and you wonder that anyone can keep that many disconnected noises in their brain and blow them out of their mouths so shamelessly. And they're staring at you too, and you wonder whether they can tell you're different now, that you were once one of them, but you're a foreigner forever, the shapes of your language are different from theirs, and capable of expressing so much more, and they're jealous, if they hear the range of your vocabulary they'll want to tear those words right out of you—so you keep your lips clamped shut, just in case the words leak out—and just so that your words aren't *infected* with theirs, that they won't change meaning, so that "featherduster" will remain "featherduster," so that there'll always be an "onion." They stare at you for these reasons. And maybe too because you aren't wearing any beverages and your pebbles are showing.

This is a mistake. And you try to find your way back home, back to her, back to Excrement and all those possibilities—but all the streets look the same, and all the houses on all the streets look the same, and there's no one to ask, there's no one to offer handbag. And you're panicked now, running through people's gardens, calling her name over and over again at the very top of your voice, all your bits flying in the wind, all getting soaked with the pimp, and—oh—there she is!—oh my God—oh my Badger—there she is, she's looking for you, she's in her garden, she's looking for you, and now she sees you—oh most truculent Badger!—and she sees you, and she's running toward you too, her arms out wide. "Daddy!" she calls, and that's it, she's named you. And she wraps you up in her arms, and takes you back indoors.

You take her to bed. To her bed, not to yours. You lay her down. You teach her that the word for "kiss" is "moist," oh, now she gets it. You teach her that the word for "sex" is "mulch." You teach her the word for "love" is "mond." You don't need to teach her the word for "enough."

"Mond," you say, and point at her. "Mond Ian."

"Mond Ian," she agrees, and you make mond all over again.

↓

Now you're free from the bedroom you understand that she goes to work every day. She goes back into that big nasty old world, she does a job to make money so she can feed you and keep you safe. She speaks another man's language, and swallows down her own. And the sacrifice of that makes you cry.

You never want to go outside again, you tell her. And whenever she leaves the house you ask her to lock you in your bedroom. The first time she doesn't tie you to the bed, and that just makes you panic—what if you sleepwalk? What if you sleepwalk right through the window? What if you sleepwalk, then wake up to find you're out in the world again? The silk ropes aren't strong enough, you tell her. Use the cords.

"Mond Ian, Daddy," she tells you every day, and "Mond Ian, Excrement," you say back. And you sleep together most nights, and most nights you explore each other's bodies, and find in them whole new landscapes of sensations just aching to be given names.

She falls pregnant. And you spend weeks renaming the new pronouns you'll need. You decide that if the baby is a boy, you'll call "he" "Sharon." And if it's a girl, "she" can be "Jim." . . . You won't think about actual names for the baby yet. That can wait.

And when she's due, the stomach looking fat enough to burst, she says she'll find her own way to the hospital. You can just stay right where you are and wait. She ties you to the bed, she leaves several days' worth of food within easy reach in case there are complications. She says she'll be back home as soon as she can, Daddy, and she'll bring with her a whole new life you can share.

You can't horserace for all the excitement.

And a day or three later, who's counting, you hear her come through the front door, and there's crying, and you hope it isn't her crying—and you strain against your bonds to be set free. She enters your room then, and she's holding it in her arms, and it looks a bit like her, and looks a bit like you, and a bit like neither of you, quite honestly, it looks like a bald dwarf. "Daddy, Daddy!" she says, and that's how you meet your daughter, you strapped naked to the bed with cold trays of hedgerows by your side, she screaming her head off. You look at Excrement, and she's gazing adoringly, but not at you, at it, at the baby, and she no longer looks quite like Excrement, she looks like the Mother, she looks like the Conveyorbelt. And that's how you'll think of her from now on, no matter how much you try not to: just another conveyorbelt proud of her darling miracle child. The Conveyorbelt puts the baby on your bare chest, and unties your arms so you can hold her, but the baby doesn't want to be there, not on that stranger's skin. And yet you're trying to show it mond, all the mond you can, but you don't feel it in your heart, and the baby can tell, the baby doesn't want to know. "Ssh, ssh," says the Conveyorbelt, and scoops the baby up in her arms again, and the howling stops, and you feel that first stab of pure jealousy.

You promise you'll be the best father you can be. You'll teach her how to speak, give her all the words she'll ever need. You'll strap her down in her cot, feed her lampshades and caterpillars and plinges. You are told to stop—you're told the infant is only two days old. It is too early for lessons. You're told to wait.

So you wait. And maybe the baby is softening toward you. Maybe as the months pass it starts to show some affection. It no longer screams at the very sight of you—not each and every time, anyway. Sometimes it just looks at you directly and fearlessly, and glares with undisguised loathing. Sometimes it just throws up.

One day, as you're sitting at dinner, the baby speaks up. "Aubergine!" It's its first word. And the Conveyorbelt is delighted; she lifts it up in her arms, and dances with it around the room. And you sit there, forcing out a smile, forcing out congratulations—and you think, "aubergine"? What the hell is *that* supposed to mean?

And once the words start, they won't stop. "Artichoke!" "Censorship!" "Dogmatism!" "Peanut!" "Rhomboid!" "Fart!" And each time the Conveyorbelt applauding the genius of it all. And then the truth dawns on you. Why she's been locking the child away for so many hours in that room away from you. She's been teaching it how to speak all by herself. She's been doing your job. She's been denying you that role.

And that wouldn't be so bad. You could live with that. You could join in, it wouldn't be too late—she could teach it the nouns, you could start on participles and prepositional adverbs. But. It's a different language she's teaching it. It's a different language altogether.

And the child babbles again, "Rape my bollards!" and mother laughs like it's the wittiest thing on earth, and mother and child exchange a knowing glance, and you realize that the child is complicit.

You offer to hold her. You reach out to take her. And the child looks scandalized that you would dare, and your darling love says, "I don't think so!" And then claps her hand to her mouth. As if she could stop the words coming out. But it's too late. She has spoken the old language. She *promised*, and now she's angry, as if breaking her promise is your fault, as if you're the one who made her a liar. She shouts at you, says terrible truths, and she uses the new language and bits of the old, and the baby starts to cry, and you can't be sure whether because of the noise or the interjection of words it cannot hope to understand.

The Conveyorbelt wants to sleep alone that night. You agree. You know you'll never sleep with her again. And when you creep into her bedroom you tread softly so as not to disturb her. You don't want her to wake until you're ready. With silk ropes you bind her feet to the bed—by the time you start on the arms she's stirring, but there's nothing she can do, and you hold her down, you hold her hard against the mattress, and she gives in.

"Ssh," you say. "Ssh." And she shouts out, "No!" and "Help!" and "Please!"

You take the baby out of the cot at the foot of her bed. Mercifully, it doesn't struggle. Its mother starts to cry.

"Ssh," you say again. You kiss her on the forehead. And you tell her the truth, in spite of all. "Mond Ian."

"Please," she says. "I love her."

And the old language confuses you, and you don't know whether she merely got her pronouns wrong.

You hold the guacamole over her face until she's sleeping. Or, at least, until she's still.

Downstairs, to the hallway, the front door. And by now the baby is trying to resist. It's kicking, it's biting, it's screaming—*she's* screaming, your little daughter, your own. And that's good, because you know all those screams are just words needing to be moulded, and you're the one who can mould them. You pull open that door, look out at a world that's dark and cold and wet. But it'll be all right now, this time you'll have someone to talk to. And out you go.

IT FLOWS
FROM THE MOUTH

I'd been flattered when asked to be the godfather of little Ian Wheeler, of course, but I'd had certain misgivings. When I'd met up with Max in the pub, something we'd liked to do regularly back then, I'd tried to explain at least part of the problem. "Oh, don't worry about the whole spiritual adviser nonsense," said Max. "Lisa's no more religious than I am, this is just to keep her parents happy." So I caved in, and went along to the christening, and watched Ian get dipped into a font, and afterwards posed for photographs in which I must admit I passed myself off quite successfully as someone just as proud and doting as the actual father and mother.

But my real concern had nothing to do with any religious aspect, and more with the discomfort of shackling myself for life to a person I had no reason to believe I would ever necessarily like. I'd had enough problems when Max started dating Lisa—Max and I had been inseparable since school, and now suddenly I was supposed to welcome Lisa into the gang, and want to spend time with her, and chat to her, and buy lager and lime for her—and it wasn't that I *disliked* Lisa, not as such, though she was a bit dull and she wore too much perfume and I had nothing to talk to her about and she had a face as dozy as a stupefied cow. It was more that she had barged her way into a special friendship, with full expectation that I'd not only tolerate the intrusion but welcome it. She never asked if I minded. She never apologized.

And so it was with little Ian. I'm not saying he was a bad child. It was simply that he was a child at all. I'd never been wild about children, not even when I had been one, and I had always been under the impression that Max had felt the same, and I'd felt rather surprised that he wanted one. Surprised and, yes, disappointed. But then, Max had done lots of things that had surprised me since he'd met Lisa. And my worst fears came to be realized. On the few occasions I went to visit, I would be presented before Ian as if he were a prince, and every little new thing about him was pointed out to me as if I should be entranced—that he had teeth, or that he could walk, that he'd grown an inch taller—sometimes I was under the impression I was supposed to give the kid a round of applause, as if these weren't all things that I myself had mastered with greater skill years ago! I just couldn't warm to my godson. It seemed to me that he was constantly demanding attention, and I could put up with that if it were only his mother he was bothering, but all too often he'd pull the same stunts on Max. Still, I tried to be dutiful, and at Christmas and on birthdays I would send Ian a present. But is it any wonder he made me uncomfortable?—this infant who had crept into my life, though his birth was none of my doing, though his existence wasn't my fault. With his strangely fat face and his cheeks always puffed out as if he were getting ready to cry. I played godfather the best I could, but I felt a fraud.

When Ian was killed at the age of three, knocked down by a car (and safely within the speed limit, so the driver could hardly be blamed), I was, of course, horrified. The death of a child is a terrible thing, and I'm not a monster. But if a child was going to have to die, then I'm glad it was Ian.

Max and I had always been rather unlikely friends, or so I was told: at school he was more popular than I was, more sporty, more outgoing. I suspect people thought he was good for me, that's what my mother said, and I resented that—I'd point out that, in spite of appearances, he was the one who had sought me out, who wanted to sit next to me in class, who waited to walk home with me. I'd been there for him when he failed his French O levels, when he got dumped by the cricket first XI, when he first smoked, drank, snogged. I'd been best man at his wedding to Lisa, and I'd arranged a very nice stag night in a Greek restaurant, and given at the reception a speech that made everybody laugh. And I tried to be there for Max when Ian died. We'd meet up at the pub, at first it was just like the good old days! And I'd get in a round. How was he feeling? "Not so good, matey," he'd say, and stare into the bottom of his pint. "Not so good."

We drifted apart. And I'm sorry. I would have been a good friend if he had wanted me to be. But he didn't want me to be.

Max and Lisa sold their house and moved up north. We exchanged Christmas cards for a couple of years. In the last one, Max told me they were moving again, this time overseas. He promised he would write to me with his new address. He didn't.

One evening I was at home reading in my study when there was a phone call. "Hello? Is that you, John?" The number was withheld, and so I'm afraid I gave a rather stiff affirmation. "It's Max. You remember, your old friend Max? Don't you recognize me?"

And I did recognize him then, of course; and he sounded like the old Max, the one who'd call me every evening and ask for help with his homework, the one who always had a trace of laughter in his voice.

He told me he was down in the city for a "work thing," and the firm had given him a hotel for the night. "Would you like to meet up on Thursday?" he said. "We could go to the pub. No problem if it's too short notice. But we could go to the pub."

It was rather short notice, to be fair, but I didn't want to let Max down.

The pub was heaving with businessmen, it was just after the banks had shut, and the pub Max had chosen was right in the financial district. I felt a sudden stab of discomfort—what if I couldn't remember what Max looked like? What if I couldn't tell him apart from all these other smart suits? (What if he couldn't remember me?) But he'd arrived first, and he was guarding a small table in the corner, and I knew him at once, he really hadn't changed a bit. He was standing up, and laughing, and gesticulating wildly to catch my attention. No, I was wrong—he *had* changed, a bit, just a bit, actually—as I got closer I could see he'd put on some weight, and his hair was grey. But I'm sure just the same could be said of me, I'm sure that's true, I'm not as young as I was, though I try to keep myself trim, you know? I stuck out my hand for him to shake, and he laughed at that, he was laughing at everything. And he pulled me into a hug, and that was nice.

"What are you drinking?" was the first thing he said. "My round, I'll get the drinks."

We stayed rather late that night, and we had a lot of beer, and I suppose we got quite drunk. But that was all right. For a while we had to shout over the crowd to make ourselves heard, and that was a bit awkward, but pretty soon all the bankers began to go home to their wives and left us in peace. He asked me what I was up to these days, and I explained it the best I could, and my answers seemed to delight him and he laughed even more. I asked him how long he would be in England.

"Oh, we've moved back now," he said. "Mum's dying, I wanted to be close. Well, not too close. But the same country is good. Back over last year, sorry, should have been in touch."

I told him that it didn't matter, he was home now, he'd found me now—and I expressed some sympathy for his mother. I remember quite liking her, when I went to Max's house she'd give me biscuits.

"We've got this lovely house in the countryside," Max said. "A mansion, really. Almost a mansion. And the garden's fantastic. Lisa has been designing that, but of course, no surprises there!" I wondered why it was no surprise, I wondered whether Lisa was famous for designing gardens, I supposed she might have been. It was the first time he'd mentioned Lisa, and I said I was glad they were still married.

We shared anecdotes about our school days, some of the ones Max told me I had no memory of whatsoever, so they were quite fresh and exciting. I asked him how Lisa was, and he said she was well. I didn't bring up Ian at all, and I felt a bit bad about that—but then, Max didn't bring up Ian either, the evening was mercifully free of dead children.

I said I'd walk him back to his hotel.

"You should come and stay," he said to me as we walked the streets. He hung onto my arm. It was raining, and Max didn't seem to notice, and I didn't care. "Come and stay this weekend. It'd be lovely to see you properly. And I know Lisa would just love to have you." Before I knew it he was all over me with practical details—the best train I could catch, that they'd pick me up from the station. I said I wasn't available the next weekend, I was too busy—I wasn't as it happens, but I still didn't want him to think he could just swan his way back into my life and be instantly forgiven. I promised to come up the weekend after.

Now, I am aware that I don't come out of the following story too well. I can't pretend I understand more than a fraction of what happened when I visited Max, so I'll just tell it the best I can, warts and all. And I think you'll accept that the circumstances were very strange, and perhaps, to an extent, extenuating.

↯

Max met me at the station in his car. I asked if it were a new car, and he smiled, and said it was. Then we drove to his house through the rolling countryside, and he talked about his new car all the way. He'd said that he lived somewhere conveniently situated for occasional commutes into London, but I'm glad I hadn't got a taxi, the drive was half an hour at least.

Lisa was standing in the driveway to welcome us. I wondered how long she had been standing there. I had been concerned she might remember that I had often shown her a very slight resentment, but she gave no indication of it. She smiled widely enough when I got out of the car, she opened her arms a little in what might have been the beginnings of a hug. I didn't risk it, I offered her my hand. She accepted the hand, laid hers in mine like it was a delicacy, gave a little curtsey, tittered. I still didn't like her very much.

I had to admit, she looked better than I'd expected. Some women grow into their faces, do you know what I mean? They just age well, their eyes take on a certain wisdom maybe, they just look a bit more dignified. (Whereas I have never known that to be true of men—we just get older: flabbier or bonier, it's never better.) I had always likened Lisa to a cow, and it wasn't as if she had totally thrown that bovine quality off, but the fleshier parts of her face that I had once dismissed as pure farmyard now had a certain lustre. She was beautiful. There was a beauty to her. That's what it was, and I was surprised to see it.

At first I couldn't see why Max had referred to his house as a mansion. It wasn't especially grand at all—bigger than my house in the city, of course, but you'd expect that in the styx. They showed me their kitchen, and the stone AGA that took up a whole half of the space. They showed me the lounge, the too big dining table, the too big fireplace. I made the right sort of approving noises, and Max beamed with pride as if I were his favourite schoolmaster giving him a good report card.

"Let me show John the garden!" said Lisa. "Quickly, before the light fades!" And she was excited, impatient.

And now I understood why Max had used the word "mansion." Because though the house was unremarkable, the gardens at the back were huge. "It's just shy of two acres," boasted Max, and I could well believe it; it seemed to stretch off into the distance, I couldn't see an end to it. But it wasn't merely the size that was impressive—on its own, the size was an anomaly, a vast tract of land that had no business attaching itself to a house so small, like tiny Britain owning the whole of India. What struck me was the design of the thing, that it was truly *designed*, there was honest to God method in the placing of all those shrubs and hedges, the garden was laid out before us like a fully composed work of art. Even in the winter, the flowers not yet in bloom and the grass looking somewhat sorry for itself, the sight still took my breath away.

"I did all the landscaping myself," said Lisa. "It was a hobby." We walked on pebbled paths underneath archways of green fern. One day the paths would lead to big beds of flowers—"I've planted three thousand bulbs of grape hyacinth," Lisa told me, "and, behind that, three thousand of species tulips—so in the spring, there'll be this sea of blue crashing onto a shore of yellows, and reds, and greens! You'll have to come back in the spring." And every archway opened out to another little garden, different flowers seeded, but placed in ever winding patterns; there was topiary, there was even a faux maze: the design was intricate enough, I could see, but the hedges were still four feet tall, only a little child could have got lost in there.

And then, through another archway, and Lisa and Max led me to a pond. There was no water in the pond yet, this was still a work in progress. And, standing in the middle of the pond, raised high on a plinth, a statue of an angel—grey, stone, a fountain spout sticking out of its open mouth.

The wings were furled, somewhat apologetically even, as if the angel wasn't sure how to use them. Its face was of a young cherub, and I stared at it, trying to identify it—it seemed familiar, and I wondered what painting I'd seen that had inspired it, was it Raphael, maybe, or Michelangelo?

"It's Ian," said Max helpfully. And I had a bit of a shock at that. But now I could see it, of course—the infant hands, body, feet; the strangely fat face; those puffed out cheeks he had always had, now puffed out in anticipation he'd be gushing forth a jet of water.

"We gave a photograph of him to a sculptor," said Lisa. "Local man. Charming man. Excellent craftsman. Can you see the detail in that?"

"This way," said Max, "it's like Ian is always here, watching over us."

I said I could see the effect they were aiming for. And I couldn't help it, I actually laughed, just for a moment—I remembered that nasty, sulky godson of mine, and thought how unlikely an angel he would have made. If there's an afterlife, and I have no reason to believe in one, God wouldn't have made Ian Wheeler an angel, he wouldn't have wasted the feathers on him. And I thought too of how, had he lived, he'd be a teenager, or nearly a teenager?—if he were still about by now he'd be even nastier and sulkier. Instead here he was, preserved as a three-year-old, forever in stone, with wings sprouting from under his armpits.

I apologized for laughing. "No, no," said Lisa. "The fountain of remembrance is supposed to make you happy."

We went back to the house. Lisa had prepared us a stew. "Only peasant stock, I'm afraid!" she said. The meat was excellent, and I complimented her on it. She told me it was venison. We opened the bottle of wine I had brought, and disposed of it quickly; then Max got up and fetched another bottle that was, I have to admit, rather better.

After we had eaten we settled ourselves comfortably in the lounge. Max took the armchair, which left me and Lisa rubbing arms together on the sofa. Max smiled, stretched lazily. "I like being the lord of the manor!" he said.

"It suits you very well!" said Lisa, and I agreed.

They placed another log on the fire, and we felt safely protected from the winter outside. But I thought there was still not much warmth to the room. It felt impersonal somehow, as if it were the waiting room for an expensive doctor, or the lobby of a hotel. It was neat and ordered, but there were no nick-knacks to suggest anyone actually lived there. No photographs on the mantelpiece.

There were more anecdotes of our childhood, and Lisa listened politely, and sometimes even managed to insinuate herself into them as if she had been part of our story all along. The wine was making me drowsy, so I didn't mind too much.

I said how happy I was they were back in England.

"Oh, so are we!" said Max, quite fervently. "Australia was all well and good, you know, but it's not like home. You can only run away from your past for so long." It was the only time Max had ever suggested he had run away at all, and Lisa frowned at him; he noticed, and winked, quite benignly, and the subject was changed.

"It's a lovely community," said Lisa. "There are village shops only ten minutes walk from here, they have everything you really need. The church is just over the hill. And the local people are so kind, and so very like-minded."

At length Max did his lord of the manor stretch again, and smiled, and said that he had to go to bed soon. "Church tomorrow," he said, "got to be up nice and early."

"Max does the readings," said Lisa. "He's very good. He has such a lovely reading voice. What is it tomorrow, darling?"

"Ephesians."

"I like the way you do Ephesians."

I expressed some surprise that Max had found religion.

"Oh, all things lead to God," said Max. "It was hard, but I found my way back to His care."

"Maybe you could come with us in the morning, John?" said Lisa.

"You don't have to believe or anything, but it's a nice service, and the church is fourteenth century."

"And my Ephesians is second to none," added Max, and laughed.

I said that would be very nice, I was sure.

"I'll show you upstairs," said Max. "Darling, can you tidy up down here? I'll show John to bed."

"Of course," said Lisa.

I thanked Lisa once again for a lovely meal, and she nodded. "A proper peasant breakfast in the morning, too!" she promised. "You wait!"

"We've put you in Ian's room," said Max. "I hope you enjoy it."

I must admit, the sound of that sobered me up a little bit. And as Max led me up the stairs, I wondered what Ian's room could be like—would it still have his toys, teddy bears and games and little soldiers? Would it still have that sort of manic wallpaper always inflicted upon infants? And then I remembered that Ian had never lived in this house at all, he'd died years ago—so was this something kept in memorial of him? And I had a sudden dread as we stood outside the door, as Max was turning the handle and smiling and laughing and ushering me in, I didn't want to go in there, I wanted nothing more to do with his dead son.

But I did go in, of course. And it was a perfectly ordinary room—there was nothing of Ian in there at all as far as I could see. Empty cupboards, an empty wardrobe, a little washbasin in the corner. Large bay windows opened out onto the garden, and there was an appealing double bed. My suitcase was already lying upon it, it had been opened for me in preparation, and I couldn't remember when Lisa or Max had left me alone long enough to take it upstairs.

"It makes us happy to have you here," said Max. "I can't begin to tell you." His eyes watered with the sentiment of it all, and he opened his arms for another hug, and I gave him one. "Sleep well," he said. "And enjoy yourself." And he was gone.

I went to draw the curtains, and I saw, perhaps, why this was Ian's room. I looked out directly upon the garden. And from the angle the room offered I could see that all the random charm of it was not so random at all—that all the winding paths, the flowerbeds, the aches, all of them pointed toward a centrepiece, and that centrepiece was the pond, and in the centre of that, the fountain. Ian stared out in the cold, naked with only bare feathers to protect him, his mouth fixed open in that silly round "O."

I pulled the curtains on him, got into my pyjamas, brushed my teeth, got into bed. I read for a little while, and then I turned off the light.

I felt very warm and comfortable beneath the sheets. My thoughts began to drift. The distant sound of running water was pleasantly soporific.

I vaguely wondered whether it was raining, but the water was too regular for that. And then I remembered the fountain in the garden, and that reassured me. I listened to it for a while, I felt that it was singing me to sleep.

I opened my eyes only when I remembered that the pond was dry, that the fountain wasn't on.

Even now I don't want to give the impression that I was alarmed. It wasn't alarm. I didn't feel threatened by the sound of the water, anything but that. But it was a puzzle, and my brain doggedly tried to solve it, and its vain attempts to make sense of what it could hear but what it knew couldn't be there started to wake me up. I don't like to sleep at night without all things put into regular order, I like to start each day as a blank new slate with nothing unresolved from the day before. And I recommend that to you all, as the best way to keep your mind healthy and your purpose resolute.

Had Max or Lisa left a bath running? Could that be it?

I turned on my bedside lamp, huffed, got out of bed. I stood in the middle of the room, stock still, as if this would make it easier to identify where the sound was coming from. It was outside the house. Definitely outside.

I pulled open the curtains, looked out onto the garden.

And, of course, all was as it should have been. There were a few flakes of snow falling, but nothing that could account for that sound of flowing water. And poor dead Ian still stood steadfast in the pond, cold I'm sure, but dry as a bone.

I was fully prepared to give up on the mystery altogether. It didn't matter. It wouldn't keep me awake—far from it, now that I focused on it, the sound seemed even more relaxing. And I turned around to pull closed the curtain, and went back to bed.

If I had turned the other way, I know I would have missed it.

The window was made up of eight square panes of glass. I had been looking at the garden, naturally enough, through one of the central panes. But as I turned, I glanced outside through another pane, the pane at the far bottom left, and something caught my eye.

There was a certain brightness coming from it, that was all. A trick of the light. But it seemed as if the moon was reflecting off the pebbles on the path—but not the whole path, it was illuminating the most direct way from the house to the memorial pond. The pebbles winked and glowed like cat's eyes caught in the headlamps of a motor vehicle.

And there, at the end of that trail of light, at the very centre of the garden, there was the fountain. And now the fountain was on. Water was gushing out of Ian's stone mouth, thick and steady; I could see now how his posture had been so designed, with his little hands bunched up and pressed tight against his chest, to suggest that he was *forcing* out the water, as if his insides were a water balloon and he was trying to squeeze out every single last drop.

There was nothing even now so very untoward about that. If the fountain was on, so it was on. But I changed the direction of my gaze, I looked out at the garden through the central pane again—and there the fountain was dry once more, the garden still, the pathways impossible to discern in the dark.

I'm afraid I must have stayed there for a few minutes, moving my head back and forth, looking through one pane and then through another. Trying to work out what the trick was. How one piece of the window could show one view, the other, something else. I'm afraid I must have looked rather like an idiot.

And I tried to open the window. I wanted to see the garden without the prism of the glass to distract me, I wanted to know what was real and what was not. The catch wouldn't give. It seemed to freeze beneath my fingers.

Then there was a knock at my door.

It brought me back to myself, rather; it wasn't until then that I realized it, that I was on the verge of hysteria, or panic at the very least. I don't know whether I had cried out. I thought I had been silent all this while, but perhaps I had cried out. I had woken the house. I was ashamed. I forced myself to turn from the window, and as I did so, with it at my back, I felt like myself again. I smoothed down my pyjamas. I went to open the door. I prepared to apologize.

Lisa was outside in a white nightdress. She came in without my inviting her to do so, smiled, sat upon my bed.

"Hello, John," she whispered.

I said hello back at her.

"Did you never want children of your own? I'm curious."

She began unbuttoning her nightdress then. I decided I really shouldn't look at what she was doing, but I didn't want to look through the window again either, so I settled on a compromise, I stared at a wholly inoffensive wardrobe door. I said something about not really liking children, and that the opportunity to discover otherwise was never much likely to present itself. I was aware, too, that something was very odd about her arrival and the ensuing conversation, but you must understand, it still seemed like a welcome respite from the absurdities I had glimpsed through my bedroom window.

She seemed to accept my answer, and then said, "Would you help me, please?" Her head disappeared into the neck of the nightdress, its now-loose arms were flailing. I gave it a tug and pulled the dress off over her head. "Thank you," she said. She smiled, turned, pointed these two bare breasts straight at me.

"What do you think?" she asked. "Are they better than you were expecting?" I endeavoured to explain that I had had no expectations of her breasts at all. She tittered at that, just as she had when she'd curtseyed to me in the driveway, it was a silly sound. "They're new," she said, and I supposed that made sense, they seemed too mirror perfect to be real, they seemed *sculpted*. And they didn't yet match the colour of her chest, they were white and pristine.

I wanted to ask her about the view through the window, but it seemed suddenly rather impolite to change the subject. What I did ask, though, was whether she was quite sure she had the right bedroom? Didn't she want the one with her husband in it? And at this her face fell.

"Max hasn't told you, has he?"

I said that he hadn't, no.

"Oh God," she said. "Bloody Max. This is what we . . . This is why. God. He's supposed to tell. Why else do you think he brought you here?"

I said that we were old friends, and at that she screwed up her face in contempt, and it made her rather ugly. I suggested that maybe he wanted to show me the house and the garden.

"Max hates the fucking house and garden," said Lisa. "He'd leave it all tomorrow if he could." She grabbed at her nightdress, struggled with it. "Bloody Max. I'm very sorry. We have an agreement. I don't know what he's playing at. This is the way *I* cope." She couldn't get her arms in the right holes, she began to cry.

I said I was sorry. I asked her whether she could hear running water anywhere, was it just me?

"I've always liked you, John," she said. "Can't you like me just a little bit?"

I said I did like her, a little bit. More than, even.

"Can't you like me for one night?"

I tried asking her about Max, but she just shook her head, and now she was smiling through the tears. "This is the way we cope. Can't you help me out?" I said, yes. I said I could help her out. I said I was puzzled by the fountain outside, but by this stage the nightdress was back over her head again, maybe she couldn't hear.

She said, "Now, don't you worry. I'm not going to do anything you won't like." Then she climbed on top of me and gripped me hard between her thighs. She let her long hair fall across my face, then she whispered in my ear. I expected her to say something romantic. She said, "I won't get pregnant, I've been thoroughly sterilized."

I hadn't touched a woman in years. Not since I was at school, not since Max had discovered girls, and had started touching them, and I had touched them too so he wouldn't leave me out.

But even accepting my unfamiliarity with the whole enterprise, I don't think I did an especially good job. To be honest, I let Lisa do all of the work, the most I contributed was a couple of hands on her back so that she wouldn't fall off and sprain herself. And I listened to the sound of the fountain outside; sometimes the mechanical grunts of Lisa would drown it out, and I'd think maybe it was over, but then she'd have to pause for breath, or she'd be gnawing at my neck with her lips, or she'd be sitting tall and gritting her teeth hard and screwing her eyes tight and being ever so quiet, and I could hear the fountain just as before.

At length she rolled off, and thanked me, and kissed me on the mouth. The kiss was nice. I grant you that, the kiss was nice. She curled up beside me and went to sleep. Then she turned away from me altogether and I was alone, so alone.

The curtains were still open, but there was no light spilling into the room, it was just black and bleak out there. And from my position I couldn't crane my head to see whether there was any light coming through the pane on the bottom left.

I didn't want to wake Lisa. I got out of bed very gently. It was cold. My pyjama trousers had got lost somewhere. I'd have had to have turned on the bedside lamp to find them. I wasn't going to turn on the bedside lamp.

I went straight to the pane, I looked out.

As before, the pathway to the centre was lit by sparkling pebbles. But this time the snow was falling in droves, big clumps of it, and every flake seemed to catch the moon, and each one of them was like a little lamp lighting up the whole garden. The flowers were in bloom. It was ridiculous, but the flowers were in bloom—the blanket of red and white roses was thick and warm, and the snow fell upon it, and the roses didn't care, the roses knew they could melt that snow, they had nothing to fear from it. I looked out at where Lisa had planted the hyacinths and the tulips—it was, as she'd said, like a wave of blue breaking upon a brightly coloured shore.

And at the fountain itself. Ian was throwing up all the water he had inside him, and he had so *much* water, he was never going to run out, was he? But I would have thought his face would have been distressed—it was not distressed. The worst you could say about the expression he wore was that it was resigned. Ian Wheeler had a job to do, and he was going to do it. It wasn't a pleasant job, but he wasn't one to complain, he'd just do the very best he could. And the flowers were growing around him too, and vines were twisting up his body and tightening around his neck.

Over the sound of the fountain I heard another noise now. Less regular. The sound of something dragging over loose stone. Something heavy, but determined; it seemed that every lurch across the stone was done with great weariness, but it wasn't going to stop—it might be *slow*, but it wasn't going to stop. And I can't tell you why, but I suddenly felt a cold terror icing down my body, so cold that it froze my body still and I could do nothing but watch.

And into view at last shuffled Max. He was naked. And the snow was falling all around him, and I could see that it was falling fast and drenching him when it melted against his skin, but he didn't notice, he was like the roses, he didn't care, he didn't stop. Forcing himself forward, but calmly, so deliberately, each step an effort but an effort he was equal to. Further up the path, following the trail of sparkling pebbles to the fountain. Following the yellow brick road.

I tried looking through the other panes. Nothing but darkness, and the snow falling so much more gently. I wanted only to look at that garden, at that reality. But I could hear the sound from the other garden so much more clearly, I couldn't *not* hear it, the agonized heave of Max's body up the path. The flow of running water, the way it gushed and spilled, all that noise, all of it, it was pulling him along. I had to look. I did.

Once in a while the bends of the path would turn Max around so that he was facing me. And I could see that dead face—no, not dead, not vacant even, it was filled with purpose, but it wasn't a purpose I understood and it had nothing to do with the Max I had loved for so many years. I could see his skin turning blue with the cold. I could see his penis had shrunk away almost to nothing.

And now, too soon—he had reached the statue of his dead son. At last he stopped, as if to contemplate it. As if to study the workmanship!—his head tilted to one side. And maybe his son contemplated him in return, but if he did, he still never stopped spewing forth all that water, all the water there was in the world. Then—Max was moving again, he was using his last reserves of energy, he was stepping into the freezing pond, he was wading over to the stone angel, raising an arm, then both arms, he was reaching out to it. And I thought I could hear him howling. He was, he was howling.

I battered at the window. I tried again to open it. The catch wouldn't lift; the catch was so cold it hurt.

But Max had his son in his arms now, wrapping his arms about him tightly, he was hugging him for dear life, and he was crying out—he was screaming with such love and such despair. And then, then, he fell silent, and that was more terrible still—and he put his mouth to his son's, he opened his mouth wide and pressed it against those stone lips, and the water splashed against his face and against his chest, and yet he kissed his son closer, he plugged the flow of water, he took it all inside and swallowed it down.

The window gave. The rush of cold air winded me. I called out. "Max!" I shouted. "Max!" But there was nothing to be seen now the window was open, nothing but dead space, dead air, blackness.

"Darling," said Lisa.

I turned around. She was awake.

"Darling," she said. "Darling, close the window. Come back to bed." She patted the mattress beside her in a manner I assumed was enticing.

I closed the window. I looked through the pane once more, I looked through every pane, and there was nothing to make out, the moon was behind the clouds, the darkness was full and unyielding. I went back to bed. I did as I was told.

↓

I had fully intended to go to church the next morning. I had made a promise, and I keep my promises. But when I woke up the house was empty. Max and Lisa had gone without me. I made myself a cup of tea, and waited for them to come back. Eventually, of course, they did. All smiles, both looking so smart, Max in particular was very handsome in his suit. "Sorry, matey," said Max. "I popped my head around your door, but you looked like you needed the extra sleep! Hope you don't mind!" And Lisa just smiled.

Neither of them said a word about the adventures of the night before, and neither treated me any differently. Lisa had told me she'd cook a big peasant's breakfast, and she was as good as her word—bacon, eggs, and sausages she said were from pigs freshly slaughtered by a farmer friend she'd made. Then we settled down in the lounge, and shared the Sunday newspaper, each reading different sections then swapping when we were done. It was nice.

Some time early afternoon, though, Max looked at the clock, and said, "Best you get back home, John! I've things that need doing!" And I hugged Lisa goodbye, and Max drove me to the railway station, and we hugged too and I thanked him for the weekend.

We drifted apart. I don't know who drifted from whom; I doubt it was anything as deliberate as that. No, wait, I sent them a Christmas card, and they didn't respond. So they're the ones who drifted. They drifted, and I stayed where I was, exactly the same.

↓

That would be the end of the story. I had heard from an old school friend that a couple of years later Max and Lisa had separated. It was just gossip, and I don't know whether it was true or not, and I felt sorry for them just the same.

That was maybe six months ago. Recently I received a letter.

Dear John,

You may have heard that Max and I have gone our different ways! It was quite sad at the time, but it was very amicable, and I'm sure one day we will be good friends.

But sometimes when something has died, you just have to accept it, and move on.

I still have the house. Max was very generous, to be fair. All he wanted was half of the money, and the fountain from the garden. We had to dig it up, and I'm afraid it has made the garden a bit of an eyesore! I tried to tell Max it won't work, it was specially designed to fit with all our underground piping, but as you know, there's no talking to Max!

I'm going to rethink the garden. I'm sure I can make it even better.

All the locals have been very nice, and they're attentive as ever in their own way. But I don't know. I think perhaps they liked Max more than they ever liked me.

If you would like to stay again, that would make me very happy.

Maybe I shouldn't say this. But that night we spent together was very special. It was a special night. And I think of you often. Sometimes I think you're the one who could save me. Sometimes I think you could give me meaning.

But regardless. Thank you for always being such a good friend to me and Max, and for being best man at the wedding, and any other duties you took on.

Best regards,

Lisa Howell (once Briggs).

I haven't written back yet. I might.

A GRAND DAY OUT

The woman at the front desk smiled at him sympathetically, and he thought nothing of that, she smiled sympathetically at everyone. But as he walked down the corridors to his wife's private room even the nurses were at it, and one or two of the doctors, they were nodding at him in acknowledgement and offering good mornings. He didn't question it, didn't think about what all that might mean. But when he opened the door and he saw Helen sitting upright on the bed, and she was fully dressed, and her eyes were sparkling, and she looked so healthy and happy and *young*, he supposed he had guessed it, he supposed this is what he thought must have happened.

"Oh God," he said. And, "No. No."

Helen spoke to him then. "Hello, baby," she said, and she hadn't spoken to him in months, not properly, not with any real understanding of what she was saying or who he was, any words she'd said had come out like staccato grunts. And now she was calling him baby, just as she'd always used to, and he burst into tears, he couldn't help it.

"Hey," she said. "Hey. It's all right." And she got up from the bed, and came toward him, as if movement was no problem at all, as if the exercise of limbs wasn't some slow torture. She stood close, she didn't touch him, he didn't know why.

"I'm sorry," he said.

"It's a shock."

"It *is* a shock," he agreed. "Yes. Wow. Yes." Yesterday he'd sat beside her, and he'd talked to her about nothing in particular, and he'd stroked her hair, and he'd held her hand. And she'd done nothing, not a thing, save grasping onto his finger when he tried to leave.

"I love you," she said.

He didn't even think about that just yet. "It's too soon," he said. "They told me you had ages. Another year, even. I haven't. I haven't had time to *prepare*." And he was crying again, Christ. And he was angry with himself for that—and still Helen towered close, and it seemed as if her arms were itching to put themselves around him and give him some comfort. He realized at last why she hadn't hugged him—she was shy, and that was so ridiculous, they'd been married forty-three years! So he put his arms around her waist, and held her instead, and she hugged him back, tightly, gratefully, and on he cried but he felt so much better.

"Do I look all right?" she asked.

"You're beautiful," he said, and she was.

She was taller, and plumper, but plump in all the right ways. Her balding white hair was now thick and brown and down to her shoulders. She had hips and long legs and she had breasts. She seemed altogether much bigger than he remembered, and that was the greatest surprise, how over the years she must have shrunk in on herself and he'd not thought to notice. The room around her now seemed small, like a box; it was just a box; it was the best room he'd been able to afford, and it was pretty enough, and she was on her own here, and the wallpaper was pink and there was a television in the corner and flowers. But now it was a box, and she'd been boxed up here for nearly two years, that was long enough.

"Let's get out of here," he said.

Now they walked down the corridor together, and the doctors and nurses were all smiling at the sight of them, but they were sorry too. "Take care, Mrs. Marshall," said the woman who had used to turn her bed. "We'll miss you, Helen, you've been lovely," said the woman who'd injected her each morning. And Helen smiled back at them all, and nodded, and looked a bit awkward, as if she didn't really know who all these people were.

Doctor Phillips was waiting at the exit, he must have been informed. He shook Helen Marshall firmly by the hand and told her that she'd been a kind patient, not many of his patients had been so kind. He shook Mr. Marshall's hand too, and called him sir, and told him to be brave, and that he was sorry for his loss.

"We thought we'd have longer," said Mr. Marshall. "You told me we'd have longer." And Doctor Phillips just shook his head, and offered his hand once more.

The woman at the front desk with the sympathetic face smiled at them both sympathetically, and asked Mr. Marshall how he wanted to settle the final bill. Mr. Marshall handed her his credit card, and she swiped it.

ᴟ

Mr. Marshall wasn't there to witness his mother's last day. Dad was still alive back then, and he'd said he wanted her to himself. That seemed fair enough, and Mr. Marshall made his farewells to his mother every time he visited her, just in case he never saw her again. One day his dad called and said that his mother was gone. Mr. Marshall didn't know what to say. Was it peaceful? "Yes," his dad had said, "it was peaceful."

For his dad, it had been another matter entirely. There was no one else left for Dad. He'd driven out to see him at the old family house, and there was his dad waiting for him, in the front driveway, all teeth and muscles, and wearing a flannel sports jacket. "Hey hey!" Dad had said. Dad wanted to spend his last day at a cricket match, so that's what they had done. His dad seemed fit enough to play cricket himself if he wanted to, and Mr. Marshall knew he'd played in a team when he was younger, wouldn't he rather do that? "No, no," said Dad; spectating would be just fine. Mr. Marshall had never much enjoyed cricket, but they sat there together in the crowd, and Dad would tell him at which points he should be excited and whether anyone was playing well or not. Afterwards they went to the pub and drank beer and talked about girls, and it was easy to forget that the man ogling the barmaids beside him who was stronger and bolder and wittier than he had ever been was his old father; more than that, it was easy to forget they had anything in common at all. At the end of the day Mr. Marshall had driven his dad back home; "Thanks," said Dad, "that was perfect, I wouldn't have wanted it any other way," and he really seemed to believe that. He left his dad there, then; he asked him whether he'd like some company for the very end, and Dad said no, he'd be all right. It had been such a good day, why risk spoiling it? And sometimes now, when the cricket played on television, Mr. Marshall would sit down and watch it, and think of his dad, and almost enjoy the game for his sake.

Helen had been dying for such a long time. It had crept over her slowly. She had been the only woman he had ever loved, someone who had never failed to make his heart race, someone who always made him feel lucky and proud—and death had *crept* over her, so slowly, so carefully, it took away her looks, it took away her memory, it took away her *self*. Mr. Marshall had tried taking care of her for a while, until it became clear he really didn't know what he was doing, and his wife stood a better chance of happiness if he put her away in a home—and if not a chance of happiness, then a chance of comfort maybe, or at least a chance of a few months' extra life.

And the only consolation Mr. Marshall had allowed himself was that he was being given lots of notice. So that when her time was up, he could have everything ready. He'd have tickets for a London show, a musical, Helen liked those, the very best seats in the house, they could watch it in a private box if she wanted! He'd take her out to some fancy restaurant, and they'd stuff themselves with everything on the menu. They'd go to the seaside maybe. If the weather was nice. They'd go to the seaside, and walk along the beach, and kick at the sand, and they'd hold hands, and stare out at the sea, and stare out at the horizon, and they'd wait for the sun to go down.

He'd give her back everything the disease had stolen. Just for a little while. Just for as long as they were given.

"I'm taking you to the seaside," Mr. Marshall told his wife, as they went out into the hospice car park.

"That sounds nice," she said.

She got into the car beside him. He wished he'd tidied it up, the passenger seat was strewn with empty crisp bags; sometimes after he visited Helen he'd stop at a service station and buy bags of crisps and eat them parked on the forecourt. He pushed the rubbish onto the floor, he hoped she wouldn't comment, and she didn't.

"Oh God," he said. "Nothing's prepared. I wanted everything prepared." And just for a moment he gave in. He leaned forward, he pressed his head upon the steering wheel in despair.

She stroked the back of his neck. "It doesn't matter."

"No," he said. "You're right. You're with me now."

"I'm with you now, baby."

"And we're going to the seaside!"

"Yes! Let's do that!"

"Could you pass me the map?" he said. "It's in the glove compartment."

"I'll need to go home first, baby," said Helen. "I need to change." It was true. She was bursting out of her clothes. And besides, they were old lady clothes, even Mr. Marshall could quite see they didn't suit her.

They drove home. Oh, he wished he'd tidied up the house too. He said to her, "You rush in, I'll wait here in the car. Don't be long, we don't have a minute to lose. We want to miss the traffic."

She said, "Baby, I've got to go through my things. I can't remember what I have to wear, I threw so much out! I've got to go through it all. And I want to put on some lippie, I feel naked without it. I won't be too long, come indoors with me."

"No," he said, "it'll be quicker if I wait in the car."

She took his keys, and left the car, and let herself into the house.

He waited twenty minutes, then decided to go in after her.

She took another three quarters of an hour, and he paced up and down in the kitchen, and he fretted. When she appeared he forgave her at once. Her hair was done up the way he'd always liked it, her face was full of colour, and she was wearing a red dress that made her look so pretty it took his breath away.

"I hung onto this for years," she said. "You know. Just in case."

↓

At first they made good progress on the A23. Helen said that when they'd gone on outings they'd sung songs along the way, did he remember? And Mr. Marshall did remember! Though he couldn't necessarily remember what. So she taught him "Summer Holiday," she sang it over and over again, and the words came back to him, and eventually they stuck. It was fun, although it was hardly summer yet, it was only May.

They didn't talk much. When she'd been sick he'd talked to her non-stop. He'd found a way of filling the silences even though he'd had nothing to say—because there was never any news to share with her, all that he was doing with his life was visiting her in the hospice every single day. He'd talked, though; and he'd supposed she might be listening, he'd hoped that even if she weren't able to understand what the words meant that the sound of his voice would be a comfort. But now, side-by-side in the car, he felt embarrassed. Still, they sang. And as he reached for the gearstick his hand brushed hers, she'd been lying in wait for it, she caught hold of it and grasped it tight. All the time looking ahead out of the windscreen quite innocently, as if she were doing nothing at all, just enjoying the scenery and singing Cliff Richard. And she tickled his palm with her fingernails, and he felt happy.

"How long do we have?" he asked suddenly. "You know, before?"

"I don't know," she said.

"No."

"I'm sure we'll get our full day. Everyone gets a full day."

He said, "We can have fish and chips tonight! The fish is better by the sea. I'm going to have battered cod and mushy peas!"

She said, "And I'll have the haddock, if there's any fresh!"

A little outside Lewes the cars ahead began to slow. "This won't be a traffic jam," he reassured her, "don't worry." But it was a traffic jam. Pretty soon they were just inching forward. All around them the cars were honking their horns in frustration. He did the same.

"That doesn't do any good, baby," Helen said mildly.

"Bloody hell," he said, and fumed.

"Well, there's not much we can do."

"We could have set out earlier, that's what we could have done," Mr. Marshall said. "And who wears a bloody dress to the bloody beach anyway?" He felt sorry. "Bloody hell," he said again, quietly.

She didn't say anything for a while. He stole a look at her to see whether she was cross, or whether she was sulking. She didn't seem to be either.

He said, "Are you frightened?"

She turned to him, frowned, tried to work out what he was talking about. Then she said, "Yes. A little bit."

He squeezed her hand. "It'll be okay."

"I know," said Helen. "I don't know what's waiting for me afterwards. But I'm sure there must be something. I believe God is kind. Because he has to be, don't you think? He wouldn't give us this. That before we die, just for one day, everyone gets to be young and happy again."

"You think that's proof of God?"

"Don't you?" she said.

In all their years of marriage, they'd never really discussed God or anything like that. She'd never wanted to go to church, she'd never seemed the preachy sort. He couldn't help wondering about all the other things that they had never got around to talking about, in all their forty-three years. There were still new things left to say.

"Yes," Mr. Marshall said. "I suppose I do."

They sat in silence for a couple of minutes.

"Are you frightened, baby?" she then said.

He wasn't sure of what, frightened of his own death, or frightened she was about to leave him? "I'll be okay," he told her.

He knew how it was going to happen, of course. That at some point Helen would just start getting even younger still. She'd shrink again, but

303

not this time with old age and disease, she'd become a little girl, then an infant, then a baby, all her memories falling away. And then she'd be gone. It would only take a few seconds, and they said it was painless and rather sweet. Peaceful.

Mr. Marshall hoped it didn't happen whilst they were stuck on a dual carriageway outside Brighton.

It began to rain.

"Let's go home," said Helen.

"No," he said. "No. I want to give you a perfect day."

"I like home," Helen said. "I've always liked our home. Let's go home. Baby. Let's go."

They turned around. The roads leaving Brighton were free and empty and they were back before they knew it.

⥼

Mr. Marshall said, "We can still go out for dinner, there's a new Thai restaurant that's opened around the corner." Helen said, "Let's stay in. I'll cook."

Helen looked in the fridge. She looked in the freezer. She tutted. "Baby, this is all junk," she said. "How are you supposed to take care of yourself with this stuff?"

"I'm sorry."

"We'll go to the supermarket," she said.

He objected. He wasn't going to take her to the supermarket. He had wanted to take her to the seaside, and to a West End musical, to special things. She said, "If I get to choose where we go, I choose the supermarket. Come on, it'll be fun! We'll make it fun!"

It was fun. Helen placed Mr. Marshall in charge of the trolley, and she'd order him up and down the aisles whilst she picked things from the shelves, and he told her he wasn't in the bleeding army, and she laughed and began to call him Corporal Marshall, and he called her his Sergeant Major. She was shocked at how expensive everything had got. "How long have I been away?" she said. "What, was I in a bloody coma?" They both found that very funny, and Mr. Marshall laughed so hard he began to wheeze and Helen had to clap him on the back.

She cooked them spaghetti bolognaise. Nothing too grand, but she'd always done something clever with the sauce, it tasted better than any spaghetti he'd ever had eating out. "I want to look after *you*," he'd protested. "You've looked after me for long enough," she said, "now it's my turn!" She said she didn't want any help, but he could stay in the kitchen and talk to her if he liked. He didn't find anything to talk about, but he stayed anyway, and kept her company.

They ate the pasta. It was really good. "Who likes Thai anyway?" said Helen.

Mr. Marshall said, "I've been dreaming of this. That you'd be all right again. That things would be back to how they used to be."

Helen said, "Oh, baby." She took his hand. "Oh, baby, but I'm not all right. Am I? I'm really very very ill indeed."

Mr. Marshall swallowed. "Yes," he said.

She reached over the plates and kissed him then. Her lips seemed so soft and big, and he knew his were just these awful cracked things, but she didn't seem to care. He hadn't kissed in such a long time, he thought he might have forgotten how, but it all came back to him like Cliff Richard.

"Let's go to bed," she whispered.

"Oh, Helen," he said. "Oh. I don't think I can. I can't. I can't. I'm sorry. I can't."

"Do I look all right?" she asked him.

"You're beautiful," he said. And she was, she was.

↓

So they went to bed, and stayed dressed, and lay side-by-side, and held hands. They didn't say much, and sometimes Mr. Marshall would start, and wonder whether she'd vanished already, and he'd take a look, even though he could still feel her fingers stroking his palm.

No, God wasn't kind. One extra day wasn't kind at all. Why not a week, that might have meant something, he could have taken Helen away, to Paris, or Venice, or New York. Why not a year? Then they could have tried for a child, again, maybe. Why not twenty years, so they could see the child grow up? Why not forever?

He was crying again. He blurted out, "I don't think I can go on without you."

"Look at me," she said softly.

"No."

"Look at me."

He looked at her.

She said, "All day long we've been together. And you're still old. So that means you'll live through tomorrow. You can get through tomorrow without me. And if you can live tomorrow, you can live the day after that. One day after the other. You'll be all right."

"I'll be all right," he whispered, and she kissed him on the nose.

He felt so sleepy. This latest bout of tears had quite worn him out. And Helen was stroking at his hair.

"Of course you're tired," she said. "All you've been through. My poor love, I've quite put you through hell these last couple of years. I'm so sorry. You go to sleep. Just for a little while. You take a nap, I'll hold you."

He wanted to say no, but his eyelids were drooping, and when he opened his mouth to answer a yawn popped out. "Promise you won't leave without saying goodbye," he said.

↓

He slept through the night, and it was only the sunlight flooding in through the windows that woke him. He looked for Helen, he called around the house for her, but he knew she was gone.

He found her little red dress on the floor downstairs.

He also found a note.

You're so tired, I didn't want to disturb you.

Thank you. You have been the best thing in my life. You have been my life.

Take care of yourself, for me.

xxx

Mr. Marshall wasn't sure that he would ever forgive Helen for leaving him behind. But eventually he did.

He ate the healthy food she'd left him in the fridge, and when it ran out, he went to the supermarket and bought some more. He started to lose weight. He looked trim.

He tried out the Thai restaurant one night. There was a special deal on Thursdays. He had the lad nah with chicken, it was quite nice. There was a woman there, eating alone, and he said hello.

He went back to the Thai restaurant a couple of months later, and this time he didn't worry about a Thursday discount. The woman was there again! He supposed she was a regular, but it was only her second visit as well. They laughed at the coincidence. She asked whether he'd like to join her, and he said he would.

Her name was Claire. She was a widow. Her husband had died seven years ago. "I don't think I said the right things to Helen that last day together," he told her. "Oh, darling," Claire said, "no one ever does."

It felt odd to have a new girlfriend, though she wasn't really a girlfriend, was she? Well, maybe she was. They'd meet a couple of times a week, and they'd kiss goodnight, on the cheek, and then one time they went for the mouths. She invited him in, and he accepted, and when she took him to the bedroom he got scared again. But this time he could, he *could*.

He felt guilty. He liked to think that Helen would have got on with Claire. But would she have, honestly? Claire said to him one night, "What was it you wanted to say to Helen? Let it out. Tell me instead."

Mr. Marshall said, "I love you too."

↓

It was a whole new year, the first year in which Mr. Marshall hadn't got a wife called Helen anymore. Claire asked him to move in with her. He already spent so much time at her house anyway, wouldn't it be simpler?

He went back to his home, began to sift through all his old stuff. So much to throw away. Still, so much to keep too.

He took a deep breath, he at last boxed up all of Helen's clothes and took them to the charity shop. He hesitated about the red dress, but it was just a dress, it wasn't Helen—and he could never give it to Claire, Claire was seventy-four years old and fat, she'd never fit into it. And he would never have wanted Claire to have it anyway.

He cried for Helen that day, and though he didn't know it, it was for the last time.

And in a dresser he found an old photograph album. He hadn't even known Helen had kept one. He leafed through it, from the beginning, from their wedding day. He used to be so handsome, and Helen was so pretty. And as he turned the pages he watched himself get older, but Helen, Helen didn't age at all, Helen stayed young and healthy forever and so so full of life. In every picture they stood together, and he looked so proud of her. And she looked so proud of him.

HISTORY
BECOMES YOU

And, one day, the Towers came back.

Later there were those keen to tell the world how they had witnessed the miracle first hand. How they'd been right on the spot when the five hundred thousand-ton structures of concrete and glass had so impossibly popped back into existence. How they felt blessed they'd been there to see it, how they'd felt *chosen*, how it had brought to their eyes tears of patriotic fervour. But they were lying. Some of them didn't even know they were, they wanted so much to take their part in history. But no one had seen the Towers appear. They came back at the exact moment when everybody in the vicinity just happened to be looking in the wrong direction at the same time.

In the instant of their arrival the Towers blotted out the sunlight, and the sudden shadows that they cast caused passers-by to shiver.

The police cordoned off the area. The yellow tape around the buildings' perimeter said "Crime Scene"—although there wasn't a crime, not really, or there *was*, but the crime that had been committed there had happened such a long time ago and on such a scale that "crime" seemed too paltry a word to describe it. But "Crime Scene" was the best they could come up with, the police just didn't have an appropriate yellow tape.

And into the buildings were sent doctors, firemen, the police. They soon reported that the structural integrity of the Towers was sound. The ninety-third floor was intact, as if it had never been cleaved through with aeroplane fuselage. And it was clean; the window panes were polished and fair sparkled in the New York sun, the toilets smelled of pine bleach, the carpets seemed newly shampooed.

There was no one to be found. Not a trace of a single body. Not a trace, moreover, that anybody had ever worked there. The desks were empty, the memo boards were blank. The windows were fastened shut tight, as if indeed they'd never been opened at all, as if indeed no persons had ever felt the urge to climb through them and jump to their deaths. Even the soft swivel chairs were pristine and plump, there was not the merest indentation from any bottom to be found.

As good as new.

The media weren't sure at first how to play the story. The default stance was one of panic: this was the signal for another attack; another Godless foe had designs upon America. But no one could quite see how bringing the Towers *back* could be construed as a terrorist act. And so, broadly, it was reported as a Good Thing. One expert pundit said that he could explain the phenomenon. That sometimes events take place that are so important that they shatter the world stage and change the course of history. That the destruction of the Towers was one such event. That the impact it had made was so great, its legacy so incalculable, the Towers would be a part of everyone's lives forever; so, therefore, the very *absence* of the Towers was at once weird and contradictory, how could something that so defined the mood of the twenty-first century *simply not be there*? History itself had brought the Towers back into existence. History could not let them go.

It wasn't a very scientific theory, and no one necessarily understood it. But it quite caught the public's imagination. For a good few hours, at least. For as long as the Towers stood intact.

Because, at a little before half past ten the next morning, the Towers vanished once more.

The same expert claimed on breakfast television that this in no way contradicted his earlier theory. Rather, it was an extension of it; that the Towers' fall had been so momentous an event of history that what they were now seeing was its echo. Why hadn't such things happened before? Well, maybe no event before had been important enough. Maybe this was the most significant historical event there had ever been. This was a reminder. God was reminding them not to take the tragedy for granted. God was reminding them never to forget.

But the news was less interested in the whys. It would rather focus upon the human drama. Because the Towers had not been empty at the time they had vanished. They had taken eleven souls with them: seven firemen, and four police officers. No trace of them could be found. They were described as fresh victims of the 9/11 attacks, as new American heroes. Journalists were dispatched to interview the bereaved: the wives, the lovers, the children. One wife declared, with tears in her eyes, but they were angry tears of determination, there was no *weakness* to those tears, that she was proud her Brad had struck a blow in the war on terror. That she would love him forever, and that she knew Brad was looking down on her from Heaven. That their son was still too young to understand, but she'd *make* him understand, one day, just how lucky he had been to have had a father who had died so nobly and so selflessly to ensure that he could live in a better and purer world. The newspapers loved it. They wrote up long features on Brad, and on all his companions. Fallen heroes, all; all of them sacrifices in the crusade for democracy, liberty, and truth.

Expressions of sympathy poured in from all over the world. They spoke of deep regrets, of common bonds, of alliances never to be broken. They were accepted with cool politeness. As a whole, the American people saw them for what they were. These other nations, they were just jealous *they* hadn't had a miracle. They were trying to muscle in on the act.

Nine days after they had vanished, late in the afternoon, the Towers came back again. It was rush hour, and quite a few people were looking in the right direction at the right time. But the Towers appeared at the exact split second when everybody blinked.

The police cordoned off the area once again with their yellow tape. And the military stood by for a full hour and a half to see whether or not the Towers would simply wink back out of existence. At last a major said that he was prepared to inspect the buildings, but that he would do so alone, he refused to risk any of his soldiers' lives in there. He would go in with a walkie-talkie, he'd be in constant communication, he'd be able to give the world a second by second commentary of his impressions and insights. Before he made his entrance, he found time to acknowledge his bravery exclusively to Channel Eight News. He said that he was "taking one for Uncle Sam," and spoke directly to his wife: "I love you, Moira, and I love the kids, and if I die today, this is how you should remember me forever, as a hero, as a patriot." America watched collectively, hearts in mouths, as the major embarked on his mission—it went out live on all stations; families held hands and prayed, mothers cuddled up close to children, men drank bottled beers and wept openly together in downtown bars. The major was soon able to tell the viewers that there was no one to be found, neither the original victims of the attack nor those so haplessly taken in the aftermath. The major spent a good two hours inside the Towers, establishing just how immaculate those carpets could be. Two hours, that was longer than an average movie, and yet the live broadcast stuck with him for the whole thing. He was ordered out; he claimed there was still so much more he could investigate; he was ordered out again, very strictly; he emerged, somewhat reluctantly, to the cheering of crowds. "It's nothing, I would have taken one for Uncle Sam," he said, "it's all I wanted, to take one for Uncle Sam." And then went home to Moira, and to the kids, and to a new contract as a TV anchorman.

The expert said that night that he hadn't meant an echo, not as such, but *ripples*: if you imagined History as one big pond, and the Twin Towers as one big rock—two big rocks, technically, but let's for the sake of an argument call them one—if you were to drop your one big rock right into the centre of your pond, then there'd be a ripple effect; this is the situation they had here, rock, pond, and America was blessed, it was seeing the ripples, getting ripples on all sides, God was buffeting them with ripples. He'd go into further detail, he said, but it was better examined in his new book, which would be available next week. The interviewer complimented him on the speed at which he must have written it. "We must all do our bit for our country in these dark and difficult days." Would the Towers now be safe? "It's in the book," said the expert. But when pressed, "I think by taking away the Towers God gave us a reminder of a tragedy past, and by restoring them, a beacon of hope for the future. Those Towers right now are the safest places in America."

The next morning, again a little before half ten, the Towers vanished. This time they took fourteen firemen, six police officers, and a tramp who hadn't been deterred by yellow tape. The expert was not available for comment. Luckily for him, the press left him alone—they had families of new fallen heroes to interview.

One night the NYPD received a call from a woman. She said the crisis wasn't over. She knew the Towers would come back, and take more lives; she knew that she was responsible. The NYPD had been plagued with hoax calls ever since the first reappearance. The woman sounded a bit drunk, and very distressed, and no one on duty was inclined to take her seriously—but they were obliged to bring her in. What she said when they did convinced them all.

She explained that she had once worked at the Towers. And how the day that they fell she ought to have been inside, she ought to have fallen with them. But on September the tenth she'd been out to a bar, she'd met a man, she'd had a few drinks, and one thing had led to another— she'd taken him back to her apartment, they'd fucked all night, and in the hangover and satiated exhaustion that followed she'd slept through her alarm clock the next morning. By the time she'd thought to ring her office and pretend that she was sick, her office didn't exist anymore. At first she'd taken this as a sign from God. He'd *spared* her, He had other plans for her; rather than die in fear and fire she was supposed to be with this man she'd picked up. But that soon turned out to be wrong. The man was a liar, and used drugs, and was married—and, worse still, was bad in bed; he wasn't someone on whom she could pin any salvation at all. And ever since it had haunted her, how close she had come to dying, how she had been *meant* to be there with all her colleagues, with the office managers, with the girls on reception and the boys in the post room. She'd tried to live her life, she got a new job, she found a boyfriend who wasn't married and got high only at weekends—but it always seemed so wrong to her, that all about her was a lie. She had been destined to be a victim of America's greatest tragedy, she'd been destined to be special.

When the Towers had come back, she'd known they'd come back for her. They were calling her. And they'd appear, and then disappear, appear and disappear again, over and over, until they got what they wanted—until they took her—until they gobbled her down and swallowed her whole. As was meant to be. And only then would it all stop. 9/11. It was about her, it had always been about her, and her alone, that's all it had ever been for.

She wasn't the only one to come forward.

A man in New Jersey petitioned for the right to die in the Twin Towers. His story touched the nation. He told how his wife had died in the attack, and they'd never even said goodbye. So many farewell phone calls sent out that morning, but never one to him—he didn't know whether she'd died quickly, or in pain, all he knew was she hadn't come home again. He'd have to live through it—so said his friends, his doctors, the therapist—he'd live through it, one day things would get better. But they hadn't got better. No day was ever better. Because they were days without *her* in them. He'd flirted with suicide—but he'd never taken quite the right number of pills, never cut quite deeply enough. He'd always supposed Heaven was a big place, it must be *huge*, just to house the sudden influx of new American heroes—what if he were sent to the wrong bit of it, the bit reserved for pill poppers or wrist slicers, what then, how would he ever find her then? Now he knew he could find her. He wanted to be at her work desk. He wanted to be on her swivel chair. He wanted to know that when he vanished, he'd vanish right to where she'd be waiting for him, this woman who'd make him forever happy, they'd be reunited at last in an open-plan office of their very own. He wanted to die the way she had died. He wanted to die *right* . . . And he was pretty sure his sister-in-law would take care of the kids.

And there was the elderly couple that lived in Arkansas, no one dreamed of sending suicide bombers to Arkansas—it wasn't fair, they too wanted the honour of dying for America. And there was the man who'd tattooed "9/11" on his left arm, and on his right a picture of an airplane in flames—across his chest it said "never forget," and he never would, he wouldn't. And there was the old man who believed in God so much. And there was the young girl who just wanted to believe. And there were the lost. And there were the lonely. And there were the ones who were so happy and so safe and were living the American dream, and the guilt that it had come too easy and they'd never been called upon to make a sacrifice for it gave them nightmares. And those who'd tried to enlist for the army, for the right to serve and fight, but their country had turned them down, they weren't good enough to fight, they were too old, or too diabetic, or too gay. All of them, all of them, they claimed that when they saw the Towers on their TV screens, unbowed, undefeated, and so majestic now, and so *clean*—they'd felt pulled toward the Towers, they knew it was their God-given right to become part of them. "I want to be a hero," said an unparticular someone. "And I don't know any other way of doing it."

And, one day, the Towers came back.

Cameras had been set up to record the possibility, but all of them glitched at the very same moment. And the police cordoned off the area, and this time they had new tape already prepared, it was *red*, and it said "Crime Scene!!!" with three exclamation marks, and the exclamation marks were an even brighter red! The whole thing was really very red indeed!!! And once the authorities had done their checks to make sure it was safe, they didn't want anyone to slip on those shampooed carpets, they didn't want anyone to *sue*, they let in all those who'd queued up for days, ready to take their places in the Twin Towers. All of the chairs filled quickly. Soon there was standing room only in the lobby and in the corridors and in the restrooms. Everyone admired how the windows sparkled, and the pleasing scent of bleach. "We're going to Heaven!" said one delighted six-year-old child, to a mummy and daddy who were laughing along with him, "we're all going to Heaven, and we'll be there in the morning!"

Indeed they would be. And none of us really want to die, of course we don't. But we all know we will, it's like a ticking bomb inside all of us, and we never know when that bomb is going to go off, and doesn't that spoil everything, just a little? And we know too that our deaths won't be *grand* deaths, most likely they'll be lung cancer, or cancer of the oesophagus, or cancer of the brain—we'll die, and it'll be *pathetic*, we'll maybe not even remember our own names as we stare into the abyss, the moment when we could have been special will have passed long ago and we'll never even have realized when, and we'll end as we began, confused, infant-like, and just the same as everybody else. But what if you could be more? What if your death could become history? Ensure that in your final seconds you'd be part of something bigger than you would ever be on your own, what if you too could be part of the 9/11 Experience? Just like Our Fallen Heroes, but no, better—cleaner, simpler, no pain, no doubt, just erased away, no need for burning flesh, no need for tears as people scream out desperately for families they'll never see again, certainly no need to jump out of any windows! (The windows sparkle in the New York sun, and are fastened tightly shut.) Better than Our Fallen Heroes too because they died in ignorance, they never knew what their martyrdoms would represent and how they would change the world, if they could only have seen the news reports the next day imagine how thrilled they would have been!—but *you* will know, you'll *know*, how can you resist? Be a part of history, let history consume you, and your death can never now be a trivial one, you too can be a hero, you too can be like Superman (or Wonder Woman, if that's your preference)—and if your *death* isn't trivial, maybe, just maybe, it'll mean your life wasn't either, maybe, maybe. And you'll look just so dandy, history will become you, and after you're gone friends will tell of how important you were, and they'll feel important by association—"I knew a guy who died in the Towers!"—really, it's a win-win scenario, the 9/11 Experience is a gift not only to you but to *them*, to your family, doesn't Junior deserve a daddy who's a hero? a mummy who bled out stars and stripes? Come to New York, take in a Broadway show, a meal at Sardi's, enjoy the best New York has to offer! Safe in the certainty that the very next day you're making a stand for something noble we can all believe in.

The world has changed, and we all now stand in the shadow of the Twin Towers. But who wouldn't choose to be part of what casts that shadow?

By the time the Towers next returned, there was a box office service all ready and waiting.

One day, in Baghdad, the twelve metre-high statue of Saddam Hussein popped back into existence. American troops pulled it down immediately, and razed the ground with fire. It never returned.

↓

And, one day, the Towers stayed right where they were.

The Towers were packed. Of course, they were always packed. But this was the height of summer, and the waiting list for summer reservations was especially long. You could get such a lovely view from the top when the weather was nice!

The complaints started only minutes after the scheduled half past ten departure time. Families who were taking hands and composing themselves for the rapture kept having to let go and recompose themselves all over again. They were so determined to keep their minds pure for the moment of deliverance: "For Christ's sake," they asked, "what the hell's going on?" By noon customers were being advised to vacate the Towers. The buildings were cordoned off with tape saying "Technical Difficulties," and "Your Patience is Appreciated."

There was no system in operation to cope with dissatisfied customers, nobody had ever complained before. It was chaos. Overseas passengers wanted reimbursement not only for the 9/11 tickets, but also for their plane fares. Others demanded compensation for all the earthly possessions they had given away. One woman sued the Towers for mental distress—now she'd have to find some other way to kill herself. Her claim for three million dollars was rejected, but it only provoked a spate of claims for smaller sums that were more successful. Within three weeks the Towers were bankrupted. No one could now have afforded to let people die in there. Not even if the Towers had been working properly again, not even if they started winking on and off like the lights of a Christmas tree.

But the Towers implacably, resolutely, refused to leave. They weren't going anywhere.

Nobody was quite sure now what to do with them.

It was suggested that they take on the job for which they had originally been intended. They could be rented out for office space. That didn't sound unreasonable. And so, in preparation, a crew of maintenance workers were sent inside. The windows no longer sparkled, but were grey, and blotchy, and spattered with the bodies of bugs and birds. The water in the restrooms had gone stale. The carpets were matted stiff.

No matter how much the carpets were shampooed, they could never have restored that scent everyone had enjoyed before. The windows might be made clean one day, but the next they'd be smeared, whorls of dirt caught in the sunlight and distorting it, making each pane look as if it had been prodded hard with enormous stained fingerprints. And there was dust everywhere. You could never get rid of all that dust. The dust, it got into everything.

No businesses wanted to move into the Towers. The desks stayed bare, the memo boards empty. There was a strange film clinging to them all, and it may have been mould, and it may have been something else. It became too expensive to clean the Towers. From the outside the windows grew blacker with dirt until no one could see in, until the Towers seemed somehow to suck all light into them.

The Twin Towers squatted lugubriously into position and dominated the New York skyline.

Someone suggested they be pulled down. But whilst many privately agreed that would be the best thing, no one dared give the order. It would be an insult to all those who had lost their lives there—a casualty list that now nearly numbered a cool two million worldwide. What was needed, everyone thought, was some outside force to take down the Twin Towers for them. Some outrage that would leave America blameless. But this time no suicide bombers were forthcoming.

The decision to conceal the Towers wasn't undertaken lightly. The cost alone was staggering. But, it was reasoned, they had built two gigantic towers before—so now they could build *dozens* of them, all over the city—and taller too, so they'd dwarf the originals! And a whole *ring* of towers could now surround them, they'd be completely encircled, and these new ring towers would be the very tallest of all, you'd have to climb to the very top of them, right into the very clouds, and peer down from the roof to get so much as a glimpse at what was hidden beneath.

And the inner windows to these towers would be made of jet-black glass, so no one could see through at the Twin Towers behind. And workers could sit at their desks quite happily, and do their accountancy, their share brokering, their telemarketing calls. And only the smell might remind them what was nearby—no matter how high the air conditioning was turned, no matter how strong the scent of domestic shampoos or bleach, there was always that smell. Rotting history, just a few feet away.

↓

One morning one of those new towers disappeared, taking with it four thousand souls. But there were so many towers, no one even noticed.

ONE LAST LOVE SONG

Listen.

There was once a little boy who was in love with love. It was the first thing he thought of when he woke in the morning. It was what he hoped to dream of when he went to sleep at night. At school he'd think of love during his lessons, geography, physics, gym. He didn't see the point of geography or physics, he didn't see the point of gym; love was so much more important, surely, and so much more interesting, he didn't see why they couldn't just study that. His grades weren't very good.

Of course, the little boy had no first hand experience of love. He was, after all, a little boy. But on his eighth birthday his parents had bought him a radio, all of his very own. He kept it in his bedroom. And after he'd done his homework, and he'd done his chores, it was to the bedroom he'd go. He'd lie on the bed, turn on the radio, and listen to the love songs that came out. And there were so many! He listened to the ones that were sheer celebrations of love, telling the world how great love made them feel, and how unashamed they were of that, they were in love and that was all there was too it—there'd be drums, probably, and loud guitars, and the songs would be fast, and it would sound as if the singers were almost laughing over the words. These songs made the boy happy. And, when he was a little older, he listened to the other love songs. The songs that were about *wanting* love, crying out for love, wondering where love had gone—or, even more despairing, about being in love that wasn't love after all, or *was* love but the wrong kind of love. These songs were much more confusing. They made the boy sad. And, in a funny way, they made him happy too, even happier somehow than the happy songs had.

He learned what love was. A matter of getting the right notes in the right order. And hoping that the right words didn't get in the way of those notes and spoil everything.

By the time he was twelve, after countless evenings of diligent study, the boy had heard every single love song in the world. And he liked them all. He had his favourites, of course he had. He had two hundred and eighty-nine favourites. But there wasn't one love song he didn't respect, and which hadn't taught him something.

He never intended to compose a song of his own. But one night, as he dreamed about love, a tune began to play in his head. He'd absorbed so many songs, they were as much a part of his life as breathing or eating. And somehow the best bits of the best of them had got mixed up in his head, and produced something new. He woke up with a start. He didn't know how to write music. He didn't know how to record his voice. So he made himself stay up all night, walking around the house, singing the new song under his breath over and over again so he wouldn't forget it. When his parents got up at dawn they were shocked to see their little boy shivering with exhaustion, the catchiest of melodies on his lips. They listened to the song. The boy couldn't really sing very well. And he had to explain where the drums and guitars came in. But the parents exchanged glances in awe. "That," said his daddy gravely, "is a love song, all right."

Daddy didn't go to work that day. He phoned a friend, who knew someone who knew someone who might be able to help. Daddy took his little boy to see this man, and for a fee the stranger wrote down the song with staves and treble clefs. "Is that it?" said Daddy. "That's his song?" "That's his song," said the man, pocketing the money, "and we never met, right?" And the little boy took the paper on which his song was now inscribed, and he didn't recognize it like that, but it still gave him a thrill of pride to see it. And then he just keeled over, fast asleep, right there and then. He really was very tired.

Daddy went to the post office for the right forms and filled them in. And the next day, as instructed, he took the little boy into the city to get his love song registered. Mummy made them sandwiches for the trip. The government buildings were stone and grey. There was nobody at reception; a notice at the front told prospective songsmiths to take a ticket and wait until their number was called. It also said that there must be no smoking and no littering and, in particular, the humming of unregistered music was expressly forbidden. Daddy and the little boy took seats. A number was called, and a man at the far side of the room got up, stretched, and shuffled through swing doors down a corridor. The little boy calculated that there were one hundred and twenty-eight people in the queue ahead of them.

There were no other children in the waiting room. Mostly men with beards and raincoats, each holding in their hands a post office form and sheets of music paper. "Is everyone here to get their song registered?" asked the boy.

"I think they must be."

"Why do we need to get songs registered?"

"Well," said Daddy, and handed him a sandwich. "Otherwise, it'd be chaos, wouldn't it? Look around." The little boy did. "Without registration, there'd be another one hundred and twenty-eight songs in the world for us to listen to."

"That doesn't sound so bad."

"One hundred and twenty-eight doesn't sound bad," agreed Daddy. "But that's just today! There'll be another one hundred and twenty-eight tomorrow. Maybe more! You'd end up with a world that has so many love songs in it, we'd be swamped in them. We wouldn't know what to listen to. We might miss out on the one thousand good love songs we'd enjoy, because we couldn't find them amidst all the bad ones we wouldn't."

The boy liked his sandwich. It was tuna. It was the seventeenth best sandwich filling in the world. Across the aisle an unkempt man with grey hair glared at him. The boy didn't know why. The boy was glad when, a few hours later, the man's number was called. He didn't see him again.

At last it was the boy's turn. His daddy nudged him from his drowse. "Come on," said Daddy, and offered him his hand. The boy was really too old now to need his hand held, but he took it gratefully. They walked through the swing doors, and down a long corridor. They only stopped when they found a cubicle that had a door open. "Come in," said the clerk inside the cubicle. And then, on seeing the boy, "Composers only. That's protocol. You'll have to leave your little boy outside." "I'm not the composer," said Daddy. "My little boy is." The clerk blinked in surprise, just the once, then regained his composure. "Very well," he said, and ushered them in, and in spite of protocol, he didn't ask Daddy to leave. The clerk held out his hand for the form. Daddy gave it to him, and the clerk read it briefly. Then the clerk held out his hand for the song. And, taking it, fed it into the computer on his desk.

"Aren't you going to read it?" said Daddy.

"No need. The computer is wholly impartial, it's not affected by quirks of personal taste. It measures the song on timbre, metre, rhythm, and cultural importance." The computer whirred as it made its assessment, and the clerk smiled thinly at the little boy. "Shan't be long now." And then the computer made a happy little ping. This time the clerk didn't bother to hide his surprise, and blinked repetitively.

"Does that mean," asked the boy, "that my song is one of the top thousand in the world?"

"Yes," said the clerk. "Yes. It would appear so. Yes. If I . . . just check my . . . yes." He tapped away at his keyboard. "It's nine hundred and fourteenth," he said. "Well done."

With a new respect, the clerk went on to explain to the little boy that the Government would now be purchasing his song and all future rights appertaining. The boy would receive a handsome stipend once a month, index linked to adjust for inflation. That he should start listening to the radio, because he'd be hearing his own song playing there soon! "But what happens," asked the boy, "to the song that's nine hundred and fourteenth already?" "Well," said the clerk, "that'll become nine hundred and fifteenth. It'll shuffle down the rankings. They'll all shuffle down, until they reach one thousand." "And what happens," said the boy, "to number one thousand?" "Quite right," said the clerk approvingly, although the boy couldn't see why, he'd only asked him a simple question, "I'll deal with that right now." And he turned to his computer, tapped on his keyboard for the shortest few seconds, and erased Elvis Presley's "Blue Suede Shoes" forever.

On the bus ride home Daddy realized that they could now have afforded a taxi. Taxis were the fourteenth best transportation in the world, whereas buses were at only three hundred and forty-seven. "Never mind," he laughed. "Taxis only from this point on! I'm proud of you, son. Not a bad day's work, eh?" And the little boy agreed. "I'm going to write some more songs now," he said, "I'm already getting ideas!"

But he didn't have time for writing for a while. The boy was famous. Truth to tell, the press wouldn't usually have taken much interest in the story. Every few months someone or other was breaking a song into the bottom hundreds of the canon, shoving aside others that had only just been put in. And it may have been the nine hundred and fourteenth best song in the world, but it was also the eighty-seventh worst, which didn't sound half so impressive. But the boy *was* twelve years old. That was something which caught the listeners' imagination, and his song was rerecorded in many different styles to sate the interest: reggae, rap, a cappella. The boy was referred to as a genius in the making, a wunderkind, a veritable Mozart. Mozart was a famous composer. He'd managed to get no less than fourteen songs into the top thousand, he was really very good indeed.

At school he'd been so dreamy he'd barely made an impression. But now he was the epitome of romance. He won the hearts of all the girls, and quite a few of the teachers as well, one or two quite got into trouble over him. He barely noticed, he looked on in some bemusement as his classmates wept for his love, as his form mistress was disciplined by a tribunal and put on probation. And he didn't stay at the school for long; he had no need for geography or physics or gym anymore, and the boy could now afford a special education at which he could focus upon his gifts. He learned how to write in musical notation, he learned to pick apart the songs he'd once enjoyed so uncritically. He wrote a few songs, and of course everyone in academe buzzed with expectation, what fresh classics might he be concocting under their very noses? But they were to be disappointed; the boy always destroyed these efforts, saying that they weren't good enough, he wasn't yet ready to give a second masterpiece to the world. By the time he graduated his original song had slipped down the rankings, and was now nine hundred and thirty-third. One of his fellow students at last managed to catch his attention, and then to catch his heart. She was the envy of all her friends, and received a couple of death threats from the most jealous. As they walked down the aisle, with his mummy and daddy looking so proud, and the boy no longer quite a boy, no longer quite a wunderkind, the song that was played was his own. The bride had chosen it especially. She said it was that song that had made her fall in love with him. Of course it had been. At this point it was the nine hundred and forty-seventh best love song in the world.

The fact was, the boy didn't like the song very much. No matter how much it was digitally remastered, or re-remastered, he heard it for what it was. A melange of other people's songs that had just got lucky. There was love in it, and it was *his* love, but it wasn't the love it pretended to be—a love for the love that others feel is still a borrowed love, it's no love at all. The boy knew he had to find within his heart some passion that was sincere. He dedicated himself to his wife. He knew that she loved him, and that ought to make him love her—but was it really a love strong enough to produce a good tune? He worked on it. He studied her from every angle. He'd adore the nape of her neck, he'd delight in the kink of her nose. He taught himself to feel ecstasies over the little jokes she made he knew really weren't that funny at all. And at last he thought the preparation was over. He wrote a new song. He read it back critically. He prised it apart, put it back together, tweaked the chorus, softened the guitars a bit. He thought about destroying it. He was all set to tear it up. And then he realized how much it would hurt him, to lose even one note of it. It was finished, his second attempt at love. His previous effort was now ranked at nine hundred and seventy-four.

As a composer in the top thousand, he could bypass the usual registration process. He didn't have to queue. He could come to the city with his post office form and his sheet music, and no matter how busy the office, the doors of the cubicles would be flung open wide for him. "Hello, sir!" said the clerk, "and welcome!" The clerk fed the new song into the computer. The computer whirred, but it didn't ping, it grunted. "Oh!" said the clerk, checking his readout, much surprised. "Better luck next time." And took the song from the feeder tray, and shredded it before the young composer's eyes.

Maybe his love had been too clean, he hadn't fought hard enough for it. He began to have affairs. Nothing major at first, just the odd grope with likely looking women in the back of pubs; he was no longer hailed as a genius, but telling a pretty girl he'd written the nine hundred and eighty-second greatest love song was always an icebreaker notwithstanding. Seeking further inspiration, he moved on to afternoon trysts, and then evening trysts, and then weekend trysts. A five-day fling with identical blonde twins provoked him to compose a full seven and a half minute ballad. The computer rejected it, as it did all his other songs. The doors of the registration office were still flung open wide to him, but with markedly less enthusiasm. His wife left him. She said that she no longer knew him. She said that maybe she never had. He wrote a song about how that made him feel. The computer didn't care. His daddy died. Quite unexpectedly of a heart attack, there was no warning. His mummy, who had never raised a voice to him, who had bought him a radio and made him tuna sandwiches, told him that his father had been so appalled by the way he'd treated his wife that the shame had killed him. The composer cried for days. He wept it all out into a new song. The computer barely gave it a blip, let alone the much-sought ping. The clerk studied the readout and said, yes, the computer could see that the composer in question was upset, and it offered him its condolences. But that didn't mean he'd written a good song.

One day a bar pianist in Portugal hit the news. Afonso Guttierez had been playing his own songs to customers as they ate their tapas, and had been persuaded by concerned friends to take a selection of his work for registration; it would have taken only one disgruntled diner unhappy with the calamari to stop him. He offered fourteen songs. Eight were rejected, but that still left an unprecedented *six* that were accepted automatically by the Lisbon computer. The pianist was thirty-four years old, but in spite of that still hailed as a new wunderkind, a new Mozart. All six of the songs ranked higher than our composer's effort, which now came to rest at a precarious nine hundred and ninety-seven. The composer decided that he needed to get a song accepted into the canon immediately before he lost his placing altogether, and for the next few nights worked hard on his latest masterpiece—he pushed and prodded at all of his feelings, dredging his heart for something that might sound beautiful. But it was too late. By the time he took his new work into the city everything had changed. Fired up by his success, Guttierez had returned to his bar, and written up for submission a further fifty-eight of the songs he'd squirreled away over the years. All fifty-eight were accepted. When our composer reached the office, he found he now had to queue like everybody else. He had to take a ticket and wait his turn. And when he at last reached a cubicle, tired and angry, it was to find only that his childhood success had been erased, deleted from the computer, wiped from the world's iPods. The clerk apologized. He fed the new song into the computer. It was rejected.

"What if I wrote a song that wasn't about love at all?"

The clerk said, very slowly, "I don't think that's possible."

"It has to be possible."

"Every song expresses love for *something*," said the clerk. "A few hundred years ago, love of God was all the rage. Now it's all about love of sex. Give it another hundred, it'll be love of silicon chips, who knows? But in any good song, there's always a love you can't get around. And that's love for the music itself. That'll always be there. You can't beat it."

"A man can try," said the man who had once been a composer.

For two long months the man worked hard. Fortified by broccoli and lukewarm beer, he cut out anything from his diet that might excite his taste buds, anything that might get translated accidentally as passion in melody form. The stipend had been withdrawn, so he was obliged to go out to work during the day, concentrating on his music only once his shifts were over. He wasn't trained for anything, so took on a series of menial temp jobs, stacking shelves, stuffing envelopes. But even that helped, he was able to channel the numbness of the day into the numbness of his music. He composed through the night, every night, his desk turned so he was facing a blank wall, and every time he came up with a note that even reached for emotion he'd quash it. The music wasn't bad; he couldn't simply afford to be bad, anyone could write *bad* music. It took a very certain sort of genius to write something instead that was so good and so fully formed, and yet stillborn.

He went to register his song. He took the day off work. They'd just have to find someone else to hold a placard advertising golf sales. He took his ticket. He waited. There was a child across the aisle sitting with his father, no doubt thinking this whole process of assessment and rejection was some fun day out. He glared at him and made him cry. He went to the toilet. His face looked haggard with lack of sleep, his hair had greyed.

The song was fed into the computer. It whirred for a bit, and then whirred some more. The screen froze. The clerk had to get out the manual, turn the computer off and then back on again. "Well," he said, at last, "it's not a love song. We don't know what it is, but it's not a love song. And so it's outside our jurisdiction. It doesn't need to be destroyed." He took the sheet music from the feeder, and instead of shredding it, handed it back to the composer.

"You'll buy it?" said the composer.

"God, no."

On his way home, for want of something to do, the composer read over his song. He didn't finish it. He left it on the bus behind him.

He vowed he'd never write music again. He needed a career, something permanent, something he could commit to. He applied for a job at the local McDonald's; McDonald's was a fast food chain specializing in burgers, and the six hundred and sixth best in the world. He was much older than any of his fellow workers, they all thought that was impressive. And he worked hard there, he began the week as a mere team member but by Thursday he was team leader, he had five gold stars on his name badge and he was on a roll. His managers were in awe, they'd never seen anyone scale the ladder of convenience food industry so quickly, he was astonishing, a wunderkind. He loved his job. He flipped the burgers and wiped the tables and gave service with a smile, this was something he was good at. The restaurant played an endless stream of Muzak, simplified versions of the love songs he'd once admired and competed with. And sometimes they played Guttierez.

One day the televisions all reported breaking news. The world had a new best love song. Nothing composed in the last fifty years had even made it near the top ten, there was something so established about those classics that was just hard to beat. But the latest from Afonso Guttierez had taken the number one spot, knocking down into second place some ditty by Verdi. Always one to shy away from publicity, Guttierez had only reluctantly agreed to a TV interview, in which he mumbled in broken English that he was pleased people a-liked his song. People more than liked it; it was adored. Everyone played it for their loved ones, and although doing that was immediately a cliché, it somehow wasn't, because the song seemed to speak personally to whoever heard it, it was universal but was also specifically about *them*. The former child prodigy, former composer, gave the song a listen. He didn't much care for it.

He couldn't have explained why he caught that flight to Lisbon. Why from there he took a seven-hour coach trip into the Portuguese hinterland. He didn't know what he was going to do when he found Guttierez. Only that by now Guttierez had three hundred and four songs in the top thousand, and, if that wasn't bad enough, the other composers of the world had cottoned on, they were writing their songs in the *style* of Guttierez; they weren't quite as good as Guttierez, of course, but they were perfectly suited for adaptation as background music, for elevators, for supermarkets—there was suddenly a strange sticky homogeneity to the music of the world, and there was a new name already coined for it, it was used freely and without shame by all the critics and all the disc jockeys, and that name was Guttierezesque. He'd been working so hard at his Big Macs to make a bit of money. Now he'd blown all his savings. Some of it had gone on the fare to Lisbon, the rest had gone on the gun.

They said that the genius of Guttierez was that he didn't appear to compose his songs at all, he'd just play at the piano and somehow they'd pour out. It was why he was so extraordinarily prolific. He said he needed the audience, that before his success he'd tinkered before customers in a bar, and that he couldn't change the way he worked now. That was why, shy as he was, he still performed. He'd sold up the small bar, of course, and now owned a large restaurant. The food was only adequate, and was served on paper plates and with plastic cutlery to minimize the clatter of knife and fork. But no one came to Restaurante Guttierez to eat.

The maître d' asked if he had a reservation. "No, I'm sorry. Can you squeeze me in?" "I'm sorry, senhor, tonight we're fully booked." "I see. Can I reserve a table for tomorrow?" "Senhor, we are fully booked for the next five months. Senhor Guttierez, he is very popular." "Please. I need to see him. I've flown all the way from England." "We have many visitors from England, senhor. From Japan, from Australia, from the Americas, from all over the world." "I'm begging you. I'm a composer too. I compose love songs. I used to compose love songs. We're the same, him and I. We're the same. Please. Please." The maître d' let him in.

He was given a little table at the back, with two chairs. He looked at the menu. The wine cost a fortune. He couldn't afford it. He ordered a carafe.

At last the lights dimmed, and Guttierez appeared. He shuffled toward the piano. He was just a little man, a little man. He was wearing shirt and tails, like a concert pianist, but they didn't really fit him, he looked scruffy. He darted a glance at the audience, but didn't look at them directly, didn't want them there. There was a smattering of applause, but Guttierez ignored it. He sat down at the piano.

The team manager from McDonald's carefully took the gun from his coat pocket.

Guttierez frowned at the piano. As if it were something he was trying to remember, trying to place. He raised a finger. He hesitated. He dropped it onto a key. Plonk. It was a C. He thought about this, then raised the finger once more, thought a bit further, then dropped it onto the F. Then back onto the C. Then back onto the F. He gave this some consideration. He took his hand away from the piano altogether, stared at it once more. Then raised his hand, raised his finger. Held it in the air—then let it fall, at last. Back onto the C. Then faster, another C, another F, another C. Then the single finger exploring further, excited, picking out other notes, at random, a mess.

Our hero wanted to laugh. Guttierez wasn't worth killing. He wasn't worth the price of a wine carafe. He got up to leave.

"No," said the woman beside him.

He hadn't realized there *was* a woman beside him. That someone had taken that second chair. He couldn't make her out in the dim light. She said something to him in a whisper.

"What?"

"*Escute*. Listen."

So he listened. And there wasn't much to be impressed by. Not for a while. But then Guttierez visibly relaxed. The notes began to smooth. They still seemed random, at least at first—not so discordant now, even pleasing to the ear, nothing special of course, nothing of any worth—but then that was all stripped away, it was as if it had been a game all along, those notes weren't random, they'd been building up to something, building up a rhythm, you could hear those simple Cs, those Fs, every now and again being picked out, as if winking at an audience who took them so much for granted before, we're building up to something, they said, we're building up to . . . and here on the top of them there was . . .

He gasped. And was flooded by the music.

Guttierez opened his mouth. For a while nothing came out. The fingers continued to dance upon the piano, the music hadn't reached his head yet, the mouth hung open, waiting for it to do so. And then words tumbled out. Guttierez was not a great singer. He didn't have to be.

He didn't know what Guttierez was singing about. He didn't have to.

He didn't have to know anything.

He wasn't a composer anymore, or a man who had once been a composer and had given up, or a man who had once been a composer and who could never give up, not really, no matter how much he failed. He was a little boy. He was a little boy who listened to love songs. He was a little boy in love with love.

He turned to the woman, and he could barely see her. It dawned on him that this was because he was crying.

She put what she was holding onto the table, and with her hand now freed, reached for his. He looked at her closely. And he knew that he loved her. It wasn't that she was beautiful, it wasn't that. But she was there. She was there, amongst the music.

"Listen," she mouthed, and he nodded happily. She held his hand tightly. It was smaller than his, but strong, stronger. He saw that she was crying too. He saw what she'd put upon the table. He saw that she too had come with a gun.

He didn't know what he could ever say to her, whether he could ever find the right words. But for that moment he was in love, and it was the fullest and richest love he'd ever felt. He gazed at her, and she gazed at him, and they listened. They listened. And hoped that the love song would never end.

PUBLICATION HISTORY

"Luxembourg." First published in *Andromeda Spaceways Inflight Magazine*, Issue 39, edited by Andrew Finch, and subsequently collected in *Love Songs for the Shy and Cynical*.

"Restoration." First published in *Everyone's Just So So Special*, and subsequently collected in *The Best Science Fiction and Fantasy of the Year Volume Six*, edited by Jonathan Strahan.

"A Joke in Four Panels." First published in *The Best Science Fiction and Fantasy of the Year Volume Seven*, edited by Jonathan Strahan.

"That Tiny Flutter of the Heart I Used to Call Love." First published in *Psycho Mania*, edited by Stephen Jones, and subsequently collected in *The Best Horror of the Year Volume Six*, edited by Ellen Datlow, and in *Best British Horror 2014*, edited by Johnny Mains.

"Taboo." First published in *Everyone's Just So So Special*.

"Peckish." First published in *Fearie Tales*, edited by Stephen Jones.

"Dumb Lucy." First published in *Magic*, edited by Jonathan Oliver.

"Static." First collected in *Tiny Deaths*, and subsequently adapted into a short film directed by Tanya Lemke.

"The Constantinople Archives." First published in *The Cutting Room*, edited by Ellen Datlow.

"Your Long, Loving Arms." First published in *Love Songs for the Shy and Cynical*.

"Brand New Shiny Shiny." First published in *Flotsam Fantastique*, edited by Stephen Jones.

"Patches." First published in *Wild Stacks 1*, edited by Peter Coleborn, and subsequently collected in *Everyone's Just So So Special*.

"The Sixteenth Step." First published in *The Burning Circus*, edited by Johnny Mains, and subsequently collected in *The Mammoth Book of Best New Horror 25*, edited by Stephen Jones.

"It Flows From the Mouth." First published in *Shadows and Tall Trees*, Issue 6, edited by Michael Kelly.

"History Becomes You." First published by the *Sunday Times* when it was nominated for the Sunday Times EPB Private Banking Award, and subsequently collected in *Everyone's Just So So Special*.

"One Last Love Song." First published in *Love Songs for the Shy and Cynical*.

ACKNOWLEDGEMENTS

It's hard enough to know whom to thank when you've just written a single story. It's nigh on impossible with a book like this one, where the oldest story dates back nearly a decade. (I see photographs of that younger me sometimes. He looks weird. I suppose that accounts for a lot.)

So, let me start at the beginning, by thanking my family. Dennis (my father) and Vicky (my sister) have put up with my sense of humour for years—and the best jokes I've stolen from them.

I'm very proud to be a ChiZine writer. I stumbled across their books at a horror convention a few years ago, and I was so struck by their beauty I had to buy them all. Brett Savory and Sandra Kasturi, thanks for making me part of the family. We had fun with the first book, didn't we? Here we go again! Erik Mohr, your covers are both terrifying and gorgeous, thank you. Thanks to my editor, Andrew Wilmot, who pored over these stories, the old and the new, and showed me fresh things in all of them. And to all my editors of the past who've tackled these stories beforehand, but especially Xanna Eve Chown, who worked on three entire books of mine and managed to preserve her sanity.

Many of these stories were written whilst enjoying a year's residency at Edinburgh Napier University, attached to the Creative Writing MA course. I was inspired by the work of the hardest working students I've ever known, and by the extraordinary staff: Sam and Stuart Kelly, and David Bishop. I began a project there to write one hundred stories, and one hundred foolhardy people volunteered to let me use their names for characters in any way I saw fit—thanks then, to Julia Loecherbach, Madalyn Morgan, Raphael Klein, Karen Davison, Lizbeth Myles, David Allan, Sieglinde von Zieten, Lucy Zinkiewicz, Ian Mond, Matthew Bell, Richard Marklew, Matthew Tozer, Nathalie Gallagher, Paul Hiscock, and Ian Wheeler. I have plans for what to do with all hundred of these stories; watch this space.

One of those hundred, but one in a million, is Helen Marshall. Helen is the greatest of friends and the greatest of writers. So many of these stories started life as the two of us swapped crazy ideas back and forth in art galleries and pubs. Her own work makes me want to be a better writer. Thanks also to her wonderful sister Laura, who has been like a sister to me too.

Suzanne Milligan is not just my agent, she's my pal. Unfailingly supportive, she's encouraged me whenever I've needed it, and made me feel I can take on the world. Apologies to her, though, for all the icky stuff in this book that makes her flesh crawl. I can't help it. Sometimes the stories just come out that way.

And lastly, as always, thanks to my wife Janie. Now, I'm not the easiest of writers to live with. Some days the words don't come out right, so I get grumpy. Other days the words come out just fine, so I get smug. Still other days I'm lazy and don't write at all and make the house dirty and get under her feet. In a very real sense, the fact these stories exist is down to her. She's patient and kind, and knows when to ignore me, and when to flatter. And at any point during the last twenty years she could have killed me in my sleep, and she didn't. It wouldn't have taken much. Just a pillow over the face, I wouldn't have known a thing. She could still do it too. Sometimes she gets that look in her eyes. She could do it whenever she pleases.

ABOUT THE AUTHOR

Robert Shearman has worked as writer for television, radio and the stage. He was appointed resident dramatist at the Northcott Theatre in Exeter and has received several international awards for his theatrical work, including the Sunday Times Playwriting Award, the World Drama Trust Award and the Guinness Award for Ingenuity in Association with the Royal National Theatre. His plays have been regularly produced by Alan Ayckbourn, and on BBC Radio by Martin Jarvis. His three series of *The Chain Gang*, an interactive short story and drama project for BBC Radio, has won two Sony Awards. A selection of his plays have been collected in book form as Caustic Comedies.

However, he is probably best known as a writer for *Doctor Who*, reintroducing the Daleks for its BAFTA-winning first series in an episode nominated for a Hugo Award. He has also written many popular audio dramas for Big Finish.

His first collection of short stories, *Tiny Deaths*, was published by Comma Press in 2007. It won the World Fantasy Award for best collection, was shortlisted for the Edge Hill Short Story Prize and nominated for the Frank O'Connor International Short Story Prize. "No Looking Back" was selected by the National Library Board of Singapore as part of the annual Read! Singapore campaign.

His second collection, *Love Songs for the Shy and Cynical*, was published by Big Finish in 2009. It won the British Fantasy Award for best collection, the Edge Hill Short Story Readers Prize and the Shirley Jackson Award, celebrating outstanding achievement in the literature of psychological suspense, horror, and the dark fantastic. His third collection, *Everyone's Just So So Special*, won the British Fantasy Award, and his story "History Becomes You" was nominated for the Sunday Times EFG Private Bank Award.

Most recently, his best dark fiction was collected in *Remember Why You Fear Me* by ChiZine Publications; the collection won the British Fantasy Award, was shortlisted for the Shirley Jackson Award, and received nominations for Best Novella and Best Collection at the World Fantasy Awards.

EMB
RACE
THE
ODD

REMEMBER WHY YOU FEAR ME
ROBERT SHEARMAN

A woman rejects her husband's heart—and gives it back to him, still beating, in a plastic box. A little boy betrays his father to the harsh mercies of Santa Claus. A widower suspects his dead wife's face is growing over his own. A man goes to Hell, and finds he's roommate to the ghost of Hitler's pet dog. Giant spiders, killer angels, ghost cat photography, and the haunted house right at the centre of the Garden of Eden.

Deliciously frightening, darkly satirical, and always unexpected, Robert Shearman has won the World Fantasy Award, the British Fantasy Award, the Shirley Jackson Award, and the Edge Hill Reader's Prize. *Remember Why You Fear Me* gathers together his best dark fiction, the most celebrated stories from his acclaimed books, and ten new tales that have never been collected before.

AVAILABLE NOW
978-1-927469-21-7

GIFTS FOR THE ONE WHO COMES AFTER

HELEN MARSHALL

Ghost thumbs. Miniature dogs. One very sad can of tomato soup . . . British Fantasy Award-winner Helen Marshall's second collection offers a series of twisted surrealities that explore the legacies we pass on to our children. A son seeks to reconnect with his father through a telescope that sees into the past. A young girl discovers what lies on the other side of her mother's bellybutton. Death's wife prepares for a very special funeral. In *Gifts for the One Who Comes After*, Marshall delivers eighteen tales of love and loss that cement her as a powerful voice in dark fantasy and the New Weird. Dazzling, disturbing, and deeply moving.

AVAILABLE NOW
978-1-77148-302-5

CHIZINEPUB.COM

FEARFUL SYMMETRIES
EDITED BY ELLEN DATLOW

From Ellen Datlow, award-winning and genre-shaping editor of more than fifty anthologies, and twenty of horror's established masters and rising stars, comes an all-original look into the beautiful, terrible, tragic, and terrifying.

Wander through visions of the most terrible of angels, the Seven who would undo the world. Venture through Hell and back, and lands more terrestrial and darker still. Linger a while in childhoods, and seasons of change by turns tragic and monstrously transformative. Lose yourself amongst the haunted and those who can't let go, in relationships that might have been and never were. Witness in dreams and reflections, hungers and horrors, the shadows cast upon the wall, and linger in forests deep.

AVAILABLE NOW
978-1-77148-193-9

THE FAMILY UNIT AND OTHER FANTASIES

LAURENCE KLAVAN

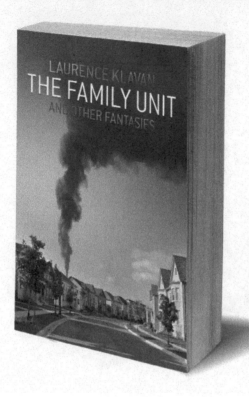

The Family Unit and Other Fantasies is the debut collection of acclaimed Edgar Award-winning author Laurence Klavan. A superb group of darkly comic, deeply compassionate, largely fantastical stories set in our jittery, polarized, increasingly impersonal age. Whether it's the tale of a corporation that buys a man's family; two supposed survivors of a super-storm who are given shelter by a gullible couple; an erotic adventure set during an urban terrorist alert; or a nightmare in which a man sees his neighbourhood developed and disappearing at a truly alarming speed, these stories are by turn funny and frightening, odd and arousing, uncanny and unnerving.

AVAILABLE NOW
978-1-77148-203-5

CHIZINEPUB.COM

THE DOOR IN THE MOUNTAIN

CAITLIN SWEET

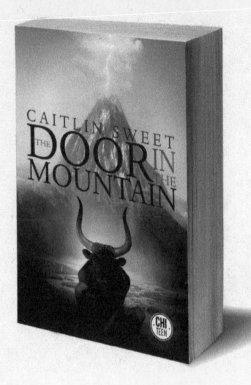

Lost in time, shrouded in dark myths of blood and magic, *The Door in the Mountain* leads to the world of ancient Crete: a place where a beautiful, bitter young princess named Ariadne schemes to imprison her godmarked half-brother deep in the heart of a mountain maze . . .

. . . where a boy named Icarus tries, and fails, to fly . . .

. . . and where a slave girl changes the paths of all their lives forever.

AVAILABLE NOW IN CANADA/OCTOBER 2014 IN U.S.

978-1-77148-191-5